28 QUESTIONS

28 QUESTIONS

INDYANA SCHNEIDER

SCRIBNER

LONDON NEW YORK SYDNEY TORONTO NEW DELHI

First published in Great Britain by Scribner,
an imprint of Simon & Schuster UK Ltd, 2022

A CIP catalogue record for this book
is available from the British Library

Hardback ISBN: 978-1-3985-0109-6
Trade Paperback ISBN: 978-1-3985-0110-2
eBook ISBN: 978-1-3985-0110-2

Typeset in Palatino by M Rules
Printed and bound by CPI Group (UK) Ltd, Croydon CR0 4YY

For GPS

CHAPTERS

YEAR 1

YEAR 2

Kissing you now, the waves begin
And evermore divide me:
Before and after you.

—'Before and After You',
The Bridges of Madison County,
JASON ROBERT BROWN

Reader, imagine yielding to someone with a power so strong she has the ability to slice time. Before. Her. After.

Imagine being so scarred, creativity wilts and words flee. The after-her was filled with her even though she wasn't there. But now that I have my voice back, I want to share our story. Is it possible to enjoy a love story when you know it will end in the kind of heartache that slices time? I think so.

YEAR 1

1

WHAT BRINGS YOU PLEASURE?

I made my way to our College Bar, drunk, and spotted the silhouette of new friend Eve, seated, with a bunch of women. All the women who studied French and Italian (I say 'all' – there were four women spread across all four years) were sitting in the little cave-like corner of the bar, drinking. The bar had only one light, right in the centre, leaving the corner buried in darkness. Eve was leaning against a wall, thick black hair pressed up against it.

Walls in our College Bar were rough on the eyes but smooth to the touch, years of history hidden by new coats of paint. Eve smiled when she saw me – carefully painted red lips framing perfect orthodontic white teeth – and gestured that I should join her. Alcohol has robbed me of much of the conversations and introductions that followed. But, of course, I remember meeting Alex. I was struck by her voice, so rich, even velvety, like Baileys or Merlot. There was something so mesmeric about the way she spoke. I was drawn to her subtle Australian cadence, her delicate, almost musical consonants.

There in our College Bar, I drunkenly studied her. Barely-there eyebrows. Dark hair in a constant state of flux as she absentmindedly put it up and took it down during conversation. Three perfect freckles in a line along her arm. Eyes the colour the sky should be – the Australian sky I knew, not this foreign English white. I acknowledged and dismissed that this was an odd thought to have about a stranger or a new friend.

Eve and I stumbled back to our adjacent rooms arm in arm, new allies. In the dark hallway:

Eve: I'm not a sentimental person
Me: Okay

I paused.

Me: I think I am

She nodded. I wondered whether this was a bad thing in Eve's books.

Eve: Yes, I think you are
Me: Why did you bring up sentimentality?
Eve: As a disclaimer

I waited.

Eve: I'm really glad we're neighbours

She pulled me into a hug, squeezed, then let herself into her room. I drunkenly fumbled with my key as I did the same.

———

I must have been charming, despite my inebriated state, because the next day I received a friend request on Facebook:

Alex:
Hey,
It was lovely to meet a fellow Aussie last night.
It would be really nice if you and Eve came over for dinner one night next week? What do you think?
Alex x

What did I think?

Amalia:
Hey,
Lovely to meet you too!
I'm at a concert in chapel until 8pm on Tuesday (music student duties!) – would after that be too late?
Amalia x

Alex:
After that would be perfect!
I'll message Eve.
X

Eve and I never really discussed the dinner. Tuesday arrived and I attended the concert I'd told my Renaissance Music tutor I'd attend. The chapel was magnificent – gothic and resonant – and the music hit me behind the knees. I was glad to be sitting because music that hits you behind the knees can leave you unbalanced. Five singers stood in a row. The tallest, a man with a boy's face, sang the solos in a set of Renaissance music and, though his voice was soft and gentle and sweet, the chapel acoustics rubbed his sound warm, inflating it until it filled the ancient space. During a particular Gesualdo madrigal, a balloon of sound lodged itself inside me. I'd never heard music like it before. An ignorant First Year, I'd assumed Renaissance music was too rule-abiding in its harmonies to achieve this intense emotional expression. How could they express such anguish in such simplicity?

'Io pur respiro' ('I still breathe') – Carlo Gesualdo, 1611

The ethereal introduction morphed into something breathless. Wildly chromatic. Everything began to hasten. Voices overlapping. Faster. The balloon of sound burst. Shivers overwhelmed me then left me raw.

About halfway through the concert, I felt her sit beside me. It was the second time we'd met in all of time and I was struck by how close she was sitting. Very close. The music faded from foreground to background. It was like a concerto where she was the soloist – the scraping of her chair, the shuffling of her feet, the rhythm of her breathing. She whispered to me, accompanied by the music, 'I smell of herbs and spices. I'm sorry.' I laughed because she was funny and she did smell strongly of coriander. I love coriander. We watched the rest of the concert together in silence.

I say watched, but suddenly everyone was clapping so I clapped, too, because that's how clapping works. She was whispering to me again, 'Oh, but I thought *you* would be singing.' I contemplated making a joke, but couldn't follow through because she really did look disappointed. She smiled when I said, 'Alex, I can't think of anything worse than some-one seeing me perform before they get to know me.'

———

Alex's books were stacked in a neat pile beside her desk, which overlooked the college deer park. Alex, Eve, and I sat around a circular table in this, her study. The door to her bedroom was closed. The air was flavoured with chicken and coriander and all the right spices. This was before we both became vegetarian. In the centre of the table was a colourful salad. It struck me that the food wasn't typically English – starchy or heavy. It was something I would have at home in Sydney.

Alex made me nervous. Not in an uncomfortable way, but I felt I wanted to impress her. University stretched our two-year age difference, so she seemed older, wiser, almost glamorous. I was grateful for Eve's relaxing company. I found her very straightforward, non-judgemental. She was the first in her family to go to university, but she never made a big deal about it. I wondered how many students found a best friend in their first-year college neighbour.

Alex told us both about her American boyfriend, Oscar,

who was studying for a Master's in law. I had a vague memory of meeting an American who fit his physical description at some international students mingle evening early on. I remember thinking that he laughed a little like Professor Umbridge: closed mouth, high-pitched. But I decided it couldn't have been Alex's Oscar because the man I met was too arrogant, too opinionated. It didn't make sense to me. Anyway, I'm digressing. The three of us sat on the floor to eat. Within an hour, Eve was lying on her back. She looked in pain, but said nothing. Migraine. She'd warned me about these. I didn't know how to behave, how to be, which I'll admit felt unusual for me. This was before I'd read and reread Sheila Heti's *How Should a Person Be?*, an Alex recommendation. Though I'm not sure that would have helped me here.

Me: This chicken is really good, much nicer than
   eating in hall–

Fumbling, awkward words. Childish. Mundane.

Eve: I'm sure that's meant as a compliment ...
Her: Is food something that brings you pleasure then?

For me, the short answer to this question was no. Almost an aggressive NO. Food actually brought me a lot of pain growing up because eating disorders are rife in my family and I'd only just dropped out of the Who Can Eat The Fewest Calories At Dinner competition we all secretly played. I never won.

Eve: I like food, but I'm not sure I'd say it brings me
    pleasure. What do you mean by pleasure?

I breathed out.

Her: Have you read that pleasure–joy article?

I would come to learn that, among circles of friends, it was kind of a given that everybody had read the same articles and books. They became the common language at most social gatherings. I would also learn that Alex and Eve weren't really friends. In fact, after that night, Eve, Alex, and I never had dinner again just the three of us. So it was a strange combination of guests at this First Dinner. I'll let you decide why Alex organised it in the first place.

Eve: No?
Me: What?
Her: Zadie Smith, who I love, wrote this interesting
    article, which distinguishes between joy and pleasure.
    For her, pleasures are, like, simple things that could
    happen every day. I think she uses the example of
    eating an icy pole–
Eve: A what?
Me and her: Ice lolly

Eve laughed through her nose – I'd never heard her laugh like this and it tickled me – and I think she muttered something like 'Australians ...'

Her: Anyway, joy is something much rarer and more,
um, intense? Kind of ecstatic actually. Zadie talks
about taking drugs with a stranger and giving birth.
Big moments of Joy, with a capital J

In the years to come, I would read almost everything Zadie
Smith ever published. I would also know Joy by Zadie's definition: 'that strange admixture of terror, pain, and delight'.

Me: So what brings you pleasure?
Her: Definitely not icy poles in this weather
Eve: It's such a funny image – licking an 'icy' 'pole'. Like,
I get it! I can picture it!

Still lying on the floor, she made quotations with her fingers
when she said 'icy' and 'pole'. It never fails to amuse me how
baffled English people are by the slightest idiosyncrasies in
Aussie vocabulary.

Her: I think finishing a good book is up there for me
Eve: I really like running – it makes me happy and I do it
often, so I guess that counts?
Her: That definitely counts
Eve: That said, I guess I also use running to combat
stress, so it's not entirely a pleasurable thing
Her: But you use it because it brings you pleasure, right?
I still think it counts

I didn't know what I was going to say before I said it.

Me: I think it would probably be wanting really badly
   to listen to a piece of music and then listening to that
   piece of music. Yeah, I guess that'd be mine
Her: So you like when desire is satiated?

She said the word 'desire' like it felt good in her mouth. Desire.
I didn't blush.

Eve: I'm actually in quite a bit of pain. Fucking migraines
Her: Ah, I don't even have any painkillers to offer you
Eve: No, that's okay. Thank you for a wonderful dinner. I
   think I'm going to go

Eve has a funny way of behaving. Once she has made up her
mind about something, she will just block everything out
and do it, kind of forgetting where she is and everything else.
It's difficult to describe, so I'll use this dinner as an example.
After saying she was going to go, Eve stood, hugged Alex,
hugged me, and left.

Me: Maybe I should get going, too
Her: Please don't feel obliged. I have no other plans this
   evening apart from getting to know you
Me: And you plan to do that all in an evening?
Her: I plan to start this evening. Yes

The wine had oiled my initial fumbling and I could feel my
charisma swell as I surfed the alcoholic wave. I let it swell. I
leaned in.

Me: And how do you usually get to know people?

Her: I don't usually want to get to know people the way I want to get to know you

I didn't blush.

Her: Besides, I only get to hear you sing once I know you properly, right?

Me: Right. But what if I'm a terrible singer?

Her: You're not a terrible singer

Me: I could be terrible. Can you imagine? Would you tell me? How embarrassing–

Her: I've heard a recording, you're great!

Me: What recording? How did you–

Her: Not that I know much about opera, but–

Me: Did you look me up?

Her: Sure! You weren't difficult to find. Don't you google people?

Me: I do google people

Her: Exactly! I watched a clip of you singing something from *Carmen* and it was extraordinary

Me: That's not fair! What's your secret talent then?

Her: Your opera-singing talent isn't exactly a secret

Me: Alright, detective

Was I teasing or flirting? What's the difference?
I paused.

Me: I want to get to know you, too

I stayed for seven more hours. Alex told me that she saw herself as more of a dancer than a linguist, which she found odd given she'd never wanted to dance professionally. She'd spent the time in between school and university teaching herself to code, though she didn't seriously believe she'd ever need the skill. At 2 a.m., we made peppermint tea in a kettle so small we had to boil it twice to fill two cups. We sat on her sofa and discussed the following:

1. James Blake's music – how it sounds both so angsty and so sexy and how often those two particular adjectives are used together
2. My father's work in artificial intelligence
3. The diagnostic manual for mental health – why was the threshold for diagnosable anxiety lowered in the latest version of the manual? More stressful world? More forthcoming people?
4. Moral bucket lists – the experiences one *should* have in order to live a Good Life. I suggested trying again at a task you've failed. She countered this with being able to let go of something that isn't working. Me – actually putting someone before yourself. Her – actually keeping a secret you said you'd keep
5. Our greatest fears. Her – losing her mind and memory. Me – losing loved ones. She asked me what it was like to fear something that was likely, if not inevitable. I told her I tried not to think about it
6. Why we both left Australia. Neither of us could really answer this question. Me – it just felt right to

leave Sydney. Her – she'd always known she would
leave Melbourne

7. Friendship deal-breakers. Hers – liars, but only if the
lying is malicious. Mine – people who hate people

8. The sound of brass instruments in jazz. She thought
they sounded tinny and alarming. I disagreed,
feigning horror

9. Personality tests. She quoted an article she'd read:
'People can be separated into two categories.
Those who believe people can be separated into
two categories and those who don't.' I chuckled.
I'd never taken a personality test. She asked me a
question from a test she'd taken: 'When reading
for pleasure, do you prefer unusual/original ways
of saying things or when authors say exactly what
they mean?' I refused to answer because I didn't see
how the two were mutually exclusive. She seemed
pleased with my response

And lots of other things.

We forgot about the tea and we didn't boil the tiny kettle again.

At 3 a.m., she brought up a psychological study about a
list of 28 questions that, when answered in full, are meant
to make strangers fall in love. We didn't answer all of the
questions together, so we didn't fall in love, but we did look
through them on her laptop and answer a few. Some were
more intense than others.

- Is fashion a statement? What does yours say?
- Is there a person who has changed your life the most?
- When did you stop being a child?
- How would you describe your relationship with your parents?

Me: Ooh, this is a good one! How do you feel about politically incorrect jokes?

Her: Oh, that's easy. I don't like them. And I don't really care about being called an oversensitive snowflake. Like, if what you're going to say is going to make someone feel small, just don't say it? And it's always the minorities that are made to feel small, right? The trans community or people of colour or Jewish people–

I flinched.

Her: –and, if people think offence is at the heart of good comedy, I feel sorry for their senses of humour. Okay, sorry. Rant over

Me: Fair enough

Her: Another good question: if you could learn something about the future, what would you want to know?

Me: Oh, I want to say nothing, but maybe that's not true ... I think I'd like to know when my parents are going to die. Is that awful? I'd probably move back to Sydney if I knew it was any time soon, which does make me question why I'm not in Sydney now

Her: Because you can't live life like that, surely?

Me: Maybe not. What about you?

Her: I don't really know how to answer this. Isn't it a bit *Macbeth*-y? Self-fulfilling prophecies and all that? My initial thought was that I'd like to know whether I'll succeed in whatever career I choose – but, if the answer was yes, would I become arrogant and slack? If the answer was no, would I give up? That kind of knowledge could be dangerous!

Me: Oh, now I feel like I answered too simply

Her: No, not at all! You didn't ask about yourself, you asked about other people. I think your answer was very clever and very telling

She looked at me very intently.

Her: You're a very compassionate person, Amalia

This time, I blushed.

Her: Okay, what about this one: would you like to be famous? My answer is absolutely not

Me: This is going to sound arrogant, but, yes, I would

Her: Go on

Me: Well, I want to be an opera singer and success in that career comes with fame. So, in order to be successful, I need to be famous. If that makes sense . . . ?

Her, calling my bluff: Okay, but, if you could be a successful opera singer and not be famous, would you prefer that?

Me, laughing: Fine, fine, you got me, I also like the idea
   of being famous

Then she asked me to tell her more about my singing, 'what
it means' to me. I paused. I tried to explain that, just as music
communicates without words, how I feel about music is
somehow tied up in that ineffability.

So she asked me to choose a piece of music that sum-
marised how I felt about music. I paused, taken aback by
her perceptiveness. I wondered whether this was a gift of
hers, the ability to communicate effortlessly with people in
their own language, or whether we shared a special type of
communication.

We opened Spotify on her laptop. I mulled. I told her about
this scene from Mozart's opera *The Marriage of Figaro*. The
opera itself is very hectic, full of antics and plots. The Count
tries to cheat on his wife, the Countess. Musically, the opera
revels in its chaos for three hours until this glorious moment
of silence – and then *'Contessa, perdono'* ('Countess, forgive
me'). It is the most simple and beautiful melody and, in the
midst of all this farcical turmoil, you do forgive him. Music
has this unique ability to humanise this man beyond words,
beyond actions. Then, after another stretched moment, the
Countess sings that, like you, she forgives the Count. And
the chorus sneaks into this intimate musical texture and
you weep because Mozart's melodies awaken within you
something that is Real in a way that the real world and real
people are not.

Silence. *Did I go too far?*

Her: Wow

She thought for a moment.

   Her: And singing, specifically?
   Me, earnestly: You know when you've got the flu and
      you lose your voice? When that happens to me, I feel
      like I've lost my entire identity and sense of self

She cocked her head. At first, she looked at me curiously; then she looked at me like she loved me. I don't know how else to describe it. Her face softened. Her mouth opened, just a little. Her eyes grew warm, then misty. We said goodnight soon after and I walked back to my room, dizzy with conversation.

   I had music in my head. It was dance-like, seductive. Wanting. I wrote it down.

Then I googled her back. She played the saxophone in high school and scored extremely highly – unsurprising, who here didn't? She danced salsa, tango, the Viennese waltz. I found these videos of her dancing on YouTube. I watched them over and over because I was interested in the dancing. And the music was beautiful. Well, okay, I knew the music already because the music was Beyoncé – 'Sweet Dreams'. That's important. Remember Beyoncé's 'Sweet Dreams'. But this whole focused investigation was completely platonic because

I was completely straight. Oh, I haven't mentioned yet: I was completely straight. Sorry, 'completely' 'straight'.

As a teenager, I used to invent thought experiments at the beach – maybe it was something to do with the faraway horizon or the comfortable silence. I remember once imagining a world in which being gay was the norm. I asked myself: would I 'come out' as straight? Simple question: was my attraction to men so innate that I would defy expectation and face social marginalisation and declare my deeply rooted, irrepressible heterosexuality? Simple answer: probably not. But I figured that being straight was simpler and I *did* like men, so that was that. I mean, no, it obviously wasn't.

2

DO YOU EVER THINK ABOUT
MAKING TIME FOR COMPASSION?

I was having a bit of a hard time when I first arrived in Oxford, for all the normal reasons. I'd thought so much about getting in, I hadn't paused to consider what it would actually be like to study there. The work was grueling and there was too much of it. I was admonished for reading too slowly. I felt like I knew nothing about music. I seemed to have fewer opinions than my peers and I was suddenly in a place where strong opinions were valued, prized. I was exhausted by the contagious, masochistic appeal of working into the night. I felt under pressure to actively 'self-discover', but couldn't find the time to do so, so I felt I knew nothing about 'me'. And, amid this pressure and chaos, England didn't feel like home.

Just before I'd left Sydney, my friend Jack's dad had died. I mention his name, but you don't have to remember it. I'd never met his dad. He'd killed himself and Jack had found him lying dead in their home. I've always wondered if those creatures in *Harry Potter* – the ones you can only see if you've seen death, Thestrals – I've always wondered if there is a real-world Thestral equivalent. If you've seen death, what else can you see that the rest of us can't? I never asked my friend.

Jack used boxing classes to hurt himself in a way that wasn't immediately obvious. He started picking fights he wasn't ready for. He got hurt. His fingers, which I'd seen wrapped around drumsticks and guitar picks and birthday presents, coffee cups, steering wheels, were bruised. And then I left. I left my friend with the bruised fingers.

I decided I wanted to tell Alex about Jack and his dad. We messaged and met in town at a café above a bicycle shop. Exposed floorboards, bicycles hanging from the walls, an acoustic guitar album on loop. I ordered my usual coffee, an Americano with hot milk, and she smiled. She ordered the same. I asked her if it was her usual coffee order, too. It wasn't.

She asked me if I'd share some lemon polenta cake with her. Coming from my calorie-counting home, it was so foreign to me that she would order something sweet. We chose a table by the window overlooking St Michael's Street. I took the first bite of the lemon polenta cake. I thought I'd feel rebellious, somehow defiant, chewing the cake, but it felt completely ordinary.

Me: Can I tell you a story?
Her: Please

She waited while I watched the milk cloud the black coffee. Then I told her all about my friend, who she didn't know, and his dad, who I didn't know. She cried. *When was the last time I cried at something completely outside myself?* It was the first time I'd felt 'listened to' in the way she can make people feel 'listened to'. I can't describe it. It felt as though she were hugging me. I felt held, warmed. I'm trying, but I can't describe it. It was a good feeling.

You know the way moments sometimes attach themselves to places? After I had read everything Zadie Smith ever published, I moved onto Ben Lerner. Just like Zadie forever defined the way I think about pleasure and Joy, Ben forever navigated the way I store memories. Ben reflects that, since he received a lot of his important personal news via smartphone while out and about, he could plot the major events of his early thirties on a map. Subtracting Ben's 'smartphone' from the equation, I've often fantasised about drawing my own map of Oxford, straight from my head onto paper, but, instead of labelling places with their names, I would label them with memories. I've never followed through.

The café above the bicycle shop was renovated soon after this moment, so our Lemon Polenta Memory was kind of frozen in space. Though I'm not sure how it would appear on my memory map. I didn't fall in love with Alex at this disappeared café – I didn't feel out of control the way people feel when they fall in love. I felt like Alex was invested in me, like I was invested in her. My inner monologue had morphed into a dialogue – her voice, a new character. Those moments felt important and intense, but not maddening or overwhelming the way romantic love often is. Perhaps this is where I fell in friendship.

Her: Do you ever think about making time for
   compassion?
Me: Not actively, no
Her: There's a study associated with the parable of the
   Good Samaritan that really got me thinking once
Me: I'm not sure I know what you mean

She paraphrased for me. The basic idea is that three people are given various tasks that involve crossing town.

The first is told that they need to be across town by, say, 10 a.m. for a meeting.

The second is told to deliver something across town before lunchtime.

The third is told to cross town by the end of the day.

Each passes someone on the street asking for money.

The first person doesn't notice.

The second gives a little money, maybe lingers for a while.

The third stops and has a conversation with the person on the street.

Her: I think that, in a place as stressful as Oxford and the
   way it kind of breeds a culture of selfishness or at least
   self-absorption, it's important for me to remember to
   make time to be kind

I was scared to be living in a place where you had to remember to make time to be kind. *Is that also true of after-Oxford, adult life?*

Her: What's been the strangest thing you've come across
   so far here?

Me: I had a Music Psychology lecture this morning where
   the professor opened with: 'What is it like to be a bat?'

Her: And?

Me: I still don't know

Her: I'm sorry to say, but I think you never will

Me: Sadly not

Her: Do you think it's possible to know what it's like to
   be anything or anyone other than yourself?

Me: Are you asking me if empathy is possible?

Her: True empathy, yeah

I paused because I didn't know and because I'd never considered this before.

Me: Actually, I don't know

Her: That's perfectly okay, neither do I. My friend
   Harry – you should meet him, he's great! – thinks
   empathy is overrated

Me, finding my academic feet: I think it's probably very
   problematic to deny the importance of empathy . . . Is
   your friend Harry a psychopath?

Her, laughing: Far from it! Just a keen philosophical
   intellect . . . but, sorry, you were saying about a bat in
   your lecture?

Me: Oh, there's nothing more to say really, it was just
   really bizarre . . . You never said: what's the strangest
   thing *you've* come across here?

She went quiet and her eyes glazed over.

Me: I'm sorry, I didn't mean to–
Her: There's nothing to be sorry about, of course

Then she was back. Sun-in-the-sky eyes.

Her: I'm worried to play the older, I've-been-here-longer
   card. I don't want to
Me: I don't think that's something you need to
   worry about
Her: Sure, but that's not how I see us. I'm not your
   'buddy', I'm your friend
Me: I'm not sure what you're getting at?
Her: This place can be – well, I don't think I know the
   right word
Me: Testing?
Her: No. Sorry, I'll answer your question. The strangest thing
   I've come across here is probably also the hardest thing
   and it's probably been knowing people who aren't okay
Me: If you'd rather not talk about it–
Her: The strangest thing I've come across is seeing what
   'not okay' really looks like

I was scared to be living in a place where I would see what
'not okay' really looks like. She didn't elaborate and I didn't
ask her to.

———

There was more new music in my head that afternoon. Seductive, still, but with a trace of sadness or loneliness.

I started to panic. It was the kind of panic I often experience after opening up to somebody. I tried to work: *The peaceful mood of Schubert's lyricism is repeatedly disturbed by brutal, violent contrasts.* Jack's dad was dead. I tried to work: *An example of the relationship between serenity and violence can be found in the slow movement of Schubert's A Major Piano Sonata (D959).* I felt far away from Sydney. I scrambled eggs. I gave up. I paced. I stopped pacing and leaned against the windowsill – clichés, like staring out the window to gain perspective, can be comforting in moments of panic. My room had a view of Longwall Street, so named because it consists of a street and a long wall. Maybe. Cyclists in Oxford seemed to match the architecture – same colours, same postures. I worried that Alex felt awkward that I'd let her in on something so close to my heart. She'd hinted at her own vulnerability, darkness, but she hadn't gone into detail like I had, which was fine. We don't need to trade vulnerabilities with our friends. Though people do. What a weird game.

———

Dear Alex,

I hope you don't mind me writing you a letter. I really enjoy writing letters and felt like I had something to say that would look better on paper.

Thank you for the lemon polenta cake. I don't mean the cake. Thank you for listening to me. I really appreciate being able to talk about things with you.

But, also, I haven't known you very long and I opened up to you in a way I'm not used to doing with new friends. It feels like things got very intense very quickly, which isn't a bad thing. I just realise that this might have been a bit of a burden to place on a new friendship and I really don't want you to feel burdened.

I hope at least part of this makes sense.

Amalia xxx

Dear Amalia,

Thank you for your letter – I also really enjoy writing letters. Things do sometimes need to be articulated with a pen.

I want to start by saying that I don't feel at all burdened by your sharing. I think one of the things I've found about this place is that things happen very quickly and intensely here. It's like a pressure cooker (though please excuse my banal simile) – we all seem to befriend, to be inspired, to crumble, to fall in love, so quickly.

If it helps, there's this quote in Chinese, yī jiàn rú gù, which describes a kind of falling in love that happens in friendships, which is kind of how I see us.

Like old friends at first sight.

*Please don't worry about sharing too much or
too little. That said, if you'd like some space,
I would completely understand that, too.
Sometimes it's good to take a breather.
    Love,
    Alex xxx*

I studied her writing because I'd never seen it before and because its elegance attracted me. I fell in silly, school-crush love with my high-school maths teacher because he drew perfect circles on the whiteboard. Effortlessly. Alex's every letter was perfectly proportioned. Every letter slanted a little to the right. The way she penned cursive made it look like the letters were dancing with each other, holding hands or linking arms. The way they leaned made it look like someone had paused the dance in the midst of some weight-shifting move. Didn't Zadie Smith write something about dancing and writing? I don't think she meant it like this. I loved Alex's writing.

3

DO WE DESIRE BECAUSE WE'RE INCOMPLETE?

A boy called Tim studied music two years above me. He looked like an uglier Leonardo DiCaprio. He dressed very well, was predicted a high First, and sang in the choir. It surprised me that the choirs in Oxford seemed to claim the same social status as the rugby teams back home. Tim was captain of the choir. He hosted great parties. One night, he invited me. The very casually ripped piece of paper in my mailbox read:

PARTY
8PM
RM V.3
TIM

Eve sat cross-legged on my little bed while I tried on different outfits. She played with the holes in her tights. We had soft rock music playing and Eve was drinking gin and tonic out of a can.

> **Eve:** Why exactly were you invited to this party?
> **Me:** Because Tim studies music

I paused. Then I added:

> **Me:** And maybe he knows I'm friends with Alex? Aren't
> they in the same year?
> **Eve:** I haven't even seen Alex since that dinner

She scratched her head.

> **Eve:** You know, the Greeks used to try to treat migraines
> by drilling a hole into the skull to release evil spirits

I didn't know.

———

Tim lived in a room with two levels joined by a spiral staircase. The echoes of the party boomed through his building, so I followed the sound vibrations – musical breadcrumbs. I recognised no one there and decided it would be easier to dance with strangers than to talk with them. I've always thought that musicians without inhibitions make good dancers. The beats tell us how to dance. Those who can anticipate the changing beat, who can tailor their dance to each piece of music, are the most beautiful.

Tim crossed the room to dance with me. His dancing made me think of liquid – like his bones were missing. I danced longer than I normally would. Eventually, I helped myself to someone's beer, ignoring a cautionary warning from home. My mother's voice: never drink from a bottle you didn't see opened. *I should call her.* The bottle was cold and I massaged the condensation into my palms. From where I stood, alongside the makeshift dancefloor, I could easily survey the party. The lower level was filled with bodies that moved less fluidly than Tim's. People up the spiral staircase were attempting conversation over the music. I could see the veins pressing against their necks as they strained to be heard.

Among those up the staircase, I spied Alex with a group of strangers. They were mostly dressed in black. Alex wore a gold skirt and a light scarf tied around her neck. She was nodding along to the shouts of the people in black. I was overcome by the urge to dance again. *Watch me dance, Alex.* I rejoined the sweaty bodies with beer still tingling my tongue. I danced bonelessly like Tim. Then I let my bones reform and I spun and popped and laughed with the strangers I didn't want to speak to. I glanced up the spiral staircase and caught her eye. *How long have you been watching, Alex?* I think she looked surprised to see me there and we held eyes for a long time before either of us smiled. She motioned that I join her upstairs and I was introduced to the people in black. I asked Alex whether Oscar was at the party, but she said this wasn't really his sort of thing. Alex talked and breathed in time to the music. I watched her neck to see if I could see veins straining. I couldn't. Occasionally, she'd glance at the dancers below and roll her shoulders or sway her hips.

Tim messaged me the next day thanking me for coming and suggesting that we grab a drink in town some time soon. I told him I wanted to try out this cocktail bar I'd heard about from Eve that only let you in if you correctly answered a riddle. It was called The Mad Hatter.

————

Door to cocktail bar: What has an eye but cannot see?
Me: Pie!

Tim laughed and offered 'a storm'. The door was laughing, too, and insisted both answers were 'technically correct', though one was 'certainly more original'. The door welcomed us into a small cocktail bar. The design was like nothing I'd seen before – wannabe speakeasy meets Alice's Wonderland. The chandeliers shimmered next to oversized top hats pinned to the low roof. The thick, rouge curtains were freckled with hearts, clubs, aces, spades. A saxophone rendition of *'La Vie en Rose'* played at the perfect volume. Tim hummed along in harmony. Something smelled of mint. We found a table in the corner.

Tim looked urbane in his black trousers and black turtleneck. He'd slicked back his Leonardo DiCaprio hair and smiled what I think he thought was his winning smile. It *was* a good smile. We decided to share a teapot martini, which arrived in a matte black teapot with matching teacups. Tim asked a lot of questions and leaned in when I spoke. I explained the parallel I'd drawn between Australian rugby players and English choral singers; he laughed and flexed his choir-quarterback biceps. *This is flirting.* When he asked me what I thought of Oxford so far, I told him that it was exactly what I had expected. He raised his eyebrow and I felt silly, so I confessed. I told him that I'd been completely thrown by the place and by the people, that I felt like I'd fallen down the rabbit hole. I imagine you'll think this clichéd, but it pretty much summed it up – like most clichés do. He gestured to the chandelier/top hat ceiling.

Tim: Welcome to Wonderland

Tim was very charming. He'd decided to study music because he was 'through pretending he was cool enough to study economics', though he'd probably end up working for a bank. He was an only child, like me, and appreciated the way his upbringing had helped forge such an intimate relationship with both his parents. His mum was the star of a British TV drama. Had I heard of it? No, but I would check it out. Tim had heard me singing scales through the practice room walls and couldn't believe that scales could sound so musical. I didn't blush. I told him I sang scales in the shower and his eyes twinkled along with the chandeliers. *Is it wrong to mention what you do in the shower on a first date?* When he asked me what I thought of the people, I told him about Eve and her holey tights and that the Greeks used to try to treat migraines by drilling a hole into the skull to release evil spirits. He smiled a less good smile and told me I could use a few good allies in a place like Oxford. When I told him about Alex, he seemed taken aback. It was the first time I'd caught him off guard all evening and I wondered how many first dates he'd been on. I decided he'd likely been on the same number of first and second dates. Tim did not consider Alex the type to befriend First Years. I wanted to ask if he was the type to ask out First Years, but decided against it. He asked whether Alex and I were from the same part of Australia, if we'd known each other before. No – I'm Sydney, she's Melbourne. He asked how we met and I told him and he paused. 'Interesting.' It was my turn to be caught off guard, so I panicked and invited him over for dinner with Alex and maybe Oscar, who I was yet to meet. Tim thought that sounded like an excellent idea. *When did coping mechanisms take the form of impromptu dinner invitations?*

We stood to leave and my brain hummed with martini overtones. We strolled back to college, singing. Tim laughed when I danced on the empty road. I told him his laughter was more resonant than I'd expected from a choirboy. He reminded me that he was choir-quarterback. He placed his hand on my lower back for the last few steps before my door. I nearly assured him that I wouldn't get lost without his guidance, but decided against it. Instead, I told him I'd had a lovely time. Then he kissed me. He pulled me close to him so most of my body was pressed against most of his. I kissed him back. I wondered where the college positioned its security cameras, how many romances the porters watched blossom and die over the years. I wondered where Alex and Oscar had shared their first kiss. I wondered whether

Eve was awake, what she was doing. Then I remembered I was kissing charming Tim and wondered what he was thinking. His lips were soft and warm. Eventually, I pulled away and we said goodnight. He reminded me that I'd invited him for dinner with Alex and Oscar and I told him not to expect much from my cooking. From my window, I watched Tim saunter away. Was he deliberately walking so slowly or were my martini eyes seeing in slow motion? Eve didn't respond when I knocked on her door so I collapsed on my bed.

———

Eve:
So, how was the date?! E x

Amalia:
Eve!
It was fun!
I really like him ☺
How are you doing?

Eve:
Fine, fine, have fuck tons of reading to get on with this morning . . .

Amalia:
Ah damn, hope it's all okay?

Eve:
Yeah it'll be fine.
Also I think your mum added me on Facebook?

Amalia:
Oh god ...

———

I held the phone against my ear while I made the bed. I was
tucking in the sheet when they answered together.

   Dad: Mali! She lives!
   Mum: Hi, baby, you've caught us at the perfect time!
       Dad and I have just finished a movie and are getting
       ready for bed
   Dad: You would have loved the film. You know
       Ben Affleck?
   Mum: Let her speak! How's Oxford, Mals?

I finished making the bed and threw the pillows against the
wall haphazardly.

   Me: It's good, fine so far. I spent the first few weeks
       thinking they'd accidentally accepted the wrong
       person, but actually I'm managing to keep up, just ...
   Dad: That's my girl!
   Mum: And are the people nice?
   Me: They're lovely. Though you would know that, since
       apparently you're adding them on Facebook?

Dad: I told her not to. I said it would be weird
Me: It *is* kind of weird
Mum: Oh, I'm sorry, Mals. Do you mind?
   I was just missing you and I saw a photo on
   Facebook of you and this Eve and she looked
   so sweet
Me: No, no, it's fine, but maybe don't do it again, if
   that's okay?
Mum: Got it! No more interfering parent
Me: Thank you

Silence.

Mum: So ... do you have a boyfriend yet?
Dad: Diane! No! Your old man doesn't want to know!

I imagined them together in our kitchen, leaning over the speakerphone. I felt the punch of homesickness.

Me: I went on a first date last night actually. With a guy
   called Tim

By this point, I was brushing my teeth.

Dad: Tell me his last name and address
Me: Very funny
Dad: What is he studying?
Me: Music, but he wants to go into banking
Mum: Nice boy?

Me, mouth full of toothpaste: Very. Actually, I'm having
　　him and two other friends – a couple – over for dinner
Mum: How very sophisticated

She'd interrupted her broad Aussie accent with a posh British
caricature. I spat into the sink.

Me: I don't know what to cook
Dad: Have you asked their dietary requirements?
　　Apparently that's the thing to do these days
Mum: What about a nice white fish? You can bake it
　　with balsamic vinegar, tomatoes, and olives like we
　　do at home
Me: Oh, thank you, that's actually a great idea. How are
　　you guys doing anyway?
Mum: Fine, fine. Couples still fighting, so I'm
　　still in work
Dad: All good here, too – just missing you, Mals
Me: Missing you guys, too

———

My first dinner party – I drowned Tesco's finest white fish in
balsamic vinegar, topped it with tomatoes and olives, threw
in the herbs Eve had given me for the evening, and popped
it in the oven. I'd invited Eve to join us, but she was watching
a film in town.

　　I cut my finger while trying to put the knife away. Then I
heated some chocolate in the microwave. It was rich and thick
and the smell of it flavoured the air in the tiny communal

kitchen. I breathed it in. I dipped strawberries into the melted chocolate without washing them because my mum raised me to know that water kills chocolate, though I was also raised to wash fruit – we take advice when it suits us. I was about halfway through the chocolate-inhaling-strawberry-dipping when Alex stuck her head into the tiny kitchen. She was 'in the neighbourhood' and thought she'd pop by to see if she could lend a hand. I laughed because, like me, she lived in our college and because she was funny. When we took the food into my room to set the table, I was embarrassed because, rather than the dinner party playlist I'd prepared, my favourite Chopin piece was playing. Waltz No. 3. I assured her the music would be better suited to the evening when the evening officially started, but she wasn't listening. She closed her eyes and swayed in triple time with the waltz. I watched her sway.

Tim arrived with Oscar, who I quickly recognised as the arrogant American from the international students mingle evening. Of course. I was surprised, almost appalled, at Alex's poor taste in men, though he was friendlier than I'd remembered – all smiles and thumbs-up. Tim greeted me with a slow kiss on the cheek. I blushed. Alex threw me a glance. I threw it back. She smiled. We all sat on the floor. By this point, James Blake was playing, as angsty and sexy as ever.

When Alex spoke, she would touch my arm, shoulder, back, casually. I used to wonder whether her touches were instinctual or intentional. It was strange speaking to Alex with other people present. I felt like we were always a few

steps ahead of the conversation and there was only room for
two on our step.

Oscar played a lot of tennis at university. Alex had shown
him videos of my singing, which he complimented without
knowing what to say. 'They were very nice.' Thanks, Oscar.
He insisted that, to 'level out the playing field', I had to watch
videos of him playing tennis. I didn't know if he was joking.
Even Tim noticed Oscar's clumsy conversation, raising his
eyebrows and running his fingers through his Leo DiCaprio
hair. Oscar's sentences kind of petered out. He sounded like
slime feels. Cold and wet. *How did his slime ever mix with her red
wine?* My dislike of Oscar was visceral. But the conversation
became richer with the wine.

> **Tim:** But do we desire because we're incomplete?
> **Oscar:** I don't think there has to be something missing
>   for you to desire it

His mouth curled around the 'r' of 'desire'.

> **Tim:** Well, you can't desire something you already have
> **Oscar:** No, but I don't think you are incomplete just
>   because there are things you still desire
> **Tim:** Do you think desire is ubiquitous?
> **Her:** Do you think the fact that most sex workers
>   are women and most of the people who hire sex
>   workers are men says something about
>   male desire?

I laughed. She made me laugh. We all settled back in our floor cushions. Alex put her hair up.

Later, we were talking about something less intense when Tim asked, 'Yeah, but what is irony?' I replied, 'Irony is slicing your finger open while putting on the knife protector.' I showed them my bandaged finger and Alex gasped and grabbed my calf without thinking. Instinctual? This time, Oscar and Tim laughed with me. Tim's laugh was deeper and more resonant. Oscar's was nasal and tense. If they were colours, they would have been maroon and puce respectively. I smiled at my synaesthetic diagnosis. Alex's hand left my leg. It cooled.

We spoke about whether good leaders need to have firm opinions. Oscar and I thought they did. Tim and Alex thought they needed to represent the opinions of many. Then we discussed our opinions on confidence. It felt like a very University Conversation. I felt a little young, almost naïve, but consciously tried to brush off feelings of inadequacy. I'm not sure if Alex noticed my brushing, but she rested her hand on my back, then on the floor behind me. Her hand was so warm. I envied the floor.

By the end of the dinner, we were full of balsamic-soaked fish, chocolate-dipped strawberries, wine, and University Conversation. Alex yawned and grew quiet. Tim asked us all what we had planned for the rest of the week, a gentle segue towards the end of the evening. Oscar didn't take the hint and diatribed for another 15 minutes about the rest of his week. Eventually, I started clearing away. Oscar and Alex left together. They hugged me goodbye one at a time. Alex thanked me 100 times and told me what a lovely evening she'd had. Tim hung around. When it was just the two of us in my room, we kissed until I felt less tired. This time, my thoughts didn't wander. Tim didn't stay over.

———

Mum:
So, how did your friends like the fish?

Amalia:
They loved it, thanks again Ma!

Mum:
Fun evening?

Amalia:
Yeah, mostly! I met my friend's boyfriend, who was kind of weird

Mum:
It's very common to like a friend but not a couple. I imagine the dynamic was different to what you're used to?

Amalia:
Yeah, exactly

Mum:
Just remember to keep in touch with old friends too – I'm sure Cali would appreciate a phonecall . . .

Cali, my oldest friend (in time, not age).

Amalia:

Yeah, good idea.

You and dad still good?

Mum:

Still good xxx

4

WHAT'S THE DIFFERENCE
BETWEEN DRAWING AND ART?

I decided to join the poetry society despite always having been a closet poet. The society met once a fortnight behind a plain door, hidden among many in our college cloisters, in a small room atop a spiral staircase. Famous poetry was read and wine was drunk and thoughts were shared. Most society members wore baggy, light, colourful clothing, despite the cold. It was all very fitting. I often left feeling inspired, intimidated, quiet, thoughtful. One particular evening, the president of the society asked for anonymous submissions to be left in her mailbox 24 hours before the meeting. The idea was that your poem would be anonymously prodded and dissected. I had never shared my poetry, but, on this occasion, I decided to bite the bullet. I submitted a musical poem I'd written from the perspective of melody – it kind of read like an unrequited love poem from melody to harmony. There weren't supposed to be hidden meanings.

I didn't expect to have to chew and swallow the bullet I'd bitten.

The president of the society was a tall redhead who wore her hair in two loose plaits that framed her face in a messy love heart. Her fingers were very long and her nails were very short. I didn't realise the significance of this. We all sat together – there were probably a dozen of us – and poured the wine. There was only red wine. Six bottles. I couldn't remember the names of any of the society's members and I was sure they couldn't remember mine. I felt the warm blanket of anonymity I sometimes use for comfort. Someone had brought 70 per cent dark chocolate to the meeting. It was my favourite. Though no one knew. Safe in my blanket, I wasn't nervous.

Three poems had been submitted anonymously. The first was about ashes in an urn – the poet likened the urn to a genie lamp. The second was about feet – I didn't get it. The third was mine – a love letter from melody to harmony. I was part of the Passive Half of society members. When the president read my poem, I kept my face still. I held the anonymity blanket tight. I clung to it.

> *I am melody, you my harmony*
> *But they don't notice how you lead*
> *You lead, I follow.*
> *I flutter beneath your power*
> *I trill and dance and sing and fly at your command*
> *You control my pulse. You choose my direction.*
> *You are dark imagination*
> *I, your fantasy.*

President: I find this third poem really peculiar

Active Member 1: How horrible to feel so powerless

Active Member 2: This is definitely about power

Active Member 1: Isn't everything?

Active Member 3: What is 'dark imagination'?

Active Member 4: I think it's the persona's dark
    imagination

President: Their inner, hidden desires

Active Member 4: It's sexy

Active Member 2: What's sexy about having your pulse
    controlled?

I wasn't sure how I felt. For me, this was a simple exercise in writing about music. If you forced me to reach deeper, I could probably have spun some tale about what it's like to be the simple melody-singer on top of a rich sea of harmony. But it didn't really get deeper than that for me.

President: I think it's about sexuality

What?

Active Member 3: Oh, yes, of course!

Active Member 1: The powerlessness of secret
    homosexual urges!

Active Member 5: 'You lead, I follow'!

Active Member 6: It's all in the imagery – leading,
    fluttering, commanding, control, direction ...

Active Member 5: Fantasy!

Active Member 4: Sexual fantasy!

Me: I don't think it's about sexuality

President: What do you think it's about?

Me: I think it's about music

The president licked her lips. She took my anonymity blanket in her teeth and ripped it from me. I was completely exposed to the prodding and dissecting. I suffocated the need to shiver and kept still.

Active Member 3: But what's it *really* about?

Active Member 4: Lesbians!

What?

Active Member 2: And power dynamics in lesbian relationships

Active Member 1: Exploring the homosexual power dynamic–

Me: What if it's about how people give melody too much credit?

Active Member 1: –and the powerlessness of homoeroticism

Active Member 3: Power dynamics in homosexual relationships are fascinating

President: I think it would be interesting to see harmony's response to melody

Active Member 2: It would make a great dialogue

I was naked and confused.

When I got home that evening, feeling drunk, naked, and confused, I scribbled harmony's response to melody in the notebook I kept next to my bed. Then I slept. The next morning, Alex came to my room to pick me up. We were going to work together on our college lawns because 19 degrees was warm by English standards. She looked around my bedroom while I put the last of my books in my tote.

Her: What's this?
Me: What's what?
Her: On the notepad?
Me: Oh, no! Don't read that!
Her: Who makes you feel fleshless?
Me: I went to poetry society last night
Her: Clearly
Me: Nosy!
Her: I couldn't help myself, it's just lying here and–
Me: I don't even remember what I wrote. It was a late-
    night drunken scribble

So she read it to me. Very. Dramatically.

> *Without you I am not naked*
> *I am fleshless. I have no muscle.*
> *No strength.*
> *I am bare bone. And it's cold.*
> *And I'm detached.*
> *You are not perfection. Simply mine.*

When you dance and extend your hand
I cannot take it
I simply move beneath you
I close my eyes
And dance alone.

Me: It's harmony's reply to melody
Her: What did melody say?

I gave her melody's poem to read.

Her: Wow
Me: Stop
Her: No, I think this is beautiful
Me: They told me to write harmony's reply
Her: I think I identify more with melody, but, I agree, it
makes for a nice dialogue
Me: Oh, is that because you're secretly a lesbian?
Her: Sorry?
Me: They all thought the poem was about sexuality and
lesbianism and homoerotic sexual fantasy
Her: But it's about music
Me: Exactly
Her: Poets are weird

We set up in the middle of the lawn between between the handsome, sand-coloured New Building and the cloisters. The grass was warm and vividly green. I lay on my front, typing slowly on my laptop. Beside me, Alex read on her back.

Unbeknown to me, while we were working together, Alex bought us tickets to that evening's life-drawing class at the Pitt Rivers Museum. This made me nervous for two reasons:

1. Life drawing involved naked people, which made me nervous
2. Life drawing involved drawing, which made me nervous

———

We began in the museum part of the museum, where we drew little figures and totem poles from different angles. They were 'timed' drawings, warm-ups – six minutes on a little figure, 24 minutes on a totem pole. Then they told us to wander around the room and pick something, anything, to draw for half an hour. Alex went left, so I went right. I found an arm-length statue of a naked woman. Her jawline was pronounced and her eyes were hollow. Her nose was too small for her face. Her hands were too big for her arms. She was smooth and grey and I wanted to touch her. I touched her. She was cool. I spent far too long staring at her. My drawing didn't do her justice, of course. We discarded our drawings. We were given large sheets of brown paper when we moved into the non-museum part of the museum.

An old, round man in a robe was sitting on a stool, phone in hand. 'Meditative music' was playing – cymbals, gongs, pentatonic scales ...

The man removed his robe and sat naked in front of us. Alex whispered to me between gong beats, 'I've kind of always wanted to pose in a life-drawing class.' At first, I felt strange looking at the robeless round man, so I looked at Alex instead. She was deeply immersed in him. She was studying his outline, 'breaking him up into shapes' as she'd later tell me. I watched her eyes trace him. Then I traced him. His roundness made him easy to trace. My mind wandered while I put the man on my paper. Alex looked over at my drawing and smiled. I blushed. She couldn't have known no one had seen me draw before. What did this man do when he wasn't sitting naked in front of me? I started thinking about something I'd read that kind of upset me.

Her, whispered: Hey, are you okay?

Me, whispered: Yeah, sorry, I'm just thinking about something I read today that kind of upset me

Her: What is it?

Me: I was reading an essay about this motet from the 14th century called 'Why does my husband beat me?'

Her: Oh. Wow. Humans are disgustingly consistent

Me: I've found this essay-reading really affects my mood

Her: That's because you're extremely empathetic

Me: So it *is* possible to be extremely empathetic!

Her: You've convinced me!

Me: I think you are extremely empathetic

Her: Hey, when we're done here, can I tell you a story?

We drew in silence. Alex's every line was fine and precise. The man on her paper clearly matched the man on the chair. Then, in the last few minutes, I watched her smudge each perfect line with her fingers. Blur. It would have been quite an aggressive action if not for her determined elegance. I smiled, asking, 'What's the difference between drawing and art?' She scoffed at my sarcasm. She told me she was going to throw her blurry man away, which shocked me. She told me it was about the act, not the art. I insisted on keeping both of our men. Later, I taped them to my bedroom wall.

On the slow walk home, Alex told me a story about a friend who was no longer at university with us. They'd become fast friends after they met at the language faculty in their first year. Her friend, Martina, was unique and pure and beautiful. She always wore a bright-red beanie and refused to eat pre-packaged food. She experienced something dark during university that had made everything else dark – Alex didn't want to speak about it. It seemed she'd felt her friend's hurt the way extremely empathetic people do – all over, around, inside her body. On her skin. It was strange for Alex to be in Oxford without Martina, who'd gone home to Italy and probably wouldn't return. They hadn't really kept in touch. Her eyes were dark and watery. They were the sea. I'd grown up by the beach and I loved the sea. I reached for her hand and she grasped mine. I drew perfect circles on her skin and she sighed. That day, the music she gave me was bruised into the minor key.

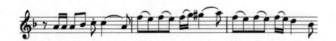

On the way to my room, I passed a poster advertising a clinical trial.

MOOD SWINGS

Does your mood often fluctuate?

Have you ever felt so hyper that
you've acted out of character or
done something you regretted?

Do you sometimes have more
energy than usual or get so irritable
that others are concerned?

Volunteers aged 18–25 years are required
for medication study investigating
the role of calcium channels in
mood stability. Volunteers will be
reimbursed for time and travel.

I cried.

———

Alex wanted to show me the only shop in Oxford that sold tofu (I later discovered that lots of shops sold tofu) and I was appropriately very excited. We walked together up Cowley Road, annoying passers-by because Alex also liked to dance in the street.

Then she stood in front of me, blocking my way so that I had to slow down dramatically. She returned to my side and looped her arm through mine as though she hadn't just been very weird. I asked her why she had just been very weird, as I brought my hand up to meet hers, and she blushed and told me that a smoker was walking directly towards us and she wanted to stand between me and the smoke. I think I laughed because she was smart enough to know that she was being ridiculous. But I also wanted to scream or sing.

> **Her:** So many people try to quit smoking in January. Like, there are spikes in Nicorette patch sales and all that. And then they all join gyms. Why do people make New Year's resolutions?
>
> **Me:** I guess a lot of people don't make time for reflection, right? And the New Year is kind of this universal signpost? People think about their lives in an active kind of way
>
> **Her:** I think people should always actively be thinking about how to better themselves
>
> **Me:** It's strange that we don't make birthday resolutions
>
> **Her, chuckling:** Haha, yes, that's true. I like the idea of birthday resolutions

She put up her hair.

> **Me:** I really hate New Year's Eve
>
> **Her:** That surprises me
>
> **Me:** Really? Why?
>
> **Her:** You love celebrating and spending time with people. I bet you love silly holidays like Valentine's Day
>
> **Me:** I love celebrating and spending time with people and the idea of a day set aside to celebrate love makes

me smile, though I've never spent Valentine's Day in a
relationship

Her: You're really not missing out

Me: How do you and Oscar spend Valentine's Day?

Her: We don't

I didn't know what to say. Maybe the sequel to Sheila Heti's
How Should a Person Be? should be *What Should a Person Say?*

Me: Well, New Year's is different because everyone is
drunk and tired

Her: Being drunk and tired is the worst

Me: Yet people are so often drunk and tired

Her: I definitely get more drunk when I'm tired

Me: The worst

Her: Do you know what would make New Year's better?

Me: You?

Her: Tofu

———

I spent the afternoon reading an article, which quoted a music
theorist: 'To write poetry after Auschwitz is barbaric.'

Unprepared for the Holocaust reference, I shut my laptop
and took a brisk walk around the college grounds – past the
brick walls dressed in wisteria, the swirly wrought iron gate,
the stone bridge, the gravel trail, the tree-stump chair, the
leisurely deer. Flowers shivering with the occasional rush
of wind. It all suddenly felt familiar, almost comforting. I

wondered when this shift occurred. In my first poetry society meeting, we'd read a C. S. Lewis poem set on this very walk:

This year, this year, as all these flowers foretell,
We shall escape the circle and undo the spell.

I tried to read the tulips like a fortune teller, but saw nothing.

———

I took the tofu to Tim's. His room hardly resembled the room in which I'd danced without talking and then talked without dancing. I hadn't noticed his framed posters – the Rolling Stones, Marilyn Monroe, David Bowie, *La Bohème*. In a line by the window stood a row of bottles dressed in paper bags. Tim flavoured his own gin. We took the dinner ingredients to the kitchen. He insisted on cooking because he didn't want me to expect him to expect me to cook. He suggested we open some wine and took a bottle out of the cupboard, but he was embarrassed – someone must have opened it and it was the only one he had. Did I want him to go grab a bottle from up the road? No, that's okay. Did I want to sample some gin? No, I was fine without.

Tim seemed more considered with his words than he'd been over cocktails and again over dinner. He spoke slowly, clipping each word with consonants, and he seemed to close each sentence with a physical gesture.

Tim: Has anyone ever told you that you look really sexy in glasses?

Tim leans forward.

He told me he was preparing to cycle across the country because he wanted to abuse his body while he was still young.

Tim flexes biceps.

He asked me my opinion on extreme sports and I scrambled for opinions on extreme sports.

Tim flicks floppy hair.

We sat without touching and ate the tofu, a flavourless addition to a vegetarian pasta. Tim told me he'd written 50 facts about himself when he first started university so he could track the ways university would change him. He thought it probably hadn't changed him all that much.

Tim shrugs.

Then it was quiet and I couldn't think of anything related to add, so I panicked and attempted University Conversation by asking Tim whether he thought that desire was conditioned. He laughed and leaned back in his chair. He ran his hands through his hair while I clumsily rearranged my words, as though that would make the segue smoother: 'Do you think it's possible to condition desire?' I'd been thinking a lot about how something as personal and intimate as desire could be influenced by our surroundings. It was something I wanted to speak to Alex about, though I wanted to be firmer in my own thoughts before sharing them with her. Tim didn't have anything to add to my thoughts, which disappointed me. He might have noticed my disappointment because he started talking more, compensating with confidence. The discussion felt rough. It was the first time I'd noticed an

interaction where alcohol's conversation-lubricating quality
was missing, which worried me.

Tim moved closer to me and kissed my neck. His kisses felt
good, warm, strong. He pulled me up off my seat. We kissed
the short way to his bed. We undressed. He stopped kissing
me to look at my body, which made me feel self-conscious,
not sexy. *Does alcohol make me feel sexy?* But I pushed through
it. I looked at this naked British man in front of me and I
wanted to touch him. I wanted him near me and all over me.
I was reassured by my wanting. Though I wasn't sure why
I needed reassuring. Sex with Tim was how I'd imagined it
would be – safe, caring, gentle. I lay on my side and he ran his
fingers over my curves and told me my body was a skyline.
I liked that, the image of bodies on beds, silhouetted against
walls, looking like skylines. I wondered what I looked like
to Tim. I wondered whether Tim wondered what he looked
like to me. His kisses were slow and deliberate. We explored
each other with our tongues for a long time before he came
and I felt each lick all over me. I didn't recognise the way he
made my body feel. *Do we get to know our own bodies through
the bodies of others?*

———

I decided to try writing 50 facts about myself but quickly
grew bored, so I decided to try to write 50 facts about Alex:

1. She loves James Blake's music
2. She considers herself more of a dancer than
   a linguist

3. She doesn't want to be famous
4. She cannot stand lying
5. She's very politically correct
6. She's very tactile
7. Opening up doesn't come easily to her
8. Keeping secrets is important to her
9. She wouldn't describe herself as 'naturally confident'
10. She wants to pose naked in a life-drawing class

5

WHAT SONG MEANS A GREAT DEAL TO YOU?

Harry was one of those tall, dark, handsome types. Chin shrouded in stubble. His hands were very bony, constantly adjusting his tie. We sat next to one another, opposite Alex and Oscar.

I'd brought with me to Oxford just one formal dress, pale pink and flowery, which made me feel like a bridesmaid. It contrasted wildly with the long black gown I was having to don for Formal Hall. Before leaving my room, I balanced my phone against a stack of library books and took a picture for my parents, though they would still be sleeping. Sending the photo, I felt more excited than ridiculous.

The hall was softly lit and almost ethereal. We stood as the High Table entered from some seemingly secret passage. Bang. I jumped. Alex chuckled. A booming male voice: *Benedictus benedicat.* The scraping of chairs as hundreds of students sat, the tinkle of cutlery as they buttered their bread. Gazing down the long table, the ratio of wine bottles to people seemed to be 1:1, which felt excessive. Oscar filled our glasses.

Oscar: Welcome to Formal Hall, Amalia

I had been to Formal Hall before, though this was my first 'Sunday Formal', which was extra formal.

Me: Thank you, it's lovely to meet you, Harry
Harry: And you. Alex speaks about you often

She does?

Her: So, down to business, Harry. Explain your
empathy theory to Amalia. You think empathy is
overrated, right?
Harry: You don't waste any time, do you, Alex?

She smirked. I already liked their dynamic.

Harry: Yes, well, I think people put too much
emphasis on the importance of empathy. For
instance, Amalia, what are three characteristics you
value in a person?
Her: No need to put her on the spot
Harry: I'm sure she's okay
Me, stumbling: Okay, um, I'd say honesty,
kindness and, um–

Harry, smiling: Empathy perhaps?

Me: Maybe, yeah, but I don't see what's wrong with that

I felt like I'd walked, willingly, into a trap, like Harry had asked me to choose a card from a deck that he would use to baffle and amaze a crowd at my expense.

Harry: Okay, let's start by defining empathy as putting yourself in the shoes of other people or, better yet, climbing inside someone's skin and walking around in it

Oscar: Atticus Finch, *To Kill A Mockingbird*, 1960

Harry: Very good. I argue that relying on empathy as a moral guide for decision-making is a mistake. Firstly, some people are more empathetic than others, so, if we think empathy is at the root of morality, then empathetic people would have more stringent moral duties than non-empathetic people. Secondly, we empathise with some people more than others. So, in relying on empathy to make moral decisions, we'll inevitably prioritise suffering that we can relate to over another that seems further away

Oscar: Well put

I excused myself to the bathroom. I sat on the closed toilet. It was early in the morning in Sydney, but I tried my luck.

Me: Hey, Mum, sorry, did I wake you?

Mum: No, no, I'm just having coffee in my favourite
  mug – the one you made me, remember?

Me: Ma, I'm in this big conversation about empathy and I
  have no idea what to say. Can you help me?

Mum: Sure, sweetheart, though it's okay to admit you
  don't know what to say

Me: I know, I know, but not now, okay?

Mum: Okay, what are they speaking about?

I was running out of time.

Me: Basically, this guy Harry thinks that empathy, as a
  tool for moral decision-making, is overrated because
  different people have different levels of empathy
  and because we empathise more with some people
  than others

Mum: He sounds very philosophical

Me: He's third-year PPE

Mum: I don't know what that means

Me: He studies philosophy, politics, and economics

Mum: Why don't you come at it from a psychological
  perspective, darling? You can tell your friend that the
  value of empathy isn't about deciding how to act, but
  it's a valuable way of relating to those you love

I considered this for a moment.

Me: Right, so less utilitarian and more about being
  present and connected with others?

Mum: Exactly. You're so clever, sweetheart
Me: Okay, awesome, thank you, got to go

She sounded concerned.

Mum: Love you, Mals. Hope you're being looked after
Me: Love you, too

When I returned, we were served by waiters. They looked our age, which was a little bizarre and uncomfortable. Looking back, the extravagant eventually became routine and that bizarreness and discomfort faded with time. What a strange world.

I explained my mum's argument to Harry as my own. He seemed impressed, even raised his glass my way. His smile was genuine. I breathed out. I decided I liked Harry, despite the initial intimidation. Alex asked me about an essay I'd been writing about artificial intelligence in music. I think she was trying to show me off, which I at once disliked and appreciated. I'd called the essay 'The Musical Turing Test' and explained how I tried to question whether 'musicality' was something machines could possess. If a musical robot can analyse the pitch and velocity data of musicians and then respond accordingly, is the robot musical?

Me: And so Turing's assertion – that a machine that behaves as intelligently as a human being is as intelligent as a human being – could kind of apply here, too?

Harry: So a machine playing as musically as a human is
  as musical as a human?
Me: Exactly, well, that's what I was trying to say. Not
  sure I succeeded, but anyway
Harry: Back yourself, Amalia!

Despite all the alcohol, Oscar was quiet for much of the meal and quickly excused himself after 'pudding'. Harry had a tutorial early the next morning, so drunkenly sauntered away soon after. Alex suggested we take the remaining bottle of wine back to my room and play a musical game. I was intrigued. On the way to my room, I confessed that I'd called my mum in the bathroom. Alex didn't judge. She complimented the 'lovely relationship' I had with my parents. I worried aloud that my only strength seemed to be synthesising someone else's knowledge and passing it off as my own. I told her that I felt like a phony. She put her hand on my cheek, sweetly, almost maternally, and said that my synthesising was a valuable skill here at Oxford. I felt soothed.

In my room, Alex suggested we each choose and play songs that 'mean a great deal' to us. It was my turn first.

'Who Wants to Live Forever?' – Queen

I tipsily told her there was something about the way the song grew, like humans grow, that mimicked life, and that the song ended with this sudden quietness, just like death, which was amazing given the song is called 'Who Wants to Live Forever?' Like, this song was this tiny microcosm of life. Plus Cali, my best friend from home, loved the band Queen, so the song reminded me of her. *I should call her.* Alex swayed from side to side as it played until she lost balance and fell off her cushion. I'd not realised how drunk she was. I asked her, 'What song means a great deal to you?'

I hadn't heard of the songs Alex chose. Most were electronic pieces – not unlikeable, but, in my opinion, not emotive. This surprised me. She said these songs helped her find a flow state where she could almost detach from reality. They made her feel peaceful. I eased into them and tried to join her flow.

Bill Withers was playing when she left. I could barely keep my eyes open.

———

The number you have called is not recognised. Please check the number and try again.

Oh.

I had to add a country code – +61 – to get through to Cali. *You're not in Sydney any more . . .*

Me: Cali, hey, you're up!

Cali: It's about fucking time you called. I had to check with your parents that you were still alive

Me: I know, I'm sorry, time zones suck for calling

Cali: We are not going to be those childhood friends who fall out of touch and see each other awkwardly at family weddings and funerals

Me: No, we're not

Cali: So, tell me, what's Oxford like? Is everyone there a know-it-all? Or is it just you?

Me: Nope, just me

I was not a know-it-all. I was a forget-it-all at best and a don't-know-anything at worst. But it felt good to be reminded of my former academic glory.

> **Cali:** I'm really jealous that you're out in the big wide
> world while I'm stuck in Sydney
> **Me:** Oxford isn't exactly the big wide world, but I know
> what you mean
> **Cali:** I'll get out of here, too, I reckon
> **Me:** I'm sure you will. Where do you want to go?
> **Cali:** Honestly? Anywhere

——

There was a morning when my breath smelled of coffee and my jeans smelled of beer. They were clearly the jeans I'd worn to Tim's party and they clearly hadn't been washed. The morning's lecture was 'Techniques of Musical Composition'. Counterpoint, 'the foundation of music', was likened to 'the fat in food'. I did not understand the comparison. I had a bit of a headache and realised that my reading glasses were probably out of date. Vision deteriorates at an alarming level when you've read more than you can understand. I arranged an eye test that afternoon because I felt guilty for not having washed my jeans.

The optomotrist was younger than I expected. Shy, awkward, she almost seemed embarrassed when she explained each test to me. She would start by bouncing a puff of air off each eye – fine – then we would test my focus. Eventually, I read from the test chart. Very good, she told me, and I felt more competent than I had in weeks. She took a photo of my eye and paused. Wait. She could see something 'peculiar', too 'peculiar' not to 'warrant a little concern'. *Do people really say 'peculiar'?* She consulted with a colleague, made a phonecall. I was at the hospital later that same day. The walls were too white and too shiny. If you stared hard enough, you could make out the faintest outline of your own reflection. The waiting room looked like a TV set – I half expected the cast of *Grey's Anatomy* to barge through the doors. They didn't. I worried the doctors would smell my beery jeans.

Someone who'd been taught bedside manner from a bad textbook put drops in my eyes that made them numb then blurry. Flashes made everything red. Everything stayed red. My polluted tears stained the tissues placed in my hands an alien, fluorescent yellow. Line and edge had been removed from my vision – everything was colour. My pupils were balloons blown up by the drops. Flash. The photo flashes went over, through, past my eyes. My throat was hot, like when I sing, but I was struggling to breathe. It felt like breathing through a straw, sucking. I imagined my own big, lightless black eyes and felt alien like my tears. There would have to be another scan. Then I was free to go. They'd be in touch.

The way doctors speak is so mechanical, detached. Understandably. Only when I couldn't see did I realise how much I'd relied on the compassion in their human eyes and on their human faces. When the lines and edges disappear, all you're left with is that voice.

———

Alex came over that night. She wanted to see me. She needed time away from her room and her books. I told her that she was welcome, that I probably wasn't going to be much company, that I was exhausted. She insisted on coming anyway and didn't ask why I was exhausted. I didn't have the energy to share. Instead, she suggested I take a nap. I think I laughed. She was less blurry than the doctor had been. Things were less red. I crawled into bed while she sat in the armchair in my room. She put her headphones in and I heard her breathing steady. I tried to slow my own breathing to match hers.

On waking, I wanted to play her a recording I'd made with a pianist, a jazzy 'Somewhere Over the Rainbow'. I poured the music into the silence without introduction. She moaned when I sang an ornament in the recording. I had improvised a little trill, a musically fluttering 'bluebirds fly', which she'd noticed. I felt birds in my stomach, much fiercer than butterflies. I rolled over to face her and was surprised to find her looking a little alarmed. Her brows were tense, her jaw was tense. I smiled into her unease until it dissipated. I told her softly about my afternoon at the hospital and she listened. She came to sit on my bed and touched my temple with the tips of her fingers.

———

By the time she was ready to leave, the nap-induced tenderness had been replaced by nap-induced vim. I punched Alex's arm and told her confidently that I was going to be fine. She danced out of my room and was halfway down the stairs when she stopped and turned to face me.

> **Her:** You really are going to be fine!
> **Me:** So fine!
> **Her:** I love you

My breath caught. It was the first time anyone in England had said they loved me. Everyone who loved me – friends, family – lived in Australia. I didn't realise how much I'd been craving that particular intimacy. I felt a little less alone. *Have I been feeling alone?* I wondered how she knew she loved me. *When and how do friends decide they love one another? How does this differ from loving a partner? Does this differ from loving a partner?* I didn't know. I'd never been in love. *Do I love Tim? No, I don't think so. How do I know I don't love Tim? It's just a feeling. Do I love Alex? Yes. How does her love for me differ from her love for Oscar? I don't know.*

Alex left before I could tell her I loved her, too.

———

The following day, I checked my phone 53 times waiting on results from the hospital. Nothing. In my tutorial, the professor asked me to read my essay aloud, so we could 'pick it apart together'. He had small, kind eyes and a forehead lined like a notepad. I couldn't imagine what he'd have looked like as a young man.

The 'prescription' of reason or motivation to an act of history differs greatly from the prescription of medicine to the sick. While the good doctor shines light upon symptoms present to determine their cause, the good historian grapples with sources in the dark.

He completemented the 'flair' of my writing and told me it was a 'pity' I didn't use enough musical examples to back up my argument. Still, this tutorial felt like a win. My first.

> **Professor:** To finish off, I'd like to have a brief discussion
>   about the topic of next week's essay
> **Me:** Okay
> **Professor:** How do we listen to music?
> **Me:** Right

He waited. I panicked. *What if I have a brain tumor? No, that wasn't the question. How do we listen to music?* I stared at the painting behind him. Dark colours, browns and burgundies, formed the torso of a woman, contorted into the shape of a cello. A locket fell beneath her breast. It was gold, almost fluorescent. I felt frustrated I would never know what was inside the locket. *I don't know how we listen to music!* Then I paused. No, there was no right answer here. No musical examples.

> **Me:** Listening to music is not a linear experience
> **Professory:** Go on

I stared at the locket.

> **Me:** We don't listen to music from beginning to end,

just like we don't look a painting up and down.
There are focal points, memories associated with
certain bits. It's an associative experience

Professor: Associative how?

Me: One piece of music can sample, or even just remind
you of, another

Professor: How else?

Me: You can associate music with a specific memory,
which would affect your listening experience?

Professor: Is this association always conscious?

Me: No, I suppose not

Professor: So?

Me: So maybe unconscious association is why music
makes us feel things. Or, like, why we associate music
with certain kinds of emotions

Professor: Such as?

Me: Like the way we associate major music with
happiness and minor music with sadness

Professor: Why do you think we do this?

Me: I think it's probably conditioned

Professor: Do you think reading is associative in
the same way?

Me: Yes, I'm sure it is, but maybe reading is less abstract,
so maybe it's less open to association in the moment

Professor: Don't say 'maybe' so much

Me: Okay

Professor: Right. You'll send me the essay 5 p.m. the
night before?

More days. More glances at my phone.

Amalia:
I'm a bit worried about the hospital results

Alex:
Hey, I know, of course.
Did they say when they'd email you?

Amalia:
'In the next few days'

Alex:
Why don't we call them? I'll come over?

We sat cross-legged on my bed while I called.

Drusen. Often mistaken for something more severe, drusen are abnormal collections of protein and calcium that amass within the optic nerve. While optic nerve drusen do not usually affect vision, peripheral vision loss can occur.

Relief shook my body. I was fizzing with energy. Instead of telling Alex I loved her, too, I decided to do something with all this music that seemed to float around her. So I wrote her a string quartet tango because she danced tango and because the music seemed to be tango-esque and because her birthday was approaching. Repeatedly, I reassured myself that a string quartet was a totally normal and lovely gift to give a friend.

I couldn't face giving her the quartet in person. It seemed too grand a gesture, one that I needed to downplay, so I delivered the score in a basic brown envelope to her college mailbox.

Alex:

Do you know what my birthday resolution is? X

Amalia:

What is your birthday resolution? X

Alex:

To be as good a friend as you

Amalia:

You're making me blush

Alex:

Amalia, I can't thank you enough!!

No one has ever given me a gift like this!!

Can I see you???

Amalia:

Yes! You need to meet me tomorrow morning at the front of college – 10am xx

Alex:

I'll be there xx

She met me the next morning at the front of college. We speed-walked the short way to the Jacqueline du Pré Music Building, where I'd organised a string quartet of muso quasi-friends to perform and record Alex's tango. The room was empty, plain, decoration sacrificed for acoustics. The quartet all wore glasses. The violinist wore pajama bottoms and a college hoodie and the rest kept their coats on during the recording. Oxford life. Alex beamed the whole way through. Even now, when people use the word 'elated', I imagine her smile in the Jacqueline du Pré Music Building.

————

Then summer came.

6

WHAT'S YOUR GO-TO DANCE MOVE?

Summertime in Oxford is glorious because all these stressed people with dark bags under bruised eyes turn into peaceful people with pink cheeks and radiant smiles. They swap the books for picnic baskets and the bikes for punts and everyone is always sunny and praising the 20-degree weather.

Tim ended up getting a job in a bank, like he said he would. He decided to travel around South America for a year before he signed away his 20s. We called it quits. I was sad because I liked Tim, but I was okay because I didn't love him. When we said goodbye, we kissed passionately, which felt appropriate.

———

In the summer, colleges host extravagant balls. They're elaborate and expensive and you dance and drink until 6 a.m. Before ours, I dressed with Alex and Eve. Oscar and Harry got ready in another room. My dress was shaded somewhere between purple and grey. It was long and hugged my figure kindly. There were two triangles missing at the waist. Eve wore a simple long black dress, complementing her black hair and red lips. She looked like a sexy Morticia Addams. Alex wore a sparkly gold dress. She looked like a sexy Academy Award. I looked in the mirror and panicked because I hadn't done anything about my wild eyebrows. No, okay, they weren't actually that wild, but they could certainly have been neater and it was my First Ball. My mum used to joke that my eyebrows were like 'adventurous caterpillars, forever plotting to take over my face'. I'm really terrible at shaping my eyebrows.

Me: Al, will you please help me fix my eyebrows?
Her: They look fine to me
Me: You're sweet. But they're a little wild. Please?
Her: You're cute. Of course. Come sit down

She was sitting on the floor, cross-legged, so I went to sit opposite her, cross-legged. I could feel her breath on my painted lips. *Is this a normal thing for me to notice?* She quickly studied each eyebrow before nodding and reaching for the tweezers. Authoritative. I didn't know where to look, so I shut my eyes. She began to pluck and casually chat. I kept my eyes closed. They started to water.

Her: So I didn't pick you as a high heel kinda girl
Me: Excuse me?

I could hear the smile in her voice.

Her: Your shoes – they're so high!

Me: I'm a performer, high heels are basically like an extension of my feet

I realised this was a weird thing to say, so I kept talking.

Still Me: No, I'm joking, obviously. I very rarely wear shoes this high, but it's a fancy ball and these are fancy shoes. Actually, to be honest–

I heard myself still talking.

Still Me: –I completely forgot about shoes until this morning, like an absolute schmuck. I actually had to traipse around town hunting for shoes to wear and these were the only ones I could afford that would kind of match. They are really high, but, like, they do match and I'm okay with pain

Pause, breathe.

Still Me: What shoes are you wearing then?

Her: You can see for yourself

I opened my eyes. Her face was inches from mine. At first, neither of us moved and I felt my breath catch. Then I caught myself. I pulled back and looked over at her classic black shoes. They were very elegant.

Me: They are very elegant

Sometimes I envied her grace. Often I envied her grace.

> **Her:** Thank you. Hey, I think I was done here like three
> minutes ago

I looked in the mirror and my eyebrows were perfect.

> **Me:** Oh, thank you! They're perfect
> **Her:** Don't thank me! It's your face

I didn't blush. When we took photos, Alex looped her hand around my waist. I felt her fingers brush my skin in the missing triangles. Pause, breathe. *Would I have paused, breathed, if it had been Eve's fingers on my skin?* I messaged the picure to my parents.

> **Amalia:**
> Ball tonight!

> **Mum:**
> What a gorgeous pair!

Switch. Alex asked me to take a photo of her and Oscar and I made sure to smile as they posed together. They moved easily with one another. I noticed they had similar smiles. I wondered how many photos they'd taken together, just like this, in the three years they'd been dating.

Let's backtrack briefly. Before this First Ball, before summer settled, I sat my first set of Oxford exams. Exams were stressful. There was a woman who also studied music two years above me, Mary, who'd lived nearby. Mary always wore her mousy hair up and owned six different pairs of gloves. Occasionally, she would mix and match. It was nice to know a woman who had done my course, who I tried to look up to, especially given the domination of male professors who taught me. Mary had the answers. She'd hit on me one time early into my degree – we were at a bar and she'd leaned in and closed her eyes and I'd leaned out with my eyes wide open – but we had both kind of laughed it off. We used to play easy Bach chorales together on the keyboard in her room. She was very good and I was terrible and I think she found this funny. Anyway, just before my exams, we were eating together at a little Japanese restaurant on a very vibrant street. There was always a queue and barely enough space for 20 hungry customers. When we finally sat at our shared table, I said something like:

Me: I think this is probably the most stressed I've ever been. But I can't tell whether I would be this stressed if I wasn't surrounded by stressed people all the time. Stress is contagious, don't you think?

Mary: You're a First Year, you have absolutely nothing to be stressed about

Me: I hear you, but one person can have three hours' sleep and another person can have no sleep and they can both truthfully say they're tired

Mary: Yeah, sure, but I'm just saying don't stress yourself
   out too early. You have plenty of stress to look forward
   to. Stock up on all the sleep
Me: I think you've handled stress extremely well
Mary: No, I haven't
Me: No, really, you have! I mean, there were those four
   weeks where you kind of locked yourself in your
   room to finish your coursework, but, like, you knew
   what you had to do and you did it. I respect that. I
   genuinely think you handled it really well and–
Mary: Does this look 'well' to you?

I didn't know why she'd raised her voice. People had turned
to look at us. I distributed a few embarrassed, apologetic
smiles and then looked back at Mary to ask her what she'd
meant. I caught sight of her hands. She'd rolled up her sleeves
to show me her wrists – they were both covered with small,
dark, horizontal scars.

Mary: Ever wondered why Third Years wear long
   sleeves in the summertime?

I hadn't really been able to get the image of Mary's damaged
wrists out of my head. It was there, floating uninvited, and
I decided not to mention it to anyone. It wasn't my story to
share. Except I did. I did tell Alex. My therapist mother had
always taught me to 'tell one trusted person your secret, so it
doesn't eat you alive'. Alex had become that trusted person.
I had told her on a walk in our college grounds earlier that

week. She'd shuddered, closed her eyes tight, held me tighter. I wondered whether Oscar was her trusted person, whether it was okay not to have my trust reciprocated exactly.

Back to the ball – six dancefloors, a Ferris wheel, countless foodstalls, all-you-can-drink pop-up bars, thousands of colourful lights. The decadence was almost overwhelming. I shuddered to think how much it had cost. Mary was quite drunk and had kind of cornered me in the cloisters to tell me about someone she'd had sex with. She slurred that, eventually, I'd learn all about 'gold rush' – this student-labelled feeling that Third Years get when, all of a sudden, they realise they will no longer have the freedom or opportunity to sleep around at university and so, reactively, sleep with everyone. I had nothing to say, so I watched her sway and soliloquise. I could taste the booze thick on her breath.

Suddenly, Alex was beside me, pulling me and sing-screaming the 'Habanera' from *Carmen* – the aria she'd heard me sing on YouTube. *'L'amour est un oiseau rebelle!'* She apologised half-heartedly to Mary as she physically dragged me away from the one-sided conversation. I joined in on the sing-scream and we were giggling as we raced towards one of the dancefloors. We passed Harry as we ran through the cloisters, who was singing an awful karaoke duet with Eve in the College Bar. The sight of them together warmed my insides.

———

We ended up on the silent disco dancefloor by the New Building. Alex winked at me. 'Sorry to drag you from the fun, but I needed someone to dance with.' I felt my warmed insides twist.

'What's your go-to dance move?' Shoeless dancers bopped and grinded to soundless music being played on hundreds of individual headphone sets. Everyone seemed to be singing along, so you had this raucous chorus of drunk a cappella singing accompanying chaotic but enthusiastic dancing. Alex and I hunted for headphones, but discovered they'd run out. I grabbed her hand and dragged her into the middle of the dancefloor as a group beside us sing-screamed Michael Jackson's 'Billie Jean'. We sang along and danced wildly. I did some sort of spin and grabbed my crotch; I think Alex was attempting a moonwalk. Then fireworks. A galaxy of golden sparks against the velvet sky, briefly illuminating castle silhouettes.

I'm telling you this because it is one of my favourite memories. Joy like Zadie Smith would describe it. The ball ended at 6 a.m.

Alex and Oscar and Eve and I had rented undergraduate rooms – two on the same floor – to crash in for a few hours post-ball. Alex was leaving with Oscar at 9 a.m. to meet his family in London. I asked her to wake me to say goodbye. I remember waking to her hand on my shoulder and the smell of banana shampoo. Eve didn't move. I sat up too quickly. Alex chuckled and pulled me into a hug on the bed. She stood to go and I stood, too, and we hugged again. She smelled like morning should smell. Pause, breathe. She put her hand on my cheek and I put my hand on hers and she winked and whispered, 'I know, goodbyes are the worst. But it's like ripping off a band-aid. And I'll see you soon.'

On the plane home, the steward asked me if I wanted pret-
zels. I really did. I told him as much and smiled my good
smile. I was dressed in a leather jacket, black as the dark
liner around my dark eyes; I wondered whether my eager
smile juxtaposed my moody 'look'. I was listening to John
Dowland's *Lachrimae or Seven Tears* through the plane's
entertainment system. I saw the steward notice, peering at
my screen. I thought what I always think when a stranger
notices me listening to classical music – that the tendency
to associate classical music with psychopathy and murder,
especially in pop culture, is really unfortunate. Just think of
Hannibal Lecter listening to his beloved *Goldberg Variations*
moments before he brutally butchers two security guards. It
was probably an unfair thought – perhaps untrue of the real
world and just something we'd learnt in Psychology of Music.
I chose red wine and the steward gave me a small bottle. Then
he paused, looked around, and offered me a different small
bottle. They were both Tempranillo and we decided together
that we couldn't tell the difference. The steward said the one
with the red label looked 'more posh' and I smiled again. He
gave me both bottles.

The posh one's label said 'sustained nose with expressive
aromas of sour cherries and macerated prunes, set off by
delicate notes of bitter cocoa and sweet spices'. The wine was
nice. The other said 'soft, easy-going red with bags of dark
berry fruit and just a twist of pepper on the finish'. That one
was nice, too.

*Fuck I love red wine. Maybe red wine is my Zadie Smith icy
pole. Less wholesome.*

A baby cried loudly. The screams were raw and painful. When I was a baby, my mum used to spend the whole plane ride in the bathroom with me because she was so mortified to be That Woman with the Crying Baby. I remembered something Alex had said about how angry it made her when people seemed irritated at babies crying on planes. I leaned into the thought until the baby's sobs were music and I was sleeping soundly. That's what she did. She made everything into music when she shared her thoughts with me. And the red wine probably helped, too.

Alex, I bought a postcard at Heathrow because I still feel like a tourist in this country. Do you? Questions don't suit the postcard genre, do they? Oh! There I go again. Yes, I'm writing on the plane (excuse my writing) and I think I'm a little drunk (excuse my writing). I'm so excited for you to visit me in Sydney – 3 weeks and counting!

I love you, too,
Your Amalia xxx

7

WHAT'S YOUR GO-TO LOVE LANGUAGE?

Australia. I was happy to be home.
Three sunny weeks without worrying about what to
feed myself.
Seven jet-lagged sunrise coffees.
Four icy sea swims.
Six punnets of strawberries, shared with Dad.
Three café brunches.
Two family Shabbat dinners.
One walk along the cliffs.
Ten hours' sleep a night, on average.
I was itching for her arrival.
Five nights with Alex.

————

I tapped nervously on the steering wheel. On the seat beside
me lay an A4 sign with her name. I parked my car and waited
in the Arrivals area. I was far too early so I sat for a while and

people-watched and cried. There is something very moving about watching families and lovers and friends reunited. Cinematic happy endings played over and over again. I just sat there crying while I waited for her.

Confession: sometimes at university, when I was feeling low but couldn't quite 'feel' properly, I used to search on YouTube for videos of soldiers surprising their families. The soldier sneaks through a primary school, cut to a classroom full of children, cut to classroom door, the soldier knocks, cut back to children working at their desks. But one child recognises the soldier ...

The videos would trigger my tears so that I could go full-on catharsis and let it all out. YouTube, a therapy tool. Anyway, the Arrivals area had a similar effect on me. It's probably something I'd mention to a therapist if I ever had the nerve to see one.

Alex was carrying a comically big suitcase. I waved and held up my sign, but her eyes didn't leave mine and we hugged close and tight. I wondered whether anyone cried while they watched us hug. She was warm and smelled of summer, even though it was July – Sydney's coldest month. Having one foot in each hemisphere is strange. She insisted on buying flowers for my family and spent way too much money on way too huge a bouquet. She chose flowers the colour of fire. Alex had been staying with Oscar and his family in London. In the car, she recounted an anecdote: 'And then we all sat down to watch golf and I let out this huge sigh because, well, golf – and they all just looked at me, disappointed, but honestly I don't care because watching golf is stupid.' I smiled and agreed. I took a wrong turn and then some more wrong turns and we ended up crossing the Harbour Bridge three times for no reason, which made her laugh my favourite laugh, but also meant we were running very late to *La Bohème*, the opera I'd organised for us to see.

Me: Surprise!
Her: You're kidding
Me: I'm not. Is it too much?
Her: It's ridiculous, but brilliant
Me: You're not too tired? Sorry, I really didn't think this through, I was just so excited for–
Her: As am I

In the car, Alex quickly changed into a light grey dress that gave no appearance of having just been unpacked. She put on earrings as we climbed the steps.

Her: Do you think I have time to run to the bathroom and splash my face?

———

Christmas Eve in Paris. In the dark, lavish auditorium, we met Puccini's Bohemians and watched love blossom from our dark seats.

Sì. Mi chiamano Mimì ...   *Che gelida manina ...*
La storia mia è breve ...   *Chi son? Sono un poeta ...*

Son tranquilla e lieta . . .   E come vivo? Vivo . . .
Lei m'intende?   Sì
Do you understand me?   Yes.

At the interval, we queued to get Alex a coffee. She yawned twice before we were served.

Her: Do you think there should be mics in opera?
Me: That is an incredibly complex question
Her: I'm flattered
Me: So the short answer is: I don't know
Her: That's a terrible answer for an incredibly
    complex question
Me: Okay, fine, I don't think there should be, but then
    that goes against other beliefs of mine
Her: Go on?
Me: Are you really interested?
Her: Of course I'm interested. I love the way you talk
    about music
Me: Okay, stop me if you get bored
Her: Go on
Me: So I think amplification in opera would allow a lot
    more people to make it onto the big stages
Her: That makes sense
Me: Which is great because openings for more
    singers, evening out the playing field, yay for equal
    opportunities, fight the–
Her: I get it. But you disagree?
Me: I guess I disagree on two levels. I think there's

something insanely beautiful about the raw opera
voice – the way it can hit you in the chest and sort of
vibrate right through you

Her: I told you I like it when you speak about
music, right?

She let down her hair.

Me: And I think amplified sound really does lose
that effect

Her: Hmm. And the other reason?

Me: Well, I guess I don't really like the idea of evening
out the playing field

Her: Oh?

Me: For starters, it would worsen my chances of making
it if amplification became the vogue. And also, like, on
a less selfish level, I think it's important that we keep
the big voices for the big stages. There are smaller,
more intimate spaces for the smaller, very beautiful
voices. And I think it's cool that both can exist.
Actually, a third thing, microphones are arguably
one of the distinguishing factors between opera and
musical theatre

Her: Because musical theatre singers use mics?

Me: Exactly – and it definitely affects their vocal
colour and style

Her: So you think the introduction of microphones
might change the sound or, like, production of opera-
singing in the long term?

Me: Yes, exactly

Her: Interesting

Me: Do you agree?

Her: I'll have to think about it more

———

Sitting beside Alex in the darkened auditorium was thrilling. I felt it in my chest, the thrill, an almost nervous energy. She leaned into me to whisper, 'Thank you so much for organising this.' She rested her hand on my shoulder. Slowly, it slid down my arm towards my wrist. Our fingers touched lightly.

When Mimì collapsed, Alex gripped my hand. I felt my own throat tighten, my jaw grow tense. The orchestra whispered the melody of Mimì and Rodolfo's first duet as she died.

Vedi? . . . È tranquilla. Che vuol dire quell'andare e venire,
quel guardarmi così . . .
Coraggio!
Mimì . . . Mimì! . . .

There was a moment of silence before the audience roared.

———

I offered her my bed or the couch. She chose the couch, which was fine. Sort of. Okay, I was a little disappointed, but only because I enjoyed late-night chats with friends – the kind of chats that only really happen when you're sharing a bed and you're a little sleepy and a little vulnerable. At least, that's what I told myself. But, yes, the couch was fine and we were excellent conversationalists anyway. No late-night vulnerability or bed-sharing required.

Her: Can you enjoy the kind of love story you know will
    end in heartbreak?

I smiled.

Me: That's opera

———

When Alex met my parents the following morning, she seemed nervous, which I hadn't expected.

Her: I feel like they're going to base their entire
    perception of the typical Oxford student on me!
Me, sarcastically: Yep, probably, gosh, I don't think I
    could handle that pressure

My parents were already in the kitchen drinking orange juice my dad had made from scratch like he always did. They'd chosen their most colourful tie-dyed tablecloth.

Dad: Morning, girls! Sorry we missed you last night
Mum: Alex, it's so lovely to have you with us – are you
    exhausted?
Dad: I can't believe Mali took you to an opera after a 26-
    hour flight

Mum: And you're going kayaking this morning! Come,
   have some orange juice

Alex: Oh, thank you. And thank you for having me! I'm
   actually not too tired, thankfully, though I've had a bit
   of practice travelling back and forth from London to
   Australia. And the opera was a pleasure

Dad: That's right! Your parents live in Melbourne!

Her: My mum lives in Melbourne, yes, exactly, so I'm
   heading down there next week

My mum was about to ask more, but my dad interrupted her
interrogation.

Dad: Well, we're very happy to have you with us. Now,
   important question: how many Weet-Bix will it be?
   You'll need some fuel for your kayaking

I breathed out. I'd been nervous, too. I felt my mum's eyes
examining me while we breakfasted.

————

We kayaked close together. Her strokes were elegant, as
though in slow motion. I wondered whether I'd ever seen her
in sunglasses before.

Me: What do you think has changed the most about you
   since you left Australia?

Her: So much. But I don't really see it as change. I mean, I
   don't really see my younger self as myself

Me: What?

Her: Like, child Alex and school Alex and adult Alex are
just different people

Me: What? No, they're all Alex. It's just that time
has passed

Her: I just don't really identify with earlier versions of
myself. I don't see the point

She strained her voice as the waves knocked us together. We
waited for the wind to pass. The air was scratchy with salt.

Me: So you don't think you're a product of your
upbringing?

Her: Sure, but I'm a new product, a reinvented product

Me: That makes no sense to me

Her: Are you the same person you were when
you were 5?

Me: Yes, obviously

Her: Okay, so there's a kayak–

Me: Right . . .

Her: –and it stops at a beach and replaces its seat. Then
it stops at the next beach and replaces its bow. And it
keeps stopping at beaches and replacing various parts
until it has none of the same parts as when it started
its journey. Is it the same kayak?

Me: Um. No, I guess not

Her: Then at what point would you say it became a new
kayak? How much would it have had to change for
you to see it as a new kayak?

Me: Fine, I see your point, but I'm not a kayak! I'm not
   just parts! I have a soul!

Her: Okay, so you're saying that, if it were possible to
   substitute every part of your body – every organ
   and bone and all the rest – with another, you would
   still be you?

Me: Yes

Her: Why?

Me: Because of my memories and my personality

Her: Is someone with severe dementia still the
   same person?

Me: Good point

Her: What if you managed to download your brain onto
   a computer and your body died – is that you?

Me: No, I guess not

Her: Right, so, for me, defining identity is so messy it just
   seems pointless. I just consider myself a new person
   when I feel significantly different

Me: I just find that really weird

I licked my lips, seasoned salty by the sea.

———

Late that night, we shared a giant passion fruit mojito bucket
at an empty bar on Bondi Beach and talked until it closed.
Outside, umbrellas were draped with rainbow bulbs. The
beach was dark and empty. Inside was warm and candlelit.
Amy Winehouse was playing.

Her: What's your go-to love language?

Me: What do you mean 'love language'?

Her: It's how you express your love for another person –
there's gift-giving or quality time or acts of service or
physical touch or ... words of affirmation

Me: And you have to choose one?

Her: For the sake of this conversation

Me: I guess probably acts of service or gift-giving. Oh,
God, does that make me a really superficial person?

Her: Absolutely not. And which would you want
to receive?

Me: I think I need physical touch more than I realise

She made a point of brushing my leg with hers under the
table. I laughed and kicked her off. Amy Winehouse crooned
about a man who was impossible not to love.

Me: What's your language of love then?

Her: I think I give physical touch

Me: And quality time

Her: And probably feel loved when people do thoughtful
things for me

Me: Haha! Perfect match!

Her: Did you doubt it?

The waiter came to check on our progress with the mojito
bucket. Bulging Bondi muscles and a movie-star smile. I wondered if he'd been watching us chat given the rest of the bar
was empty. He wore a sleeveless vest under a denim apron

and flexed his biceps as he handed us two cocktail menus 'just in case'. His tan almost looked fake. I smiled at him and Alex raised her eyebrows.

Me: A lot of people in England have called me flirty, which I'm not sure I like

Her: You are flirty!

Me: I'm really not!

Her: No, you really are, you're just missing the distinction between 'flirty' and 'flirting'

Me: Go on

Her: Like, by English standards, the way you act is flirty. So is the way I act. Because we make eye contact with people and touch them and lean in when they speak

We both leaned in. I rested my elbows on the table and cupped my face with my hands. She mirrored me.

Me: I like this distinction. So flirting implies intention?

Her: Exactly, which you don't have

Me: Most of the time

She cupped *my* face with her hands and squeezed. My smile fought my squeezed cheeks as I struggled to stop laughing. I must have looked like a cartoon.

When we finished the mojito bucket, she insisted we order two glasses of red wine. Alex called the tanned, buff waiter to our table and asked for his 'finest house red'. She winked at me. 'House is my favourite flavour.' I felt my cheeks rouge. When he returned with our wine, clearly filled beyond the prescribed 250ml line, Alex asked him to take a photo of us. To my surprise, she came to stand behind me, threw her arms over me in a drunken hug, and squished my cheek with hers. She thanked the waiter, checked the photo, zooming in on our smiles, then put her phone away.

Her: You know, apparently even just leaving your phone on the table lessens the quality of conversation

Me: Interesting

Her: What do you do with the photos you take?

Me: I guess I send them to my parents?

Her: Oh, so they knew what I looked like before I arrived?

Me: Absolutely! This is Alex, she's a languages student two years above me. I think she's super cool and fun and–

Her: Very funny

Me: What do you do with the photos you take?

Her: Well, I don't really know! Which is why I ask. Social media isn't really my vibe, but I take so many photos. I guess they just stay on my computer. And I show them to my mum when I see her

She took a photo of me on her phone. I deliberately looked at her instead of the camera.

Her: Oh, you are so beautiful

Me: Are you sure your language of love isn't the words
  of affirmation?
Her: Yes, I'm sure

She touched my leg under the table again. I didn't kick it away.

8

How would you describe your family in three words?

I got the last parking spot at the fish market. Briny air. Everything was in motion: the sea next door, hooting cars, hundreds of bustling people. The market was too loud to continue chatting, so we ventured from stall to stall deciding our lunches through elaborate mime. As it happens, there are many fishing-related mimed actions. Purse your lips and suck in your cheeks? Cast your rod? Hook your finger in your cheek? The stall-owners enjoyed our charades. Eventually, we found an outdoor table and tucked into our fish and chips, steaming in the salty winter air.

Her: What stresses you out?
Me: Conversation
Her: You're kidding. You're the conversation queen
Me: It's a difficult title to bear
Her: Shut up

Me: No, seriously, I have a really good memory for
conversation and often replay them in my head, so I'm
pretty pedantic about what I say. Most often I analyse
where I went wrong ...

Her: That doesn't actually surprise me

Me: I can't help it

Her: It's probably why you're so good at talking to people

Me, chuckling: Thank you

Her: I love you

Me: I think you mean 'you're welcome'

Her: No. I love you

She drew swirls on her chips with ketchup, taking care to
make the pattern symmetrical. I preferred mine plain. She
leaned back in her chair and closed her eyes. The bustling
market exaggerated her stillness. Eyes still closed:

Her: Tell me something I don't know about you

Me: I once murdered a turtle

Her: Excuse me?

Her eyes flew open in alarm. Silence.

Her: You know killing animals during childhood is
classic psychopath behaviour, right?

Me: It was the class turtle, Bubbles

Her: Poor Bubbles!

Me: It was my turn to take him home and I took him out
so we could play together and I don't know what I did,

maybe he was out of water for too long or something, but he just died in my hands

Her: Oh, God, that's horrible! Though that doesn't sound like murder to me. At a push, it sounds like manslaughter. Sorry, *turtle*-slaughter

Me: I've never cried so much. I never felt entitled to love the class pet again

Her: God, this is dark and unexpected!

Me: Well, there you go. I'm half-expecting you to launch into some deep, philosophical discussion about what it means to feel entitled to love

Her: Sorry, I guess I'm just mourning Bubbles. So young, so full of hope, so much potential–

Hand on heart. Lips fighting a smile.

Me: Not funny. What don't I know about you?

Her: Oh, you know everything

Me: That's not fair

Her: Okay, you don't know the code I use to unlock my phone. It's the same as my credit card pin. It's 6254

Me: I don't think you should tell me that!

Her: I trust you

Me: You're bizarre

Her: Fine. Maybe I'm 'bizarre', but you're the turtle-murderer

She licked her fingers clean of ketchup. Triumphant.

———

Alex showered while I laid the Shabbat table, enjoying the familiarity of the task. I decided to make place-setting cards so I could control where everyone would sit. Do people make place cards for any other reason?

ALEX	COUSIN BEN	DAD
MUM		
ME	GRANDMA	GRANDPA

Soon, Alex joined me in the living room. Her smart navy skirt and black turtleneck were amusingly juxtaposed with her flushed cheeks and the towel wrapped around her hair.

Her: I feel like I should have prepped more. So your
　　　cousin's name is Ben, your mum and dad are
　　　Diane and Ron, and your grandparents – oh, fuck,
　　　I've forgotten
Me: Roz and Philip. Though, if you're worried, you can
　　　call them Gran and Gramps like me
Her: No, I think I'll stick to Roz and Philip, thanks. What
　　　else do I need to know? How would you describe your
　　　family in three words?
Me: Good question. Um. Loud, loving and … involved?

———

My family sat at their prescribed seats and complimented the setting of the table and the 'lovely choice of candleholders'. A bat mitzvah gift from my grandparents, the fire-coloured candleholders at the centre of our table were made from the glass smashed at my parents' wedding, which had been re-sculpted and hand-blown by an artist in Melbourne.

Dinner would be 'served in ten' and I was in charge of the background music. My family preferred music without words to accompany Shabbat dinners, so I'd chosen generic flamenco guitar to start. Not dissimilar to the café above the bicycle shop.

Her, to my mum: How's your today been, Diane?

Mum: Long. So many arguing clients – too many, if you ask me!

Her: I'm sorry, but I'm not actually sure what kind of therapist you are?

Mum: I'm a relationship counsellor

Her, to me: Hang on, how has this not come up?

I'm sure I blushed.

Ben, to my mum: So what's the latest trend in your clients?

Grandma: Ooh, I love this segment of the evening

Me: Is this a new segment?

Dad: You've been away

Me: Presumably you're not going to disclose confidential client information?

Mum: Of course not, Your Honour

I rolled my eyes. She winked at Alex, who was watching the backs and forths like an eager sports fan. I was watching, too, exploring our family dynamic through her eyes. We were quite funny.

Mum, excited: Actually, there's been a theme this week
Grandpa, sarcastic: Here we go ...
Mum, authorative: The latest trend is that couples keep
  repeating the same thing and then being surprised by
  the outcome
Dad, mocking: Shocking!
Her, fascinated: So what do you tell them?

The oven beeped and my dad disappeared. The male members of my family covered their heads with napkins. Alex leaned into me.

Her: What's with the napkins?
Me: The men cover their heads, but only during the
  prayers. I don't actually know why we don't use
  real kippahs
Her: Why don't the women?
Me: Actually, I don't know that either. I don't really
  engage much with Judaism. Long story

Barukh ata Adonai Eloheinu melekh ha'olam borei p'ri hagafen.
We cheersed.

Her: Story for later?

Me: Maybe, though it's not a nice one

Barukh ata Adonai Eloheinu melekh ha'olam hamotzi lehem min ha'aretz.

My dad disappeared and returned with a tray of foil pouches of salmon, which he served while my mum continued.

Mum: So I begin by sharing some Einstein wisdom–
Grandpa: Amen
Mum: –that insanity is doing the same thing over and
    over again and expecting different results
Me: So you call your clients insane?
Dad: Very, very subtly

My cousin snorted. Through Alex's eyes, I watched my dad and Grandma pull apart the challah bread like a Christmas cracker. Alex was eager to share a piece in the same fashion. I readied myself for the secret Who Can Eat The Fewest Calories At Dinner competition, but Alex filled her plate, so I did the same.

Mum: In my humble opinion, a lot of couples throw sand
    on a relationship when they should throw cement
Her, chewing challah: So why did you become a
    couples' counsellor?
Dad: Oh, she loves this question
Grandpa: Alex, you're very good at asking Diane's
    favourite questions

Mum: It's an excellent question! Well, Alex, I used to
be a children's counsellor, which I loved, but I found
that so often the problem stemmed from the parents.
So I started seeing the parents together before my
session with the child and found the work not only
more interesting, but actually more beneficial to
the children

Grandma eyeballed my cousin, who was messaging on
his phone.

Grandma: Don't you have a new girlfriend, Ben?

My cousin put his phone away.

Ben: Actually, I might keep this one to myself for
now, thanks
Grandma: Diane, why don't you offer Ben some
unsolicited advice?
Ben, looking up, laughing: Okay, what have you got for
me, Diane?
Me: Here we go
Mum: Well, a good thing to bear in mind is that you
shouldn't define your partner by saying they *are*
something. Rather say they are *acting like* something.
Calling someone an idiot is a personality judgement,
whereas saying someone is *acting like* an idiot is an
isolated judgement
Ben: That makes sense, cheers!

There was almost a moment of stillness before my cousin posed a question to the table. I adjusted the music with the conversation. Glitzy jazz piano.

Ben: Okay, so I want to get everyone's opinion for my latest assignment

Grandpa: Ben, we're all going to be qualified lawyers by the end of your degree

Ben: Okay, so we've got an assignment based on this famous case in English criminal law called R v Blaue. They've edited the story for the assignment, but basically there's this couple and, one night, the guy loses his temper and stabs the girl four times in the chest. But he freaks out and is filled with remorse and rushes her to hospital. At the hospital, the doctors say they can save the girl, but they have to do a blood transfusion. If they do it, she'll live. If they don't, she'll die. She refuses treatment because she's a Jehovah's Witness and she dies. What should the guy be charged with?

Mum: What a great assignment!

Grandpa: Wouldn't it be manslaughter? He tried to kill her and failed

Me: But that's attempted murder!

Dad: But she died!

Grandpa: And her death didn't have to do with him directly

Me: I mean, he did stab her

Grandpa: Yes, but, in the end, she died because of her beliefs, not because he stabbed her

Mum: What a great assignment!

Her: How long had they been dating?

Ben: Um, I don't know, why?

Her: Well, did he know she was a Jehovah's Witness?

Everyone looked at her. She continued:

Her: If he knew she was a Jehovah's Witness and he
wanted to kill her, he could've stabbed her so that
she lost a lot of blood, but in a non-fatal way, and
then rushed her to hospital knowing she'd deny the
transfusion, so he'd get away with it

No one spoke. Then:

Dad: That is some seriously criminal thinking, Alex

Ben: Oh, that's such a good point – thanks, Alex!

Me: What was he charged with?

Ben: Manslaughter in the end

––––

Alex and I sat together on the edge of my bed.

Her: Your family is so ... functional

Me: You're kidding

Her: No! I love them. They're all so warm. And I love
that you guys get together once a week for Shabbat

I liked the way she said 'Shabbat' – slow, precise, brightening each vowel, taking care with each consonant. I confessed to her that I always felt a little guilty about the way I behaved in family gatherings. Even now, it can bring out a nasty, childish side of me. She reassured me that we were all our worst selves with our parents.

I fell asleep wondering where she'd learnt to think the way she does.

———

When I took her to Centennial Park, Sydney's Central Park, she suggested we go tandem bike-riding. I hadn't ridden a bike since I was seven. She didn't know. I made sure to hide my shaky hands and insisted she take the steering seat of the tandem bike. We cycled for the whole hour without stopping, through swamps and wetlands, manicured landscapes, past dog-walkers, barbecuing families, passionate teenage soccer players.

She was surprised each time I declined her offer to have a go at the front. I was sweating. My neck ached. My hands were stiff from clenching. When we finally stopped, I fell off grace-lessly. I stayed lying on the grass, laughing, gulping, laughing.

Her: Mali! Are you okay? What's so funny?
Me, in between laugh-gulps: Yes! *GULP* I'm sorry
     LAUGH it's just that *GULP* I haven't *LAUGH* actually
     been on a bike *GULP* for a good 12 years
Her: You're joking!
Me, calming down: No! Because I cycled when I was
     very little and then there's that saying

Her: Do you mean 'it's like learning to ride a bike'?

She joined in on the laughter because she thought I was ridiculous.

    Me: Yes! I just assumed I'd remember! Because of
      the saying
    Her: You're a schmuck
    Me: That's my word!
    Her: I like sharing words with you
    Me: Okay, we can share 'schmuck'

She joined me on the grass and we laughed until we stopped. Her shoulders pushed against mine.

    Her: Do you ever think about family languages?
    Me: What do you mean? Like in bilingual families?
    Her: No, like the way families seem to have their own
      ways of talking – their own vocabularies, sentences,
      references, that sort of thing – that wouldn't make
      sense to other people. Like little dictionaries of
      family lingo that develop over time?
    Me: I haven't really thought about it before, but I guess
      history and time spent together means that families
      have this network of references to–

An impressive rainbow lorikeet perched on my shoulder. I froze. A man with a glove called out from far away telling me not to worry. I didn't move, worrying. Then the bird flew back to the man. Alex looked at me strangely. The week had been perfect and here was this impressive rainbow lorikeet to prove it. Neither of us brought it up. Instead, we brainstormed a few words in our own family languages.

Alex's family phrases:

- We say 'you're driving me WiFi' instead of 'you're driving me mad', simply because my mum drives me mad, forever asking for WiFi passwords
- 'Find the funny' is a phrase my aunt developed in order to get through difficult moments

Amalia's family phrases:

- My parents refer to 'Mali droppings', which are things I tend to leave around the house
- To get 'Passover drunk' means to get catatonically drunk, which my cousin did one Passover after being out with his friends all day. He threw up all over our bathroom floor

There, on the grass, it occurred to me how little I knew about Alex's family in Melbourne. She told me she was raised by her mum and her aunt, who were both teachers – thankfully not at her school. Her dad lived in America with her much older half-brother, who she didn't really know very well. *How did I not know this?*

Me: You're a surprisingly private person, you know

Her: Not really, I just don't find my own family
    background particularly interesting, so I assume no
    one else will

She puzzled me. She intrigued me.

Me: Because you're a different kayak?

Her, laughing: Exactly. Actually, do you want to meet
    my mum now?

Me: What?

Her: We can call her now, together. I've told her so much
    about you, she'll be thrilled!

Me: Oh, no, I mean, I don't know enough about her!

She'd started to dial.

Her: She's a maths teacher, she's really into her garden,
    and her favourite colour is blue

Me: Great, thanks

We sat next to one another while the FaceTime call rang.
I liked the look of us together on her phone screen – our
pink cheeks, my messy curls, her neat ponytail. She read
my thoughts and smiled, taking a screenshot just before her
mother answered. I realised I didn't even know her name.

Alex's mum: Ally! I'm so glad you called! And is that the
    famous Amalia?

Her mum was very beautiful. Light eyes, like Alex's, but with sharper facial features and short blonde hair.

Her: It is indeed. Mals, this is my mum, Laura

Me: Lovely to meet you, Laura

Laura: Where are you girls? What are you up to?

Her: Actually, we'd just finished tandem bike-riding when Amalia confessed she'd forgotten how to ride a bicycle!

Laura: Don't be rude, Alex. Have you never ridden before, Amalia?

Me: Not since I was little, no

Laura: Oh? I thought it was impossible to forget how to ride a bike

Her, laughing: Who's being rude now?

Me: No, no, she's right! Because of the saying! That's what I thought!

Her: Apparently it is! What are you up to, Mum?

Laura: Oh, never mind about me, I'm just glad to see you girls. You both look so happy

I looked at our little faces in the corner of the screen. We did look so happy.

Me: Alex tells me you're very proud of your garden?

Alex smiling, whispering: Well played

Laura: As a matter of fact, I was just heading there now. Would you like a little tour?

It struck me that, at university, you don't get to know your friends' families the way you do at school. This moment felt special.

————

On her second-last evening, Alex and I went salsa-dancing in town. There was an hour-long class for beginners followed by social dancing. Salsa music, hot and zesty – the beat thuds deep inside you. You can feel it pumping the blood around your body.

Contigo una noche de pasión, sin tí una vida de dolor.

The whole exercise is extremely heteronormative in a way I expected Alex to have more of a problem with. Women wait on the side for men to ask them to dance. Men lead. Women step backwards first. Dancing led to some weird conversations in between the beats.

Salsa Partner 1: I've fallen in love many times tonight
Salsa Partner 2: *La vida es como una caja de chocolates*
Salsa Partner 3: I have a feeling you're a mathematician

It was sweet of Alex to come to the beginners' class with me. I didn't realise just how sweet until the social dancing began. She danced with a heavily tattooed man in black with cropped curls – the whole floor cleared in a kind of messy oval to give them room to fly.

Una mirada furtiva de amor y caigo desplomado en
tus brazos.

There was this one moment when he spun her and, instead
of extending her hand in a kind of bird-like shape, as she'd
been doing, she laid her hand on her stomach. She flicked
her head to meet his eyes. Her hair whipped around her face,
catching on her slightly ajar mouth. He used both his hands
to move her hair from her face as they rolled their bodies into
one another. It was like watching a story.

Labios infames ingratos, delincuentes
Aun así los amo,
Aun así te extraño.

They gave me shivers. *She* gave me shivers.

We walked to the station together far later than we'd
planned. It was too dark for her to see how much I blushed
as we spoke. I wasn't sure why my face was so hot. Probably
the dancing.

Me: I did not expect you to be able to dance like that
Her: I thought you'd seen videos of me dancing
Me: I have, but it's different live. You're amazing
Her: You're sweet
Me: No, really, that was breathtaking!
Her: Well, thank you. I don't do it enough. How did you
    find the dancing? I thought you were wonderful
Me: Are you being cruel?

Her: No! For real!

Me: It's really sensual

Her: It's funny you say that

Me: Why?

Her: Because it just really, really isn't for me

Me, laughing, blushing into the dark: You'd think otherwise if you saw yourself dance

Her: I started social dancing with my auntie when I was 14. It was just a thing we did together. I had to get special permission to enter the bars so I could dance

Me: That's really cute

Her: Occasionally, the men would get a little close for comfort and my auntie or I would tell them I was 14 – you should have seen the looks on their faces. But no, it's always been an incredibly platonic thing for me

Me: Oh, right, I can really see how that'd take the sensuality out of it for you – starting so young and dancing with much older guys

Her: What did you find sensual about it?

Me: Maybe I found it intimate rather than sensual. I'm not used to having strangers' bodies so close to mine. It's actually kind of nice

Her: I always find it so startling when someone makes an advance at a salsa club

Me: Does it happen often?

Her: Hardly ever, actually. It's just not what's done and most people know that

Me: How do you feel about the heteronormativity of it all?

Her: Ah, I don't know. It's shit, right? I have friends who
    are gay who won't do it because of that. I'd actually
    really like to learn to lead better
Me: So you could ask a girl to dance?
Her: In theory, yeah! Why not? I'm just a rubbish leader
Me: Never say that in a job interview

She properly laughed. We linked arms and we went home.

———

Walking along the cliffs between Bondi and Bronte beaches
in perfect weather. Warm sun, sea breeze, the dramatic
soundscape of waves smashing rocks. Two men overtook us,
holding hands.

Her: Why can you sometimes tell a man is gay by the
    way he walks?
Me: It could be a kind of signalling thing, like a way of
    telling other gay men that you're gay?
Her: It could be a way of feeling like you're part of some
    gay community

I told her about my best friend in high school, a closeted gay
man called Felix. Felix came out to me months before he came
out to the world. I told her about what he'd said to me when he
first came out – that all men secretly wanted to act camp, but
that society only made it acceptable for gay men to act camp,
so only gay men acted camp. I'd found that really bizarre. I
wondered whether his views had changed since simple 16.

Alex and I decided that: 1) this was probably Felix's way of rationalising his camp mannerisms; 2) it was interesting when considering whether this behaviour comes more 'naturally' (but not really) to gay men; and 3) we probably weren't really in the position to make judgements and have too many opinions on this because we weren't gay men.

I didn't tell her the other part of my conversation with Felix. He'd told me he was gay in my car one night when I dropped him home after we'd been at the gym. We were both still sweating. We went into his empty house and chatted about it some more – how long he'd known he was gay, how he'd pretended to fancy a hot popular girl in our school, how he'd learnt all about gayness from threads on Reddit. Felix offered me tea and I asked for peppermint. He snorted and told me that I'd chosen Lesbian Tea. What?

What is Lesbian Tea? Why did I want it? Was he kidding or was he hinting that I was a lesbian? Why would he think that I was a lesbian when I'd clearly had a lot of boyfriends? Why were we talking about my sexuality anyway?

Of course, we weren't talking about my sexuality. Liking peppermint tea didn't make me a lesbian.

———

That night, we watched a film about a musician falling in love. We sat very close and narrated the film with our thoughts.

'No one actually takes a guitar with them to a café. Wait, have you?' Her foot touched mine. 'Was that really the actor singing? It seems so different from his speaking voice. I hate how they do that sometimes. Just cast a bloody singer!' Her leg touched mine. 'Do you ever write songs?' Our legs inter-twined. She put her head on my shoulder and I touched her collarbone. Tentative. She leaned further into me so I could feel her breath, light on my chest. I let my fingers move along her collarbone, across the base of her neck. She flinched then slowly sat upright. I felt a little rejected. We carried on watching, but with fewer interjections. 'Anne Hathaway is great.' Her foot touched mine. 'Oh, they ended up together. Who saw that coming?' We called it a night. I went to bed. She went to couch.

———

I couldn't sleep, so I added to my facts about Alex:

11. She is an exquisite dancer
12. She is very feminine, but hates high heels
13. She's not a very good singer, but I don't think she cares
14. She doesn't pack light
15. She thinks golf is ridiculous
16. She doesn't identify with her childhood self
17. She feels loved when people do thoughtful things for her
18. She's a confident cyclist
19. She doesn't watch films in silence
20. She doesn't hate opera (!)

———

Her final day.

I took her to my favourite spot in Sydney, down Dumaresq Road. There is a tiny strip of park right on the water that you can only find if you zigzag down lots of little back streets. There, the water is always clear and sparkling and everything smells of flowers and the sea. Salty frangipanis. On my Ben Lerner memory map, it might be marked 'Friendship with Alex First Questioned'. She loved the strip like I knew she would. We sat together on a sunlit bench.

> **Her:** This has been so wonderful, thank you so much, I
>   really can't thank you and your family enough
> **Me:** Oh, it's been so wonderful having you. I'll really
>   miss you when you're gone! They'll all be asking after
>   you the next time I visit that salsa bar, I'm sure!
> **Her:** I'm sure you'll make do

Silence. She looked at me.

> **Her:** It really has been perfect
> **Me:** 'Rainbow lorikeet' perfect

She smiled.

> **Her:** Hey, I never really told you about how my
>   relationship with Oscar started

I didn't think I'd invited Oscar to the park.

Her: It was so early into uni, like first week, and I only
   really went on one other date

Me: I didn't know you'd dated someone else?

Her: Well, I'm not even sure it was a date really, but this girl –

Me: A girl?

Her: – this girl asked me to go to this party with her and
   I guess it probably was a date, but I was already kind
   of seeing Oscar at that point and I dismissed it

Me: Oh, are you bi? You haven't really mentioned before?

Her: Ah, I don't know. My friends at school used to joke
   that I was bi, but I think I'm just confident and, I don't
   know, flirty? I'm a really attentive listener

Me: You really are an attentive listener

Her: And I guess I probably am bi, maybe, but I'm really
   in love with Oscar and I plan on staying with Oscar,
   so I guess it doesn't really matter

Me: I don't know if I could stay in a heterosexual
   relationship at this age if I thought I was bi but hadn't
   ever, you know, been with a girl

Her: Oh, are you bi?

Me: What?

Her: I mean, have you thought about it?

Me: Sure, I've thought about it. No, I'm straight

Her: Oh, okay

Me: I mean, I'm confident and I'm flirty. And I'm a really
   attentive listener

Her: You are a really attentive listener

Me: And I've never even kissed a girl, except for this
   once in a drama play in high school

Her: No, it's okay! You're not bi!

Me: I mean, no, I didn't say that

Her: You literally just said 'I'm straight'

Me: I was hit on by a few girls while I was still at school, which was strange

Her: Good strange?

Me: What?

Her: Did you enjoy being hit on by girls?

Me: I mean, being hit on is flattering

Her: Did you want to get with any of them?

Me: No, never

Her: Right. So what was last night about?

Me: Sorry?

Her: I really do love Oscar

Me: What?

Her: It's just that I plan on staying with Oscar as long as I'm in love with him and I am in love with him

Me: I know, you've said

Her: This week has been really perfect

Me: Yes, it has

Silence. Everything was fuzzy. Probably because I'd stopped breathing. I breathed. Her eyes matched the sky in my favourite Sydney spot.

Me: I'm not sure what you're getting at, but, regardless of my sexuality, I'm not attracted to you–

No, that wasn't what I meant.

Still me: –and, even if I was, I would never hit on
  someone in a relationship. Never.

Silence. Why had I added that last 'even if I was'? She was just
my friend. She was thinking the same thing. More silence. But
I really hate silence. So I broke it.

Me: Why are you bringing this up?
Her: I just thought I should
Me: I'm sorry if I gave you that impression. It makes me
  feel sick to think that you felt uncomfortable or, like, I
  don't know, like being here was difficult or hard

I was starting to feel sick.

Her: No, not at all! This week has been perfect. It's
  just, last night, when you, I don't know, what was
  that about?

She seemed irritated.

Me: What?
Her: Forget it. Sorry for bringing this up when it's clearly
  something you haven't thought about. Oh, I feel
  like an idiot
Me: You're not an idiot
Her: What am I then?
Me: Wonderful

My brain obviously needed oxygen and I knew before I said it that it was the wrong thing to say. I said it anyway. She looked at me intently and then she looked at my lips. I'd stopped breathing again. Maybe that's why she'd looked at my lips.

> **Me:** I, um, maybe I have given off those signals, maybe, but, like, I haven't meant to and really don't think about you in that way

Do I?

> **Her:** Okay, well, I'm glad that's sorted

She laughed a new laugh. Awkward. Forced.

> **Her:** What a beautiful place to be having such a strange conversation

I couldn't help myself.

> **Me:** Have you had those thoughts about me?

Silence.
More silence. Fuck.
But I was resolute. I was going to let her reply.
So
I
Waited.

Her: Yes, well, no, not explicitly. I guess part of our
    friendship has made me question my relationship
    with Oscar
Me: What?
Her: Not in any real, tangible way, but yeah, ah, to be
    honest, I'm not sure this is a conversation I want
    to be having

At this point, I admitted to myself that I wanted her to stop looking at my lips and just kiss me. Which she didn't. Obviously. I don't know what worried me more – that I'd accepted I wanted to kiss her or that she hadn't kissed me. Perhaps this spot should be labelled 'First Admission of Wanting More' on my memory map. Or even 'Not First Kiss'.

Me: I guess parts of our friendship are a little intense
Her: Please, Amalia, can we not go there?
Me: Okay

We talked about other things and everything felt a little forced, a little unnatural. Alex didn't bring it up again, so I did because that's what I do.

Me: Okay, no, maybe I wasn't being 100 per cent honest
    with myself or with you. Maybe there's something
    here that I wasn't acknowledging. You're not a
    normal friend
Her: You're right. You're my Person

I now wondered why her boyfriend, the person she was so in love with, wasn't her Person.

Me: What does it mean that I'm your Person?

She considered the question carefully.

Her: Well, it's like you're my best friend, but you also feel
  like family
Me: Yeah, you're right, it does kind of feel like that. But
  now I feel like you've stirred up all these thoughts
  and questioned all these feelings and then, like,
  walked away and–
Her: Hey, I'm sorry. You're right. I shouldn't have brought
  things up if I didn't want to get into them. I guess,
  when I brought them up, I didn't realise what getting
  into them would look like

She was wearing a new face, one I would come to recognise. She looked tired and beautiful and sort of exposed, vulnerable. She breathed out. I hadn't realised she'd been holding her breath. I wondered whether things were fuzzy for her.

Her: Mals, can we stop? This conversation is making me
  feel a bit vulnerable
Me: Vulnerable how?
Her: I feel vulnerable that I'm admitting to you that parts
  of our relationship and how I feel about you aren't in
  line with the fact that I'm dating Oscar

When Alex looked at me like that, I'd do whatever I could to make her smile. So that's what I did.

Me: Wait, what, you're dating Oscar?! How could you lead me on like that?

It worked. She smiled. I continued.

Me: Hey, I don't want you to feel like that and also, up until today, I hadn't really thought about us as anything more than best mates. I'm happy to think of us as each other's Person and leave it at that
Her: Thank you. No, yes, you're right. Thank you.
    I love you
Me: I love you, too

I watched her hand hover over mine, wanting to touch me, then thinking better of it.

Lei m'intende?   *Sì*

———

We sat in my car in the airport car park. She didn't want me to walk her in – it would be 'expensive and unnecessary' – so we had 10 final minutes together before my short-stay parking expired. We discussed next steps, my second year, her Master's programme. We didn't discuss Us. We said a heartfelt 'rip the band-aid off' goodbye. We hugged, she held me, I swore I heard her breathe me in. She paused before she kissed my cheek.

Me: We'll be okay, right?
Her: Of course we will

She didn't look back as she walked away with her comically big suitcase.

———

My parents told me they really liked her. I said I really liked her, too.

———

I'd already ordered a peppermint tea at our favourite bookshop café, Gertrude & Alice, when Cali called to say she'd be late. We used to call the bookshop's design 'Parisian' – a maze of little rooms and jutting dark-wood shelves overflowing with colourful stacks of books – though neither of us had been to Paris.

Cali: Mals, hey, I'm going to be late, I'm sorry
Me: Yeah, I figured. We *have* met before. I've already ordered a tea
Cali, distracted then shouting: Shit! Far out, I very nearly just ran someone over. Can you get me a spelt scone or something?
Me: I still don't understand how I failed my first driving test and you passed

Cali: I told you, the examiner wanted to fuck me. See
   you in a bit

Cali walked into the café looking lost, though we'd been there together hundreds of times before. It was just a general look she had about her. She sat across from me and took her sunglasses off. Same thick hair. Same big blue eyes.

Cali: I am insulted you didn't call more this year
Me: To be fair, you didn't call either, but we'll be better
   next year, yes?
Cali: Yes. Now stop complaining and tell me how
   you've been

I told her about Oxford – the architecture, college life, the ball, class and culture shock, a few of my essays. I formed a sentence about Alex in my head multiple times, but it never made it onto my tongue because I never knew how to finish the sentence: *My closest friend's name is Alex and ...*

I asked her about herself, how she'd been. Fine, busy with university, trying to leave Sydney as much as possible. She'd stopped making art, which saddened me, but I tried not to let on. We didn't do any of the 'remember when's I'd been expecting. We were both Adult People, changed from child-hood, wisened by university.

Cali: Okay, new fact about me, not a big deal, but
   I'm bisexual

What?

    Me: Really? When did that happen?

    Cali: It's not a big deal – I just really wanted to sleep with
        this woman, so I did and it was great. We don't have
        to talk about it

    Me: We can, though, if you'd like to? Have you told
        your family?

    Cali: Yeah, they don't really care, though I'm not sure
        they believe me

    Me: What do you mean?

    Cali: They just think it's a phase. I'm tempted to bleach
        and buzzcut my hair so my grandma takes my
        queerness seriously

I laughed. Cali hadn't changed, not really. Here was my chance.

    Me: ...

———

I got home late and tried to make sense of everything by
consulting Google. I learnt that the Greeks had eight words
corresponding to different types of love. Eight.

    – *Eros*, sexual passion, requires a loss of control, which
      frightened the Greeks
    – *Philia* was friendly love, virtuous and far more
      valuable than Eros

– *Ludus*, a playful love between children, even casual lovers

The list went on ...

I thought to message Eve, but, as with Cali, I was unsure what I'd say. I didn't know how she'd react. I wondered whether she had her suspicions. She'd probably already started her second year abroad in Paris and she was probably asleep.

———

In the kitchen, my mum was making a zero-calorie hot chocolate in her 'I HEART MUM' mug. I hopped onto the tabletop beside the mug.

Mum: Try not to knock it over! It's my favourite mug!

The skin around her eyes was creased, her forehead carved with lines. I couldn't remember if she'd had so many when I'd left for university. I wondered whether I looked different to her, whether we'd have to update the memory we had of one another's faces and bodies each time we saw each other. Surely I'd age faster, more obviously, since ageing slows down with time? Like everything else.

Mum: Why the frown?
Me: I'm not sure, trying to work something out
Mum: Are you sad about Alex leaving? Can I help?
Me: Yeah, I guess I am

Her lips were pursed. As a child, I would stare in the mirror and try to imagine what I'd look like as an adult. I'd mind-photoshop my face clear of blemishes, thicken my eyelashes, deflate my cheeks and slice them with cheekbones. I'd purse my lips and wear my best Adult Face. I realised I'd been mind-photoshopping my face into hers.

Mum: You two have a really lovely dynamic
Me: Yeah, I think so, too
Mum: I think she adores you
Me: Really?
Mum: Yes. Is that something to do with what you're
    trying to figure out?
Me: I don't know
Mum: Sometimes it's difficult to know how we feel and
    what we want. Comfort, affection, sex ...
Me: Okay, TMI, I'm not one of your clients
Mum: It's okay not to know know how you feel. That's
    all I'm saying
Me: Thanks, Ma

I left her to her zero-calorie hot chocolate, taking her words with me to my bedroom. I sat at my piano and tinkered with the keys, mulling over the different types of love and attraction I recognised: familial, friendly, romantic, sexual ...

I found myself playing a melody from Wagner's *Tristan und Isolde*, the last opera we'd studied at university. A memorised quote for a practice exam, Wagner on *Tristan und Isolde*:

Henceforth no end to the yearning, longing, rapture, and
misery of love ... longing, longing unquenchable, desire
forever renewing itself ...

I played each note one at a time: F B D# G#

Music, like living, a series of tensions and releases.

Ali Smith taught me that I'll never be able to convey two
simultaneous events or emotions using words. No matter
what I do, you're going to hear or read one word after
the other. But, in music, that's not the case. I played all
four notes together – F B D# G# – Wagner's Tristan chord,
renowned for a unique kind of musical tension, released
and resolved in myriad ways. The chord that altered the
course of Western music – could I use it to untangle my
own feelings? I played the notes again. *What if this chord
represents Alex and my friendship as it stands? Could it move to
another chord? Should it? Which?* I didn't understand. I took
my hands off the keys.

I tried again.

*Let's say we're in C Major. How does friendly love sound? What
about a G7 chord?*

G D F B – friendly love

Friendly love

Rich, full, warm. Sure, it could exist on its own, but it could lead somewhere, too. Most obviously back to C Major.

C E G C – familial love

Familial love

Richer, fuller, warmer. Simple, comfortable C Major. But that's not the only direction it could take.

G7 could move to something more . . . exciting? Gripping? Raw? F9? F A C Eb G?

It sounded sharper, spicier. Good. But it was missing something. Some danger. I added a sharpened 11th.

F A C Eb G B♮ – sexual love

Sexual love

Yes.

But G7 could also move to something more . . . wistful? Relaxed? Almost jazzy? AMaj9? Ab C Eb G Bb?

Doesn't it need to share some of the excitement of sexual love, another sharpened 11th?

Ab C Eb G Bb D♮ – romantic love

Romantic love

Yes.

While my sexual-love chord sounded like a fiery relation of friendly love, romantic love was something entirely new – a kind of sublimation or modulation. But both began with friendly love. I wrote in my notebook:

Familial love – C
Friendly love – G7
Sexual love – F9 (#11)
Romantic love – AbMaj9 (#11)

Fine. I lay on my bed.

———

When I tried to rationalise my feelings for Alex, I couldn't distinguish between how I felt about her and how I felt about music, like my love for music melted into my love for her. Consuming, euphoric.

I am melody, you my harmony

She made me want to dance, she gave me shivers, she made my heart beat faster like music did. She made me think in music and music made me think of her. Blur.

> *When you dance and extend your hand*
> *I cannot take it*

Why do we have so many variations on coffee orders and only one word for love? If I felt about Alex how I felt about music then I didn't need to kiss her, I just needed to be near her.

> *I trill and dance and sing and fly at your command*

I dream about music a lot and I've recently started calling myself a musician.

> *You are dark imagination*
> *I, your fantasy*

We messaged every day for the rest of the holidays and every day I did not let myself think about what kind of love I felt for her.

> *I close my eyes*
> *And dance alone*

YEAR 2

9

WHAT WAS THE LAST DREAM
YOU REMEMBER?

I continued to live in college because I was still excited to be living in a castle, though my second-year room was grander, like I'd been promoted. Dark-wood finishes, a reading nook beside my window. Alex's letter was balancing on my door handle as I arrived. Term 1, Round 2.

Dear Amalia,

I like using your full name when I write to you – I hope that's okay.

I wanted to be the first to welcome you back to Oxford! I hope you're settling in again and to see you soon.

I've decided that I need a break from college accommodation (it's my fourth year after all!) and have moved into a lovely little semi-detached with Oscar in

*Jericho. You'll have to come visit once we're
both unpacked.*
Love to you,
Your Alex xxx

My Alex?

I was surprised and a little upset that she had moved in with Oscar without discussing it with me.

Amalia:
Thank you for such a lovely letter!
I'd love to come over and see your new digz x

———

Term began and soon I met Cate – Welsh, single, beautiful Cate. Finally, with more of a handle on Oxford, I felt I could engage in a hobby or two. I chose jazz because I liked the feeling in my throat when I let the notes slide. I liked the cold smoothness of the mic on my palms. I liked experimenting with colours, changing my voice into sandpaper, then into rum. The band 'jammed' together once a week. I crooned lines like 'you give me fever' while Cate scratched at the cymbals with those especially-for-jazz drumsticks.

I didn't know Cate was gay because she didn't look how I expected 'gay' to look, though I'll leave her appearance to your imagination. Maybe. She was a third-year theology student and she described herself as a 'frustrated atheist'. She'd chosen to specialise in Judaism. I found this especially strange because she wasn't Jewish and I couldn't understand

how someone outside my religion could want to devote so
much time to learning about it.

During Alex's time in Sydney, I'd never told her why it
was I didn't engage much with Judaism. I'd struggled to
understand Judaism after I'd visited Auschwitz as a teenager.
I didn't know how to think about the Holocaust. Maybe I'd
struggled to understand the Second World War and my
Judaism was locked up in my lack of understanding. I knew
it was cowardly not to want to think about Auschwitz, but
I couldn't really think about that either because it made me
want to throw up.

I found out Cate was gay early into our friendship. Dan,
the guy on keys, told me.

Dan on keys: Dude, I just asked Cate out
Me: Okay, so why do you look so horrified?
Dan on keys: How was I supposed to know she was
 a lesbian?

That same night, I stayed up late to watch a recording of
our 'jam' on my computer. I used to film our sessions so as
to study our improvisations in my own time. I once spoke
to a saxophonist who had decided not to pursue a career in
music because music wasn't 'inside him'. He could 'never
really be a "true musician"'. He told me that he could copy
and rehearse and 'improvise' learnt figures to perfection, but
that he was missing some special musical *je ne sais quoi*, which
would allow him to improvise freely, passionately, creatively.
Anyway, I was watching a snippet of the song 'Misty' because

I had tried to copy Ella Fitzgerald's ornaments (apologies to
the saxophonist *sans le je ne sais quoi*) and I wanted to see
whether I had pulled them off. I couldn't help but notice
the glances that Cate and I shared throughout the song. The
lyrics began:

> *Look at me*

She looked at me. The drums entered at that point, so she was
probably looking to get her cue. Fine. Or maybe she was just
responding to the lyrics. People do that. The song continued.
I looked at her. Fine. Maybe I was acknowledging the beat
she'd brought. Jazz is a musical conversation. People do that.
But there was another look.

> *I can't understand, I get misty, just holding your hand*

We were grinning at one another. I'd have thought it was
quite beautiful if it hadn't been me. If I'd seen a couple in the
street grinning the way we grinned, I'd have grinned, too.
Why hadn't I clocked this at the time? I watched it three or
four times to be sure and then began my Sexuality Crisis,
which mostly consisted of running away from thoughts
that chased me into sleep. Though they always caught me in
my dreams.

———

Dream example 1: I looked down at my hands, which had
turned into jazz drumsticks. I tried to type up my lecture

notes, but couldn't because my hands were jazz drumsticks. Everything was hot and fuzzy. I tried to open my window to let fresh air in, but couldn't because my hands were jazz drumsticks. The dream carried on in this fashion until Cate appeared in a long, floral dress and sucked on my jazz-drumstick hands. I woke up, sweating.

———

Amalia:
Al, what was the last dream you remember?

Alex:
Good question ...
I had a typical stress dream a few nights ago.
It was really lame actually – I dreamt I was in a library
and couldn't find a book I needed before an exam ...

Amalia:
That is ... very lame.

Alex:
What about you?

Amalia:
I had a really weird, almost surrealist dream about someone in my jazz band

Alex:
Sexual?

Amalia:
Kind of?

Alex:
I am *very* excited to hear more ...

———

Cate and I started going for long walks together. She talked
about Judaism in a way that made me want to talk about
Judaism. She was learning the Hebrew alphabet and took
pleasure in discovering that there were separate scripts – or
'fonts', as she called them – in Hebrew handwriting. She
took a pen from her bag and wrote the first two letters of the
alphabet in 'print' and 'cursive' script on my hand.

א *lc*
ב *ə*

She celebrated the artistry of the cursive alphabet, calling it a
'Picasso approach'. She laughed to herself. She explained that,
generally, everything published in Hebrew – books, newspapers, street signs, menus – was written in the print alphabet,
while everyone actually wrote in cursive. I pretended not to
know this already.

She gesticulated passionately, describing the way vowels
are written as dots and dashes beneath letters and sometimes
aren't included at all. She added dots and dashes beneath the
letters on my hand. The tip of the pen caught on my skin.
Cate admired her work. She asked me whether I had any

tattoos and I paused before I told her I did not. In the pause, I contemplated lying and saying I had a tattoo on my inner thigh, somewhere sexy and hidden.

Cate lifted her shirt to reveal the outline of Hokusai's *Great Wave* breaking on her ribs, just below her breast. Without thinking, I traced the swirls of the wake with my nails. I thought I heard her breath catch, but, when I looked up, her face gave nothing away.

———

Dream example 2: Cate and I were drawing with markers on a long whiteboard in the room we used for jamming. We were in bikinis and Cate kept saying that, if we drew enough waves, we'd be able to go swimming. I was drawing squiggles on the board and, when I looked over, Cate was naked and laughing and the whiteboard was filled with Hokusai.

———

Amalia:
Eve, what was the last dream you remember?

Eve:
Hi to you too.
I've been dreaming more in French lately?
I can't really remember any atm – why??

Amalia:
I've just been having some super weird dreams recently

Eve:

Super weird how?

Amalia:

Like kind of sexual??

Eve:

You know a sexual dream isn't always about sex right?

Amalia:

Yeah yeah I know

———

I visited Alex in her new accommodation, but struggled to find our conversational flow with Oscar constantly around. Speaking with the two of them felt like listening to a bad cover of a favourite song. I didn't mention Cate.

———

Cate and I started meeting before rehearsals. She unashamedly loved old musical theatre show tunes and had a framed picture of Julie Andrews hanging on the wall above her bed. I told her without breathing that Julie Andrews was the most beautiful singer I had heard, that I didn't understand how she could possibly sing four octaves, that her vocal tone reminded me of crystals and clear seas and the colour of pink Champagne. She raised her eyebrows. She looked at my lips. She had a habit of looking at my lips while I spoke, which made my stomach drop. I told her that, despite my slight obsession with Julie Andrews, I was straight, which felt appropriate and not at all defensive. She smiled and said that was fine, that we could still be friends. I laughed. She was funny. Soon we were spending all day together.

I dug out the letter Alex had sent me the previous year, the one likening Oxford to a pressure cooker, which I'd kept in a shoebox under my bed along with a few other important notes and bits of jewellery. I read it again and wondered whether, once I'd graduated, I'd ever have the experience of getting to know someone so quickly, intensely or fiercely as one is able to do at university. Is there time to fall in love alongside inevitable housemates and a full-time job? I supposed there must be. I wondered what had drawn Alex to me in the first place, whether Cate saw those same parts of me. I wondered whether, if I was aware of my most magnetic characteristics, I could use them to my advantage.

Amalia:
I'm feeling the heat of the pressure cooker again . . .
How are things with you? X

She took a long time to reply. Alex and I hadn't seen each other much during these first few weeks. I felt rejected and worried it had something to do with our Not First Kiss conversation in Sydney.

Alex:
Hey!
I've been thinking about you a lot!

I'm sorry I haven't been around as much lately.

Wanna tell me more about these pressure cooker feelings?

Things are good here, fine, blah.

Fourth year almost feels like one year too many ...

So Ox is feeling more like a fridge than a pressure cooker for me atm – things are slow moving and I'm really cold!!

(too tired for a more creative analogy – apologies!!)

Xxx

She followed up with a letter in my mailbox.

Dear Amalia,

I'm sorry we haven't seen each other as much as I would have liked. I hope you don't think I haven't been thinking about you. Of course I have. It's been difficult moving in with Oscar and finding time for myself. And for you. It's just something I'm going to need to get better at, especially with my Finals at the end of this year.

I miss Harry, too. He'd always said he was going to go into investment banking, but I never thought he'd actually do it. I'm sorry you guys only hung out that once last year. I don't think I showed him off in his best light. You must be missing Eve, too. You said she was in Paris, right? Would you go visit? Oh, I'd also love to hear more about your sexy surrealist dreams?

I'm sorry, I'm rambling, which is unlike me. Sometimes I plan letters before I write them, sometimes I don't. And they look like this. Anyway, just to say I'm thinking of you. Your Alex

I felt better knowing she was thinking of me.

———

Amalia:

Oxford's really not the same without you Eve

Eve:

I can't really say I miss it ... Paris is fucking cool

Amalia:

What have you been up to?

Eve:

Eating a lot of bread

Amalia:

And cheese?

Eve:

Of course. I even bought myself a special cheese knife

Amalia:

Classy. How's the French?

Eve:

A lot better and it's honestly so great to break up studying with a year out

Amalia:

Yeah, I wish every subject had the option to do a year abroad

Eve:

Where would you go?

Amalia:

I don't know? Somewhere musical like Vienna?

Eve:

Nice

Amalia:

Random question – do you ever keep letters?

Eve:

No one writes me letters Mali

Amalia:

Oh. I could write you letters?!

Eve:

Hahah no thanks – I prefer messenger

Amalia:

Fair enough

Eve:

I've gotta get back to work – prepping for a job interview

Amalia:

Oh, good luck! What's the job?

Eve:

It's a Parisian estate agent near the Jardin des Tuileries

Amalia:

Ooooh okay! Fingers crossed

Eve:

——

She got the job.

——

Dan on keys suggested our jazz band get together for a make-shift karaoke gig. Most of the band members enjoyed singing, so he figured: 'Chuck a keyboard, mic and amp in a bar, sheet music on an iPad, and we're good to go – the ultimate Scratch Night. Maybe we could raise money for a charity or something.'

The audience was mostly close friends of the band, though Alex couldn't join because she was doing something somewhere with Oscar. Rejected again. Actually, band aside, I knew no one there.

The bar was foreign to me and the lights were a little low for comfort, even for jazz. In fact, it was just really dark. I was singing first. I'd picked a song called 'Stars and the Moon', which is about searching for the perfect man. No, it's about materialism and never finding true love. No, it's about decision-making. I don't know what it's about. When I stood up to sing the song I didn't understand, the front row of audience members, who were other members of our band, shone torches around me. The light tinted my silhouette without touching me. It must have made my skin look smoother, my eyes darker, and my lips softer. I felt ethereal. Not quite Zadie Smith's Joy, but certainly enjoyable.

There was a tall, handsome man with a thick, red-tinged beard in the front row who clung onto every note I sang. I watched him watch me. I could tell he was transfixed by the melody by the way he leaned forward with each phrase. He didn't give a shit about the harmony.

> *I am melody, you my harmony*
> *But they don't notice how you lead*

He was extremely handsome and the absurdity of it all very nearly made me laugh. In fact, muted giggles wobbled my last note, which was very unlike me. I thought he might stand to clap. He didn't. The challenge he presented would have excited me two years before this Scratch Night. I bowed and looked for Cate, but it was too dark.

I have a strange relationship with my stage presence. I do believe that onstage me and offstage me are both me and that neither is fake. Same kayak. However, I generally don't like people to see me on stage before they get to know me off it. Voyeur–performer is not a relationship. But, when I looked for Cate, I wanted her to see and know onstage me. Onstage me, who is glamorous and powerful and confident and impressive and talented; onstage me, who knows and shows what she wants, even if she doesn't really understand what she's singing about. I wanted her to see. I sat down and breathed out. I was done for the night. I picked up a torch, ready to make the next performer glow.

I didn't expect Cate to sing in the Scratch Night. Of course she did. Her song was called 'An Old-Fashioned Love Story' and she was mesmerising. Her skin was soft under the torchlight, far softer than I'd imagined mine to be, and she stood perfectly still as the music began. It reminded me of the beginning of the musical *Chicago* in that it was enormously sexy. Cate sang sultrily about a girl sitting alone in a bar. But then the song took a comedic twist as she begged the audience for a 'good-natured, old-fashioned, lesbian love story!' with sweet girls and swell music.

I've always imagined bravery as something external, something that you have to dig for and don. Where did she find the nerve to sing this?

But her voice was so sweet and the music really was swell and I quietly thanked this Foreign Bar for its shitty lighting because my mouth was open and my whole face was probably the colour of my tongue. When the song ended, I felt the need to stand and clap, which would have been mortifying, so I consciously imagined lead in my ankles and, thankfully, stayed seated. I left as soon as the Scratch Night ended. I thought to call Alex or Eve on my way home, but decided against it. *What would I say?*

————

Dream example 3: Cate was swimming in the sea by my house in Sydney. She kept asking me to teach her to surf, though we couldn't find any surfboards. I didn't know how to surf, so I was secretly relieved. She had these sunglasses that allowed her to change the colour of the waves, like a camera filter. She told me the waves were the same red as my lips. She told me she liked my lips. She licked my lips in a circle. She put her hands inside my swimming costume and touched me softly, slipping her fingers inside me. Mirroring her, I kissed her. I touched her and explored her, copying the circles of her soft lips on my mouth.

————

In bed, I googled 'lesbian sex dreams'. I wondered how my search would affect my targeted advertising. What do you sell to sexual, dreaming lesbians?

Despite having googled 'lesbian sex dreams', the first article I read described a woman's sex dream about a horse. The interviewee, Sandra, has no waking interest in horses: 'I was in a forest and in front of me was this beautiful white stallion. I felt panicked because I was unsure as to whether to feed, groom or ride the horse. Jacob – a married colleague I fancy a little – appeared and told me not to worry. He helped me mount the stallion and told me it was here for my pleasure. He walked the horse through the forest. The up- and downwards motion was stimulating me and I started to moan about how good it felt. I begged Jacob not to stop.' The author suggested that Sandra felt guilty about her growing attraction to Jacob. An alternative reading was also offered – that women often dream of sick or neglected horses when they are not taking enough care of themselves. Next.

The second article was about Bea, a divorced 32-year-old lawyer who dreamt about ordering a glass of Champagne in a bar. While she waited, she basked in the sunshine streaming through the window. A waitress brought her the Champagne and sat beside her. Bea tried to sip her Champagne, but ended up spilling it down her front. The waitress leaned over and started licking Bea's mouth and neck clean of Champagne. 'All of a sudden, we were kissing each other. It felt won-derful.' The article countered: 'Nothing subtle here. The bubbling Champagne clearly symbolises Bea's sexual needs bubbling up inside her and the woman licking her face is a symbol of her desire for a woman to perform oral sex on her.' Apparently, Bea had been having lesbian thoughts through-out her relationship with her ex-husband. 'The sunshine breaking through the window was symbolic of a new life awaiting Bea.' Right.

I browsed a little longer, until I encountered the following ideas on a chat site:

- If you've never consciously fantasised about sex with a woman, a lesbian sex dream could mean that you are embracing a part of yourself you have lost sight of
- Dreams about gay people could mean that maybe you feel marginalised like gay people
- Dreams come purely from our unconscious. However, they are not always what they seem. For example, a woman could represent a man if you analyse the dream with a therapist
- If you're feeling attraction to women outside of your subconscious, then the sex dreams can mean you *are* attracted to women. You should go for it because LOVE is LOVE xxx

10

ARE YOU OKAY?

I told Alex about Cate the afternoon before she finally came to see the band play. I wasn't sure what to say.

Amalia:

Okay Al, it's not just dreams, I definitely feel *something* towards Cate (the drummer from my band I've been hanging out a lot with)

Alex:

That's exciting!! What do you feel?

Amalia:

Something strong and also sexy

Alex:

Ooooh that sounds promising!! To be discussed tonight! Can't wait xxx

Amalia:
Xxx

The gig venue doubled as a theatre and the band decided unanimously to take advantage of the revolving stage. We played the whole show as it spun around and around, until the stage faltered during a trumpet solo. It stopped spinning. *Can a stage have stage fright?* No, but the thought calmed me. Something about the acoustics made the lower brass rumble in my chest as I sang. I tried to ignore the feeling. Then I tried to sink into it.

After the show, Alex joined the band in the Kings Arms. She was already quite tipsy, having drunk thoughout the gig.

Her: That was amazing!
Me: The stage went mad!
Her: But you were amazing!
Me: I'm so glad you could come!
Her: You all sounded so good!
Me: You say all the right things!
Her: You looked amazing, your body in that outfit and all the lights
Me: Okay, shush, now you just sound like you're sweet-talking me

At the pub, we sat me–Alex–Cate. Alex made me swap seats with her while Cate bought us all beers, which horrified me. I'm sure Cate noticed. But she also looked pleased. I managed the better part of a pint – the unstable stage had dizzied me too much for the last few sips – and Alex had a little over two. I didn't realise until we left together that she was *wasted*. Trashed. Binned. *Why do we associate drunkenness with garbage?* We left together at midnight.

> **Her:** Can we go to the falafel van?
> **Me:** You're kidding
> **Her:** FA-LA-FEL
> **Me:** I don't buy it
> **Her:** HUM-MUS
> **Me:** Nup
> **Her:** CHIL-LIIIIII
> **Me:** There's absolutely no way you would order food
>   from a falafel van

She ordered food from a falafel van. Then she started saying things and I didn't know whether the right thing to do was to listen or to tell her to stop.

> **Her:** I think you should go for it with Cate
> **Me:** I think it's more complicated than that
> **Her:** Maybe, baby. Maybe I'm trying to live vicariously
>   through you
> **Me:** What?
> **Her:** I've wanted to tell you this for agezzzzz
> **Me:** To go for it with Cate?
> **Her:** No, that I would want to–
> **Me, panicking, interrupting:** Maybe we should talk
>   about this when you're sober?

Her: My friend Martina used to tell me I was
   probably gay
Me: That's an odd thing for her to say given you've never
   dated a woman
Her: Maybe I am
Me: I think you're drunk
Her: This falafel is the best
Me: Yep, definitely drunk
Her: No, you really need to try this

She shoved the falafel at my face and I took a bite. There was hummus all over my mouth. She laughed and wiped it off with her fingers. She licked her fingers.

Me: Thanks for that
Her: Isn't it the best?
Me, sarcastically: Yep, you're right, it's the best

She paused.

Her: Seriously, though, what if I want to date women?
Me: I don't think we should have this conversation
   right now–
Her: No no no no no, but I neeeeed to
Me: –though you definitely shouldn't cycle home just
   yet either

We sat on a bench. It was cold, so we sat close. I threw my legs over hers, then wondered whether this was inappropriate.

Her: I really want to talk about this with you

Me: Okay

Her: I do love Oscar, but I don't know if I'm
attracted to him

Friendly love

I didn't know what to say. I thought maybe she was just trying
to air her thoughts, so I played the washing line.

Her: Fine. I'm not attracted to him and I think I probably
like girls and you're talking to me all about this new
girl in your life and you and I started speaking about
it when I was in Sydney and–

Me: But in Sydney you said you were bi?

So I didn't exactly play the washing line. I was freaking out a bit.

Her: I know what I said

Me: Look, I think I'm freaking out a bit. I want to be a
good friend to you and I feel like you wouldn't be
telling me this if you weren't drunk and I don't want
to take advantage and–

Her: Can we go to your room?

Me: Of course

I paused.

> **Me:** Are you okay?
> **Her:** Honestly? I don't know. But I do know that I am
>   Passover drunk!

'Passover drunk', from my family dictionary.

I walked her bike while she ate the rest of the Best Falafel. When we got to my room, she took off her scarf and then her coat and then her jumper and then she stopped. She lay on the floor. She asked me to put on some James Blake music, so I put on some James Blake music. *Are you feeling angsty and sexy, Alex?* I went to get a blanket from my bed and covered her with it. She asked me to join her under the blanket, so I joined her under the blanket. But I promised myself nothing would happen. She rolled onto her side, wrapping one of her legs around both of mine. I looked at the roof.

> **Her:** I wish I wouldn't need alcohol so much for courage
> **Me:** I'm surprised you feel like you need courage. You
>   know you can say anything to me
> **Her:** But I'm afraid of saying this to myself
> **Me:** I'm sorry for not letting you talk about it. I'm just
>   trying to do the right thing
> **Her:** I know. You always have my back

We talked around the topic of her sexuality for a little while longer. Then we spoke about Cate, the show, the point of university, and the point of love. Then it was 4 a.m. Neither of us had realised how late it was. We decided she had better leave or stay the night. She'd never stayed the night before. We hugged goodbye and goodnight when she left.

I slept without dreaming.

The following morning, she texted me unnecessarily so that I knew she knew we knew we were okay and things weren't weird.

Alex:

Hello!

Did you do the right thing and sleep in?

I did! X

Amalia:

Hey! Absolutely YES! X

Alex:

I'm impressed and pleased and also apologetic!

Haha I can't believe it was so late and I kept you up!

But it's okay because neither of us realised how late it was.

Okay, sorry, ah, it's so sunny

But we didn't see each other.

———

Cate and I went to the Kings Arms again and I got drunker than I'd expected to get. We were sitting next to one another, close enough that it felt okay to put my arm

around her. Somehow, while chatting, I found myself drawing small shapes on her bare neck. I sloppily interrupted
our conversation. I said something like, 'What's going on
here?' She looked at me. I wanted her to kiss me. 'You're
the one stroking my neck.' I was. I didn't say anything and
we left it there.

No, that's not true. That's not what happened. Here's
what happened.

Me, sloppily: What's going on here?
Cate: You're the one stroking my neck
Me: I'm straight
Cate: So you keep saying
Me: Right. What if I'm not straight?
Cate: Are you sure you want to be having this
      conversation?
Me: No
Cate: Okay, then let's talk about something else
Me: No
Cate: Okay, so what if you're not straight?
Me: I really like spending time with you
Cate: I think we should talk about this when you're sober

How often is alcohol involved in coming out?
When we left the pub, we hugged goodbye and she looked
at my lips. My head did its spinning thing, stomach dropping.
She walked away. Her hair was all glossy in the streetlight
and I watched her walk for a while and my head was still
spinning and then my feet started running towards her and

she must have heard my boots tap-tapping on the ground because she turned around just before I reached her. I put my hands on her shoulders and looked deep into her eyes and said, 'I want to kiss you.'

Did you see that coming? Well, that's not true either. I did run up to her, I did put my hands on her shoulders, but here's what I actually said:

Me: I do like you

Cate: I'm glad. What are you doing?

Me: We spend all day together

Cate: Amalia, I'm serious, you should go to–

Me: And I didn't realise I wanted to bring it up and I thought maybe I should just kiss you

Her face softened and glowed as though lit by torches again. Neither of us spoke. Her lips looked tender and she hesitated for a second before she kissed me gently.

Cate: Let's talk about this in the morning

———

Amalia:
Alex I kissed Cate and we're going to talk about it in the morning!!!!

Alex:
!!!!!! xxx

———

We didn't talk about it in the morning, nor did we talk about it in the afternoon. She didn't message me, so I didn't message her. In the evening, the whole band went clubbing together. The music was loud, but the speakers were the bad kind that sacrificed the bass. Instead of pounding my chest, I felt the loudness slap my face. It wasn't pleasant. We all danced badly, which felt odd for a group of musicians. I held hands with Cate. Her hands were soft and small and light. I'd kind of expected her to hold my hands like she held her drumsticks – firm, powerful. She didn't. No one really noticed that we were holding hands.

Cate asked if I wanted to go outside for a cigarette with her. This was strange for two reasons:

1. It was very cold
2. Neither of us smoked

I told her I didn't want to go outside and that I didn't think she should smoke. She touched my face and whispered in my ear. I couldn't hear what she said because the music was slapping too loudly. Her breath was hot. She pulled me outside, around a corner, down a little alley. She kissed me against the wall. Her lips were softer than any boy's lips. There were scribbles in my notepad again when I woke.

———

Do we twist and do we twirl?
How do you slow-dance with a girl?

Chest to chest and eyes aligned,
Her fingers slipping down my spine,
They're smooth and sweet and soft and cold
'Til she steps close, tightens her hold
Then chest on chest and hands caress
And fingers in my curls
I think I do, I must confess,
I like her painted nails and dress,
And slow-dancing with girls.

Cate messaged me a screenshot of Banksy's Queen Victoria sitting on a woman's face. The backdrop was a blazing red. Both women wore heels and suspenders.

Cate:
Don't panic! This doesn't have to mean anything, just thought you'd enjoy x x

I didn't respond, so she sent me another picture I didn't recognise – a painting of two women reading together. The women were made from simple geometric shapes; peaceful, pastel block colours.

Cate:
If you'd like, we can have dinner? x x

The tips of my fingers were hot, pulsing with blood as I typed my response. I watched my fingers closely. I waited for my nails to buckle from the pressure of the pulse, to crack down the centre as blood started to seep from my fingertips, slowly covering my phone screen in thick, sticky red.

Amalia:
Dinner would be lovely x

She suggested a pizza pub. I hadn't realised pizza pubs were a thing.

———

I had Eve on speakerphone while I paced in my underwear. Something was different about her English accent, like the vowels had bent.

Eve: So you're going on a date with a girl?
Me: I am going on a date with a girl
Eve: You sound like you're trying to reassure yourself
Me: It's gonna be fine
Eve: Again with the reassuring . . .

A bird squawked outside my window and it sounded like it was laughing at me.

———

Cate waited for me outside the pizza pub, leaning against the wall, scrolling on her phone. The sun bronzed her face but left her body in darkness, like an Instagram filter. She looked up as I approached her and smiled as though she were posing for a photo. She had a Hollywood smile I hadn't noticed before.

Me: Hey! What are you reading so intently?
Cate: Oh, it's only BBC News – this app has just been
  banned for creating fake nudes – very disappointing

I wanted to sway along to her Welsh lilt. It was very soothing.

Me: I can't keep up with technology
Cate: Nor me. You look smashing, by the way
Me: Thank you

Do I say 'you too'?

Me: You too

I followed her into the restaurant. The design was ordinary –
white walls, scratched wooden finishes – but the charm lay
in the rolls of lopsided fairy lights and decorative vibrancy
of the customers. We were welcomed by a waiter who was at
least our age, probably younger. He walked us to our table
and stood awkwardly as we sat down and opened our menus.
I ordered a glass of house red wine, making the same joke
Alex had made in Sydney: 'House is my favourite flavour.'
The familiarity of the comment relaxed me, though Cate
didn't giggle like I had. Neither did the waiter.

Before the drinks arrived, Cate took her phone out of
her bag and scrolled through our messages to find the art
pictures she'd sent me. I panicked that she'd ask me what I
thought of the art, which of course she did.

Cate: Right, I've gotta ask you: did you prefer the Banksy
    or the Picasso?

Luckily, I had enough sense to be able to distinguish the two.
I had preferred the Banksy. It was so obviously scandalous
and the blazing red background made me feel something –
energised? I tried to think of something clever to say – red,
a revolutionary colour? A colour of change? A statement
colour? But I was too nervous for honesty.

Me: I think I prefer the Picasso. The colours kind of relax
    me and I like the fact that two people seem so intimate
    doing something that's normally done alone–

She didn't say anything, so I continued.

Me, higher pitch: –reading

Fumbling, awkward words. Childish. Mundane. She seemed
disappointed.

Cate: The thing is, I agree, there's something 'calm' about
    the whole thing

Her eyes flashed.

Cate: A lot of scholars suspect the woman on the left of
    being Picasso's mistress and the woman on the right
    of being his wife

Her voice lowered.

Cate: I like to think he was planning a threesome

I swallowed.

Me: How do you know these things?
Cate, dismissively: Well, art interests me, so I read about
    it. What about the Banksy? What did you reckon?
Me: It's Queen Victoria, right?
Cate: Okay
Me: I think it's ... sexy
Cate: Yeah, obviously. What else?

She seemed less disappointed, which encouraged me.

Me: Well, for starters, I never thought I'd find Queen
    Victoria sexy

At this, she laughed. I was finding my charm. I clung
on to it.

Me: I also find the red really exciting? Actually, it's the
    kind of thing I'd hang on my wall

It wasn't. She smiled.

Me: Alright then, expert, tell me what you know
    about this one

Cate: You've got me there, gorgeous. Actually,
not so much. It's obviously linked to Queen
Victoria's old tidbit of wisdom – women aren't
able to be gay. Originally, it sold for like 50 quid!
That's wild, that is. And now I reckon Christina
Aguilera owns it

Me: Presumably she didn't pay 50 quid. Is Christina
Aguilera gay?

We found a conversational flow and relaxed into it. I remembered how much I liked her company and decided to calm down and be more honest.

Me: I don't think I'd really hang the Banksy on my wall
Her: Oh, I know

By the time our food came – Cate had insisted we each order separate pizzas – we were smiling and laughing and it felt like a Real Date. I wondered whether other people in the pizza pub thought we were just friends hanging out. A young guy in a kippah sat down, alone, at the table next to us.

Me: I need to tell you something and you're going
to think it's really weird that I haven't brought it
up already

Cate clasped my hands in hers, faux earnest.

Cate: You're actually a Welsh girl like me?

Me: I am, unfortunately, not a Welsh girl, but I am Jewish
Cate: You're bloody joking!
Me: It's actually one of the reasons I was so drawn to you
Cate: You were drawn to me then?
Me: I just can't get over how much you love Judaism
Cate: What? How are you only mentioning this now?!
Didn't I 'teach' you about the alphabet?

At the end of the meal, both our cheeks were pink. I excused myself to the bathroom and Cate stood, saying she had to go, too.

As I was closing the cubicle door, her open palm smacked against it. I jumped and almost screamed. She shoved open the door and locked it behind her as I took a small step back. Her hands were on my shoulders, pushing. My back hit the wall. My mind moved slower than real time. *What's happening?* Then she kissed me hungrily, running her hands over my body. She lightly tongued down my neck, onto my chest, looking up at me as she slid her tongue between my breasts.

She kissed back up to my lips as her fingers fiddled with the top of my jeans. She undid a button. 'May I?' I nodded again, closing my eyes. She slid down my body, dragging her nails down my torso until her mouth reached my zip. She opened my jeans with her teeth and pulled them down my legs. My mind was misty with pleasure and lust. She breathed hot air onto my underwear and I moaned out. She looked up at me, shaking her head. 'No moaning, okay?'

She pulled down my wet underwear and set me on fire with one long lick up towards my clit. I tried to grab the wall, but there was nothing to hold onto. My nails scratched at the paint. She sucked me, flicking her tongue, and I couldn't help it, I moaned again. Then she slid my underwear back up and stood to face me. Cool air tickled where her lips had been and I shuddered.

    Cate: Just want to make sure you don't forget me over
       the holidays

She left the cubicle and I quickly locked the door behind her. I put my head in my hands, then I touched where her tongue had been. I was soaking.

    Cate:
    Thanks for a lush night Amalia!
    Looking forward to date number 2 x

    Amalia:
    Thank you! And me too! X

I also messaged Cali in Sydney.

    Amalia:
    So ... turns out ... I'm probably bisexual too

    Cali:
    Thanks for telling me Mals, but I can't say I'm
    surprised ...

    Amalia:
    What???

Cali:
Your childhood obsession with Natalie Portman was pretty gay ...

Amalia:
Hahaha oh god, don't

Cali:
You gonna tell your parents?

Amalia:
Yeah, I guess so? I'll call them soon ...
Don't think it'll be a big deal

Cali:
You're lucky

I was right. The phonecall wasn't a big deal.

Me: Guys, I think I'm going to start dating
women as well
Mum: Any woman in particular? Someone we
know perhaps?
Me: No, as a matter of fact
Dad: Mals, thanks for filling us in. Though the idea of
you dating anyone still makes me nervous ...

———

Then term ended.

11

WHEN DO YOU NEED TO BE BRAVE?

Neither Alex nor I mentioned our discussion from the night of the Best Falafel. I thought it best to let her bring it up, sober, if she wanted to. She didn't. She did insist on spending more time together and suggested we spend a weekend in Italy, just us two. Cate was going away with her family and wasn't at all fazed by the intensity of my friendship with Alex. So either she didn't consider Alex a threat or she really wasn't that into me. I still don't know. Oscar didn't seem to be fazed either, but probably because he was too secure to feel threatened. Neither of them had anything to worry about.

———

The second-hand markets in Bologna were quite extraordinary. I plunged my hand into a bucket of door handles in hundreds of colours and patterns. I pretended the handles were quicksand, pulling me in. Alex laughed beside me. The air was warm and the wind was rough, but the handles were cold and smooth. I felt my senses celebrating. *Italy for the week-end, when did this become my life?* I photographed Alex from behind as she took her time browsing silk scarves, letting the fabric run through her fingers. Sometimes I envied her grace. The scarves didn't interest me much.

A woman caught my attention. Her hair was almost buzzcut short and auburn and she had two small cartilage piercings. She wore round, coloured sunglasses and a long coat made of suede patches, many of which matched her auburn hair. She was leaning against a wall reading from a thick book. She was very beautiful. A man opposite me noticed, too. He was old and took a few seconds too long to crouch down. He had the kind of face that someone who could draw would want to draw. So many lines. He took a photo of the woman. She glanced at him above her glasses and then carried on reading. I must have looked like I felt because he glanced at me and shrugged. '*Artistico!*' She looked at me, shrugged, and said nothing. Alex came over and we continued browsing. I didn't ask whether she'd noticed the woman.

Her: Tell me a story

Me: Okay, we're in the 17th century

Her: Of course we are

Me: I think we're in the 1630s. A song is written that is only performed in the Sistine Chapel. The Vatican keeps the composition a secret for 150 years!

Her, dramatically: Dun dun dun!

Me: Enter 14-year-old Mozart, who spends an Easter in

the Vatican, listens to the piece twice, and transcribes
it from memory
Her: Fucking Mozart
Me: It wasn't even a simple song, it was a choral
composition! Many, many vocal lines!
Her: What's the piece, do you know?
Me: It's Allegri's *Miserere*
Her: Sounds cheerful

We opened Spotify and listened together. It was an Oxford college's recording. The world felt small and I felt like I was part of it. I closed my eyes and fell into a darkened room. Allegri's *Miserere* – some voices embraced me, some surrounded me. The opening swells, a peaceful mist I was happy to be lost within. The soaring treble solos were candles, breaking through the mist with light and heat. The strong basses, the steady floor beneath me. It was a dizzying, almost spiritual experience, listening to a choir from my new home sing secret, hundreds-of-years-old music, here in Italy – the place where it was first composed and then discovered – with Alex beside me.

———

We spent the afternoon at a piano concert in a small hall where the little orange floor tiles continued onto the walls and onto the ceiling. It was like being inside a small, ornate box. All rooms are boxes, but this room really felt like one. The acoustics were enveloping. When the pianist played the *Andante* of Clementi's First Sonatina, I felt like it was already summer and I was back by the sea. When she bowed, she touched the piano as though it were sharing the applause. I clapped for them both.

We sat on a bench next to a teenage couple after the concert ended. They kissed without speaking.

Her: I've been thinking a lot about words and identity
and gender-queerness

Me: Go on

Her: Like, I've been wondering what it would have been
like for someone who identified as gender-queer to
exist in a world without the vocabulary to describe
their identity

Me: Yeah, I really don't know. I mean, vocabulary is
obviously very important, but surely also knowing
people who identify the same way is huge, right?

Her: Like a role model?

Me: I mean, yeah, but even just a model

Her: Sorry, sorry, I'm sure you want to discuss the
concert and–

Me: I've been thinking a lot about sexuality and
gender. Like, I don't understand how someone
can be attracted to just one gender, except for
societal pressures

Her: Well, this is the sex–gender split/not split
thing, right?

Me, hesitating: Right?

Her: Like, I know gay women who won't have sex with
women with penises

Me: But isn't that transphobic?

Her: That's the way this conversation usually goes, sure.
But I guess I'd rather talk about bodies. Like, is sex
with Cate all that different from sex with men?

Her voice changed when she asked this. She sounded more
than intrigued, almost excited.

Me: Well, yes, it would be different, but also arousing.
Her genitals don't really have anything to do with my
arousal. It's the pleasure her genitals can bring her
that's arousing

Her: Pleasure or joy?

Me: Pleasure

I decided not to mention explicitly that I hadn't yet had sex
with Cate.

Me: In *NW*, Zadie Smith wrote something about the
imprecision of desire. It's not final

She blushed. I didn't understand.

————

We overtook Italian after Italian as we powerwalked along
the cobblestones.

Me: I've been thinking–

Her: Dangerous

Me: –about alcohol–

Her: Lethal

Me: –and about social lubrication

Her: Go on

Me: Well, I didn't drink until I was 18 because I didn't feel I needed to. Drunk Amalia and overtired Amalia are human synonyms

Her, laughing: Yes, that's probably accurate

Me: And then I started drinking at university because, well, I just did – and I really, really like the taste

Her: Which is completely fine, understandable, and not at all a concern. Go on

Me: And I don't think I drink too much

Her: You don't drink too much

Me: But then I went over to Tim's for dinner one night

Her: Oooh la la

Me: Shhh. And the wine he was planning for us to drink had been open for 20 years and it was so acidic it would have dissolved our tongues

Her: I'm glad you didn't drink it. I like your tongue

Me: What?

Her: I was being silly, go on

Me: And, for the first time in my life, I noticed the absence of alcohol! Like, conversation seemed harder

Her: For him or for you?

Me: What do you mean?

Her: I think you're perfect socially without alcohol. I think you probably noticed that he wasn't 'lubricated', so to speak

She laughed at herself – or me – while I considered this.

> **Me:** I hadn't thought of that
> **Her:** Really? It seems pretty obvious to me
> **Me:** Alright, Detective!
> **Her:** No! I'm sorry. I just mean that I think you're great with and without alcohol, truly, and you were probably noticing the absence of alcohol on his end! I really don't think you need to worry
> **Me:** Actually, you might be right
> **Her:** I don't drink to be better socially, but I think I drink to be brave

Like that time you told me you were probably gay?

> **Me:** When do you need to be brave?
> **Her:** A discussion for another time! We're here!

I didn't understand how she could say the things she'd said on the night of the Best Falafel and then pretend she never had. Even if she had been Passover drunk.

––––

The Museum of Modern Art was filled with people and their mobiles. Each painting was framed by small electronic duplicates as tourists took photos of the art. I struggled to see the point. We surveyed the art separately. I always feel a little inadequate in art galleries because art doesn't move me. I had a childhood friend who could stare at a painting and cry. I can listen to music and cry, which is something I'm strangely proud of, but I could never stare at a painting and cry. It took me many years to admit I preferred learning about art to looking at art. Anyway, I was staring at this painting of a large red geometric shape for a long time, not crying.

Man in gallery: English?
Me: Yes
Man in gallery: Excellent! I was hoping you would say yes. What brings you here?
Me: Just travels, yourself?
Man in gallery: Also. I'm from Portugal originally. Where are you from?
Me: I live in England
Man in gallery: I want to tell you I think you are more beautiful than these paintings

It would have been more charming if we weren't in a room where the art consisted of large coloured geometric shapes.

Me: Thank you
Man in gallery: Are you here alone?

I'd been travelling alone enough to know the answer to this. I saw Alex across the room and tried to catch her eye. She was busy being moved by art.

Me: No, I'm actually here with my partner

At this point, Alex turned around and met my gaze. She got the message. She came over.

> **Man in gallery:** Oh, wait, is this your partner?
> **Her:** Yes, that's me, hi, is everything alright?
> **Me:** Yes

The man in the gallery looked excited, which made me feel sick.

> **Man in gallery:** Hi! Nice to meet you! Oh, I'm going to be very forward, I don't normally say this, I'm embarrassed, but, um, your partner is very beautiful
> **Her:** She is. I think we're actually going to get going now
> **Man in gallery:** Before you do, I can't believe I'm asking this, but are you two monogamous?

The lie felt too weird, so I backed out.

> **Me:** No, we're not, but we're going to leave now
> **Man in gallery:** Can I at least add you on Facebook?

We walked away before he'd finished unlocking his phone.

———

We saw an opera that night – Bellini's *I Capuleti e i Montecchi*. Sitting in the lush, bell-shaped auditorium felt like falling back in time. I wondered whether opera houses 100 years from now would maintain the tradition of crystal chandeliers, rich red carpets, ornate golden finishes. The opera was in Italian without English surtitles. We thought it would be fine because we knew the story. Turned out, it was a liberal reworking of the *Romeo and Juliet* we knew. We were very confused.

Her: What is the right amount of violence when
　　responding to violence?
Me: If you respond to violence with violence, it
　　never ends
Her: How else can you respond?
Me: Okay, maybe if people responded with less violence
　　and then that was responded to with less violence,
　　eventually the violence would cease to exist
Her: What is less violence?
Me: Like subtler violence?
Her: Can violence be subtle?
Me: Isn't some comedy kind of like subtle violence?

————

We slept in after the opera. I hadn't been sleeping well because I was intent to keep to my side of the double bed we shared. I didn't want to be accused of any more-than-friendly behaviour. It takes quite a lot of effort to sleep next to someone without touching them, but I managed.

————

In the streets, we walked past a lot of graffiti. In the centre of a fountain, there was a statue of a woman holding her breasts while water spouted from her nipples. Near the nipple fountain, a man who had tattooed his face was singing into a megaphone over a pre-recorded track. The megaphone made his voice sound above, not inside, the music. You could buy his CDs with contactless credit card. His band was called Carne di Satana.

Her: Would you like to hear a story?

Me: About Satan's Flesh?

Her: No, but, God, great band

Me: I would like to hear a story

Her: Well, on my year abroad in France, I met a man who introduced himself as someone who won the lottery. After doing some of the 'right things' – giving money to family, charity and so on – he decided he could spend his life travelling the world learning languages

Me: Is this turning into a 'what would you spend your winnings on?' conversation? I hate those conversations

Her: Absolutely not. I hate those conversations, too. It's just that I thought it was such a strange way to introduce oneself

Me: It's certainly memorable

Her: But maybe it's how he sees himself. Like, that's his identity. Hi, I'm a guy who won the lottery. Nice to meet you

She shook my hand.

Me: Do you think the way people introduce themselves is based on how they see themselves? Or how they want others to see them?

Her: How do you introduce yourself?

Me: Well, pretty early on people usually find out I'm a musician and that my dad works in artificial intelligence. And the fact that I can kind of speak Spanish usually comes up, too

Her: Probably because you look Spanish

Me: Right. But it's interesting now that you mention it! If how you introduce yourself is what you want people to know, then I'm like, 'Hi! I'm artsy, but I can also talk about maths and data and I'm culturally curious and sensitive because I studied another language'

Her: I mean, yep, that's you!

Me: How do you introduce yourself?

Her: I don't really know. I haven't met any new people in a while. How did I introduce myself to you?

Me: Honestly? I really don't remember

Her: Excellent

Me: I found out pretty early on that you were a dancer, that you studied French and Italian, that you had taught yourself to code …

Her, laughing: So we basically do the same thing. I wonder how many people do

She smiled at me, full of love.

Friendly–Romantic love

I didn't think it was fair that she could smile so lovingly, so easily, and I was struggling to sleep for fear of mixed midnight messages.

Me: Also that you had a boyfriend
Her: Did I mention that early on?
Me: You sure did

I waited for her to say something. Nothing. I repeated my next sentence three times in my head before I said it out loud.

Me: Do you tell many people early on that you have a
   boyfriend?
Her, thoughtfully: Actually, no, I don't think so
Me: Why do you think you told me?

I'd stopped overthinking. I felt brave. I studied her cheeks for blush. Nothing.

Her, defensively: I don't know! Maybe you asked?

I gave in.

Me: Yeah, maybe

Alex spotted her friend Martina across the square and waved excitedly. I tried to shake off our unfinished conversation as we walked to join her.

——

Martina was tall and olive-skinned and quite strikingly beautiful. She wore a red beanie and gloves to match. She had to bend down to kiss Alex and me on both cheeks. She led us through small streets without saying much, past wine glasses balanced on motorbike seats and teenagers swigging from water-filled Coke bottles. We settled at a bar that looked like many of the bars we'd passed en route. The waiter brought us a bottle of Prosecco and a plate of salty olives.

I didn't know much about Martina, only that she had been at Oxford with Alex and that something horrible had happened to her during her time there. She wouldn't go back. But none of this came up over our drink. Alex seemed relaxed in Martina's presence, Martina in Alex's. I wondered why they didn't keep in touch more. I supposed it took a certain type of person or a certain type of friendship to maintain closeness while apart. Or perhaps Martina had needed to dissociate from Oxford and Alex was caught up in that dissociation. *I should message Eve.*

Martina spoke softly and precisely. She asked Alex and I how long it had taken to get to know one another. Alex told her honestly that we had felt like old friends at first sight: *yī jiàn rú gù.* Her smile was warm. I felt like Martina was trying to understand the love between us just as I was.

> **Martina, contemplative:** I feel like, the older I become, the more emotional baggage I carry, so the longer I imagine it will take to get to know me

Me: I've thought about this, too. Like, if I meet someone
  at university, maybe I'll share with them some of the
  defining moments from my school life. But, when I
  meet someone after university, will I have to share the
  defining moments of university *and* school life? And
  then what happens when I meet someone in my 30s?
Her: I imagine that what we deem the important parts
  of ourselves will change with time. I doubt someone
  in their 30s will place as much stress on schooltime
  'emotional baggage' as someone in their early 20s

I considered this. I wondered how heavy my emotional baggage from university would be at the end of it all.

Her: I have thought of an excellent word for emotional
  baggage. Are you ready? Your 'griefcase'

Martina's laugh was delicate, mine more boisterous.

Me: You did not make that up
Her: I did not

The conversation was slow but deep and I felt calmed by
the unhurried pace. We discussed how we deal with panic.
I confessed that I felt comforted, calmed, by company. Alex
was the opposite: 'I need to be alone to process.' Martina told
us she exercised to the point of passing out. I couldn't imagine
tall, beautiful Martina in such a vulnerable state, inflicting
pain on her body, aching, screaming muscles. *Didn't Eve once*

mention using running to deal with stress? Presumably she didn't
mean it like this.

When Alex excused herself to the bathroom, Martina took
my hand in hers. Her fingers were delicate, like her laugh, and
my lack of surprise surprised me. It felt right that she should
hold my hand.

Martina: I think you're very good for her
Me: Me, for Alex? Yeah, we're good for each other, I
  think. It's useful to have good friends in Oxford

Her face darkened. Then she was back.

Martina: I think she loves you

Alex returned before I could ask what she meant. 'Loves you.'

Friendly–Familial–Friendly–Romantic–Friendly–Sexual love

When Alex and Martina hugged goodbye, they held each
other for a long time. When Martina hugged me, she whispered, 'Take care of each other.' Then she walked away.

———

Final night, steps of the Piazza Maggiore, punnet of strawberries, paper cups and a bottle of wine – a personal cliché I'd be

happy to relive most nights. The sky was streaked with all my favourite colours. Sweat behind my knees. There was a soft, semi-out-of-tune guitar strumming and beer-bottle-clink percussion all around. *Oh, this is what I want. This is my early 20s. This is adulthood. This is freedom. This is beauty.* Alex took a sip from the bottle and it startled me. I'd never imagined her as the type to sip from the bottle. Her profile was lit by soft, early-evening sunlight, silhouetted against the darkening sky. I couldn't decide whether I wanted to enjoy the moment in real time or distance myself from the enjoyment so that I could study and memorise every detail and recreate the scene for ever. I chose the former. I very rarely choose the former. My throat was hot from conversation and alcohol. *This is love.*

——

I texted Cate from the train on the way home because I felt like I should.

Amalia:
Can't wait to see you! X

——

I added to my list of facts about Alex when we returned to the UK:

21. She's not straight
22. She speaks Italian with a French accent
23. She finds it difficult to live with someone and make time for herself

24. Alcohol makes her feel brave
25. She would prefer to be alone in moments of panic
26. She sometimes plans letters before she writes them
27. She is very capable of ignoring the elephant in the room
28. She doesn't necessarily keep in touch with friends
29. She wears a bra under her PJs (or maybe only with me)
30. She *is* the type who sips from the bottle

12

ARE ALL RELATIONSHIPS
ABOUT POWER?

Cate and I reunited in her college's apple orchard. She'd set up a blanket. She lay on her stomach reading a book for fun through round, oversized sunglasses with thick orange frames and tinted orange lenses. She wore a loose, colourful button-up shirt tucked into short shorts. She was a picture I wanted to take and frame. I caught myself looking all over her. Guilt. *Are you allowed to want to look all over your girlfriend? Is that what we were – girlfriends?* She didn't notice me until I lay down next to her. She kissed me closed-lipped and it felt sweet, not sexy, which was fine. I asked her how she could spend her downtime reading when she had to spend her uptime reading anyway. She shrugged and told me she enjoyed it. The book was a memoir by Lily Tomlin, an actress she loved. I hadn't heard of her.

Me: Can I ask you a question?

Cate: Alright then

Me: What do you wish you knew that you don't know?

Cate: Is this a riddle, hun?

Me: I feel like I know nothing

Cate: Well, compared to all there is to know, you *do*
know nothing and you will always know nothing.
This still feels like a riddle

She spent time rolling the 'r' of 'riddle'. She smiled at me like
I was flirting with her, which I don't think I was.

Me: I feel like education didn't teach me enough

Cate, dismissively: Well, everyone has different gaps
in their knowledge they probably want to fill, but a
school syllabus can't cover all of it

Cate rolled onto her side, still facing me. She seemed bored
by our conversation, but I continued.

Me: What if we crowdsourced a list of major historical
events or times that a bunch of people wished they knew
more about and made the ultimate school syllabus?

She laughed and kissed my cheek.

Cate: You're very cute, but sometimes I don't understand
the way you think

————

I decided to join a philosophy discussion group as part of some then-overwhelming urge to learn and find out more about myself and what I thought of the world. Fifteen or so keen, questioning philosophical intellects and myself sat around a wooden oval table with 20 white baguettes, hummus, Tesco's finest Cheddar, salami and apple juice. A tall German man presented: '"Philosophy should leave everything as it is" – Wittgenstein. Should it?' The keen philosophical intellects questioned the point of knowledge for a long time. Somehow, during my short time with this group, each conversation ended in a debate on the existence of absolute truth. One point that stuck with me was that the practical ramifications of philosophical thinking (ethics? I don't know) *do* need to be constantly renewed. I called Alex that afternoon because I was worrying about truth and life and death. Socialising with philosophers is dangerous.

Me: Socialising with philosophers is dangerous

Her: Oh no, what's happened?

Me: Do you have a minute to chat?

Her: Always for you

Me: It's about ... death

Her: Of course it is. Shoot

Me: I've just been thinking about the point of it all

Her: Okay, this sounds serious. Are you alright?

Me: Sorry, I didn't mean to scare you, it's not really so serious. I've thought about death before, but the thought of it's never really affected me. Now I feel really scared of it all of a sudden

Her: Has something changed?

Me: No ... It's just, we're all going to die

Her: Yes, we are

Me: Doesn't that terrify you?

Her: No, I guess not, there's nothing we can do about it

She paused. I wondered whether she was choosing her words carefully.

Her: And, even if there was, I wouldn't do
anything about it

Me: Nor would I. And it's not like I'm unhappy or
unsatisfied with life or anything, but I can't help but
think what's the point of things?

Her: Like what?

Me: Like stargazing

Her: What's the point of stargazing?

Me: Or doing the right thing? Or doing anything?
Or learning anything? I've got this overwhelming
feeling that it doesn't matter what I do or what
anyone else does

Her: Okay, I hear you, but can I ask a question: do things
matter to you?

Me: Sure

Her: Like what?

Me: Like family, friends, music, social justice

Her: Okay, but, according to your logic, those things
shouldn't matter because we're all going to die anyway

Me: I'm not sure this is helping!

Her: I'm trying to say that it's what makes us human –
    things matter to us! Sure, there's existential
    nihilism – life is void of objective meaning or purpose,
    la la la – but who cares about objectivity when things
    matter to us?! It's just how we are

Me: Okay, fine, I see your point. What about the fact that
    we'll definitely die one day?

Her: What about it?

Me: It's really started to terrify me

Her: Are you scared of dying in general or
    dying too soon?

Me: Both, but mostly dying too soon

Her: Well, the way I deal with that is I believe I'm going
    to grow old and, when the time comes for me to die,
    I'll be ready

Me: Sure, that makes sense, but can you stick to
    that resolve?

Her: So far, yes. Do you want me to come over?

Me: I'm not considering doing anything about it, it's just
    scaring me more than usual, that's all

Her: I think I should come over

Me: Okay, yes, will you?

Her: I'll be 20 minutes

When she arrived 19 minutes later, she was flushed from her
cycle and her neck was splashed red like her cheeks. Jackson
Pollock. She hugged me hello and we held each other a little
longer than necessary. A little longer than necessary later,
we parted but didn't move away from one another. Our faces

stayed inches apart. Maybe four inches. I heard her stop breathing. I don't know why I didn't move. I think I was just expecting her to move. She didn't move either. She looked at me with my favourite eyes and I smiled. I noticed my hands were still wrapped around her neck. *How long have we been like this?* I moved away.

Me: Hey, what was that about?
Her: What do you mean?
Me: Sorry, that just felt a bit – I'm all over the place today
Her: Are you talking about how close we were?
Me: How close we were to what?
Her: To each other?

She had been like this since we'd returned from Italy – more openly tactile, almost flirty.

Me: A lot of people in England have called me flirty
Her: You are flirty!
Me: I'm not!
*Her: No, you really are, you're just missing the distinction
     between 'flirty' and 'flirting'*
Me: So flirting implies intention?

I wondered whether she felt relaxed by my relationship with Cate, like she could be flirty with me – or flirt with me? – without consequence. Or perhaps she felt threatened? Jealous? Though she never mentioned anything. Of course. I'd given up trying to coax a Falafel Night conversation out of her.

I apologised again and she didn't say anything. I tried to explain to her why I hadn't moved away after our hug. I told her that it must have been because I'd recently changed the way I acted with another close female friend. She seemed satisfied by my response, though her eyes were starry, unfocused. She told me not to worry. I did.

We discussed life and death and existentialism a little more and I told her about the philosophy society I'd gone to. She'd been a few times in her first year, after which she'd decided it probably wasn't for her. She'd studied philosophy at school, which made me envious. Do people in the know about philosophy have a general life advantage over those who aren't? I asked her whether she thought her studies of philosophy had given her a general life advantage and she said that, if I was going to think about it like that, then any sort of thinking or reading or conversation would give someone a general life advantage.

Suddenly, she asked me whether I'd had sex with Cate, which startled me because I had not yet had sex with Cate. I was nervous to have sex with Cate. I didn't want to tell Alex I was nervous to have sex with Cate, so I laughed and changed the topic.

Me: Another philosophy discussion topic came up that
    worried me – are all relationships about power?
Her: Oh, this
Me: Yes, this
Her: Like, sure. In the way that lots of things are about
    lots of things. For me, it's never been useful to think

about relationships in terms of power, though I
suppose it's interesting to consider differences in the
power dynamics of different kinds of relationships,
especially when it comes to gender, class, race, maybe
even age. Actually, do you want to hear a weird story
about one of Harry's friends?

One of Harry's friends, another PPE student, is quite the
ladies' man. Very clever, very handsome. He's always been
hyper-aware of the power dynamics in his relationships with
women and is uncomfortable with certain powers he feels
he has 'as a man' in those relationships. Alex and this guy
had a few conversations about how to reverse those power
dynamics and she teasingly suggested he fix things by dating
older women. He agreed – he was really into the idea that
age could counteract gender in power battles, so he started
dating women in their late 30s and early 40s. He found that
the power dynamic shifted entirely, away from him, and he
loved it. Now he only dates older women.

Alex had to leave because she had a tutorial. I lay on the
floor and stared at the too-high ceiling. I felt less interesting
than Alex's friends. Although Oxford seemed more man-
ageable, more earthly, in my second year, I still felt my own
inferior schooling like a sting. I knew nothing about philosophy. I didn't do interesting things to experiment with theories
of power. Scratching these insecurities aggravated others and
soon I was also feeling sexually naïve.

My inner monologue went something like: *There are so
many things I should have spent time learning when I still had*

time to learn, which is a strange thought to have at university. At school, we spent hours on 'moral studies' – how to be nice – in physical health class. I also learnt about a lot of STIs and how to put a condom on a banana.

We learnt about flaccid and hard penises, too. It was a little strange how that teacher used her arm to demonstrate: flaccid – hard – flaccid – hard. We all found it very funny. She was weird. In hindsight, she was probably hungover a lot of the time. Actually, what the fuck? We learnt so much about male pleasure in high school! I don't even remember learning about the clitoris! Surely that's not right? When did I first masturbate? How did that happen? How did I know what to do? Why is masturbating something every woman has to learn on her own? Is it weird that I can't remember my first time masturbating? Surely your first time masturbating is as important as your first time having sex? Can you use the term 'wanking' to talk about a woman masturbating? Why haven't I thought consciously about female pleasure like this before? Far out, I am going to be a shit gay. Is it common for lesbians to use sex toys? Presumably you have to clean them. Maybe just in hot water? Or with disinfectant? I'm sure it'll say on the packet. Is there a special condom or something similar to stop lesbians spreading STIs? Are there STIs women can only get from sex with other women? Why don't I know all of this?

After my panic, I did some research and learnt (among many things) the following:

- In 1559, Italian surgeon Realdo Colombo officially identified the clitoris. *Good man*
- The concept of a vaginal orgasm (as a separate phenomenon) was first proposed by Sigmund

Freud. Incidentally, Freud also talked about clitoral orgasm as an adolescent phenomenon and that a proper response of a mature woman was 'progress' to vaginal orgasms. *It was clear that Sigmund Freud had never experienced a good clitoral orgasm*

- In 1974, Helen Singer Kapan reported that stimulation of the clitoris is usually experienced in the vagina, which has since been confirmed anatomically – clitoral tissue extends a considerable distance inside the body and around the vagina. *Cool*
- In 1996, Masters and Johnson published their work about the phases of sexual stimulation – the physiological stages before and after orgasm. They observed that both 'clitoral' and 'vaginal' orgasms had the same stage of physical response and that clitoral stimulation is the primary source of both kinds of orgasms. *NB: focus on clit*
- The G-spot has not been scientifically identified. *Hmm*
- Dental dams protect against STIs that can be transmitted orally: infections like gonorrhea, chlamydia, HPV, Hep A and B, and syphilis. They can also protect against HIV transmitted via oral sex. *Do lesbians use dental dams? Does Cate have some?*

———

Amalia:

Do you think I'm a knowledgable person?

Mum:

Yes, I do, please don't let people tell you otherwise

Amalia:

No one is telling me otherwise.

I just feel so naïve here

Mum:

British and Australian schooling systems are very different, so I'm sure your friends know a lot more about certain topics than you do.

But I bet they don't know about Aboriginal history or Japanese Shintoism or the spiritualism involved in Balinese architecture?

Amalia:

True

Mum:

You okay sweets?

Amalia:

Yeah yeah I'm fine.

Just having a moment

Mum:

Here if you need me

Amalia:

I know xxx

———

Dear Amalia,

Me again ... I'm sorry, I'm not sure I handled our existential chat so well the other day. My head is a little all over the place worrying about my Finals.

I've been thinking a lot about our 'it's important to remember to be kind' conversation. When I'm stressed like this, my natural response is to shut off from everyone and everything and let my work absorb me, which isn't fair to the people I care about. I'm sorry.

Unrelated (read: sarcastically), I've bought us tickets to a play at the Keble O'Reilly this Friday. I really, really hope you're free. I can't wait to see you.

Your Alex xxx

———

I was pleased with my response.

Dear Alex,

No need to apologise – I've heard how stressful Finals can be. I hope you're managing okay.

I'm knee-deep in an essay on sacred polyphony and the English Reformation – I'll confess, I've read more

interesting articles – so the play will be a welcome
distraction! And, of course, I'm excited to see you, too.
    Your Amalia xxx

———

Cate:
Meet me at the Ashmolean tomorrow?
There's something I want to show you

Attached to Cate's text was a piece of art titled 'Gilbert Cannan and his Mill' – Mark Gertler (1916). A man, presumably Gilbert Cannan, stood in front of a windmill with his two dogs. He almost looked like a doll. The colours were ordinary, dull. The message was unlike Cate's usually overtly lesbian art texts, which worried me, especially given our clumsy apple orchard chat.

Amalia:
Sure? Everything okay?

Cate:
More than! See you 4pm xx

———

I'd walked past the Ashmolean Museum on Beaumont Street a few times on the way to tutorials, but had yet to venture inside. The building was almost intimidating in its grandeur. Muscular pillars lifted its ornate roof. It began to rain while I waited for Cate and I quickly found cover for fear of frizz.

Cate smiled as she approached me. She strolled over – back straight, head high – and kissed me hello. I looked around, curious to see whether anyone had noticed. It appeared no one had. Cate held my hand as we walked into the museum. I was still intrigued by her lesbian-art-free message, but she gave nothing away.

Cate walked without pause, as though she were showing me around her childhood home. The first room she pulled me through was filled with marble statues, like some grand, old-fashioned Madame Tussauds. We paused amid the figures.

Cate: Have you been to the Ashmolean before, then?
Me: Actually, no, this is my first time
Cate: Okay, well, you have to come back because there
are a few really specific things I want to show you
Me: Okay, exciting!
Cate: I had to write an essay a few weeks back: 'What
defines an object as Jewish?' My tutor wanted me to
come to the Ashmolean. Apparently there are quite a
few Jewish artifacts assimilated into the collection –
hidden in plain sight

First, she showed me a handful of stone shekels, the currency in the Kingdom of Judah in the 6th century BCE. Nearby, there was a gold coin, minted 60 CE, made by the Romans following the destruction of the Second Temple.

Me: We've never been a loved race, have we?

Cate: Persecution is a frighteningly huge part of your
   history, yes
Me: Why is this coin a 'Jewish artifact'?
Cate: Perhaps because it sheds light on Jewish history

It was funny seeing this academic side of Cate, void of flirti-
ness and innuendo.

Cate: I thought of you while I was reading for this essay
   because so much of the reading involved music

This surprised me – it wasn't a connection I'd drawn between
myself and Judaism before.

Cate: I read about a viola da gamba made in 17th-century
   Italy by a Jewish convert to Christianity – probably not
   strictly a Jewish artifact – but then I spent the rest of the
   evening on a Wikipedia deep-dive reading all about Jewish
   musicians in Renaissance Italy and the crypto-Jewish
   musicians at the court of Henry VIII and Elizabeth I. One
   of them might even have been a lover of Shakespeare!

Again, I was astonished to find someone so enticed by my
religion. Cate spun me around, covering my eyes with her
hands. I welcomed her dramatics.

Cate: Welcome to the *pièce de résistance* of our
   Ashmolean tour!

We'd arrived at the painting she'd texted me. Like on my phone screen, it appeared very quaint and rather dull.

Cate: What do you reckon?
Me, unsure: It's a bit ... boring?
Cate: Yeah, sure is

She was smiling a flirtier smile. She wrapped her hand around my waist and I remembered we were on a date.

Cate: The figure in the painting is the writer Gilbert Cannan, a friend of the artist
Me: I don't know who that is
Cate: Well, I didn't expect you to. What's interesting about this painting is what you can't see. When it was X-rayed, they found an unfinished work beneath – a painting of a Jewish couple. I think there's something really striking, almost haunting, about the pair of paintings – it's like Gertler was painting over his complex Jewish identity with a plain British one

Is Cate trying to tell me something?
On the way to the rooftop café, we passed a forged £5 note from Operation Bernhard, the Nazi plan to destabilise the British economy by flooding the country with forged banknotes made by prisoners in concentration camps. Cate noticed me pause in front of it.

Cate: The ironic thing is that the counterfeiting team
    survived the war and a lot of the forged notes
    were used to help smuggle Jews into Palestine.
    Imagine that!

———

Cate ordered us coffees while I studied the skyline. The
rain had subsided and the sky was a pale, baby blue. We sat
opposite one another on the roof of the Ashmolean, beside a
closed umbrella.

Cate: So what did you reckon?
Me: It was great! Thank you! Though I'm still so baffled
    by your interest in Judaism
Cate: What baffles you?
Me: I think, if I'm honest, I just struggle to look my own
    Judaism in the eye
Cate: Can I ask why?
Me: You can, though it's not something I feel very
    comfortable talking about

I felt my eyes sting, throat tighten. I breathed deep like I was
about to sing. Cate didn't move.

Me: When I was a kid, maybe 14, I went on an
    educational trip to Poland that just kind of fucked me
    up. I didn't go to a Jewish high school, so my parents
    thought it would be good for me to learn more about
    our history. I'm not sure if I was too young or I didn't

know enough about the Holocaust before I went or the
whole trip was just handled really irresponsibly, but
I've been really fucked up about it ever since. We went
to three death camps in three days, which was just too
much. And the museums at Auschwitz were horrific.
Like, I get that it's important to learn and remember
this stuff, but ... I don't know

Cate: I can't imagine

Me: I'll never forget the guide who led us into a room
and told us to guess where we were and, just as I was
noticing these scratch marks on the walls, he told us
we were in a gas chamber. I thought I was going to
vomit or faint, but I didn't do anything. I don't think
my brain could really compute what that meant. I still
can't get my head around it, any of it. And, ever since
then, I've just really struggled with my own Jewish
identity and I've had this PTSD associated with all
things Holocaust

Cate: PTSD how?

Me: Like, I was watching the new *X-Men* in the cinema
and my whole body started to shake and I didn't
know why. I only realised the scene was set in
Auschwitz when it was signposted on screen. It
was so strange, though, like my body recognised
Auschwitz before I did

I was shaking. I don't think Cate knew what to say. I couldn't
look at her. But I felt lighter.

Me: Not the most pleasant of topics . . .

I stole a glance. She seemed transfixed.

Me: Have I ruined the romance?
Cate: Not at all

She rested her hand on mine.

13

WHO WOULD YOU LOOK FOR IN HEAVEN?

The bells at my college rang every 15 minutes. In my second year, I lived in a little room next to the bell tower. I loved the bells. They reminded me of Edgar Allen Poe's poem, which I also loved: *bells, bells, bells, bells, bells, bells, bells.* The bells never bothered me because, or so I thought, I grew up with a barking dog, which meant I'd learnt to block out continuous sounds.

Alex and I hugged hello at our college lodge as the bells chimed, which was perfect because it meant we were both exactly on time. She was wearing a light-blue sweater, black jeans, and I-love-you eyes. I analysed them, trying to decipher what kind of love, but I didn't know what to look for.

We'd been messaging in rap-rhyme all afternoon.

> **Alex:**
> I'll see you at 7.15
> Did I mention I'm so keen?
> X
> **Amalia:**
> I agree, I just can't wait
> Yes, I'll see you later mate!
> X

So, when we met, we continued with the rhyming.

> **Her:** Hey there, girlie, you look well! We're both on time,
> bell bell bell!
> **Me:** Your rhymes are good, but I think you should /
> Take my arm, we'll get some food

I pronounced 'food' so it rhymed with 'good' and 'should'. Her laugh bounced off the bell chimes. She grabbed my arm and we walked out of college and made a right towards one of the little theatres. While we grabbed eat-while-you-walk crêpes from a van, I told her that I thought Cate and I were going to start properly 'seeing each other'. At first, she was silent. Then she told me she was pleased for me. I studied her reassuring smile for a hint of sadness. Part of me wanted Alex to be saddened by – actually, let me be honest, *jealous of* – my relationship with Cate. But her smile was unfaltering. So I tried to seem pleased that she was pleased.

Promenade Theatre: we arrived at the play and joined the standing audience. Scene by scene, the actors led us around the small space. Everything was very intense. There was murder and love and shouting. A woman physically abused her boyfriend. In a moment of hot rage, she lifted up his shirt to reveal his bony body splashed with yellows and purples. Alex gripped my sweater and didn't let it go for a long time. I felt her cold fingers on my skin, under my sweater, just above my jeans. *Do friends do this? Would Cate be okay with this?* One character asked another, 'Who would you look for in heaven?' Alex whispered to me, 'Nice variation on the "who would you invite to dinner?" question.' I was thinking the same.

We decided to go for ice cream after the show and it was so windy that our ice cream was blowing everywhere. The wild way she licked her ice cream made me think of frantic kissing. I tried not to stare. We walked without a destination.

Her: Why do you think he stayed with her?

Me: Stockholm syndrome?

Her: Do you believe in unconditional love?

Me: I don't know. I find love so confusing

Her: What's so confusing about love?

Me: No one really agrees what love is

Her: No, they don't

Me: It's the same with music. There's all this scholarship on music's ineffability. Indefinable. Some schmucks even say that, because music is ineffable, you shouldn't write about it

Her: Can you imagine if no one wrote about love?

Me: Everyone writes about love

Her: So what is it?

Me: I think love is an action and also a feeling

Her: Can it be unconditional?

Me: Well, no, not if it's an action, but I guess I
unconditionally love my family

Her: I don't

Me: Well, I definitely started off loving my family in
a way that I don't start off loving a stranger. Like,
they're a step ahead

Her: But I think love's a choice

Me: If love's a choice, why do people talk about
'falling' in love?

Her: What do you mean? Because 'falling' is involuntary?

Me: Exactly

Her: I think people love the drama of love, like this all-
consuming loss of control. I think it's ridiculous

Me: It felt like I fell in love with you

Her: Me too

Me: In friendly love at first sight

Her: I know

Me: Like the Chinese proverb

Her: The one from the letter I wrote you?

Me: Yes!

Her: God, that feels like 100 years ago

Me: But doesn't it kind of suggest that love happens *to* you?

Her: I don't think love happens to you

Me: Me neither

Her: I'm glad you happened to me

Me: I happen *with* you
Her: Lucky me

Again, guilt grabbed me and squeezed until I mentioned Cate, who might not have approved of my conversation with Alex.

Me: I reckon I could probably fall in love with Cate

Could I? I hadn't considered this. But there I saw it – a flicker of sadness – and it excited me. Then I felt guilty again, this time for wishing sadness upon her, my Person.

Our walk finished outside college. Neither of us wanted the night to end. Neither of us said anything and she stared through my eyes straight into my mind. I worried she could read my thoughts. Then I realised I wasn't thinking about anything, so I stopped worrying.

Her: Oh, I'm sorry, I'm just memorising this moment
Me: What are you memorising?
Her: Ah, you just have the wind in your eyes and the
lights in your hair
Me: Do you mean the wind in my hair and the lights
in my eyes?

Do friends say that?
We said goodnight.

———

Amalia:
Eve, you awake?

Eve:
Yes!

Amalia:
How's Paris?

Eve:
I am yet to get over the price of apartments here

Amalia:
Oh god, I can't imagine

Eve:
How's Oxford?

Amalia:
Fine. There's something I want to talk to you about though

Eve:
Call now?

She picked up before the second ring.

Me: Hey! How's it going?
Eve: God, I miss English
Me: But you're having a good time?

Eve: It's fine. I do kind of feel like life's on pause, but, whatever, at least I know I never want to be an estate agent. Talk to me, what's up?

While we spoke, I stared at the two messy naked life drawings Blu-Tacked to my wall. One blurry.

Me, deep breath: Have you every wondered whether Alex and I are more than just good friends?

Eve: Big question – what happened to the girl you went on a date with?

Me: We're still seeing each other and I think I really like her! I just – I don't even know

Eve: Alex feels like more than a friend now that girls are an option, too?

Me: I don't know, it feels really weird saying it out loud

Eve: Would you do anything about it?

Me: What do you mean? Like tell her? Fuck no

Eve: I dunno, I'd ask myself is it worth risking the friendship?

Me: Yeah, you're right, I don't think friends should date

Eve: Harry and Sally might disagree

Me: I would not have expected you to have seen that film

Eve, with a vocal shrug: It's my mum's favourite

Me: I hardly remember it

Eve: Do you want to watch it?

Me: What, now?

Eve: Yeah, I think it's on Netflix! We can watch it at the same time?

We prepared the film on our separate laptops in our separate cities and clicked play after a 3, 2, 1 countdown. We decided to message one another while watching, each with a glass of wine in hand. Very techy, very civilised.

Amalia:
OMG I forgot about the old couples telling their life stories! CUTE

Eve:
Nah, too soppy
Carrie Fischer! I didn't realise she was in this!

Amalia:
Oh, she's kind of hot, no?

Eve:
She looks a bit like my aunt

Amalia:
He asks the story of her life! It's like the old fashioned '28 Questions to Fall in Love'

Eve:
What's that?

Amalia:
Google it

Eve:

Can't be bothered

Amalia:

This is the film where she pretends to orgasm in a cafe!!!

Eve:

Such a great scene

Amalia:

Oh god, she orders food like my mum

Eve:

And like you

Amalia:

Surely not? I order really simply

Eve:

Whatever helps you sleep at night babes

When did people stop using hairspray?

Amalia:

No idea ...

Eve:

Okay, here it is, PAUSE!

I paused.

Eve:

'Men and women can't be friends without the sex stuff getting in the way'

Amalia:

How is that relevant?

Eve:

Maybe it's the same for lesbians?

Amalia:

Bisexuals – but with that logic I can't be friends with anyone

Also, I don't want to sleep with all my female friends, like you, for example

Eve:

Ouch – but do you want to sleep with Alex?

Amalia:

I don't know?

Eve:

Let's carry on watching

Amalia:

Is infidelity a symptom that something else is wrong?

Eve:

Nah, infidelity is a symptom of people being dickheads

So is this like your friendship with Alex?

Amalia:

No, not really

Eve:

Should we stop?

Amalia:

No! I'm enjoying this!

Okay, Alex and I do talk in accents occasionally

Eve:

That doesn't mean you're Harry and Sally

OMG a man is talking about mental health

Amalia:

How avante-garde . . .

Eve:

I just read the IMDB trivia, apparently all the old couple stories are true

Amalia:

Awww! What else does IMDB say?

Eve:

Apparently Sally's picky eating was based on the screenwriter's picky eating and, years after the film came out, the screenwriter ordered food on a plane the same way Sally orders and the stewardess asked whether she'd seen the film *When Harry Met Sally*!!!!

Amalia:

Amazing

Finally, Harry and Sally slept together. Then Harry behaved terribly.

Eve:

So why do you think he reacted like that?

Amalia:

Cause the friendship was changing and that terrified him?

Eve:

I don't think you should say anything to Alex mate

Amalia:

Yeah, I think you're right

Eve:

Focus on the girl you're dating

By the end of the film, I'd drunk half a bottle of Tesco's finest Merlot.

Amalia:

Great film! Do you reckon they stayed together?

Eve:

You know they're not real, right?

Amalia:

If they were *real*, do you reckon they'd have stayed together?

Eve:

Nah, it'd be his second marriage, right? Like 70% of second marriages end in divorce

Amalia:

Always the optimist, Eve

Eve:

Let's sleep – that was fun!

Amalia:

Yeah we should do it again! I miss you!

Eve:

You too

But I wasn't ready for bed.

———

Amalia:

Cate, are you busy? Do you want to come over?

Cate:

Hey there insomniac. It's midnight?

Amalia:

And?

Cate:

Bold! I like it! But how about I come over after your opera?

Amalia:

You're coming to my opera?

Cate:

Wouldn't miss it!

Amalia:

Ah, that's great! Thank you! Okay, come over after then xxx

Cate:

Can't wait xxx

14

Do you think I'm sexy?

I sang in this one opera while at university – a production of Bizet's *Carmen* set in nightclubs near Oxford's train station. It was a week-long run, a different club every night: Park End, Bridge, Plush. The 'production budget' was more than I'd ever had in a savings account. As Carmen, I wore leather trousers and a red crop top. Red lipstick to match. The show was interactive, so I was encouraged to dance with the audience on the sticky floor. Both Cate and Alex came to the show at Plush on closing night, which made me nervous. I was excited to twist and twirl with Cate.

> *Yes we'll twist and yes we'll twirl*
> *Slow-dance with me, pretty girl*

I was nervous to play sexy in front of Alex. It made me feel ridiculous. She had just one exam – an 'easy one' – to go and was visibly more relaxed. The two of us were working together in my room before the show and I paused our work session because I needed to ask whether she thought I was sexy. This is how I expected the conversation to go:

Me: Pause
Her: Yes?
Me: Do you think I'm sexy?
Her: What do you mean?
Me: Playing Carmen has felt so strange because she's
   meant to ooze sex appeal
Her: I've probably known you too long and too closely to
   be able to say 'yes, you're sexy', but I'm sure you'll play
   Carmen absolutely perfectly. Oh, you're going to be
   brilliant. I'm so excited for tonight!

This is how the conversation actually went:

Me: Pause
Her: Yes?
Me: Do you think I'm sexy?
Her: Yes

She didn't even stop to think. I don't think I'd even added the 'y' to 'sex-y'. It took me a few seconds to find the beat.

Me: Oh. Well, playing Carmen has felt so strange
   because she's meant to ooze sex appeal
Her: Amalia, you are perfect for this role. I'm so excited
   for tonight!

———

Windowless. Charcoal-black walls. Disco balls hanging from the ceiling alongside long, green, neon lights. I had my leather trousers and red lipstick on and I was feeling good. The pianist's rich, black eyeliner made the whites of her eyes gleam. She matched her piano keys. At the start of the Habanera, I joined her on her stool. I sat on her lap. She put a rose in my mouth and I winked at the audience while I played the opening bassline on her piano. She took the rose from my mouth with hers and then took over the bassline.

L'amour est un oiseau rebelle
Que nul ne peut apprivoiser

I scanned the crowd for Cate. I wanted her to see and know onstage me. I found her and I extended my hand so we could dance together. I felt powerful and in control.

When I dance and extend my hand–

She took it. Someone whistled.

Et c'est bien en vain qu'on l'appelle
S'il lui convient de refuser

Cate danced shyly with me and I loved her for it. I'd expected her to be more overtly flirty, but she seemed perturbed by the crowd.

You are not perfection. Simply mine.

Her hands were light on my waist. They followed my swaying hips.

> *I think I do, I must confess,*
> *I like her painted nails and dress,*
> *And slow-dancing with girls*

The rest of the cast danced and swayed with one another. Only Carmen got to dance with the audience and she loved it – I loved it.

> *I am dark imagination.*
> *I trill and dance and sing and fly*

The whole room was electric.

> *L'amour, l'amour, l'amour, l'amour*

The leather trousers pressed cool against my hot skin. Out of the corner of my eye, I saw Alex. She seemed to be inhaling every note and every move.

> *L'amour est enfant de Bohème*
> *Il n'a jamais, jamais connu de loi*

I walked over to her. It was a slow walk because slow walking is sexier than fast walking. I saw her swallow, but I wasn't distracted by it. I felt possessed, like the music had injected me with a shot of sex appeal and confidence. I extended my hand so we could dance together.

When I dance and extend my hand–

She took it. No one whistled.

Si tu ne m'aimes pas, je t'aime
Si je t'aime, prends garde à toi

But she danced back.

Chest to chest and eyes aligned,
Her fingers pressing on my spine,
They're smooth and hot and soft and strong
As she steps close and plays along
Si tu ne m'aimes pas, si tu ne m'aimes pas, je t'aime

Her hand was tight in mine and she spun before I knew my fingers had asked her to spin.

Mais si je t'aime, si je t'aime

I smiled because I was Carmen. I felt like Natalie Portman in the final scene of *Black Swan* – completely consumed by the character she was playing. Alex stepped back into the crowd and I turned away.

Prends garde à toi.

Cate looked uncomfortable as we took our bows. I tried to smile at her, *for* her, but she didn't smile back. Guilt. Alex hugged me tight after the show. She told me I was phenomenal. I could see all the love in the room concentrated into small stars in her sky eyes. Cate interrupted our goodbye, grabbing my waist and kissing my cheek. I asked her to come home with me, which seemed to melt her discomfort. I wondered whether I'd imagined it. I tried to read Alex's smile, but, as usual, she gave nothing away.

Cate: You were gorgeous!

———

Cate's lips were red, so red it was like the colour was throbbing. They were beckoning lips. We kissed against the wall outside my college before I led her upstairs. I felt dizzy.

I asked Cate to wait in my room while I showered. My body ached with exhaustion. The water was as hot as the shower could manage and I let it soak through my skin into my muscles and bones. I was absorbed by the heat infiltrating my body, so much so that I hadn't noticed her enter the bathroom. Cool breeze. She opened the door and joined me in the shower.

Had I ever been so close to a naked woman? Her body was so different from mine; I was mesmerised. Her legs were longer, leaner, carved with muscle. Narrower, more delicate arms and shoulders. Her breasts were paler, slighter, they looked softer. She seemed both languid and dominant.

Showering with a lover was an exotic sensation. She washed my body with silky, soapy hands. I rubbed my own all over her, delighting in the feel of her skin, warm under my fingers.

In my bedroom, she hunted for a scarf to use as a blindfold. 'Is this okay?' She kissed my breasts and luxuriated over my legs, running her fingers along them. Each touch was a surprise, each sensation heightened by the dark. She kissed my inner thigh. I sighed. She wrapped her lips around me and kissed deeply, swirling her tongue.

Everything inside me stilled except the balloon of pleasure in my chest, which cast aside my organs and broke my bones as it expanded, filling my entire body until it pressed against my skin, threatening to explode.

She sucked me, flicking her tongue in and out, around and in, out and around, sucking and licking and flicking. I stopped breathing. My legs tensed. Just as I was about to cum, she slipped her fingers inside me and the balloon of pleasure pushing at my skin exploded.

She undid the blindfold and smiled at me, satisfied. My breathing had slowed. I spoke without thinking. 'I want to taste you.' She nodded and guided my hand between her legs. She was dripping. I moved my fingers lightly over her, gliding across the wetness. She sighed. 'Yes, exactly.' Excitement rippled through me. I traced light circles, as though I were touching myself, hardening my touch as her breathing grew louder. I felt intoxicated. I kissed her breasts while I touched her, sucking on each nipple. I felt myself getting wet again. Finally, I kissed between her legs. So sweet. I tried to remember how she'd licked me, in and out and around. I flicked my tongue and she growled, 'Yes! Just like that!' My stomach flipped. I flicked my tongue again and again, over and over. 'I want you to suck me while I cum.' Her body grew taut. As she came, I wrapped my lips around her and sucked while her body writhed on the bed.

We fell asleep intertwined.

————

Morning-after coffee. She lay with her hands behind her head, her bare shoulders peaking from under my chequered black and white duvet. All the scene was missing was a cigarette in her hand.

> **Cate:** So are you a quick study or a secret long-
>   time lesbian?

I blushed. She sipped from my mug, eyes on me, waiting.

> **Me:** I guess I'm a quick study
> **Cate:** Well, love, if you ever need a CV reference

I rolled my eyes, blushing harder.

> **Cate:** Or a LinkedIn endorsement . . .

She smiled at me, a beautiful, relaxed, pleasure-filled smile, and beckoned me back to bed.

————

After finishing her Finals, Alex spent the holidays in Toulouse working for a think tank. She wanted a change of scene before starting her Master's at our college. When we said goodbye, I told her not to forget me. She joked that, after our dance together at *Carmen*, how could she? *Is this flirting?* I didn't ask. The street was empty but for our dramatic hug. I thought she might mention Cate, but she didn't. She squeezed my shoulder and flashed reassuring eyes. She touched my cheek. 'It's like ripping off a band-aid.' I was overcome by something and told her to take my ring, which made her laugh. I worried that maybe she'd thought I was joking. Then she took off the ring she was wearing and said it was only fair to swap. She put her hand back on my cheek and I put my hand on hers and she smiled like she was in love with me. *Do I trust my lenses?* I wondered what my smile said. Both our rings were thin straps. Mine was silver with a black gem in the centre; hers was bronze with two tiny gold spheres – the kind that looked like they should spin, but didn't. No one ever noticed we'd swapped rings. We never swapped back.

Alex:
Missing you already xxxxx

Amalia:
Can't tell if you're teasing xxxxx

Alex:
I like your ring.

Amalia:
I like yours.

Before term ended, I'd spoken with my tutor about Next Steps. He warned me that, as 'one finds success in opera-singing only in one's late 20s', I should consider another, unrelated job in the meantime to learn some skills and save some money. Logically, this made sense, though it made my soul burn. So, like a good and patient opera singer, I spent the summer interning at a management consultancy company in London. On the first day, the interns were told: 'We hope you're excited for problems that will keep you up at night! In a good way!'

It was a long summer.

My daily phonecalls with her made the air taste cleaner and easier to breathe. Alex, I mean, not Cate. But you knew that. Cate was away with her family for most of the summer. They were Airbnb-ing around the UK like they did most summers. We spoke sporadically.

Thoughts before bed some nights: *I think I need to be thinking more about Cate.*

———

I was living in Borough for the duration of the internship. My accommodation was a small room in vacant student lodgings where the toilet was more or less inside the shower. You could reach the sink from the shower-toilet. Efficient.

Alex:
What's the room like?

Amalia:
Compact and efficient.
Et toi?

Alex:
There's an Eiffel Tower wall mural

Amalia:
I swore you said you were in Toulouse ...

Alex:
Oui ...

Every Saturday morning, I would walk the 10 minutes or so to Borough Market with her in my ears. We'd exchange updates and worries and musings. We talked about our new everyday pleasures.

> **Me:** In this new London life, my Zadie Smith icy pole is probably people-watching on the Tube
> **Her:** My icy pole is probably cycling at night
>
> **Her:** *Do you ever think about family languages?*
> **Me:** *Like bilingual families?*
> **Her:** *More like the way families seem to have their own ways of talking – sentences and vocabulary that wouldn't make sense to other people ...*

I marvelled at our developing language.

Friendly–Familial love

I worked in the financial sector of the management consultancy firm. The aim of the game was to imagine an employeeless supermarket and to brainstorm the ins and outs of that imagined scenario. What risks would you need to mitigate? What technologies could you put in place to replace the function of humans? Trust seemed to be the most important thing to consider: theft, how to stop people from sleeping in the store overnight. I tried not to think about what happened to the employees who used to work in the now employeeless supermarket in our imagined scenario, helped by the still-hypothetical nature of the task.

———

Halfway through the internship, we were treated to a Day Out. The boat was too white, too clean for the dirty water, I thought, taking pride in my disdain for British rivers. The air was icy and harsh. It felt as though grains of salt had crystallised in the wind, scratching as it blew.

Amalia:
AI, would you ever swim in the Thames?

There was no signal. I put my phone away.

By this stage, the interns had divided into two groups:

those who spoke only to other interns and those who fought for the attention of our superiors.

To spot an intern, you had to look for signs of forced relaxation – weight-shifting was an obvious tell, as was loud laughter. Interns were the first to say 'bless you' and the last to instigate a handshake.

I found myself standing beside a senior consultant with a rainbow lanyard. Of course I did. Her hair was blonde and straight and didn't move with the wind. Its stillness was distracting. I made to leave, but she breathed in like she was about to say something. I waited. She breathed out. I surprised myself by speaking first.

Me: I don't understand how people can swim in
   this water
Rainbow lanyard: What don't you understand?

She spoke softly with the residue of an accent I couldn't place.

Me: It just looks so uninviting – to me anyway
Rainbow lanyard: There are ponds near where I live in
   Hampstead Heath that might change your mind
Me: Really?
Rainbow lanyard: Yes. I try to go at least once a week, if I can.
   Once you're in the water, you feel like you're part of nature

I was taken aback by her earnestness, probably the only instance of this particular personality trait that I'd encountered during the internship.

Rainbow lanyard: A friend once described the sensation
  as 'being on nodding terms with nature'
Me: I like that
Rainbow lanyard: So do I

We stood in comfortable silence – a rare sensation for me, not
feeling the need to word-fill the vacuum – and stared together
at the dirty water.

Just before she walked away, she added:

Rainbow lanyard: On the rare occasion I speak to
  other women at the ponds, I don't tell them I'm a
  management consultant, so you know

Is this job something to be ashamed of?

———

My phone lit up when the signal returned.

Alex:
Didn't you say you were going on a boat today?
  Good luck – I still can't face the British water xxx

Romantic love

I let myself, for just a second, contemplate romantic love with Alex. But the thoughts were attacked by memories of the conversation we'd had in Sydney, her refusal to bring up the night of the Best Falafel, images of Oscar and of Cate. The memories denied the thought oxygen until it died.

I accepted a full-time job at the management consultancy firm, which I'd begin after my third year.

YEAR 3

15

DO YOU ENJOY TRAVELLING ALONE?

Alex:
Landed safe xxx

I was sitting in the armchair of my grand new study when Alex touched down. This college suite had good heating, lush red curtains, and two adjacent rooms – one for study, one for sleep. Small comforts, like painkillers, to ease the stress of Finals.

I was disappointed when she went to see Oscar at his place in London before she came to Oxford to see me. The disappointment was deep, deep in my chest and it ached and I felt ridiculous. She said she'd come see me the next morning before her first Introduction to Master's meeting. Fine.

Alex broke up with Oscar.

She knocked on my door late that evening holding a small bag of things, sobbing. She couldn't bear sleeping alone in a house of strangers. She smelled of sadness – an unpleasant cocktail of snot and salt. She slept on my floor for a week and I did everything wrong. I tried to talk to her about the break-up and it made her cry. I told her about my essays and it made her cry. I asked her more about France and it made her cry. I asked her about her family and it made her cry. I told her about my family and it made her cry. I made her cry all the time. When I asked her why they'd broken up, she told me she'd realiséd that she didn't love him any more. I found it strange that she cried so much if she didn't love him any more. Though here she was, living in a city where she'd loved him. Maybe it wasn't strange that she cried so much. I didn't know what it meant or how it felt to love and then not love.

I cooked for her, but she didn't speak much or eat much. She was a shell. The sea seemed far away. She told me she felt like a grain of sand, which made her cry. Later, I'd ask what she meant.

Her: I wanted to be so small and insignificant that I
could never hurt anyone like that again

Alex told me a story about her parents, how they used to fight until she was sure she could hear vocal cords tearing. She used to sit on her windowsill, legs dangling, ears concentrating on the sounds of cars passing. She tried to see if she could guess the type of car by the sound of its engine, the way some people can do with planes. I felt as though I were on the windowsill sitting beside her, watching her close her eyes then peek at a passing car to see if she'd guessed correctly. She told me she'd never understood why people marry. She thought she'd spend her life at peace without the restraints of marriage, perhaps a type of monogamy-less existence. Until she met Oscar.

———

Eventually, Alex's tear ducts dried and she moved into a shared house with a group of medical students I didn't know and wouldn't get to know. She slept with most of them and with a lot of their friends. She laughed as she told people she was 'making up for lost time'. She no longer smelled of sadness. She mostly slept with women.

———

We were sitting at Queen's Lane Coffee House, a café on the High Street that called itself the 'oldest coffee house in Europe', though the café across the road boasted the same title. Alex had left her phone on the table while she'd gone to order. The phone buzzed – Jennifer – an unfamiliar name.

Jennifer:
Hey you, how's it going?
I feel like it's been agessss.
What you been up to?
You still gold-rushing? xxx

Mary's 'gold rush': 'That feeling you get when, all of a sudden, you realise you will no longer have the freedom or opportunity to sleep around at university and so, reactively, sleep with everyone.' I felt sick.

Alex carried her wallet in her mouth while she walked, balancing two very full coffees in her hands. She arrived at our table, fingers dripping in black coffee – we had both started drinking Americanos without milk. I took the wallet out of her mouth and warned her, 'No sudden movements!' She laughed. It was a sunnier, richer laugh than the one that accompanied her new 'I'm making up for lost time' catch-phrase. I worried she was changing. That day, we decided to become vegetarian. We made a lot of decisions together – books and films we liked, jokes we found funny, favourite cafés, best walks in Oxford ...

———

After leaving Oxford, Cate no longer messaged me with lesbian-themed art, so I started texting her Georgia O'Keeffe flowers. I told you this was not the love story of Cate and me, so I won't go into detail about our break-up. She ended things with me in a letter because of the sometimes-true equation: New Relationship + Long Distance = Failed Relationship.

I sent Alex a picture of the letter with the caption: 'I don't want to talk about it.'

We didn't talk about it. I was hurting.

———

Dan on keys invited me out dancing. Sticky-floor, loud-music dancing in one of the clubs we'd performed *Carmen* – Bridge. I agreed because I didn't know what else to do and I liked the idea of feeling a beat pound through me, expelling all thoughts. I joined a bunch of people from his college on the sticky floor. I wanted to feel bodies rubbing against me. I danced with my hands around the neck of a stranger. He smirked when I pulled him close to me. I smirked back.

The group made its way to the bar and I suggested tequila shots. I felt numb. Sweaty. Anonymous. Carefree in a dangerous way. When the shots arrived, Dan licked his hand before he sprinkled the salt. Instead of doing the same, I licked the salt off his hand, did my shot, and bit down on my lime, all without looking away from him. The lime tasted old, dry. The light painted black circles below his eyes. Dan shotted his tequila hungrily and ordered us another round. We did a number of shots before we returned to the dancefloor. This time, I danced just with Dan. He spun me around by my waist so that I danced in front of him. I let him run his hands down my sides. I swayed my hips, pressing against him. I felt him grow hard, rubbing against me. I felt a twinge of disgust, knowing part of him wanted to be inside me. I danced without smiling. I swallowed the disgust. I scratched up his thighs while I danced, which made him harder.

When I turned to face him, my vision was a little out of focus. Feeling his hot breath on my mouth, I was surprised by how close we were. I grabbed his hair and rolled my body into his. His hands clasped my lower back, interrupting my dance. We kissed. His lips were too firm and too rough on mine, but I leaned into the pain. I tugged at his shirt, feeling his hard stomach with the tips of my fingers. I pulled him off the dancefloor.

We stumbled into the bathroom, kissing clumsily. He

slurred into my ear something like 'you sure?' and I unzipped his trousers.

———

I watched myself – numb, wanted, empty.

———

'First Dance with Cate' / 'First Bathroom Sex' on my Ben Lerner memory map.

———

I read aloud to my tutor while he looked out the window.

Me: Supporting the use of music within the prison system, this essay addresses two essential questions: 1. What is the purpose of prison? 2. Is music a luxury or necessity?

Tutor: Why did you choose the words 'luxury' and 'necessity'?

Because it was 2 o'clock in the morning and they were some of the only words left in my head.

Me: Because they are common conflicting views of music's role in global prisons

Tutor: For example?

Me: In the US and, um, Norway

Tutor: Umnorway? I've not heard of it

I attempted a laugh. He addressed the window.

> **Tutor:** You need to be more assertive, Amalia, not just in
> discussions of your writing, but in your writing itself,
> or you'll barely scrape a 2:1

Despite the late night, I'd been quite proud of that essay.

———

A few weeks later, Alex invited me over to her free-for-the-
night shared house for shakshouka, my favourite dish. The
kitchen surfaces were shiny, clinical, almost hospital-like. We
promised we wouldn't discuss work all evening. It felt like
a heroic task.

> **Me:** Do you enjoy travelling alone?
> **Her:** No, not really, if I'm honest. I've done it a few times,
> mostly during my second year abroad, but I didn't
> love it. Why?
> **Me:** I've been thinking ... I'd like to go travelling alone
> again when all this is over
> **Her:** Oh, good for you! I'd love to be the kind of person
> who enjoys solo travel
> **Me:** What don't you like about it?
> **Her:** I don't really know

She put the shakshouka in the oven. I pulled myself onto the
windowsill.

Me: Is it the loneliness?

Her: Maybe? I think it's the tree-in-a-forest scenario

Me: Oh! Like, if no one's there to see it, did it
    really happen?

Her: Exactly. I could take pictures or send messages,
    but I don't want to feel like I have to – like, what's
    the point?

Me: I don't mind the loneliness, I just really hate the
    unwanted attention

Her: Oh, you mean from men?

Me: Men tend to be more obvious about it, yeah

Her: God, do you remember that guy in Bologna?

She shook her head.

Her: Men are gross

Me: That's not true

Her: No, it's not

Me: I think, when you're travelling alone as a woman, it's
    like you're wearing this big sign on your head

Her: COME TALK TO ME

She gestured with her hands to the imaginary sign on her
head, framing it with her fingers. I laughed, but only a little.
She took her hair down and joined me on the windowsill
while the room heated with the oven.

Me: This one time in Melbourne, I was reading in a park
    and this guy asked me if I wanted a drink

Her: Naturally

Me: It was like 11 a.m.

Her: Yum

Me: Then he told me he didn't want to have sex with me

Her: Rude!

Me: So rude! His evidence was a full-body tattoo of Jesus Christ

Her: What?

Me: He lifted up his shirt to reveal the giant head of Jesus Christ

Her: You're kidding

Me: Nope. He told me he didn't believe in sex before marriage, so I should have a drink with him

Her: I think everyone should tattoo their bodies with their views on sex. Life would be a lot simpler

Me: I didn't join him for a drink

Her: And this is when you decided that you enjoy travelling alone?

Me, laughing: Not quite. But I do notice all these beautiful things and I write about them. Everything kind of feels like it's in vivid technicolour because I'm paying so much attention to it all. It's like, if I'm not paying attention, no one is. And I have this little narrating voice in my head because I'm not speaking with anyone, so it's sort of like I'm in a story. I don't know

Her: What are the beautiful things?

Streetlights? Buskers? Kissing couples? But I felt distracted.

Me: Hey, do you mind if I change the subject?

Her: As long as it's not work chat

Me: It is not work chat

Her: What's up?

Me: I can't stop thinking about Cate. I don't know why. It's not like we were perfect for each other, but I liked her and I feel like I haven't got closure. Like, she broke up with me in a letter

Her: Did you write one back?

Me: No, which is why I suppose I don't feel I have closure – I haven't said my bit

Her: What is there to say?

Me: I don't know

Her: Do you feel over her? Didn't you sleep with that guy recently?

Me: Oh, Dan on keys?

Her: Yes, Dan on keys!

Me: Yes, but that didn't change anything. Eve called it self-imposed gay conversion therapy, which I found a little harsh ...

Her: Of course she did

She paused.

Her: I think it's okay

Me: No, I'm not over her

Her: That's okay, too

Me: I just want to wake up one day and be over her, you know?

Her: Yes

Me: I want to do a 180

Her: It's just time, my love

Me: Like, it was just a crush! I was probably in love with
    you and now I'm not

She didn't say anything. Where had my confession come
from? I panicked.

Me: No, I mean ages ago, but obviously not now, I feel
    nothing like that towards you now, obviously, which
    is what I'm saying

She still didn't say anything.

Still me: Like, I didn't even know I was into women and
    you were with Oscar, but, well, maybe I did know I
    was into women, but not in an active kind of way –
    and it doesn't even count if it's not even in your head,
    but that didn't matter because you're my friend

She looked away.

Still me: But the point is that I just woke up one day and
    I'd done a 180. I suddenly felt nothing

Silence.

Still me: Okay, please don't be weird, I feel nothing now

and obviously wouldn't have acted on it then and I
only really thought about it being *that* kind of love in
retrospect and the point I'm trying to make is that I
did a 180 and–

I think I told her how *not* into her I was for another 10 minutes.
Then she yelled at me, which was very out of character.

Her, yelling: I get it!
Me: You get it?
Her: You're not into me!
Me: Of course not! I'm sorry, I didn't mean to upset you
Her: No, it's fine, sorry, can we talk about something
    else please?
Me: Sure

What?
She opened the oven to check on the food while we spoke
about other things. Neither of us was really there. The whole
kitchen smelled of delicious shakshouka, like the air was
buttered with it. You could taste it. Then we were talking
about it again.

Her: I didn't mean to yell at you, I'm sorry
Me: It's okay, I didn't mean to upset you, I'm sorry
Her: No, I know, of course you didn't, I'm not upset
Me: Okay
Her: As in, I'm not upset that you were in love with me
Me: Okay

She took the shakshouka out of the oven. It was perfect. My mouth watered. She wasn't looking at me. She spoke carefully.

Her: I just understand what you mean by the 180s
Me: What?
Her: I mean, I've done those 180s, too, right?
Me: What? With who?
Her: With you

I panicked. Uncharacteristically, I panicked in complete silence.

Complete silence.
Complete silence.
Complete silence.
Complete silence.
Complete silence.
Complete silence.
Complete silence.
Complete silence.
Complete silence.
Complete silence.
Complete silence.
Complete silence.
Complete silence.
Complete silence.
Complete silence.
Complete silence.

We went back to her room with the Perfect Shakshouka.

Her: Are you okay?
Me: I don't know
Her: Okay
Me: No, I'm sorry, I'm fine, I'm just surprised
Her: No, that's okay, it's fine obviously, I hadn't really
expected to tell you like this
Me: Okay

We sat down opposite one another and broke the eggs of the shakshouka. I watched the yolk seep through the tomato. Then I breathed in through my nose. Then I swallowed. She put her hair up.

Her: Do you have any questions?
Me: Yes, do you think this needs salt?
Her: No, do you?
Me: No, it's perfect
Her: Any other questions?
Me: Pepper?
Her: Amalia–

I breathed out.

Me: Yes
Her: Yes?
Me: Where are you at now?
Her: What do you mean?
Me: On what side of the 180?

This time she spoke wildly, chaotically, like her words were escaping prisoners.

Her: If you're asking me whether or nor I'm in love
with you now, which I think is what you're asking,
then yes, the answer is yes, I am obviously in love
with you now

I breathed in. She didn't move. Poise. Her stillness was elegant and her elegance was startling. I stood to check my phone on the table behind her. I was standing and she was sitting and we were back to back. My mouth was dry. So dry, I could feel my lips rubbing against my teeth, catching. My phone was empty. Everything was on pause. I watched the time change. Everything was not on pause. I thought I was going to laugh. I felt the wild, hysterical laughter mounting in my chest. I could hear my own uneven breathing in the thick silence. What I did next surprised me.

I turned, slowly, and stepped towards her. I felt the thud of my heart, almost violent, throughout my body. She stood up to meet me and I hugged her. I wrapped my arms around her and I pressed my chin against the hollow of her neck. I breathed her in, felt her pulse on my lips. I pulled away. She didn't move. We stayed there and swayed there. Then I pressed my lips against hers. She let out a surprised sound. I felt it vibrate on my mouth. At first, it was a relatively chaste kiss. Closed lips. It was a friendly kiss. Her lips were smooth and tasted of shakshouka. Then she leaned into me, opening my mouth with hers. Our tongues danced like lovers, twirling and twisting and gliding together. She knotted her fingers in my hair. I tugged on her shirt, brushing her skin with my hands. I felt my muscles tense, then relax, as years of silenced longing escaped from me, charging our kiss with desire.

I don't know how long we kissed for.

Eventually, I tore myself away because I still had work to do that evening. She was flushed when I left.

On the street, I couldn't help but glance back, but her door was already closed.

———

By establishing the musical 'other', recent scholarship has engaged deeper with questions of ethnicity and identity in music ...

I picked at my nails as I typed – a new anxious tick.

However, in the discourse, many distinct cultures are superficially united by a flimsy umbrella heading. For instance, 'Aboriginal Music' must encompass the hundreds of dialects and musics of the Aboriginal population of Australia.

I had just kissed Alex. But what if tomorrow she pretends it never happened? Maybe she'll never mention it again just like our Sydney conversation and the night of the Best Falafel. Next topic.

Many scholars concerned with the survival of classical music defend its necessity and privileged status.

What if I'm just another name on the list of people Alex wants to sleep with before we leave here? Am I part of Alex's 'gold rush'? Next topic.

The 'anything goes' maxim commonly associated with modernism inherently suggests a lack of restrictions and so cannot be definitive.

My nails were bleeding. Next topic.

Scholars discuss how music creates a space wherein sexuality and gender lose clear definition.

It was light.

Queer musical figures of ancient Greece, Orpheus and Sappho, demonstrate early mapping of queerness onto the musician's identity.

Enough.

———

I woke with a cold spider crawling in my chest. I suggested we go for a walk. We met at the meadow gates by the music faculty. My gates. I felt lost. She was smiling at me. Dorky, giddy, warm. Confused, sad, cold. She touched my face and

I smiled the smile I know she knows is my fake smile. I watched her catch on and take a step back.

Her: Oh
Me: It's not like that, I just feel – I don't even know – what if we fuck everything up?
Her: Hey, we're not going to fuck everything up
Me: Am I just another person you want to fuck in your 'gold rush'?
Her: Of course not
Me: I thought maybe you'd pretend that it never happened
Her: What? Our kiss? Why would I do that?
Me: Because that's what you do! You say things and then you never bring them up again and I'm left feeling mad, with all your confessions swirling around in my head!

Where did this anger come from?

We walked around the meadow and ignored the tourists and the cows. She spent most of the walk reassuring me. I was quiet. Part of me felt she owed me this. I asked her what kind of love she felt for me. She told me that she loved me romantically. *Like a partner?* Like a partner. I made her tell me again. And again.

Then I told her about my night of distracted studying and showed her my bandaged fingers. She gasped, loud enough for a pack of tourists to notice. She kissed my fingers.

16

WHEN IS IT OKAY TO LIE?

To go on a crew date is to make a terrible decision. Two 'crews' (sports teams, bands, theatre troupes etc.) – usually between 20 and 40 people – book some cheap restaurant with BYOB policies and long tables, where they get *hammered, smashed.*

When did I start associating drunkenness with violence?

There are games, too. If you manage to throw a penny in someone's drink while they're holding it, they have to down the drink in one. Everyone sings 'God Save the Queen'. It's England strange. Then there's 'sconcing', the Oxford version of Never Have I Ever. 'I sconce anyone who has had sex in a library' – and then everyone who's had sex in a library drinks. Turns out, a lot of people have had sex in libraries. This was my last crew date.

Cate joined our crew date as she was back in town visiting a friend. A shiver of nerves when she sat next to me. We were talking about music, which was enjoyable. I'd also managed to dodge some pennies thrown at my first, second, third glasses of wine. Mostly thrown by Dan on keys, who sat opposite me. The first sconce was funny: 'I sconce anyone who has dressed up as a Shakespearian lover during sexual role-play.' Typical artsy-type crew date question. Two people stood up, cheersed each other, and then cheersed us all.

The second sconce was not funny: 'I sconce anyone who has slept with the person sitting opposite them right now.' I glanced at Dan on keys, sitting opposite me. I tried to flash stay-seated-don't-drink eyes, but he stood up and swigged. Then he stared at me and everyone else stared at me. I stood and sipped. People were shocked, but in a light-hearted way, so it was fine. Then I saw Cate was laughing, which hurt. Either she didn't care that I'd slept with Dan and was laughing because she found it funny or she cared a lot and had to laugh to disguise that she was hurt. Either way, it hurt me. It hadn't been that long since her letter. *Am I that easy to get over?* I stopped drinking, silently vowed never to go on another crew date, and left as soon as was socially acceptable.

At home, I wondered whether I should open a tub of ice cream, because clichés can be comforting in moments of panic. Instead, I stared at my wall. It was covered with pictures of my friends and family in very typical university-wall fashion. I realised how many photos I had of Alex, which made me smile. I'd also arranged the photos so that a photo of the two of us from our time together in Sydney was in the centre. We were smiling drunkenly from that empty bar on Bondi Beach. Next to my photo collage were the naked men we'd drawn in my first year. Of course I messaged her to come over. Of course she did. What time was it? Late. I was still standing staring at my wall when she arrived. She was flushed. She'd cycled. She hugged me and she lingered a little and my stomach flipped. I told her it had been a weird night and she said we could talk about it.

Me: I went on a crew date
Her: Why?
Me: Wrong question
Her: What happened?
Me: Nothing serious, a sconce revealed that Dan on keys and I had slept together – and Cate was there and heard the sconce
Her: Oh, I didn't realise Cate was back
Me: Yeah
Her: How do you feel?
Me: Better for seeing you
Her: How did she react?
Me: She laughed
Her: That's hard no matter how you read it

She knew me so well.

Me: Yeah
Her: Tell me some of the funnier sconces?
Me: 'Find the funny'? Wasn't that part of your family language?
Her: Yes, exactly

I told her some of the funnier sconces and she laughed. *I sconce anyone who had to stop a blow job on a roof because he was scared of heights.*

I thought to notate the pitches and rhythms of her laugh and write her another string quartet. I dismissed the thought. Something happened to me then. Yes, I'd probably been falling in love with her, slowly, for a long time, but, in that moment, I think I landed. *Can most people recall the moment they went from falling to landing in love?* My brain kind of rewired. I wanted to kiss her. Like, I *really* wanted to kiss her. I told her I wanted to lie down, so she got my blanket from my bed and put it on the floor. She moved so gently as she pulled the blanket over her body. It was the same set-up as that night after my jazz gig – the night with the Best Falafel. We both noticed. I got under the blanket with her. We didn't touch. We carried on talking, lying on my floor, gazing at the too-high ceiling.

Me: When is it okay to lie?

Her: This again?

Me: Why did Dan stand up and drink in front of everyone?

Her: Probably because he's pleased he had sex with you

Me: Lying isn't always the wrong thing

Her: Sure. It's kind of funny that we're taught to tell the truth from such an early age

Me: I always told the truth, even when it got me into trouble

Her: Hmm. But sometimes telling the truth doesn't lead to the best possible outcome

Me: How do we live in a world where lying can
   further success?

Her: I don't know. I've read some stuff about what
   happens when kids figure out that telling the truth
   isn't always the right thing. Like, kids are told to tell
   the truth, truth, truth, but then they start noticing that
   adults lie. Which is probably confusing. Some kids
   start lying – 'do as I do, not as I say'

Me: Some kids start wondering: when is it okay to lie?

Her: Did you want to lie tonight? Did you want Dan to
   stay seated?

Me: Yes. Am I changing? Am I less good?

Her: If Cate weren't there, would you have minded if
   he stood up?

Me: No, I wouldn't have minded

Her: So you're just worried about hurting her?

Me: Yes

Her: I think you're still good

I looked over at her. She was looking at me, too, though we
were both on our backs. I wondered how long she'd been
looking at me. I sighed one of my long, dramatic sighs
and her eyes shimmered. I wanted to pour jazz music into
the silence. Jazz music would suit her Merlot murmurs.
I was imagining saxophones and drums. I was holding
my breath.

Her: If you want to kiss me, you should kiss me

I did want to kiss her. We kissed. Her lips were warm and soft. We held hands. We held bodies. We fit into, onto, around one another. I sighed into her kiss. She moaned into mine. It wasn't a chaste kiss. She bit down on my lip. She could have been kissing me everywhere, I felt sensation all over. The floor was hard. I had this weird urge to quote *Romeo and Juliet* at her: 'You kiss by the book.' I didn't. I noticed patches of pink on her chest that I didn't recognise. They looked like love hearts to me. Like some uber-sensual Rorschach test. I smiled into the kiss. She asked what I wanted. I didn't know what she meant. She smiled and said that was okay. Eventually, she stood to go. I stood, too. She kissed me hard against my photo wall. She left.

———

31. She doesn't unconditionally love her family
32. She doesn't like travelling alone
33. She makes the best shakshouka
34. She hates liars, though she thinks that sometimes it's okay to lie
35. She kisses by the book

I gulped dramatically, as if for an audience, though I was on my own.

———

Since Eve had returned from France, we'd texted more than we'd hung out. A hang-up from our long-distance friendship, maybe. When Eve's new boyfriend, John, was fighting in a boxing match out of town, she asked me to join her in the crowd for moral support. Eve very rarely asked for help, but was increasingly stressed about our upcoming exams. I breathed in the smell of sweat and rubber. Eve, sweaty and shaky with nerves, knew nothing about boxing. I played the good friend and bought us a bottle of wine to share. John smiled at the crowd like an actor at a curtain call. His black mouthguard matched his black gloves. I could feel Eve swoon where we stood. I passed her the bottle. I could hear nothing over the cheers. With more wine, the *whoops* melded into a thick sound-wall, like some dramatic, cheerful tinnitus. Individual voices were indistinguishable. The fight was violent. I thought about my friend in Sydney who'd used martial arts to hurt himself, picking fights he wasn't ready for after his dad had died. We'd lost touch. I felt guilt claw at me and I quickly closed that particular memory window. I thought about the café above the bicycle shop and imagined the taste of lemon polenta cake. I didn't notice that John had won the boxing match. When we went to congratulate him in his changing room, he stank of sweat. I tried not to breathe too much. Eve had her tongue in his mouth before I could open mine to say 'congrats'.

The three of us decided to celebrate and go clubbing, sharing a cab to the club. But the cab route took us past Alex's room and drunk me yelled, 'Stop!' The cab stopped. I got out. I knocked on her door. She answered in her pyjamas.

Her: Mals, what are you doing here? I mean, come in, I
was just about to go to bed

Me: Oh, I'm sorry, I can leave

I didn't turn to leave.

Her: No, don't be silly, just give me 10 seconds to
    re-wake up

She opened the door and I got into her bed while she went
to the bathroom to re-wake up. It was dark out and only her
bedside lamp was on, so, when she stood in the doorway, she
was barely lit. The room smelled of her perfume. I breathed
in. She didn't turn on the light.

Her: So what is it you're doing here exactly?

I lay on my side, propping my head up with my hand, and
spoke softly and smoothly. I tried to imitate the silkiness of
her vowels so I could feel them in my mouth.

Me: Well, I've had a such wonderful day, so I wanted to
    tell you all about it
Her: Uh huh
Me: Yes! See, I finished this essay – it's actually very good,
    it's broadly about how we define genre, but in the
    context of times when genres didn't really exist and
    everyone considered themselves a bit of a theorist and–
Her: Amalia, it's a bit late for–
Me: Sorry. So, essay done and then I went for this
    glorious walk and the sun was bright and everything,

but I've actually just been to a boxing match
and John won!
Her: I don't know who John is, but I hope you'll pass on
my sincerest congratulations

She continued, sitting on the edge of the bed now.

Her: So you came here to tell me about your essay,
your walk and that the infamous John won his
boxing match?

I knew she was trying to hint at something, but the sheer
pleasure of this impromptu visit (and the half-bottle of wine)
were stopping me from figuring it out. She smiled and I
melted into her sheets. My cheeks grew hot, fiery. I smiled
back and she sighed and came to sit next to me. I was about
to start talking about boxing when she put her fingers in my
hair and looked at me, into me, and then she kissed me hard.
We kissed in her bed. And it wasn't innocent, polite kissing.
She pulled on my hair so my head jerked back. The room was
burning, but her sheets were so cool. She knew every angle
of my face, smile, frown, walk, dance; she looked at me like
she wanted to know my body. I let her.

Her fingers moved under my clothes and onto my bra,
where she pressed down gently, her tongue still in my mouth,
and I forgot how to think. She moved her hands under my
bra, where they lingered and traced light circles. I climbed on
top of her so that my knee was in between her legs. I rocked
forwards and backwards, rubbing against her. She ground

her hips in time to mine, like a dance. I kissed her neck and licked across her body. My tongue was hard against her skin. She moaned. My hands moved down her shirt. Something inside me shifted. Animalistic. Release. I almost snarled with longing. I clawed at her chest; I bit down on her shoulder. I licked down her arms. I wanted to explore every inch of her with my tongue. I pushed down on her hips, massaging. I slipped my fingers under the elastic of her pyjamas. I bit at her neck, gently. Then harder. She pulled my hair, moved her face to mine and kissed me fiercely. Eager. Desperate. Frantic. We undressed each other hurriedly, tearing and pulling and ripping. She laughed while she fumbled with my bra strap and then everything slowed down.

The kisses were deep. I began to feel each movement of her tongue all over me. Clawing turned to caressing. Then she touched me. I tried to touch her back, but she pushed my hand away and breathed, 'You first.' A red heat spilled all over me. She wrapped herself around me, moving her fingers, slowly first, over my clit. Colours were too bright, shapes too sharp and distracting, I had to close my eyes. Pleasure was the aesthetic – I felt it in every sigh, scratch, touch. The heat seemed to slow down time. I was soaking in a bath of hot pleasure until I could only feel where she touched me, as though the rest of my body had ceased to exist.

She licked me up and down, like she knew it was my favourite way to be touched. Up and down. The pleasure swelled again, rising, fighting my skin for release. My body thrashed against the bed when I came. It was almost violent.

Instead of emptying me, the orgasm had injected me with energy. It surged through me; it attached itself to every part of me. We kissed again, I touched her, she straddled me, I slipped my fingers inside her, she rode them as we kissed, back and forth. She thrust her head back, I tongued at her neck.

With my fingers still inside her, I pushed onto her lips with mine. She collapsed on the bed. I kissed fervently between her legs, moving my fingers in time with each kiss. She began to scream, cutting off the sound with her hand. I kissed and fingered and kissed and fingered until she came. I could feel the muscles inside her squeezing my fingers, then pounding against them while she shook.

———

I left her room because single beds render sex exciting and sleep unbearable. I woke up, smiling with I-just-had-sex-with-Alex thoughts. Good thoughts. I spent the day working on an essay. It was sunny, so I sat on the grass outside the New Building with my laptop. The lawn was empty because English people seem to enjoy celebrating the sun without actually spending too much time in it. Or maybe the rest of my year just preferred working indoors, which makes sense – the sun is hot and distracting. That morning, I enjoyed it licking my skin where she'd licked my skin.

The essay was about whether the opera medium empowered or disempowered women. Is giving women a public voice empowering? What if that voice is used to subscribe to gender norms outlined in how-to manuals? I still don't know.

I was listening to a beautiful aria, *'Lasciatemi morire'* ('Let me die'), which was apparently commissioned to celebrate a wedding. Dark. Every article written about this aria cited eyewitness accounts of the first performance, at which 'there was not one lady who failed to shed a tear'. I didn't know why this was relevant. I still don't know. I decided to stop reading and listen instead. Can something that perpetuates oppression be empowering? *What do you think, Alex?*

Despite being an aria about death, it really turned me on. Please listen to it before you judge. There is this intense climb where, semitone by semitone, the notes mount one another closer and closer, but they never make it to the top. They fall. Agony. There's this sense of breathlessness, too, that heated my skin, warmed my insides. Maybe that was just the sun. I wrote the essay quickly and carelessly because I was playing back the new faces of Alex's I'd met the night before. The day passed in the heat. I knew one of Alex's new friends was throwing a house party in the evening.

Amalia:
Hey, I think I'm going to come tonight.
Is that okay? X

Alex:
Yes, of course!
Text me when you're here? X

Night arrived and I hadn't seen anyone familiar. I'd written words and listened to music – a successful and lonely day.

But I was content. It got late. I undressed and studied my body in the mirror for a long time, like someone who had just lost their virginity in an old-fashioned novel. I expected there to be some trace of the night before, a mark of ecstasy or bruise of pleasure or at least a scratch of passion. But there was nothing. My body was smooth and untouched. I wanted it touched. So I went to the party.

When I arrived, I decided not to text her. I wanted to find her instead. I walked into this loud cacophony and the music touched me everywhere. I scanned the room for her. Almost everyone was dressed in black. The lights were low and there were candles balancing on stacks of books. Everything felt on the edge, slightly chaotic. I squeezed past sweaty bodies and continued my hunt for her. She wasn't inside, but something about the music and the sweat and the fire and the chaos stirred me, so I decided to dance. I joined a group of sweaty bodies and merged mine with theirs. I grew sweaty, too. The music was loud enough that I could feel the beat in my chest. I felt touched again. Then she whispered in my ear, 'I'm glad you came,' and touched me from behind. Fuck. She slid her hands around my waist. She pushed her chest into my back. She touched her lips to my neck, then her tongue, and moved her body with mine. She licked the back of my neck slowly. She whispered again, 'You taste salty.' Cold lips, hot breath. Everything inside me was climbing like *'Lasciatemi morire'*. Her hands moved from my hips to between my legs and I think I moaned out loud. I turned around to splay my fingers on her chest while we danced. I could feel the beat pounding inside her. I felt drunk, but I had drunk nothing. She stepped back and pulled me outside into the harsh cold. We walked a little way down the street, stopping in an archway where she faced me, wrapping her hands around my neck. I shivered. She closed her eyes. I kissed her. So deeply. The rest of the night, like the day, was a hot blur.

17

How do you normally cope with stress?

My tutorial ran over by an hour because the tutor 'realised we were vastly underprepared for the upcoming exams'. Great. I jogged up the High Street, rucksack bouncing on my back. If it weren't for the pain, I would have found the rhythmic knocking quite soothing. I couldn't get through to Eve to tell her I was running late. She and John were probably already enjoying the signallessness downstairs at Raoul's Bar. Jogging to Jericho, I wondered whether John would be nervous to meet me properly, whether I was filling in for the 'meet the parents' ritual. I decided I wouldn't get too drunk. I realised I had no idea what kind of guy Eve would date. A boxer, apparently.

The upstairs of Raoul's is underwhelming. The bar takes its cocktails very seriously and claims to use more fruit than any other bar in Oxford. The décor is plain, so as not to distract from the flavoursome cocktails, and the walls are lined with certificates of the bar's various awards.

The queue to order was too daunting, so I headed straight downstairs. Downstairs was a little more 'speakeasy' – darker, rowdier – and I spotted Eve and John seated at a table in the corner. Their combined silhouette almost looked like a love heart. I barely recognised John as the topless man I'd seen boxing another topless man.

I immediately liked John. He was relaxed and thoughtful and very clearly besotted with Eve. He ran his fingers through his hair when he spoke and he interspersed his thoughts with quotes from his Classics and English exam revision. They made an attractive pair – tall, smiley, matching thick black hair. I didn't even know how they'd met? Working at 'that new café above the bicycle shop'. I asked Eve what she was drinking and she told me that she didn't know, but she'd asked the barman for his 'strongest drink that also wasn't too expensive'. I did the same. John wasn't drinking. I felt impressed and then a little ashamed.

We began with 'what have you been up to today?'s. Eve had finished an essay and rewarded herself by bathing with a gin-flavoured bath bomb – 'I think soaking myself in hot baths of gin is the only way I'm going to survive this year.' John had met his parents, visiting from Hong Kong, for lunch at Vaults & Gardens – 'A perfect view of the Rad Cam.' He 'enjoyed Oxford's splendour through their eyes'. Eve scoffed – she was 'sick of Oxford's splendour'.

An hour or so into the evening, I asked Eve and John why they were more than friends, which I think took them by surprise.

Eve: Is this the start of a deep conversation? I'm far too
   stressed about work to be in the mood for a DMC

Me: No! Just an innocent question

John: I think it's a good question. Eve, why are we more
   than friends?

She rolled her eyes.

Eve: Sex

John snorted into his sparkling water.

Me: But surely it's not just that or you'd be friends
   with benefits?

John: I think it's a specific kind of chemistry and, um,
   attraction

Eve: Are we really discussing this?

John: That said, romantic love needs friendship: 'It's
   not a lack of love, but a lack of friendship that makes
   unhappy marriages' – Nietzsche

Eve: John is really into quoting from his revision,
   I apologise

Me: No, I like it, so love has friendship inside, but not the
   other way around?

John: I suppose not. I guess, when you're in a
   relationship, you're considering building a life
   together, just you two. Or, at least, you're open to the
   idea of it

Eve leaned back on her chair. She nearly tipped over.

> **Eve:** That's a bit intense, mate
> **John:** See? She calls me 'mate'. I'm so pleased we have
> friendship as well as attraction

I decided then that I greatly enjoyed John's company. I gave Eve I-approve eyes – a subtle nod and blink. She nodded back, approving my approval.

> **Eve:** What about jealousy? You're not really jealous of
> your friends in the same way
> **Me:** That's true
> **John:** I'm assuming there's a person behind
> your question?
> **Me:** Well, I've recently started sleeping with a very
> close friend
> **John:** Ah, okay, and what's different about your
> relationship with this person and, say, Eve?

I liked that he didn't assume 'this person' was a guy.

> **Eve:** Careful
> **Me:** I think maybe it's a different kind of chemistry?
> Like, when Alex writes me a letter, there's a part of
> me that wants to frame it. Whereas, if Eve wrote me a
> letter, I ... probably wouldn't want to frame it
> **Eve:** I love you, Mali, but I'll never write you a letter
> **John:** Do you act 'couply' together?

I thought about this.

> **Me:** I don't know
> **John:** Would people think you were dating when they
>   saw you together?
> **Me:** I don't know

John and Eve held hands on the long walk back to college.

> **Amalia:**
> Do you have a favourite cocktail?
> I can't believe I don't know this!

It took her longer than usual to reply, though she'd 'seen' the message. Two and a half hours later:

> **Alex:**
> I'm a fan of classics, I think, nothing too sweet …
> Like a minty mojito xx

> **Amalia:**
> Al, I'm feeling quite stressed

> **Alex:**
> How do you normally cope with stress?

Amalia:
I'm not sure . . .
Exercise?
Talking with friends?

Alex:
Why don't you go for a run and meet Eve for a quick
coffee after?

Amalia:
Good idea :) hope you're doing okay xx

I was too overwhelmed with work to worry about her dis-
missive replies.

——

Alex and I were meant to meet for lunch, but she bailed last
minute. Too much work. Fair enough.

——

As both our theses' deadlines approached, we messaged less.

——

She stopped coming to the library with me because she found
it easier to work from her room.

——

Eve:

I think I'm going to go mad in this library.

Stress is going to eat. me. alive.

Amalia:

Eve! Hello!

Can I cook you dinner sometime this week?

Before stress eats you alive, ideally?

Eve:

Thank you for the offer, but I think I'll be living off cereal
and diazepam

Later, she knocked on my door. She'd tied her hair in a pony-tail and was wearing exercise clothes and sneakers. Her forehead shone with sweat.

Eve: Hello! I've had far too much Pro Plus to be able to sleep

I panicked when I heard her voice because I wasn't sober. I had occasionally been using tequila to sleep. Rarely, but it did the trick and I'd come to think that drinking a few shots was better for me than taking sleeping pills – at least I knew how tequila affected me. It made sense not to experiment with sleeping pills. You can convince yourself of some weird shit when stress is eating. you. alive.

Eve: I bet more Pro Plus is consumed in this city than fucking M&Ms. I bet more Prozac, too

I let her in and she sat on my couch and talked faster than my tequila-soaked brain could handle. She was too wired to notice the state I was in. I smiled and nodded and 'hmm'ed where appropriate. I don't remember what she said – something about needing time away from Oxford. I should have paid more attention. I didn't realise how bad things had become.

I thought to text Alex after she left, but worried I might disturb her.

———

It was the last night of April. I'd finished a bottle of wine at Formal Hall. University – it was a very boozy time. Probably too boozy, but I tend often to admit problems in retrospect. The plan was to forget about work for a night and go out partying later that evening until the early hours. We were going to pre(continue)-drink(ing) in someone's room, then head to a club. Alex messaged to ask whether we were meeting in my room first. To my wine-soaked mind, this made no sense because there was nothing either of us needed from my room. Plus my room was in the opposite direction from the pre(continue)-drink(ing) room. I told her as much. You can tell a lot about a person's sobriety by the number of extra letters they add to texts.

Amalia:
Noooooo, wroooooong roooooom. Party in cloister atticssssss x

Alex:

Let's meet in your room – I'll bring beer x

So we met in my room and she brought beer. When I opened the door, she pushed me inside and dropped the beer. I caught on quickly and pushed back. We made out standing up and I dragged her into the bedroom.

———

We dressed and kissed as we stumbled through the cloisters. We danced with my friends. Alex gave me her keys to hold and I drunkenly mumbled that I was upset we hadn't spent much time together. She didn't say anything, but we were dancing, so I didn't push it. On the way to the club, Bridge again, I touched her hair while we walked. Her: *Flinching*. Me: *Slapped*. Soon after, she slowed down so I was walking ahead.

Her, yelling: Hey, I think a friend of mine is going to
   meet us at the club!
Me, coolly: Cool

We got to Bridge and her friend was there – greasy blonde hair, red lips. I smiled hello – did Alex recognise my fake smile? I felt more sober. The friend smiled a big smile back. I could see both rows of teeth. We all went inside. The music was loud. Some of us danced, some went to the bar to do shots. Alex's flinching at my touch was slightly perturbing, but I talked myself down and was not angry enough not to watch her dance. I thought back to her Sydney salsa with the heavily tattooed man in black with cropped curls.

I consciously decided to let it go and joined her on the dancefloor. She seemed not to notice me, wouldn't meet my eye. I could feel the panic twist and contort in my stomach. Back off, that's what I should have done. *Let her come to you.* It's what my mum would have advised; perhaps it's what you would have done, reader. But instead I pushed harder. I put my hand on her hand and her face quickly flicked to mine. Cold eyes. Empty.

Her: Hey, can we talk outside a minute?

She led me into the smoking area.

> **Her:** *So many people try to quit smoking in January. Why do*
> *people make New Year's resolutions?*
> **Me:** *Do you know what would make New Year's better?*
> **Her:** *You?*

I began.

> **Me:** What's up?
> **Her:** Are you having a nice night?
> **Me:** Sure, it's fine
> **Her:** What's been your favourite song to dance to?
> **Me:** What are you doing?
> **Her:** I can't concentrate on work

I didn't understand.

    Me: Okay, so talk to me, what's going on?
    Her: I don't know, but my grades are slipping and my
        thesis supervisor told me he thinks I'm slacking
    Me: Okay
    Her: I think maybe it's got something to do with us. I'm
        so bad at making time for myself anyway and you
        need so much from me

I need so much from you? Are you looking for someone to blame or do you really think it's because of me?

    Me: I'm not asking you to spend any more time with me
        than we were spending together as friends!
    Her: I don't want to argue about this with you, I think I
        just need some space!
    Me: Where has all this come from?
    Her: Please, Amalia!
    Me: So you're going to abandon me just before
        my Finals?
    Her: I'm not abandoning you, I'm making time
        for myself!

She was yelling. Her red-wine words turned to vinegar and burned me. The smoke, the alcohol, and the noise hit at once and I stumbled, as though physically struck. I couldn't breathe. I think she said, 'I just can't do this right now,' but I heard, 'I just don't want you.' I remember throwing her keys

at her, leaving the club, walking home. One step in front of
the other, not allowing my brain to think.

I calmly walked through the front door and calmly sat on
my bed. My brain was still silent. It wasn't even 2 a.m. I went
to bed in my dress and make-up. I slept well. May Morning.
I woke at 5 a.m. to work on an essay – I only had referenc-
ing left to do. The choir sang madrigals nearby, but I wasn't
listening. An hour later, a knock on my door: 'Amalia?' Her.
I looked at the door like I thought it might explode with the
force of my stare. I was surprised – no, perhaps shocked and
in shock and numb.

The bags under her eyes were dark. Her lips were
chapped. Her hands were red and shaking. Her hair was wet
and matted.

Her: Can I come in?

Me: I'm working

Her: How are you working?

Me: On my computer

Her: How *can* you work?

Me: Because I've got a fucking degree to do, Alex, what
  do you want?

Her: Have you slept?

Me: Yes

She was crying, sniffing. Rain in her sky eyes.

Me: Have *you* slept?

Her: I've been walking the streets all night

Me: Do you want some water? Coffee?

She was sobbing.

Me: Hey, shh, it's okay

I hugged her tight and she buried her head in my neck. The thick smell of alcohol made me gag.

Her: My friend got me really drunk after you left
Me: Mmm, I can smell that
Her: I was already pretty drunk when we spoke outside

I didn't say anything. I almost wanted to smile because I was overcome by a weird nostalgia – she smelled like the boys I used to kiss in high school.

Her: Why are you laughing?

I hadn't realised I was laughing.

Me: You smell like the boys I used to kiss in high school
Her: Amalia, this isn't funny

She'd stopped crying. Another switch flicked.

Me: I know it's not funny. I don't know why you're here.
　　Didn't you say you wanted space from me?
Her: Because I can't go anywhere else

Me: Where did all this come from?

Her: I'm sorry, I was drunk

Me: Fine, but those thoughts must have come from
somewhere!

Her: I don't know! I feel like I'm giving part of myself
away when I'm in a relationship and I'm beyond
stressed about work

I didn't know what to say.

Her: I'm sorry, I'm just feeling under a lot of pressure

Me: Everyone is feeling under a lot of pressure, Alex!

Her: I know. Please don't shout

Suddenly, I was exhausted.

Me: Please don't make me the bad guy here

Her: I'm obviously the bad guy here. I'll go

She looked defeated. It didn't suit her. I didn't say anything.
She didn't move.

Her: Do you never want to see me again?

I'd never heard her sound so beaten. The quick shift in power
left me unbalanced.

Me: Obviously we'll see each other again, but I'm really
tired and really hurt and I think we should have some

space just like you asked for. I also can't afford to be
distracted right now
Her: Okay, if that's what you want
Me: I feel like my lover murdered my friend

She stared at me. Then she left. I let her leave and went back
to footnoting. I submitted my essay that afternoon, did two
shots of tequila and went to bed. I woke up to scribbles.

Two people walk into a bare, cold forest
They are lost and the forest is expansive
One looks around and realises they are now co-
dependent survivors
She feels trapped and panics
The other arrives at the same conclusion and reaches for the
trapped for warmth.

Tequila tears and a country song: 'Pour Me Something
Stronger Than Me'. Then I got on with my day without noticing I was wearing my night-before dress.

———

36. She can completely abandon the people she
    says she loves

———

For 18 days, we didn't speak. Days in the library. Nights filled
with the wine I did not taste. I had far too much work to do
to justify wallowing, so instead I spent my breaks walking

around the city, visiting cafés where I thought she'd be. I don't
know why. I don't know what I thought I'd do if I saw her in
a café. But that's what I did. I hunted for her. I went to the
café that replaced the one above the bicycle shop; I went to
the café called George Street Social, where everyone worked
and no one socialised. I walked past the huge window of Turl
Street Kitchen and scanned the workaholics and their caffeine.
There was one long table where chairs covered only one side,
looking out towards the road. A bunch of students in different
colours worked in silence alongside one another, like some
absurdist *Last Supper. The Last Coffee.* She wasn't anywhere.
Later she told me that, out of respect for me and the space I'd
asked for, she'd purposefully avoided the cafés we used to go
to together. I pretended I had done the same.

> *Two people walk into a bare, cold forest*
> *They are lost and the forest is expansive*
> *Neither seeks warmth from their companion*
> *Though one craves it.*

I walked home after one of these desperate city searches to an
envelope balancing on my door handle. 'Amalia' – addressed
in her perfect cursive. I tried to suck in more air than I
needed, to taste the residue of her perfume or inhale a scent
of her presence. Nothing, except for the letter.

Amalia,
    *I hope you'll forgive me for breaking our silence
just this once. My head is full of all these things*

I haven't said that I should have said. I'm so sorry for what's happened. I don't really know what's going on for me at the moment. The last thing in the world that I wanted was to hurt you, second only to hurting us.

There's this Maggie Nelson quote, something about wanting to give your partner everything without giving yourself away. I envy her because I think this is a real problem of mine. I want to give you everything, but, in doing so, I feel like I'm giving myself away. Or maybe I'm just completely overwhelmed with my work. I don't know.

I really need you to know that I do love you, so much, and that I'm so sorry you feel abandoned by me just before your Finals.

I promise I won't write again and that I'll respect your space until you're ready to see me. But I'm here whenever you are ready.

Your Alex

Alex. I wanted to write her name over and over again. The 'A' led strong and steady, but the 'l' followed soft and gentle and then the 'e' was the 'l' that ended too quickly, the 'l' that lost control and curled in on itself because the act of writing the rest of her name left the 'e' so breathless and so full of vibrations that it had no choice. I didn't get to the 'x'.

My final recital – I'd never had to sing a concert in such a ridiculous outfit: white button-up shirt, black ribbon around my
neck, pencil skirt, academic gown. Forty minutes of music. Just
me, the examiners, and an audience of students dressed like
me. I paced in the back chamber of the Holywell Music Room. I
tried to reassure myself. *This is the thing you're good at. This is the
thing that brings you pleasure.* I felt drained, corroded by nerves.
I missed my family. I heard my name being called, but I didn't
feel like I was in my body. I felt like I was next to it, unmoving,
watching my shaking hands like a frozen, concerned voyeur. I
knew I couldn't sing like this. I slapped myself across the face.
It just happened, like a reflex, without any thought.

My cheek was throbbing when I walked onto the little
stage. I smiled at my pianist because I'd been told the examiners took kindly to students who smiled at their pianists.
They sat in a row at the back of the room, notepads in hand,
there to remind you that this was an exam, not a concert. We
had to enter the stage in full academic dress before we could
'make ourselves comfortable'. I loosened the ribbon around
my neck. I wanted to unzip my skirt, which dug into me, but
I thought that might be frowned upon.

Eve was in the front row next to John. She let go of his
hand to give me an awkward, hidden thumbs-up. Despite
everything, I knew Alex would be there – she would know
how much her support would mean to me. I hunted for her
loving smile, I-love-you eyes. I thought she mightn't be in the
first row as she wouldn't want to distract me, so I searched the
middle rows. I still hadn't spotted her when my pianist began,
so I gave up temporarily and concentrated on my singing.

'An Chloë', K.524 – Mozart

Wenn die Lieb' aus deinen blauen, hellen, offnen
Augen sieht,
Und vor Lust, hineinzuschauen, mir's im Herzen
klopft und glüht;

(When love looks out of your blue, bright,
open eyes,
And with the desire to look inside, my own heart
beats and glows)

My voice was wobbly at first, which alarmed me. I felt the audience notice. I wondered how many of them were hoping I'd fuck up. Why did I think that? My knees had locked, so I tried to shift the weight between my feet.

It was only after my first set of Mozart songs that I acknowledged Alex's absence. But I survived. I gave in to the music, riding its rhythms far away from the Holywell Music Room. I was in the centre of the sound, wearing the melodies like armour. I'd label the Holywell Music Room as a 'Place of Escape' on my Ben Lerner memory map.

My first exam finished. Eve handed me a large bouquet of flowers that made me cry. She told me that I was great, that she was sure I'd top the year, that she still hated opera. She looked exhausted.

I spent the evening writing '28 Questions to Fall Out of Love'.

18

WHAT MAKES QUEER ART QUEER?

Eve had stopped coming to the library because the 'severe' atmosphere was starting to freak her out. A scraping chair had some students rolling their eyes and others sighing louder than the scrape.

Amalia:
You sure?

Eve:
I'm sure.
That place makes me feel fucking unhinged!

Scholarly discourse on sound and listening is developing at a slower rate than that of visual culture.

Be more assertive.

Unlike visual culture, scholarly discourse on sound and listening studies is underdeveloped.

More assertive.

There should be more scholarly focus on sound and listening studies.

More.

Why don't people fucking care about sound and listening studies?!

I shut my laptop and rested my head on it. My nails were bleeding. I was woken by a graduate music student I recognised from the faculty. I braced myself for a scolding – 'If you want to take up a library seat, use it for studying, not sleeping!' – but she was concerned. I'd concerned her. *When did I become this person?* She insisted on buying me dinner and I was too tired and too grateful to argue. She took me to the Itsu on Cornmarket Street.

My dinner companion was studying a Master's in musicology and really liked Wagner. I laughed when she told me that Wagner used to ask Nietzsche to pick up his silk underwear for him. She laughed more when I adamantly refused to believe her. I wasn't really there, but she didn't know me well enough to comment on my emotional absence. I enjoy spending time with strangers when I'm hurting – sometimes it's nice when they don't see the pain behind the mask.

She insisted we go for a walk after dinner. It felt good to be told what to do by someone other than my tutor. It felt good to be cared about. I didn't even notice that she was taking me past Alex's street until we were across the road from her house. I faltered.

Me: Oh, I didn't realise we were here
Master's student I hardly knew: Where's here?
Me: I'm sorry, I mean opposite that house, because my–

What was I meant to say?

Me: Because my friend, best friend, lives there and we
    had a sort of argument
Master's student I hardly knew: Everyone argues
    around this time of year, which is daft because we all
    need each other in Trinity Term

Exam term. Terror term.

Me, more honest than I expected myself to be: It's
    a little complicated because we were also – I don't
    know – we were having sex, but it was more than
    sex because we love each other and I don't really
    understand what happened, but things got bad
Master's student I hardly knew: All this on your
    mind and we spent the whole evening talking
    about Wagner?
Me: It was a lovely evening. And you're absolutely right,

there really isn't a prelude more sensual than *Tristan und Isolde*

Master's student I hardly knew: Except maybe the *Lohengrin* prelude! Next on your listening list!

She laughed, a little awkwardly I thought.

Me: Thank you for saving me from the library

I was staring hungrily at her window. At first, it was dark and empty, but then I glimpsed her silhouette. She didn't see me. The Master's student watched me watch nothing. Then she pulled me away. I wouldn't move. She pulled again and my feet shifted. We walked in silence.

———

I took a short power nap, a learnt Oxford tool, before some more thesis work in my study. I read about motets in the 14th century. The lyrics were cruel.

Motet 1: *She had a gay heart and she was singing in great distress: I have love; what shall I do about it?*
Motet 2: *To whom shall I give my love my dear if not to you?*

Then I messaged her saying we should meet up.
She replied seconds later.

Alex:
Of course.
Say the time and place and I'll be there

Amalia:
Deer park tomorrow 11am?

Alex:
See you there

I took my notebook with '28 Questions to Fall Out of Love'.

———

We didn't hug. She was cautious and precise with every word. She asked me how I'd been and I lied because I was learning to lie when it felt appropriate.

   Her: Shall we go left or right?
   Me: Right

We spoke carefully about this and that for however long until we found our rhythm. When we found our rhythm, I wanted to dance to it, but I kept on walking, past the tree-stump chair, past the leisurely deer.

When I was a kid, my mum gave me a book called *The Games People Play* and told me that reading it would give me a general life advantage. I don't know if she was joking. The book is divided into sections on common interactions – games in which humans engage. One game is called

Inverse Pride, also known as 'my misfortune is greater than yours'.

> **Person 1:** I stubbed my toe this morning and now it
>   really hurts!
> **Person 2:** You think that's bad? This morning I fell off
>   my bike and now I can't walk!

I thought break-ups prompted the inverse of 'my misfortune is greater than yours'.

> **Person 1:** I'm doing really well, thanks, really focusing
>   on all my projects and I've recently started meditating
>   and I'm just really calm and happy all the time
> **Person 2:** That's so good to hear! I actually have never
>   been happier because everything is going so well
>   in my career. I just feel like I'm really on the right
>   track, you know?

So, when Alex asked me how I was *really* doing, I tried to play.

> **Me:** I'm doing well, thank you! I've been really into my
>   studies and feel like I'm really on top of things! How
>   about you?
> **Her:** Oh, I'm really glad to hear you're doing well
> **Me:** How about you?
> **Her:** Well, it feels silly to say now, but I feel broken

Silence.

Her: I don't really understand days without you

Either Alex didn't know the game or she didn't want to play. I could feel her eyes on me, but I couldn't bring myself to turn towards her. If I looked at her, I'd lose my balance and I needed to keep my feet firmly on the ground. I needed to concentrate on my studies. I needed to finish my degree. I needed to remember to make sure my friends were doing okay because I lived in a place where you had to remember to make time to be kind.

I looked at her.

She was crying or about to cry, so I stopped walking and hugged her. The hug was meant to say, 'I forgive you,' but, without my consent, it started saying, 'I want you' or 'I need you.' I gripped the back of her hair and she held me tighter. I worried that she would reject my 'I need you' hug, but she didn't. We finished the walk quietly. She suggested we go on an outing to London to celebrate handing in our theses, with the proviso that we didn't discuss our love affair or whatever was happening between us.

Her: We'll just put everything on pause and focus on
    having a wonderful time together

I enthusiastically agreed that it sounded like a great idea, muting my doubt. I didn't mention my recital. Or my '28 Questions'.

———

Miraculously, we both finished our theses.

———

Boarding the bus to London felt like leaving on a holiday. FREEDOM. We visited the Barbican, an exhibition on Jean-Michel Basquiat. There was a physical presence to the paintings on display. I felt that they were trying to tell a story I didn't understand. Basquiat was fascinated in how individuals narrated their own life experiences, so perhaps he was telling the life stories of his subjects – Jesse Owens (American athlete) and Ishtar (ancient Egyptian goddess of fertility and war). I didn't know.

I was standing with my arms behind me, one hand gripping the wrist of the other, an open palm facing the world. I was somewhere inside my head wondering whether busking could be considered musical graffiti . . .

I felt her strong, gentle, hot palm burn mine and I nearly died right there because I'm sure my whole body caught fire when she touched me. She turned me around, unaware of my body on fire, and pointed to a poster advertising *Queer British Art*, Tate Britain.

Her: What makes queer art queer?

God, I'd missed our conversations. *Speak into my mouth, Alex.*

> **Me:** Well, I guess if the theme is queer or if it's created by
>   a queer artist?
> **Her:** But why is it queer if it's created by a queer artist?

And what about works that only look queer because
we know they're done by queer people?

Me: It's like a reading, though, right? I don't think
it's saying the art is queer, because art by itself
can't be queer

Her: Can't it?

Me: I'm thinking more about music

Her: Shocking . . .

Me: Shush. I guess music differs in that it's more
abstract – music without words, I mean. I guess you
can argue that a piece of art explicitly featuring gay
sex is explicitly queer art?

Her: What if it's done by a straight person?

Me: Okay, so let's differentiate between queer as subject
and queer as author and queer as lens

Her: Sure, but there's also the distinction between queer
in terms of sexuality and gender and queer in terms of
society and natural order

Me: Sure

Her: So queer art is art that *represents* queerness – in all
its guises

Me: Maybe, sure

Her: I'm not sure how I feel about that as a theme for
an exhibition. It's too broad. Like, also, what about
works of art that are only queer if you're looking for
queerness? What about 'queer art' that was created at
a time when homosexuality was criminalised?

Me: So it wasn't queer then, but it's queer now?

Her: Yes. And what about a straight woman painting

a naked woman in a way that kind of looks erotic –
queer or not queer?

Me: So it's just an erotic painting of a naked woman?

Her: But it was painted by a woman! What about art that
isn't thematically queer but happens to be created by a
queer person?

We were both so absorbed in conversation that we forgot that
we were on pause. We were standing in the small gift store
of the Barbican, next to the entrance. She laughed when she
noticed us standing in the same stance. One hand on hip, the
other gesticulating excitedly. She touched my arm. She was
so elegant, it felt like a caress. Sometimes I envied her grace.
Then she looked at me nervously and I knew she was going
to break the rule of the day.

Her: You know when I was in your room after May
Morning and you told me you felt like your lover had
murdered your friend?

I didn't say anything.

Her: I think you were right. I'm so sorry, Mals. I didn't
know how to be a lover and a friend to you and I
let one murder the other. It wasn't fair of me. I don't
even know what to say. My mum isn't speaking to me
because of what I did to you

My voice was strangled.

Me: What did you do to me?

Her: I abandoned you during the most stressful period
of your life. Your Finals at Oxford

I looked away.

Me: You didn't come to my recital

Her: I thought you didn't want to see me, I didn't want to
distract you

Me: I thought you'd be there

She spoke so earnestly.

Her: I really fucked up. I'm so sorry

My eyes found hers.

Me: Go on

She spoke like she'd practised what she was going to say.
Maybe she had.

Her: I've tasted life without you and I hate it and I'm terrified
to lose you again and part of me wishes we could just be
friends so we don't risk our perfect, perfect friendship,
but then I see you fiddling with the buttons on your shirt,
like you are right now, and I want to undress you

Sexual love

Unbalanced, I felt myself fall. I could feel my limbs loosening and falling off my body. First my wrists, then my elbows, my ankles, my knees. She was dismembering me with her soliloquy. Hips, shoulders. I felt my head unsteady on my neck. It fell on the floor and rolled away.

19

How do you feel when you finish something monumental?

My hands started to shake in the mornings because written exams were a week away. This was new.

Alex left food and flower packages at my door while I studied. Our messages were so full of love – romantic love – that I started to think we might be okay. I started to think that maybe our rough patch was just a tiny patch on a larger, colourful and constant love blanket.

———

Whether you're selling drugs on campus or suffering from mental health issues, the same verb – to rusticate – is used to mean suspending your studies.

Eve:
Hey,
I have been speaking a lot to my sister and I think I am
going to take a year out

Amalia:

Shit! Are you okay? What can I do?

Can I help with anything?

I'm sorry I haven't really been around

Eve:

Don't be stupid, everyone needs to look after themselves here

I didn't know what to say. I had forgotten to make time to be kind.

Amalia:

So you'll rusticate?

Eve:

Yep, I think my sister's right – I just need space from it all.

Still thinking of moving to London?

Amalia:

Yes! You?!

Eve:

Looking for a housemate?

Amalia:

Yes!?

Eve:

My cousin's flat in Stratford is free this year, though it's kind of a shithole

Amalia:

Sounds perfect xxx

———

Finishing exams at Oxford is weird. You pin a red carnation to your gown and you take a different exit from Exam Schools, an ominous-looking building supposedly designed to inspire fear and intimidation. You're greeted and cheered by all your uni loved ones and they throw things at you. Shaving cream, confetti, streamers, glitter, and cheap Charlemagne. I think the point of Charlemagne is that, if you're drunk enough, it reads like 'Champagne'. You have to be *really* drunk for it to taste like Champagne. It's a mess. But a fun, chaotic, happy mess.

I was covered in glitter and orange powder and tears and garlands of plastic flowers. People usually get really drunk because the studying has been all-consuming and it's been so long since they've had a drink and they haven't really been sleeping well anyway. I didn't get that drunk.

Alex and I had organised to meet that evening at a chain restaurant in town for dinner. I was exhausted. I wore lipstick and winked at my reflection as I left my room. I've never seen a less seductive wink. If a sexy wink is like a slut drop, my eye tripped and fell on its face.

We hugged, gently, outside the restaurant. At that stage, it felt strange to publicly greet each other any other way. As we walked inside, Alex smiled and asked the waitress who was seating us how she was. She looked startled, 'Oh, I, I, I'm fine. I'm okay. No one's asked me that yet today.' Her accent was thick – Slavic, I guessed. She sat us down by the window and brought bread and water. Alex looked at me adoringly as she played with my fingers over the table.

Her: How are you feeling?
Me: I don't know
Her: Well, you should be feeling great! You beat Oxford!
Me: Almost. I've *almost* beaten Oxford. It's hard to celebrate properly when I haven't got my results!
Her: Let's not talk about that tonight
Me: Suits me. What shall we talk about?
Her: Chain restaurants
Me: You hate them
Her: Yes, but I like you
Me: Come on, this hardly feels like a chain restaurant!

She went to the bathroom, so I looked out the window and forced reflection. I'd read somewhere that humans daydream for approximately 780 hours a year, the equivalent of a calendar month. This seemed unlikely. I couldn't remember the last time I'd daydreamed.

How strange to be here with Alex, to be finished with exams, to ...

I couldn't think of anything else because I'd used up all my words on my exam papers.

———

After dinner, she asked me what I wanted to do, but I couldn't answer because I didn't know. I didn't know anything. My mind felt too full of musical examples and theorists' quotes. She suggested we buy some more alcohol at the Tesco nearby and take it to a park. Sure. We bought two huge bottles of beer and made for a park I'd never been to before.

It felt surreal. I was with my Person/lover/best friend, having just finished a degree in this tiny, stressed city, on my way to drink beer in a park I didn't know existed. The park gate was locked, so we climbed the wall to get inside. Adrenaline flowing from the break-in, we realised that we couldn't open the beers. Chuckles grew into giggles. Hysterics. We agreed that we were terrible delinquents. She took the beers to the park's metal fence. BANG. She came back with open beers. I loved her. We sat next to one another and watched the empty park.

Me: The bags under my eyes could catch rainwater
Her: Good thing it isn't raining
Me: How do you always know what to say?
Her: How do you feel?
Me: I don't know how I feel
Her: Then tell me a story

I stared at my hands like they'd help me write the story I was about to tell.

MY STORY

There once was a stressed Oxford finalist who'd had a turbulent year. She didn't recognise her hands because they were ashen and she was used to the sun. They didn't look like her hands, so it surprised her every time they moved when she told her hands to move. The strange fingers were blistered from writing too much. They hadn't spent enough time on piano keys or music scores. They'd behaved oddly during that turbulent year. They'd typed ferociously and fought valiantly against ticking clocks. They'd touched in ways the finalist had never imagined she'd touch anyone.

A viola started to play from a window near us. Clichéd, but true.

Me: How do you feel when you finish something
      monumental?
Her: Relieved, most often
Me: I just feel empty
Her: That's okay

The viola was playing the first movement of a Shostakovich sonata, though Alex wouldn't have known. Op. 147. The last piece he wrote before his death. We were sitting next to one another, not touching.

Me: What are you thinking?

Her: I'm not really, I'm just happy to be here with you

She paused.

Her: It's going to feel strange leaving Oxford behind
after all these years, but I'm quite excited to
move to London

She hadn't told me that she was applying for a job in London until she'd got the offer. I'd found this strange – I couldn't imagine not sharing every stage of a job application process with her – but I didn't think much of it.

We talked about Oxford in the summertime and about summer plans and summer clothes and summer perfumes. Then we scaled the gate, easier on the second attempt, and walked back to college. We waltzed together in the street. She held my hand and puppeteered some glorious spins and twirls. She was singing loudly, which made me laugh. Friends were often so scared to sing in front of me, like I was judging. I *was* judging. She was terrible. But wonderful. We'd arrived at my door. I scrutinised her face, reading her skin for clues. *Are we officially lovers again? Do you want to come up to my room with me?* I started to hug her goodbye because a hug felt fitting and she put her lips on my neck without kissing me. She breathed out hot breath. The hug ended.

Her: Can I come up with you?

——

On our last night together in Oxford, we decided to take our dinner to a park. I had forgotten my coat, so I sat beside her, touching; I borrowed her body for heat. Both of us were struggling to pretend we could concentrate on conversation. I made to kiss her cheek and she read it wrong and kissed my lips and we were eating raspberries and she was biting my lip and her fingers were cold and I hoped there were no cameras as I kissed her hands and she was surprised by how much she liked it, though I wasn't. Then it was that time of night when you don't know whether to call tomorrow today or tomorrow.

Amalia:
Al, did you sleep well?

Alex:
Yes, I dreamt about you and woke up smiling

I was sitting down, but still I felt my knees weaken. The absurdity of it made me laugh. I closed my eyes and repeated our last night.

Is it heavy, Alex, walking around with my heart in your chest? It must be heavy. Though I don't feel any lighter myself. Maybe I have your heart in my chest. Maybe we've swapped hearts the way we swap rings and stories.

Year 4

20

WHAT IS THE POINT OF NON-ALCOHOLIC GIN?

Sydney Cali called the day before I was due to start at the management consultancy firm. I left the grocery unpacking to Eve and John and answered the phone in my new, naked Stratford bedroom. I straightened the stack of books leaning against the wall in anticipation of a bookshelf I'd never buy and fiddled with the leaves of my Sainsbury's pot plant.

Cali: I bumped into your mum today – so you're starting a desk job tomorrow?

Me: I am

Cali: *Mazel tov*

Me: You sound sarcastic

Cali: What happened to the singing?

Me: I can't do it yet, I'm still too young

Cali: What do you mean?

Me: Just physically, I mean, my voice needs to develop

> more before I can sing, no one will take me seriously
> at this age. So I'm using the time to save some money
> and learn some skills
>
> **Cali:** You don't sound like you believe that
>
> **Me:** Did you just call to tell me off?
>
> **Cali:** No! I called 'cause it's been ages and I want to hear
> all about your shiny new life in London!
>
> **Me:** Well, I live with Eve, my friend from uni, and her
> boyfriend John
>
> **Cali:** Very hetero
>
> **Me:** Eve's taking time off studies and working in
> a bookshop
>
> **Cali:** In a bookshop? Do Oxford graduates work in
> bookshops?
>
> **Me:** Yes, they do. And John's doing a Master's in London
>
> **Cali:** Very fancy
>
> **Me:** Tell me how things are going for you? Where
> are you now?
>
> **Cali:** No! First I want to know all about your latest
> lesbian adventures
>
> **Me:** Well, I've started dating my best friend
>
> **Cali:** That is so extremely gay. What's she like?

I told Cali about the difficult time I'd had with Alex during
Finals. She thought it sounded 'rough'. Only halfway through
the call did she tell me she was actually calling from Oslo.
She didn't sound like she was enjoying her semester abroad,
though she didn't say so explicitly. I promised I'd try to
visit. She ended the call by reminding me that my mum

was a relationship counsellor and that I should make use of
her skills.

———

My new work uniform was not dissimilar to the one in which
I'd taken my exams: button-up shirt (anything but white),
pencil skirt (the same), plain reading glasses (though I'd soon
upgrade to tortoiseshell). The shoes were less comfortable.
The office was grey – grey walls, grey desks, grey ceilings –
like the firm had proven that colours were distracting. Alex
and I had plans to meet for drinks after our First Days. A little
cocktail bar in Brixton, near Alex's new flat, was the setting
of our Debrief – Granny's Cocktails. Granny obviously liked
Rasta music, fluro colours, little umbrellas, and totem polls.
Outside, a man spat out his cigarette with such force it must
have meant he was quitting for good. *Good for you, spitter.*

She narrated my walk to the table like she was David
Attenborough.

Her: Here approaches a management consultant in her
  natural habitat

I played along, brushing off my shoulders, taking a seat
across from her.

Me: She seems to be joining a commercial executive.
  Together, they will browse this laminated menu in
  time to order before Happy Hour concludes

Friendly love

We cheersed when our cocktails arrived. She slid me an envelope across the table, which read 'Happy Graduation!' in her flawless script. I worried that I hadn't brought her a 'happy-graduation' anything. She read my thoughts and told me that it was her pleasure, that graduating from a Master's wasn't as much of a big deal. Besides, these were gifts for her, too. In the envelope were three little slips of paper, each with locations, dates and times.

One of them was today:

NUMBER 1
Granny's Cocktails, Brixton
3 July
8pm

NUMBER 2
Embankment Station
17 September
7pm

NUMBER 3
Barbican Centre
20 February (next year!)
6.30pm

Me: What are these?

Her: Treats I've organised. For example, this
        cocktail is on me

Me: This is extremely sweet

Her: It's nothing really. Harry pays more than half of
        our rent because he's got the en suite, so I have a bit of
        disposable income to play with

Me: Harry the investment banker! What's it like
        living together?

Her: Easy enough. His boyfriend is around a lot, so it's
        really like living with the two of them

I hadn't realised Harry was gay.

Me: I hadn't realised Harry was gay?

Her: Oh, really? How funny. Yes, he is very, very gay

Our conversation was punctuated by passing sirens. I
flinched every time one sounded. I glanced at the man
who'd spat out his cigarette with such force that he must
have been quitting for good. He'd lit up again. London.
Alex reached for my hand across the table. Her fingers
were warm.

Romantic love

Her: Have you decided whether or not to come
out at work?

Me: God, no, I hate that we have to do that. Like, in
theory, I'm on a new team every six weeks. Do I have
to come out to every new team? Or maybe I should
just wear one of those rainbow lanyards

Her: There's no pressure to, you know. Though you'd
look great in a rainbow lanyard

Me: Have you come out?

Her: Yeah, though I hadn't intended to. I was asked
what I was doing tonight and I said I was seeing my
girlfriend

Me: Oh. That sounds easy enough

During our Debrief, I swung between friendly and romantic
love, which I decided was okay. Maybe John and Nietzche
were right: romantic love needs friendship. 'It's not a lack of
love, but a lack of friendship that makes unhappy marriages.'

Friendly–Romantic love

———

My parents couldn't get time off work for my graduation, so
my grandparents decided to fly to London in their place. When
I think of romantic love, I think of my grandparents. They've
been together for ever and they giggle and gossip a lot and hold

hands while they walk or shop or watch films. Alex and I had planned to have dinner with them while they were in London. She called it a double date, which made my heart twirl.

When Grandpa chose the venue of the dinner – the Côte in Knightsbridge – he used a castle emoji. On the Tube, an elderly man wearing loafers was drinking from a thermo-mug that read 'Deja Brew'. He noticed me notice and winked.

Alex was a little late, flushed from a fast cycle. She was very apologetic. The waitress arrived at our table with a bottle of wine; she offered it to Grandma to taste. My gran smiled and said she'd prefer it if Grandpa tasted the wine. They exchanged wicked grins. I recognised those grins. I braced myself as the poor waitress fell victim to their prank. You wouldn't know this, but Grandpa is a very handsome, charming man with sparkling eyes. He took his time swirling the wine and smelling the wine and smiling his best smile at the waitress – all part of the act. Alex looked confused, but I knew that, if I met her eye, I'd give the game away. Grandpa brought the wine to his lips and held the waitress's stare. He took a luxurious sip, but it must have gone down the wrong way because his eyes grew round and frightened and he started to cough and splutter and he gripped the table with his free hand and my gran started to panic and the waitress was panicking and Alex was panicking and then Grandpa stopped. He smiled and told the waitress, 'The wine might just kill me it's so tasty.' Grandma giggled. The waitress clutched her chest and then our table and then she burst into laughter. Alex was chuckling, too. In the midst of all the hilarity, her leg brushed mine.

My grandparents shared a story about their wedding, a story I'd heard once or twice before.

   Grandma: –and there's a photo of a group of strangers
   Grandpa: Two couples we'd never seen before
   Grandma: And there they were, smiling in *our*
      wedding photos

Grandpa looked very serious.

   Grandpa: I'm telling you, they crashed our wedding
   Grandma: We had wedding crashers at our wedding!

They reminded me of the old couples from *When Harry Met Sally*. It felt like years since I'd distance-watched the film with Eve, Oxford to Paris.

At one point during the evening, I was moving my errant serviette across my lap and I decided to feel for Alex's leg by mine. When my hand found her thigh, she pushed into it. My chest fluttered. I felt wanted, noticed. Though my grandparents would never know, there was nothing subtle about our under-the-table game. *I want you, too, Alex.*

My grandparents hugged Alex goodbye and wished her luck for her new job. They kissed me on both cheeks and walked away hand in hand. Not two minutes later, my tech-savvy gran WhatsApped me:

Gran:
You wear your heart on your sleeve, my little one.
Keep it safe.

I checked my sleeve expecting to find my heart. It wasn't there. Alex told me I was lucky to be able to take my girlfriend on a double date with my grandparents – a lot of people from their generation 'wouldn't be cool with it'. She suggested we get a drink nearby.

Alex snorted, pointing towards the counter where a tip jar read: *If you're afraid of change, leave it here.* I grabbed a table with a tea-light candle and she disappeared back to the bar. She reappeared with two glasses of red wine. 'This is something I know you want.' She disappeared again and returned with two shot glasses of clear liquid. 'This is something I think we should try.' She placed the shot glass in front of me and smiled. 'It's non-alcoholic gin.' We sipped together.

Me: It's almost spicy and sort of grassy
Her: Have you ever thought about becoming a
  sommelier and finally putting those florid descriptive
  skills to good use?
Me: Yeah, yeah. Hey I don't mean to look a gift horse in
  the mouth, but what is the point of non-alcoholic gin?
Her: Oh, don't you know? Non-alcoholic drinks are the
  next big thing
Me: But why?
Her: Health-conscious people tired of hangovers? Green-
  juice-guzzling millennials?

Me: Okay, sold, Miss Commercial Executive!

I told Alex I'd written '28 Questions to Fall Out of Love' while we were still at university. She didn't believe me, so I showed her my notebook, which I'd begun to carry around with me. There was no room for creativity in my office at work, so I hoped to write music or something in my down moments. They never came.

28 QUESTIONS TO FALL OUT OF LOVE

The beginning and the good times

1. How did you meet?
2. Do you remember your first kiss? Discuss it
3. When did you fall in love with each other?
4. What are three facts about the other person that most people don't know?
5. Do you have a favourite memory together?
6. What do/did you like most about your partner? Do they still exhibit that trait?

Qualities and competition

7. Who is cleverer between you and your partner?
8. Who is more attractive between you and your partner?
9. Who is better in bed?
10. Which of you will be more successful?

11. What do you dislike most about each other?
12. What's your least favourite outfit that the other person wears?
13. What's your partner's most annoying habit?

Let it all out

14. What is your worst memory of your partner?
15. If you could say one thing to each other with no repercussions, what would you say?
16. What doesn't work sexually between you and your partner?
17. What's the longest amount of time you could spend together without wanting to kill one another?
18. What do you really think about your partner's family and friends?
19. Do you respect your partner's choice of study? Current occupation?
20. What is the main thing you differ on opinion-wise? Discuss it for a bit

The end

21. Why, in your opinion, did you break up?
22. Did your partner break your heart? What did it feel like?
23. Do you remember your last kiss? Discuss it
24. How do you feel knowing you will never kiss your partner again?
25. How would you describe life without the other person?

26. Who will be first to move on?
27. What are you most excited for now that you're single?
28. What do you regret most about the relationship?

Her: Well, my worst memory of you is thinking I'd lost
    you; I could spend for ever with you; I don't want our
    last kiss to be our last kiss; I don't remember the rest
    of the questions, but I guess we're not falling out of
    love any time soon

I sighed at her perfect response. She reached for my hands
across the table and I gave them to her because they were
also her hands. *Take me by your hand and I'll take you by mine.*
She brought them to her mouth and kissed them. It was the
kind of hand-kiss you'd see in a Disney film. Then she turned
my hand over and flicked her tongue across my palm, which
made my insides kink.

She stood, moved towards me, and crouched by my seat.
She tentatively brought her lips to mine and I moaned into
her. She traced my lips with her tongue. The sheer force of
wanting her was making my stomach seize. We finished our
wine and left together. She had to cycle home, so I said I'd
take the Tube to hers and meet her there. She made a spec-
tacle of kissing me while she put on her helmet. I felt almost
manic. Things had shifted so quickly. *If you're afraid of change,
leave it here.*

I beat her to her apartment building and sat waiting on
her steps. She arrived, sweating. She was eager to show me
she could cycle without hands. I watched the wheels as she

rode away to give me a better view. The swirling spokes were almost hypnotic. The tiny lights smudged against the darkness. She yelled, 'You ready?' and I yelled back, 'I'm ready!' She proceeded to pedal precariously in a circle. The frame wobbled, she *whoop*ed, shoving her fists into the air, I applauded. I was still cheering when she cycled back to me. She dismounted the bike, an athlete, and took a small bow.

Friendly love

In her bedroom, she lit candles. We danced together. We kissed deeply, like long-time lovers kiss. We undressed each other, slowly. We delayed touching each other. We scratched and sighed and pushed. When I finally kissed down her body, between her legs, I felt myself grow wet. I licked rhythmically, moaning into her so that my lips vibrated as I wrapped them around her. She screamed and shook when she came, convulsing, head smashing the pillow. I kept moaning and my lips kept hold, vibrating. She lay there, panting with closed eyes. I rested my head on her thigh.

The orgasms she gave me were kaleidoscopes. They shattered everything, they rearranged the whole world into colourful, symmetrical abstraction. Then the shards dissolved and the world came slowly into focus. Her eyes, lusty and beguiling and enchanting and seducing and consuming and–

Fuck, I was so in love with her.

Sexual love

———

I felt peculiar – proud? Self-conscious? – on the empty Tube home because I was in yesterday's clothes and because I was wearing the scent of last night's orgasms. There was an empty bottle of Bombay Sapphire gin opposite me. I took a photo of it and sent it to her.

Amalia:
Saturday mornings on the Tube
Xx

Alex:
#London
Xx

A teenager walked onto the carriage with a cello that had a 'Baby on board!' badge attached to it. She smiled at my smile. I tried to remember the last time I'd practised singing. I promised myself I would get to it soon, as soon as things calmed down with the new job.

———

Alex and Harry were similar in ways that made living together easy. I couldn't remember whether I'd noticed this before. They were both very tidy, almost pedantic. They'd read the same books and shared most of the same opinions. They even cycled into work together because their offices were both in Canary Wharf. The main thing they disagreed on was swimming: Harry loves to swim; Alex thinks swimming lengths is stupid and that everyone who says they enjoy swimming lengths is lying in an attempt to feel virtuous.

The night of their house-warming party was cold. The day before the party, Alex had decided to have a drastic haircut. I thought it was very brave and maybe very stupid to have a drastic haircut the day before a big party with all your friends. Do you agree? Alex thought otherwise, obviously. I sat outside the salon drinking coffee from a nearby café, reading with red gloves on, contented. I loved the idea of waiting for my lover, reading Ali Smith, sipping black coffee, turning pages with red-gloved fingers. Fellini-esque.

Alex's hairdresser was completely bald but for a thick rainbow plait that started at the base of her neck and ended just above her belt. Sipping my coffee, I vowed to tell Alex that I loved her hair regardless of what it looked like. When I saw her, I froze. She looked so edgy. 'So extremely gay,' I heard Sydney Cali's voice in my head. Her hair was short, dark, conditioner-glossy, parted where the hairdresser had run her fingers. Perfectly still on this perfectly windless morning. Neck exposed. She did a little spin, which I interrupted, kissing her. In the street. Wearing red gloves.

—

House-warming guest list

- Friends from college
- Bunch of people (mostly women) Alex had slept with after breaking up with Oscar while 'making up for lost time'
- Oscar
- Harry's old housemates (not Harry's boyfriend, who was on a work assignment in Edinburgh)
- Harry's investment banking colleague 'friends'
- Bunch of people I didn't know or recognise
- Me

Eve and John were invited, but wanted to make use of a me-free house to have a 'date night' and they 'didn't know anyone else at the party anyway'. Fair enough. Oscar didn't know that Alex and I were seeing each other or that we had ever been romantically involved. She'd decided not to share this with him. Early into the party, he sat down opposite me, joking awkwardly, 'Ah, Amalia, sitting opposite you, it's like we're facing off in a duel!' *Does he know?* Alex breathed in sharply and shot me a laser beam of fierce blue. Oscar laughed his Professor Umbridge laugh. I updated my reference – he sounded like Olivia Coleman's stepmother character in *Fleabag*. Nobody said anything. Great start.

I looked really beautiful that night. I should probably say, 'I *felt* really beautiful that night.' I wore a light-grey shirt, patterned blue pencil skirt, long brown boots. My hair fell in accidental ringlets, my eyes were clear and my lips were sexy, dark red and kissable. Alex did a double take when I made my grand entrance from her bedroom. She was in her loose black dress, which I loved. The material was thin enough that you could just make out the silhouette of her body as it moved beneath, though it gave nothing else away. She was pale from the winter and had lined her eyes in black. The blue didn't look like the sky any more. It was dark and a little dangerous. She'd slicked her hair back with gel, like she was embracing the gay.

As the guild of Alex's sex escapades joined the party, I panicked acutely, intensely, but silently. I reassured myself often. *When she slept with them, there had been nothing between us. I mean more to her than they do.* Still, I panicked. I wanted them to think I was cool, alluring. I almost wanted to seduce them. I'd stopped noticing that Alex was two years older than me. However, most of her friends were two years older than her, which made them four years older than me, which I did notice.

I'd heard a lot about the people that Alex slept with during her 'gold rush'. Sometimes, she'd joined couples. A few times, she'd tried group sex with a wider friendship circle. Then there were several times with another Master's student from the language faculty, Jennifer.

Jennifer didn't have social media, so I rightly assumed she wouldn't know what I looked like. I knew what she looked like because Alex had shown me a photo of her. She was thin and tall with tight, curly, auburn ringlets. The things I knew about Jennifer were:

1. She's a lesbian
2. She's Jewish

3. She doesn't like music
4. She's studying Russian and Arabic on some important scholarship
5. She once texted Alex asking her about her 'gold-rushing'
6. She's had sex with Alex several times

Me: You must be Jennifer

She smiled an 'of course you know who I am' smile. I smiled back, one of my good smiles. *Yes, I do know who you are.*

Me: Nice to finally meet you. I'm Amalia

Her response was an almost cartoon-like double take. I chuckled, one of my good chuckles, while she carefully studied my face. There was something very beautiful about the intensity of her eyes. They made me feel like the only person in the room. Cliché.

Jennifer: Wow, you even look like her. Not so much the structure of your face, but you kind of share expressions. How fascinating

I didn't expect her to say that. I think she takes pleasure in saying things people don't expect her to say.

Me: I don't think we share expressions, not really
Jennifer: They're the same faces

Me: They are?
Jennifer: This is mad!
Me: Is it?
Jennifer: This makes sense

Yes, it does. I smiled. She was warmer than I'd expected. With the new knowledge of who I was, she seemed fascinated by me and only me. The rest of the party slipped away.

Jennifer: Did Alex really date the Oscar on the couch?
Me: She did indeed

We glanced together at Oscar on the couch, who was focused on his phone.

Jennifer: Like, how did that happen?
Me: I wasn't around for that – they'd been dating for two years when Alex and I met
Jennifer: You're around now. Lucky me. Alex needs someone just as sexually radioactive as she is

Did you make up 'sexually radioactive' or read it somewhere and adopt it as your own? Almost certainly the latter.

Jennifer: So I brought a question I wanted to ask at this party. Can I ask you?
Me: Sure
Jennifer: How do you think a person should be?
Me: Oh, the Sheila Heti book!

Jennifer: Oh, you know it! Of course, it was one of the
   books on Alex's bedside table!

The image of Jennifer and Alex in bed together. Blah.
Dissolve screen.

Me: I hear you don't like music
Jennifer: I don't like music
Me: Really? No music?
Jennifer: No music. Well, actually, I've recently come
   across a Vivaldi string thing that I didn't hate
Me: Ah, so you like the textures to be super defined
Jennifer: No, I just don't like music
Me: But that's like saying you don't like breathing!
Jennifer: I don't particularly *like* breathing
Me: But you breathe
Jennifer: I need to breathe to survive

Pause. Contemplate banal cliché.

Me: I need music to survive

She laughed.

Jennifer: I like you
Me: Good, I like you, too

Just then, Alex broke into the conversation and the rest of the
party re-formed around us. It was the first time we'd properly

inhabited the same conversation space all evening and it felt good. She seemed nervous.

Her: What are we talking about over here?

Me and Jennifer: Music

Her: Oh, no

Me: No, it's okay

Jennifer: I like this

Me and her: What?

Jennifer: You two

Her: I like it, too, and it's lovely that you guys are finally getting to meet

Jennifer: Yeah, I told Alex to invite you to a party I had in Oxford, but you two weren't speaking

Her: Yes, well, luckily we are now

Jennifer: Alex got quite drunk and kept saying, 'I wish Amalia was here'

Her: Oh, let's not talk about that

Me: I didn't know you'd–

Jennifer: Oh, she spoke about you the whole night

I glowed. Alex mingled elsewhere. Jennifer and I discussed how a person should be. I told her I thought a person should be honest – a dishonest answer from someone who was learning to lie when lying felt appropriate. I quickly took it back and told her a person should be kind. She agreed, some people should be kind, but she added that a person should also be authentic and, if it is inauthentic for that person to be kind, they shouldn't be kind. I disagreed. She quoted Sheila

Heti, something about responsibility suiting one person, irresponsibility suiting another. We spoke about Judaism and lesbianism and books like Naomi Alderman's *Disobedience*, which I *had* to read. It was one of *those* books. Apparently, writing the novel had led Alderman to stop practising Judaism. I wondered whether she might find some beauty in Judaism again one day, as I had. Or maybe she could see the beauty, but wanted to remove herself from it all the same. I didn't know much about Orthodox Judaism.

Me: I suppose they're not cool with the gays?
Jennifer: Gay men, no, but lesbians were pretty invisible
   for a long time
Me: Invisible how?
Jennifer: Because our sex doesn't include semen, which
   is how sex was defined in the Talmud
Me, laughing: Lucky us!
Jennifer: Though I think the Talmud prohibits *mesolelot*
Me: I don't know what that is

She smiled, leaning in.

Jennifer: Women rubbing genitals together. But don't
   worry, I think it's only a minor infraction

I thought of Cali, my only other Jewish, queer friend, and wondered whether she'd read *Disobedience*.
There is so much I don't know.
I excused myself to go to the bathroom, though I didn't

need to go to the bathroom. It's something I began to do while living in London – after an hour or so of socialising, I escaped. It's why I question whether I'm as much of an extrovert as everyone says I am. I need regular breaks from large groups of people. I normally stare at myself in the mirror, fix my wild hair, do a few star jumps, and wash my hands, like a pre-performance ritual. *Though when was the last time I performed?* In the bathroom, I stared at myself in the mirror and washed my hands. I liked who looked back. Bright eyes, blushed cheeks. Even my hair was perfect. Unusual. I decided not to star jump for fear of ruining my perfect hair. I took four breaths and opened the door. Then I jumped because someone was leaning on the door. That someone was Alex and I was about to say, 'Woah, you scared me!', when she pushed me back into the bathroom and locked the door.

She kissed me hard against the cold wall. My stomach flipped and clenched and I felt heat rise, like the blood in my veins had started to steam, simmer, and boil. She sucked my neck, licking my jaw, nibbling my ear, whispering to me in between kisses.

Her: I can't stop looking at you

She spun me around.

Still her: Ah, I see you talking to all these different
people and I just want to grab you and touch you

I was too tipsy to feel self-conscious. I spun her so she was against the wall. I held her hands together above her head and kissed down her body. I let my hand explore beneath the flimsy, loose fabric. She moaned too loudly for the hollow acoustics of the bathroom. To muffle her moaning, I covered her mouth with mine. I felt her knees give against my body. I kissed harder, deeper. I – gently and not so gently – chewed on her bottom lip as I slipped my tongue in and around her mouth, twirling, dancing. We were flushed and breathless when we re-joined the party.

―――

Eventually, the guests drifted away and the music died and we were back together in her bed. We were both too spent to do anything but hold each other, so we held on until it was too late to still be holding each other. I rolled over and resigned myself to the quiet. Apart from her, I was very cold, but she'd spilled some of her heat beside her and I curled up to it.

> *Two people walk into a bare, cold forest*
> *They are lost and the forest is expansive*
> *At first, they hold each other. Then they part.*
> *One craves warmth. What craves the other?*

―――

37. She's a very thoughtful gift-giver
38. She wasn't afraid to come out at work
39. She's not afraid of drastic change with unknown results (e.g. haircuts)
39. I don't think she has a 'type'
40. She radiates heat in the night

21

How's work treating you?

Months pass. Happiness crumbles.

She hadn't messaged for a full 24 hours. This wasn't us.

Amalia:
Al, how's work treating you?

I waited.

. . .

She texted hours later.

Alex:
Busy but fun. Really absorbing work! You?

Amalia:
Fine fine. I've just started a new project and they're making us stay late a lot

Another hour.

Alex:
Oh no!!!

That was all.

——

The following Friday night we met up with Jennifer, the Jewish lesbian from the house-warming party, for a pottery class. We'd arranged to meet in some abandoned-something-turned-studio, as is the London way. I felt exhausted from work, panicked by Alex's 'distance', still a little weary of Jennifer, and I hadn't sung a note for more than a month. All of this, shaken together like one of Granny's Cocktails.

I arrived first and sat down beside a couple. They were both very attractive – she wore a feather in her brown curls and he wore a suit. They'd both rolled up their sleeves. I passed the time by trying to guess how long they'd been together and by imagining their backstory. They were both swigging from a bottle of red wine with no label. Neither spoke. She'd crafted a set of intricate utensils and was at work on a soup spoon. Something about the curve and the texture of the spoon made me hungry. I realised I hadn't eaten since the morning – rough new project at work. I imagined the spoon between my lips, sliding perfectly onto the shape of my tongue. Strange thought to be having in a pottery workshop. I couldn't figure out what he was making. He'd arranged a few little globs of clay monsters in a messy circle. They were quite grotesque figures, some without heads, some without limbs. They looked angry. Did Rorschach also test with clay?

Man in suit: I can't remember the dimensions
of the board

The woman with the feather in her hair rested her perfect soup spoon on the table and looked at the man in the suit. It was the first time she'd looked at him since I'd sat down and the intensity of love in that look stunned me. Somehow nobody else noticed. I wondered whether he could feel the intensity of it. It was for ever before she spoke. She told him she couldn't remember the dimensions of the board but that it didn't really matter. They would make the chessboard to suit his figurines like they'd done with the checkers. *Did couples like this really exist?*

When Jennifer arrived, she greeted me with a soft kiss on the cheek. I smiled the smile she would think was my real smile. I told her I didn't know where Alex was, but this didn't seem to bother her. She told me that she thought Alex and I made the most beautiful couple. Then she asked me how we were doing. I was caught off guard by the question so I laughed. It was not my real laugh. She studied my face. There was something almost threatening about the intensity of her stare. Tonight, I didn't want to feel like the only person in the room.

Jennifer: She truly loves you, you know. She doesn't
speak about anyone the way she speaks about you. It's
enchanting

Just then, Alex appeared and collapsed into the chair next to me. The enchantment shattered. We started massaging, moulding the clay as we spoke.

> **Jennifer:** So tell me why you chose to study music academically
>
> **Me:** Well, I love it, and it's important to know how music works if you want to be a singer and I think knowing about music makes listening and performing more enjoyable
>
> **Jennifer:** Really? Doesn't it then become more of an academic exercise?
>
> **Me:** Well, no, because musical thoughts and phrases need to be anticipated – a lot of enjoyment comes from meeting and delaying those anticipations, you know?
>
> **Jennifer:** Okay, I kind of see what you mean
>
> **Me to Alex, who was quiet:** Do you think knowing about music helps or hinders your enjoyment of music?
>
> **Her:** Well, I don't know very much about music and I do enjoy it, but I guess you enjoy it more than me, though it's hard to know whether your enjoyment comes from your knowledge of music or whether you wanted to learn more about something you already enjoyed

The evening was pleasant, though I felt out of time with Alex. I couldn't find our rhythm. Jennifer told us that she thought queer people had just 'given sexuality a bit more thought'. We laughed. Jennifer started to make a hand from the clay.

Alex took to making geometric shapes. I tried an abstract sculpture. Alex sighed dramatically because she'd just then thought about making me a coffee mug. Jennifer's clay hand was beautiful, like Alex's hands.

Jennifer: It's been so lovely hanging out with like-
    minded women
Me: Yes, it was really nice to see you again
Jennifer: It's strange, but I feel like gay people
    have sexuality in common in a way that straight
    people don't
Her: Oh, that's interesting
Me: I wonder whether that will always be the case ...
Jennifer: Anyway, take care you two

She kissed us both goodbye. Alex and I walked towards the Tube station together.

Her: Do you remember that conversation we had with
    Harry about empathy at Formal Hall in my third
    year? About empathising with things you've not
    experienced?
Me: Of course I do
Her: I wonder how often straight people empathise with
    the queer struggle, you know?
Me: Maybe someone who's felt persecuted or ostracised
    in another way – racism or sexism or something –
    would be more empathetic?
Her: I wonder if gay people immediately feel like they

have something in common on a first date in a way
straight people don't?

Me: Maybe?

Her: Aren't you curious?

Without my consent, my body started to pulse with adrenaline. *Does Alex want to date other people? Is that why she's disappearing?*

———

We didn't speak much on the journey back to her place. The weight of the silence pressed hard against my chest. Slow, stretched minutes. My skin grew uncomfortable and itchy. It suddenly felt too tight, constricting me. I tried to adjust my posture, open my lungs, uncross my legs. I focused on my breathing while she stared into the distance. *In for four, hold for four, out for four.* But soon every breath felt deliberate, manual, an effort. It was as though, if I didn't will the breath, I would stop breathing for ever. I wanted to gulp in air like it was running away from me. Eventually, she noticed something was up.

Her: Hey, are you alright?

I nodded. By this point, I was too scared to speak for fear of running out of breath.

———

I'm not proud of what I did. In fact, I feel shame. But you must understand: I wasn't me in those months. Her phone buzzed while she was in the shower and I checked it, thinking it was mine – Harry. He was still at work.

Harry:
Hey Alex, well done for surviving this week!
I promise it's going to be okay, it just takes some adjusting

What takes some adjusting? Had she spoken to him about our changed relationship? What did he mean surviving this week? Were we breaking up?

6254. I unlocked her phone and scrolled up. No mention of our relationship. Nothing. Actually, it was like I didn't exist in her life. Alex had been working towards something at work. She was falling behind colleagues on her grad scheme. She was sure she'd miss a promotion. *Why hasn't she mentioned any of this to me?*

I didn't ask. I rolled over and pretended to be asleep when she got into bed.

———

I'd been analysing our every moment like a romantic paranoiac. I decided we should go for dinner, just us two, and chose a gastropub near her house, famous for its Prosecco on tap. I was already seated when I saw her approaching through the window. I suddenly didn't know how to greet her. *Do I pretend I haven't seen her? Do I stand up? Or wave self-consciously for the minute or so it will take her to reach me?* I decided to wait and wave, a cool hand swipe from left to right, a full 180. When she finally arrived, she kissed me on the cheek with closed, dry lips. My compass didn't know how to settle.

Her: Hey! Good to see you!

Why was she greeting me like an acquaintance?

Her: How do you like the area?

Why was she greeting me like a tour guide?

Her: Have you chosen what you'd like to drink?

Why was she greeting me like a waiter?

I tried, subtly, to bring up her grad scheme worries, but she gave nothing away. We ordered separate dishes. We didn't share. She didn't even speak with her hands. No dance. Panicked and desperate, I spoke too quickly and too haphazardly. I spoke too much. Then I stopped. I sank into the silence. I drowned in it. I could hardly breathe. She didn't budge. After too long, I told her I thought we should get the bill. We waited in small-talk-fractured silence. The bill arrived. *What's happened to us?*

She tried to kiss me goodbye, but I hugged her instead. I was terrified she'd taste different, that she'd taste of rejection. Her perfect mouth, a potential weapon. I decided to go home to Stratford. We were a few steps away from each other when I changed my mind.

Me: What is wrong with us?

Her: Amalia, I don't want to do this now

Me: I'm sorry, but you cannot distance yourself from me whenever things get tough for you!

Her: I'm not distancing myself from you. I'm exhausted from work and I don't have the energy to argue

Me: I don't understand why you can't just be honest with me! Are things tough at work?

A sudden rage contorted her expression, re-sculpting her tired eyes into angry ones.

Her: Of course things are tough at work! I don't even know why I'm working in marketing, let alone why I'm working so fucking hard!

I was almost relieved she'd cracked.

Me: So talk to me about it rather than shutting me out! Since when do you shut me out?

Her: I can't do this right now

She walked away from me and I didn't follow. Then we didn't speak for a full week.

———

I don't want to break you into loving me.
How long will it take before you're shoving me
Against a wall – or out the door –

And, oh, I'm sure this war of hearts will end in blood,
And Mali, on the Jubilee, will be the first to bleed.
Don't you see what this breaking does to me,
What it's taking just to breathe
When we are beating out of sync,
And how I think is too unstable,
How I need your heart back on the table?
But first I must attack your skin,
But first I have to crack your ribs,
I have to stick my hand within
Your chest, so full of love, I pull and tug,
I pull and tug and win.
And still you say you'll stay each time before you go away.
Go away.

———

I was shocked at the women swimming in the freezing Hampstead Heath ponds. Eve didn't seem fazed. Walking together, I was reminded of Oxford's meadows. I felt far away from central London.

Me: Would you swim here?
Eve: Actually, I don't know how to swim
Me: Really? Do you want to learn?
Eve: Sure, why not?
Me: Why don't we come here in the summer and I'll
    teach you?
Eve: Sure

We sat together on the grass. She was the only person with whom I experienced Comfortable Silence the way it is romanticised by some people. I watched women greet one another with nods and occasionally a smile. More than one woman read from Maggie Nelson's *The Argonauts*. I kept my eye out for the rainbow-lanyarded consultant I'd met during my internship, though I didn't know what I'd say if I saw her. After some time, Eve broke our Comfortable Silence.

Eve: John says Keats lived around here
Me: You two seem really happy together
Eve: Me and Keats? Nah, he's not so much my type

I chuckled.

Eve: Do you want to talk about what's happening with Alex?
Me: I don't know. I just don't get how it's possible to be such wonderful, compatible friends and so ill suited as lovers
Eve: From what I've seen, you and Alex react to stress very differently. You freak out and become super-needy–
Me: Oy!
Eve: –and she needs space and time to process

She paused.

Eve: And I think relationship stress is very different
from friendship stress
Me, considering: That was surprisingly profound
Eve: People talk shit about reality TV, but I'm basically a
qualified pop psychology expert
Me: How is relationship stress different from
friendship stress?
Her: Because you have many friends and one relationship
Me: If you're monogamous ...
Her: Which you are. And your expectations of one
another are a lot higher. That's stressful
Me: Right

She shrugged and unwrapped the sandwiches we'd brought.
She took a bite.

Eve: Tomato and mozzarella, now that's a perfect
relationship

Eve spoke with her mouth full, which assuaged some seri-
ousness from our conversation. She didn't look at me while
she spoke.

Eve: I'm struggling a bit. Teachers kind of prepare you
to leave school for university or whatever, but no
one really prepares you to leave university. Not that
I've officially left, but you get me. Like, working in
the bookshop is fine, but I'm not really sure what's
next for me

I was about to interrupt, but caught myself as she continued.

Eve: I bet a lot of Oxford students who rusticate don't have to work in bookshops in their year off

Me: Yeah, you're right

Eve: I just feel under a lot of pressure to be doing something well paid and impressive

Me: Like what?

Eve: Like management consultancy!

Me: Honestly? I fucking hate management consultancy

She snorted.

Eve: I know

Me: What can I do?

Eve: I'm just quite ... lonely. Living with you and John is obviously great; I don't feel like I'm actually alone. But I have this feeling – I don't know, it sounds lame – but I've got this feeling that feels like loneliness

Me, channelling my mum: That's not lame. I think it's pretty normal, for what it's worth

Eve: John seems fine

Me: He's doing a Master's

Eve: True

Me: I'm glad you said something

Eve: Yeah, me too

Me: I'm here if you want to chat more about it

Eve: I know. But maybe not right now

I pulled Eve into a hug. We spent the rest of the afternoon in Comfortable Silence.

———

Then I met Liam.

I was on the Jubilee line Tube at 11 p.m. on a Thursday – the earliest I'd left work all week. It was empty but for a man at the end of my carriage. His concentration was almost physical as he scrutinised the pages of Nabokov. His hair was cartoon-like, spiky and light. I couldn't see his eyes. I had forgotten my headphones, my book, and all my other ways to plug in and ignore the journey, so I sat and stared and thought.

My thoughts terrified me. I'd once heard a line in some musical TED talk – 'with the torment of his own mind unleashed upon him' – and it stuck with me. It really unnerved me because I kind of got it. I felt like that was definitely a thing that could actually happen. To me. Being scared to think is probably also something I should bring up with a therapist. Anyway, I decided to stare at this man with the spiky hair. He looked gentle. I was analysing what 'gentle' looked like to me when he glanced up. His eyes were this penetrating, electric blue, disrupting his rather plain face. He smiled a plain smile.

Man on Tube: Fun night?

Oh, he was American, so the on-the-Tube chatting made more sense.

Me: Don't you know you're not supposed to talk
on the Tube?
Man on Tube: You don't look like the kind of person
who abides by that rule

I wondered what the kind of person who abides by that rule looked like. I wondered what I looked like to him. The Tube came to a gentle stop, though we were somewhere in the stretch between Canary Wharf and North Greenwich. Nothing happened.

Me: Do you know what's going on?
Man on Tube: You're the Londoner
Me: Hey! I'm offended, I'm Australian!
Man on Tube: Oh! I hear it when you say 'Australian'
Me: It's the 'l' at the back of the throat
Man on Tube: How long have you lived in London?
Me: Really not long at all. But I've lived in England for
the past three years or so. You?
Man on Tube: Oh, I don't live in London. I'm just here
visiting a friend. I'm actually on my way to Warsaw
Me: What's in Warsaw?
Man on Tube: Work
Me: What do you do?
Man on Tube: I'm a writer
Me: I need to marry a writer

It was a strange thing to say. It was a joke I used to make in high school about opera singing – that the nomadic nature of

Indyana Schneider

the career required a nomadic spouse, i.e. a writer. He smiled. Still, it was a strange thing to say.

Man on Tube: Good thing we met then. Fate, some might say

Me: I'm sorry. That was a strange thing to say. It's a joke I used to make as a teenager

Man on Tube: Why do you need to marry a writer?

Me: Because of my career

Man on Tube: What do you do?

Me: It's what I *will* do

Man on Tube: Which is?

Me: Opera-singing

Man on Tube: Awesome!

He was very American. The Tube hadn't moved.

Me: So I'm not sure what's going on with this Tube

Man on Tube: I've got nowhere to be

Me: Nor me. Just home. How long have you been visiting your friend here then?

He put the Nabokov on the seat beside him.

Man on Tube: Just a few days before I move to Poland

Me: So why does a writer need to move to Poland?

Man on Tube: I've got a job teaching English there

Me: I'm not following. Why Poland?

Man on Tube: I have a bud who moved out there for a

girl a little while back and he told me about a job. So I
went for it

Me: So when will the writing start?

Man on Tube, laughing: The writing never stopped.
But it doesn't pay the bills just yet. When will the
opera start?

Me: Touché

He came to sit opposite me. He smelled very strongly of
citrus. When he smiled, his eyes crackled. I didn't tell him
about Alex. I wasn't sure what there was to tell. The Tube
didn't move. Eventually there was an announcement.

*Attention, passengers. We apologise for the delay to your service.
We are currently working on a technical fault and will update you
in due course.*

Man on Tube: Excellent

Sarcasm.

Me: I thought you had nowhere to be?

Man on Tube: I'm not being sarcastic. It means I get to
keep talking to you

Misjudgement. Right, so he was kind of into me. Was I into
him? Of course not.

Man on Tube: Teach me about opera

Me: I'm not going to sing

Man on Tube: No one's asking you to sing
Me: What do you want to know?
Man on Tube: Why do you want to be an opera singer?

It was a perfectly ordinary, perfectly sensible question. But it was a question no one had asked me for a very long time and I couldn't remember my go-to response. There was a long pause. But I struggle with silence, so I started speaking without thinking.

Me: I'm sorry, it's actually been so long since I've sung
Man on Tube: I'm officially confused

I was tearing up.

Me: Part of me doesn't know if I can even do it any more

Where is all this coming from?

Man on Tube: Do you usually open up to strangers like this or can I count myself special?

I felt ridiculous, so I forced myself to stop crying. He leaned forward and put his hand on my leg.

Man on Tube: Hey, are you okay?
Me: Actually, can I take it all back? I remembered why I want to be an opera singer
Man on Tube, laughing: Sure you can. Why?

His mouth curled around the 'r' in 'sure'. He leaned back.

> **Me, reciting:** Because, every so often, I come across a
>   new piece of music and getting to know the music
>   kind of feels like falling in love. And the idea of
>   spending my life falling in love over and over and
>   over again . . . who wouldn't want that?
> **Man on Tube:** Is that the honest reason?
> **Me:** Yes, it's just . . . it's been a while since anyone's
>   asked me that

I'd successfully pulled myself together. I felt proud.

> **Me:** Why do you want to be a writer?
> **Man on Tube:** I read things and I think: *Fuck! I want to
>   create something like that*
> **Me:** But what's the real reason?
> **Man on Tube:** That's it, man!

Then he looked at me with love in those electric eyes. I was
startled. For a moment, I mistook the love of writing for
love of me.

*Attention, passengers. We are still assessing the technical fault
and will have more information for you shortly.*

> **Man on Tube:** That's it, I'm opening the wine
> **Me:** What?

He was carrying a brown, shiny, new, old-fashioned,

writer-wannabe briefcase. Inside was a small laptop and a bottle of red wine. It was sealed with a spin-top lid, which snapped as he opened it.

Man on Tube: Do you mind drinking from the bottle?

What would you have done? It wasn't spiked – I'd seen him open it in front of me and I'd heard the snap. The Tube had stopped and wasn't going to start any time soon and this man seemed interested in getting to know me. I felt wanted. Are you still rooting for Alex and me? Were you ever?

Me: Not at all

I drank from the bottle.

Man on Tube: Do you often talk to strangers on Tubes?
Me: Probably more often than most, but that's not
saying much
Man on Tube: I don't get the Brits
Me: A lot of Brits don't get Americans
Man on Tube: So what's your story?
Me: I'm not sure there's much to tell
Man on Tube: Boyfriend waiting for you at home?
Me: Why do you assume it's a guy?
Man on Tube: You're right, I'm sorry. Anyone waiting for
you at home?
Me: Yes, as a matter of fact, I live with my friend from
uni and her boyfriend

I passed him the bottle.

> **Man on Tube:** What's been your longest relationship?
> **Me:** That's a bit forward!
> **Man on Tube:** I think it says a lot about a person
> **Me:** I don't think it does. What do you mean?
> **Man on Tube:** My parents were together 10 years before
> my mum left my dad
> **Me:** Oh, I'm sorry to hear
> **Man on Tube:** No, it's so fine, they're better off apart
> anyway. Plus I really like Karen
> **Me:** Karen?
> **Man on Tube:** The woman my mum loves

He passed me the bottle.

> **Me:** Ah, so now you're letting me know you're cool with
> the gays. Love it
> **Man on Tube:** No! I'm obviously just opening up to you
> about my parents' divorce!
> **Me, laughing:** Oh, I'm so sorry. But I'm glad it
> worked out
> **Man on Tube:** Tell me about your family

People on Tubes in London don't say things like 'tell me about
your family'. I didn't respond.

> **Man on Tube:** Okay, then at least tell me your name?
> **Me:** Amalia

Man on Tube: Of course it is. What a beautiful
   name. I'm Liam
Me: What a beautiful name
Liam: You're funny. Hey, have you ever heard of '28
   Questions to Fall in Love'?
Me: Actually, yes, I have
Liam: They sound kind of dangerous, right? I've always
   wanted to answer them with a stranger! You down?
Me: Sure, why not? But we're not allowed to fall in
   love, obviously
Liam: Then I'm definitely not playing
Me, laughing: What? Why?
Liam: Who walks through life trying not to fall in love?

Someone already in love, Liam.

Me: Me. You in?
Liam: Fine. Let's do it!

Before we started, he pointed to the ad above me. *On average, every 14 minutes, someone finds love on eHarmony.*

Eighteen questions in and the Tube started up again. Twenty-two questions in and we were finally one away from his stop. 'Amalia, life is far easier with a hardened heart, but that's not the point.' He kissed me on the cheek and the scratch of his beard surprised me. Then he leaned in and kissed me on the mouth. I kissed him back.

22

DO YOU LIKE HORROR FILMS?

Alex:
You were right

No letter, no phonecall, just this message. Then another.

Alex:
I understand if you don't want to talk to me and I won't
push this if you don't want to, but I really think we
should talk

Her indifference nourished my anxiety. We agreed to meet
near Tottenham Court Road station. I saw a moth on the
Central line. I thought about how strange it was to see something living in a Tube. Then I looked around and wondered
why I didn't seem to recognise all these grey people as 'something living'.

I arrived very early. There was a drummer busking by the

entrance. He was playing a basic rock beat with intense fills that got me even more vexed. It was like some cruel, deviant soundtrack to my imminent break-up, this frenzied beat. I still can't look at busking drummers without faltering and flashing back to Tottenham Court Road station. 'Panic' on my Ben Lerner memory map.

The drummer looked angry, too. He was wearing an oversized hoodie and a pink bandana. I wondered if that was just his street-music aesthetic. I tried to distract myself with stories.

Maybe he's a banker Monday to Friday. Maybe he's not allowed to practise the drums in his small flat in Hoxton. Maybe he lives with his ex-girlfriend because neither of them can afford the place without the other, but they're used to the luxury and they don't want anyone else to move in. Maybe his ex-girlfriend is also a banker. Different bank, though. They're careful not to bring confidential files home. They have tinted security screens on their laptops. They only got these after the break-up. Like some passive-aggressive gesture of INDEPENDENCE. Maybe his ex-girlfriend plays the piano and they have a small, electric keyboard that she plugs her headphones into to play Brahms. No, Chopin.

No, I don't think he's a banker Monday to Friday. I think he works in marketing. No, he's the manager of a bar. And he's in a band. This is his everyday aesthetic. He lives with three friends from uni in Brixton and they get through a lot of craft beer. He got the bar gig after uni to pay the bills while he 'figured out his music'. Time passed and he realised the bar gig was a sweet gig and he was happy. He got to pick his own playlists, he was always around people, and he still had time to work on his drumming.

For another 10 minutes, I let the drums bash against my chest.

Alex:

I'm here, where are you?

Empty, dejected – she looked how I felt. We hugged and finally I felt her there with me. Why did it take drama and pain to have her present? Or had she been here the whole time? Did I completely imagine her retreat? She wrapped herself around me and we held each other for a long time. We went to a bar, though neither of us wanted to drink.

It was the first bar we found and it was called Tapas & Vodka. Every inch of wall was covered in pictures of Amy Winehouse. She was everywhere. Amy singing, Amy dancing, Amy sitting, Amy squatting, Amy eating, Amy rocking. We asked the posh waiter for water and bread. He thought we were joking – fair enough – and left with a superior huff. I spoke each line thinking only of the consequences of speaking.

Me: I don't understand how this happened again

Her: I think I'm just bad at relationships

Me: But you are so wonderful at friendships

Her: Do you want to try with me again?

Me: It's not *just* your fault

Her: Don't try to take the blame for this

Me: I'm not trying to do anything. You need space when things are difficult. I don't and I don't understand you, so I feel rejected when you need space. And I push

Her: You push because you care
Me: My pushing is in *my* best interest, though, not yours
Me: This is a very mature conversation
Her: I know, it's starting to freak me out
Me: We feel like us again
Me: We do

The waiter arrived with our bread and water. He started to offer us something else to eat or drink. Then he looked at us and quickly retreated. Good call.

Her: Things go wrong with us when we date
Me: I agree

Do I? I supposed so. I excused myself to the bathroom and she stood, saying she needed to go, too.

Me: Girls . . .
Her: What do you mean?
Me: That's the issue with dating girls! You can't even run
     away to the bathroom!
Her: I promise not to disturb your escape

The bathroom was very, very small. Amy Winehouse wasn't there. Alex and I ended up very close to one another, face to face. *There is so much I want to say, Alex.* I said nothing. She looked like she wanted to kiss me. We stood like this, inches from each other, breathing the same air for too many seconds. Still, we didn't kiss. We went back to our table and didn't kiss.

Me: The problem is that I want to grow old with you

She sighed like – what did she sigh like? Like she was resigned, like she was exasperated, or like she was in love? I didn't know. I couldn't trust my thoughts.

> **Her:** I want to grow old with you, too
> **Me:** And I'm really attracted to you
> **Her:** I know, I'm attracted to you, too, obviously, but–
> **Me:** But it hasn't worked
> **Her:** No

She looked vulnerable. Then she rearranged her face as though she were looking into a mirror. I stayed still, watching. She looked calm. She told me that it was probably better to stop hurting ourselves and each other. They were just words and she didn't look like she believed them. I felt panic bubble. I decided to disagree with her. I told her that it didn't make sense that we didn't 'work', it wasn't logical, we had everything – we obviously loved each other so much, we were attracted to one another, we were perfect friends. She seemed grateful for my disagreement. Was she bluffing? I still don't know. We chose our favourite photos of Amy Winehouse. We finished the bread.

> **Me:** So we'll try again?
> **Her:** Do you really want to?
> **Me:** Third time's the charm
> **Her:** Wow

Me: I think I should stay at my house tonight. We can take things slowly, okay?

Her: Let's be friends for a while first. I think I need my friend more than my lover right now

I didn't understand why they had to be two separate people.

Me: Okay, we will be friends first

I decided not to tell her about kissing a stranger on the Tube. Maybe one day, but not now. I felt guilty, but only partially guilty because we were partially broken up when it happened. The posh waiter looked seriously pissed off, so we asked for the bill. When we left the bar, neither of us said goodbye or goodnight, so we started to walk together in the same direction. We walked past a closed Côte restaurant.

Me: Oh, I wish it was open

Her: What should we do?

Me: I don't know – everything's closed or closing!

Her: Is it weird that I'm hungry?

Me, desperate to lighten the energy: I know a great vodka and tapas bar . . .

Sad smile, her. Desperate smile, me.

Me: 'Find the funny'?

Her: Exactly

Me: What should we do?

It was midnight. We walked past a cinema. The only film showing was a horror film about clowns. She hates scary films. I'm not a huge fan of clowns. We didn't buy popcorn and we sat close.

Me, whispering: We've never seen a horror film
   together, have we?
Her, whispering: No
Me, whispering: Do you like horror films?
Her, whispering: I hate horror films. I can't believe I'm
   about to watch a bloody horror film
Me, whispering: See? Who else would you do this for?
Her, whispering: Not funny
Me, whispering: Not at all

We sat very close. 'Remember the horror movie rule: don't get attached to any of the characters.' Her shoulder touched mine. 'Doesn't that kid know not to chase little boats down rainy streets?' My leg touched hers. 'That's actually sick. Who thinks of this stuff?' Our fingers intertwined. I put my head on her shoulder and she turned so her lips brushed my forehead. We didn't kiss. 'Why do I think you might actually be enjoying this?' She moved her lips away. 'I bet the clown industry hates films like this.' We left the cinema.

We both examined our respective 'help me get home' apps. Half an hour for her. Ninety minutes for me.

Her: Obviously just come to mine

We went back to hers and got straight into bed. She was everywhere. I breathed her in. How was it possible for her room to become such an exact reflection of her essence in such a short time? We said goodnight. We didn't kiss. I lay awake trying not to breathe her in. I vowed not to push, not to be needy, so I borrowed her underwear and left for work the next morning before she woke.

———

The following day happened to be one of the dates on the slips of graduation paper.

Alex:
Hey, do you still want to meet at Embankment station tonight?

Amalia:
Yes, I do

Alex:
Okay, see you there

I met her in the dark by the water, wearing yesterday's clothes. When she looked at me, it seemed she'd managed to concentrate all of the love in the world into the sparkles in her eyes. *Stars in my sky.* Blah. Anyway, we met and hugged awkwardly. It was the kind of hug where first you embrace intensely and then you back off by jumping in the opposite direction of the hug so that, when you've finished all the hugging, you're not left standing too close to one another.

>**Her:** So tell me all about work
>**Me:** Wow, this is such adult talk
>**Her:** That's because we're such adults

Our initial chat more closely resembled alternation than conversation. At first, Alex looked at me the way you look at family you haven't seen in too many months. Then she looked at me like she wanted to rip my clothes off with her teeth. I felt newly undressed when she looked at me like that.

Unsurprisingly.

Friendly–Familial–Sexual love

The graduation surprise was a burlesque show – part of the Underbelly Festival on the Southbank, London's Wonderground. The queue to enter the huge circus tent wrapped around a wall lined with life-size graffiti figures in 100 colours. We stood too close. We made up stories about the graffiti characters. *The purple man with the bandana was a barista who had fallen in love with the orange man holding the pineapple while on holiday on an island no one had named.* She moved closer to me, leaning in ever so slightly so I could feel her shoulders rise and fall with each breath. *The green woman on the phone was talking to her sister for the first time in months since she'd left home to follow her dreams of becoming a professional photographer.* I let my eyes rest on her lips while she spoke and I watched her throat tense as she swallowed hard. *The yellow child in the polka-dot sundress had run away from home and all she had remembered to pack was a toothbrush, an apple, and her Oyster card.*

Finally, we entered the tent. They'd gone to town with the smoke machines and coloured lighting – the whole space was very ethereal. Alex offered me a drink, which I declined, desperate to keep my inhibitions policed. We sat without touching – at first. As we continued our conversation, we moved closer to one another. She vehemently agreed with me about something – her hands told me so. I grabbed her enthusiastically. She leaned into me, arm around my chair. Our holding hands rested on her thigh. The show began with a lady dressed entirely in newspapers. Speakers shouted about FAKE NEWS as the lady undressed, page by page. Eventually, she was naked but for a diamond-studded thong and florescent pink nipple tassels. Alex whispered to me, 'Do you think the theme is political stripteases?' The next act began, a silhouette behind a huge white sheet. A short-haired figure spun around and around. Eventually, the figure's skirt was in the air and looked like it was coming apart. The cloth fell to reveal a gorgeous woman wearing a skirt made from bananas. Alex whispered to me, 'Oh! Josephine Baker! I love it!' I rested my head on her shoulder and I felt her lips touch my hair, lightly. A woman with huge boobs shimmied to a song in Portuguese.

In the interval, again, she offered me a drink, which, again, I declined. I watched her wonder whether there was a reason I wasn't drinking. We tried unsuccessfully to distract each other from the sheer intensity of each moment together, though our limbs stayed intertwined. Were we really so clichéd as to be so completely drawn to forbidden love? She had her hand on my shoulder in such a way that the tip of her finger traced my bare neck with my every breath. We breathed in time. But then the speakers played a Beyoncé song, 'Sweet Dreams', and she noticed me notice. I told you to remember Beyoncé – from when I'd first googled her and watched her dance on YouTube. As the song played, I admitted to her how I'd watched that video over and over when we'd first met. We were both taken aback by my candor. I laughed at the absurdity of all that had happened since the last time I'd heard 'Sweet Dreams'.

Her soft fingers pushed hard on my neck as she danced in her seat, rolling her body with the music. Finally, I looked at her. I really looked at her. Such intense longing clouded her sky eyes. Or were those my eyes mirrored in hers? Every part of me awoke – as though I were lit on fire, limb by limb, organ by organ – because I knew we were going to kiss and, once we did, I would be hers again, even though she was right: this probably would end in pain. As the last of me ignited, she clenched my hair and brought my face to hers and I leaned in and I started to cry because I knew her lips belonged on mine, I knew her tongue belonged entwined with mine, I knew her hands belonged in mine, but I also knew we would never be. I knew it would rip through us, ravage us, and that this fire all over me, this fire that *was* me, would turn to ash. But, still, during that exquisite kiss I think I felt Zadie's Joy.

Kissing you now, the waves begin
And evermore divide me:
Before and after you.

Is it possible to enjoy a love story when you know it will end in the kind of heartache that slices time?

The second act passed as though in fog. She kissed my neck with closed lips, then with open mouth. Her tongue danced while a group of glow-in-the-dark skeletons danced with hula hoops.

Outside, the air tasted briny. I breathed deeper because salty air took me home to the beach and the waves. A man in black flicked his cigarette to the ground. I imagined the cigarette catching fire as it hit the floor. I could see the fire spread. My jaw was clenched, palms sweating.

Me: I should probably go back to mine before the
  Tubes stop
Her: Of course, though you know you'd be
  welcome at mine
Me: To do what?
Her: Whatever you like?
Me: What about concentrating on being friends first?
Her: Fuck that
Me: I should go
Her: I'll walk you to the station

The taste of the sea on my tongue relaxed me. The way the streetlights backlit her entire body enticed me. I was reminded of the Scratch Night at university and the torches and Cate's singing: *I need a good-natured, old-fashioned, lesbian love story . . .*

Alex's perfect hands lay gently at her sides. I wanted them on my sides.

No.

I wanted them all over me. I wanted them around me. I wanted them in me. I watched her watch my wavering with interest. Or longing. Or love. Lust? We were too blurred to tell what was her and what was me. Was this blurring a gay thing? 'Call me by your name.' Exactly, André Aciman. I couldn't move. She brought her hand to my face and I nuzzled into it. My cheeks were still fiery and they flared with her touch. I moved my mouth towards her hand and kissed, swirling my tongue. I felt her knees buckle into mine.

Me: Walk me to the Tube

I wish I could say I'd had resolve enough to stick to our 'I think we should concentrate on being friends again first' reasoning. But the salty air was still in my mouth.

Me: Let's go back to yours

We woke with the sun. I told her that song lyrics had begun making more sense since our love story started. Every lyric either punched me in the stomach or caressed my hair. There was one particular song I told her about from the musical *Follies*. She wouldn't know *Follies* because she

didn't know musicals, so she wasn't burdened by the con-
text. I told her that the song 'Losing My Mind' was how I
sometimes felt.

I had to go. I can't remember why – I was probably meeting
someone for lunch – but I started to dress. Day 3, same clothes.
We chatted casually about musical theatre, like we were out
for coffee. She thought it was silly that people sang their
emotions. She thought it was illogical and took away from
the drama. I told her that life and theatre don't make enough
time for emotion, that songs in musicals put everything on
pause. Songs can stretch time. They allow you to feel in full.
She told me that she sort of understood and even agreed, but
perhaps only in some contexts. I told her that I loved musical
theatre anyway.

She asked to listen to 'Losing My Mind', so I played it
through tinny iPhone speakers while I did my make-up in
the mirror on her cupboard. Her cupboard was by the biggest
window in her little room and the light was kind to me. I was
glowing. I didn't bother with foundation. Unlike Sondheim's
quicker, pun-filled numbers, 'Losing My Mind' is a spotlight
number. A showstopping picture of love that colours every
moment of your day – as the sun rises, as you drink your
coffee, alone, in company . . .

Complete infatuation. Obsession.

I paused while I coloured my lips red and looked at her in
the mirror. She seemed completely transfixed by the sight of
me putting on make-up. I smiled goofily because everything
felt too intense. Comic relief. She had an intense look. It was
an intense song.

The song continued and I let myself get lost in it a little while. I looked again before I thickened my eyelashes black. She was still watching. She came to stand behind me then and softly put her cold hands on my shoulders as the song finished.

> *You said you loved me or were you just being kind?*
> *Or am I losing my mind?*

We didn't say anything else. There wasn't anything else to say. I knew she was crying because her lips tasted salty when I kissed her goodbye.

———

I decided to take Sydney Cali's long-ago advice and ask my mum for help. I called her on the bus to work – the Tube was down – surveying the upstairs occupants as it rang. Two men sat opposite me. Each was speaking on his own phone through headphones, but the timing was such that it sounded as though they were having a conversation with each other. Next to the men who weren't speaking to each other, a woman was feeding olives to her child that she deseeded with her mouth like a bird feeding her young.

Me: Ma, how often do people do something even though it's not in their best interest?

Mum: All the time. Why? Should I be worried?

Me: I don't know. It's just relationship stuff, but it's been going on for a long time

Mum: Oh, well, I know nothing about relationship stuff,
    so it's wise you've not called until now
Me: Ha ha
Mum: Is this relationship not in your best interest?
Me: It's with Alex
Mum: I see. And it's not making you happy?
Me: No, it *is* making me happy! I just … it's been bumpy
Mum: The transition from friendship into partnership is
    often bumpy
Me: I don't really understand why. Aren't we just adding
    sex to a perfect friendship?

A man a few seats away looked up from his book. I remembered I was in public. I lowered my voice.

Mum: No, Amalia, you're not just adding sex to a perfect
    friendship. Do you want me to wear my mum hat or
    my psychologist hat?
Me: The psychologist hat, please
Mum: What does friendship look like to you?
Me: Friendship looks like two people who enjoy each
    other's company and who are there for one another
Mum: Okay. And what needs to change between these
    two people for this to look like a relationship?
Me: Well, sex, and … a different kind of excitement
    and … I guess your partner is the person you put
    down as your emergency contact
Mum: So which of these elements is lacking between
    you and Alex?

Me: I don't think I trust her to be my emergency contact

Had I just accidentally disclosed my sexuality to the bus? I looked around, panicked, but no one seemed to have noticed.

Mum: Okay, so what are you going to do about that?
Me: Hope that it changes?
Mum: And if it doesn't?
Me: I don't know
Mum: I'd ask myself: *What am I hoping to achieve with this relationship? Where do I want it to go?*
Me: I don't know
Mum: What does it feel like when things are going well?
Me: Time stops, everything's in technicolour
Mum: And what are you afraid of?
Me: I'm afraid that this will end in heartbreak and that I'll lose my friend
Mum: I think you have already lost Alex as your friend now that she is your lover – not that she can't turn into your friend again, but, right now, that's not the case
Me: Right
Mum: So is that feeling – the time-stopping technicolour – worth the potential heartbreak?
Me: I don't know
Mum: You need to think to yourself: *What is the worst thing that can happen?* Can you survive it?
Me: I can survive it
Mum: Okay!
Me: Okay

23

How do you act in situations without a social script?

Things improved. A lot.

As I waited for her in the restaurant, a tiny woman sat down opposite me and grabbed my hand. She looked about my age. Buzz cut. She introduced herself. Her name was Beck. I was too surprised by her boldness to ask her what she was doing sitting at my table holding my hand. She smiled bizarrely at me, though I think she was trying to appear coy. I reclaimed my hand without saying anything. Why was this tiny woman inserting herself into my space? *Are you okay, Beck?* She asked me where she knew me from and I told her I might just have one of those faces. Then she said that, if she didn't know me already, she thought she should get to know me. She took a swig of my tap water and told me she'd noticed me walk in because of my short skirt and deep eyes. She said she could tell I wanted to get to know her, too. Still, I didn't speak, taken somewhat aback that this was happening and not really knowing how to respond. She was too tiny to be threatening, but here she was, this tiny gay woman called Beck, threatening me – or rather, making me feel threatened. I tried to be gentle and polite because that's what felt the most natural. I answered her questions – whether I had my mother's or my father's eyes ('My father's'), whether I came to this restaurant often ('It's my first time'), what I did for a living ('I guess I'm a management consultant'), whether I've always looked this good ('I made a special effort tonight because I'm meeting my partner'). I reciprocated the questions I deemed appropriate – not many. Beck worked as a solicitor in a firm I'd never heard of. She smiled her frenzied smile again and touched me under the table with her foot. *Alex, where are you?* The touch, though tender and tiny, jolted me into Defence Mode.

If she had been a man, I would have been brutish and brusque straightaway. I would have snarled, cursed, rolled my eyes, and told him I wasn't interested. People around me would have noticed the threat and they would have come to my aid. The lady opposite me, who was digging violently into her spaghetti, would have offered me I'm-sorry-men-can-be-dicks eyes and I would have smiled knowingly in return. I told Beck I was waiting for my partner and wasn't interested in talking further. She was angry that I'd led her on. She thought we had a connection. I apologised, pacifyingly but half-heartedly, and told her that I hoped she enjoyed the rest of her night. Beck left my table.

Alex arrived with what-was-that-all-about? eyes – which aren't all that different from I'm-sorry-men-can-be-dicks eyes – and I smiled into them as I told her about my strange encounter with Beck. We spent a while talking about how much gender impacts the way we relate to others, especially strangers, on a day-to-day basis.

> **Me:** I wouldn't know what to say in so many situations if a woman behaved inappropriately
> **Her:** Right? It's like there's no social script for dealing with these kinds of situations!
> **Me:** Exactly! How do you act in situations without a social script?
> **Her:** Like, if a woman slapped my butt in public, I'd just assume it was an accident
> **Me:** If I slap your butt in public, don't assume it's an accident
> **Her:** You wouldn't dare
> **Me:** Try me
> **Her:** But you're not really a butt person, are you?

This prompted a discussion on physical attraction, which, when dissected by two fresh-faced bisexuals, was fairly prolific. I tried to explain to us both that I wasn't really turned on by boobs or bums or pecks or genitals in the abstract, but that, in bed, everything was fair game. She told me she found breasts sexy – *why is it that people can't talk about breasts without looking at breasts?* – but that she also found men's bodies really attractive. I told her that I loved hands, that I loved *her* hands. She showed me what a sexy thumbs-up should look like and we both started to laugh. Dorky laughter. I could feel Beck sitting at the bar watching us.

Me: I'm going to confess to something
Her: You're actually turned on by breasts
Me, not blushing: No. Actually, I've been trying to
    experiment with dressing more butch
Her: Babe, you're not doing a very good job

I crossed my legs under my teal skirt, sheer stockings rubbing together.

Me: Yes, yes, I realise this. 'Butch' is the wrong word
    anyway. I've been trying to dress a little more
    androgynous, but I think my figure makes it really
    hard to look androgynous. Like, if a flat-chested,
    skinny woman wore ripped jeans and a too-large
    white T-shirt, they'd look very different to booby me
Her: So you feel like your breasts make you
    more feminine?
Me: Yes, is that the wrong thing to say?
Her: I don't think so. You're right, I've never really
    thought about it like that, but you're definitely
    right – a lot of androgynous style today tends to be
    pretty masculine-leaning. And I guess the media's
    representation of androgyny is a white, thin, curveless
    body assigned female at birth
Me: Right. Okay, it's not just in my head
Her: Can I ask why you're wanting to dress more
    androgynously?
Me: Actually, I don't know for sure. Maybe as a
    signalling thing?

Her: Signalling to whom?

Me: Maybe to myself? Is that weird?

Her: Not at all

Me: I guess when I look in the mirror, I don't really
see queerness

Her: I think cutting my hair definitely gave me easier
access to queerness

Me: And you look so hot, but I don't want to cut my hair.
Maybe I should get a rainbow tattooed on my cheek?

Her: Yes, I think that'd do it.

Our waiter had purple hair and an undercut. She took our
orders and gave us oh-you're-so-sweet-I'm-gay-too eyes
(which, for reference, are very different to I'm-sorry-men-
can-be-dicks eyes). As she left, I added a jug of Sangria to our
list of vegetarian delights. Alex raised her eyebrows at me. I
shrugged. The waiter smiled.

Her: Wow, she so approves of us

Me: That's cause we're cute

Her: I'm actually so awkward around gay
couples in public

Me: How so?

Her: I either smile encouragingly, more likely creepily, or
aggressively ignore them

Me: I think, with the haircut, you're pretty safe, babes

Her: Are you telling me my hair is gay?

Me: I think you look hot

Her: I think the chick by the bar thinks *you* look hot

Neither of us was in a particularly subtle mood, so together we looked directly at Beck by the bar, who promptly choked on her drink. We burst into giggles, unabashedly. Beck left in a huff and neither of us felt bad about it. I looked around, admiring the makeshift chandeliers, bare brick walls ...

I felt hot, aroused. Everything in that restaurant felt like an aphrodisiac. Half a jug of Sangria later, Purple Undercut approached our table.

Purple Undercut: Hey guys, sorry to bother you
Me: Don't be sorry
Her: Never sorry
Purple Undercut: I've been asked by the bar staff to ask you what the deal is?
Me: What deal?
Purple Undercut: Did you guys just get married?
Her: What?! If we'd just got married, why would we be here?
Me: Alex!
Purple Undercut: Engaged?
Me, beaming: Sorry to disappoint
Purple Undercut: Oh, are you guys just always like this? We've been calling this the Love Corner all night!
Me: The 'love corner'? That's awful
Her: Baby girl, don't fight it
Me: Who are you?

Alex and I made a show of taking off the rings that originally belonged to the other, swapping them, and placing them on our wedding-ring fingers. Purple Undercut clasped her hands together and hurried off towards the bar.

Me: Would you marry me?

Her: Yes

Me: Will you marry me?

Her: Yes

Me: But you never want to get married

Her: Oh, yeah, that's true – so no

Me: Did you know that the wedding-ring finger is the wedding-ring finger because it connects your hand to your heart?

Her: I did know that, genius

Short silence. We were three-quarters of the way through the jug of Sangria. We swapped back.

Her: I really don't want to get married, but I want to grow old with you

Pause.

Her: Mostly because I've always wanted to grow old with–

She drum-rolled on the table.

Her: –an opera superstar!

Alex sang a faux-operatic, wobbly *la*! I felt a jolt of guilt – the opera superstar who didn't sing any more. I vowed to organise a lesson soon.

Alex, growing old together would be sweet as Sangria. Are you drunk on me like I'm drunk on you? I think you are.

Actually, I might have even said that out loud because, by this stage, the jug was empty.

On the way home, we discussed whether social media giants knew we were in love by how often we called and messaged one another.

Her: Do you think they keep tabs on stuff like that?

Me: Sure! Did you hear about that shopping centre that knew a woman was pregnant before she told her family?

Her: No!

Me: It's crazy! You know how supermarkets collect information on our spending habits?

Her: Sure

Me: They use data to create 'scores'. Like, say 25 products are often bought together, that bundle allows the supermarket to assign a 'pregnancy prediction' score to a customer

Her: That's just creepy

Me: Right? They can even predict your due date and send you coupons for baby-related products at specific stages of your pregnancy!

Her: So what happened to the woman whose family didn't know she was pregnant?

Me: Actually, I think she was still at school and baby-product coupons arrived at her address, uninvited, based on her spending habits!

Her: Oh, God, that's one way to find out!

Me: I reckon Spotify thinks I'm crazy

Her: Why would it think that? Eclectic taste?

Me: No, because I'll find a track I like and just listen to it on repeat for a few hours until it's part of me

Alex, that's how I feel about you, too. First, you were music; now, you're part of me.

We arrived at her place far later than we'd planned.

Her: Would you like anything?

You, all of you. What if I trade you? I'll give you all of me for all of you.

Me: Peppermint tea, please

Her: Oh, good thinking!

She warmed those perfect hands on her mug.

———

Whenever I slept at Alex's, the sight of her bedside table would make me laugh. One of Zadie Smith's 'everyday pleasures'. Next to a stack of dog-eared books were always half-full mugs of peppermint tea that we'd made before bed and forgotten about. Without exception, every time I slept over, we would distract ourselves with conversation or sex – or both – and we'd wake up to cold peppermint tea. Surprisingly delicious.

———

In the middle of the night, Alex startled me awake by jerking upright in bed. The muscles in her forearms were tense as she yelled fast staccato French into the thick air, French that I couldn't understand. I was mesmerised. I just let her yell. Her hands were flying in a Satanic dance. They were more chaotic than the fast French. I sat up to join her and put my own hand softly on her shoulder. She stopped yelling. Her eyes were wide, but she was asleep. I kissed the curve of her neck and told her that it was okay, that she was sleeping, that I was there with her. She didn't move, so I didn't move. She started speaking French again, softly. Gently. I still couldn't understand. Her pyjama vest had moved during the night, so it hung on her diagonally. Loosely. She looked otherworldly. Angelic. I started to wonder whether I was sleeping. She turned to me and put her hand on my neck with a little more force than I was used to. Still asleep. She looked just past me and said, 'Amalia, I'm yours.' I swallowed. Everything inside me liquefied. Was this Zadie's Joy or something else? She folded down and rolled over.

———

People say that sex is great when you're hung-over. Everything is slower and things take longer to build and you're more sensitive and more raw. It's sensuous. And slow.

And languid. Waking up with someone's hot hands stroking and caressing you isn't a bad way to wake up. Plus, logically, you have more time to spare on weekend mornings.

I was still asleep when I felt her hot hands sliding up my back. I brushed her leg with mine and she wrapped herself around me. My thoughts slowed, almost stilled. Who needs meditation? We searched each other's skin for uncharted territory. I wanted to touch her, to feel all of her. The heat and the morning seemed to slow time. Every touch lasted longer than it was. She told me she loved me, so I tore off a piece of my heart and gave it to her. We lay in bed together because we weren't ready for the rest of the world.

Me: I struggle a bit with the word 'cum'

Her: You don't like it when I say I'm going to cum?

Me: I don't *not* like it, it's just not a word I really associate with orgasm

Her: Why not?

Me: Because, I guess, for me, cum is associated with ejaculation. And you don't ejaculate when you orgasm. Neither do I

Her: So, for you, 'cum' is a 'man's word'

Me: Yeah, I guess that's it

Her: Too many words are 'man words'. What if I say 'cum' over and over? Would that help? *Cum cum cum cum cum cum cum*

She'd reminded me of a song.

Come again
Sweet love doth now invite
Thy graces that refrain
To do me due delight

She looked at me.

Her: What are you doing?

I kept singing.

To see, to hear, to touch, to kiss, to die

She was laughing.

With thee again, in sweetest sympathy

Sweet, tuneful tones of laughter.

Her: What is this?
Me: It's Baroque music!
Her: Please never sing Baroque music to me while
   we're naked
Me: Why not?
Her: Because it's too ... sensible!
Me: No song can be sensible – people do not sing when
   they are feeling sensible
Her: You didn't make that up
Me: I didn't make that up – it's paraphrased W. H. Auden

Her: I'll trade you

She started to sing-rap a French song about sliding along the floor, women's thighs, fucking like turtles. She translated for me and my faced glowed scarlet. I touched her hipbone lightly and her red cheeks matched mine. We spoke about songs we found sexy until I noticed my favourite rouge Rorschach love hearts on her neck and bit them gently. We stayed in bed all morning.

24

IF I WERE MORE SECURE IN MY
PARENTS' LOVE, I WOULD BE A . . . ?

Eve and John were baking together in the kitchen when I arrived home one Sunday. The air was flavoured with sugar and butter and I breathed it in hungrily. I sat on the kitchen table while they fought over who would lick the spoon. Then the doorbell rang, so I jumped to answer it. I returned with a package addressed to me that I hadn't ordered. Eve was licking the spoon triumphantly.

Me: It's cute you thought you might win, John
John: I never stood a chance, did I?
Eve: No, mate, you did not! What's in the box, Mali?
Me: I don't know

I opened it. Inside was a pair of glossy, brown, stylish men's shoes in a size 38. There was a note in Alex's perfect handwriting: *Some androgynous shoes for my booby girl (for use until the rainbow cheek tattoo).*

   Eve: That is gross
   John: Eve means that's very sweet. I'm glad things are
      going well for you two
   Me: Yeah, I think they are

   ————

I think hosting small dinner parties is on Alex's list of 'Why I Can Call Myself An Adult'.

Dinner party guest list

   – Alex and housemate Harry
   – Harry's boyfriend, Calum, an actuary
   – Jennifer, the Jewish lesbian who doesn't like music
   – Eve and John
   – Me

Alex and I had written the invitations together.

Dear you,

You are formally invited to a Dinner Party.

Please bring either a dish or a question. Or both.

7pm, 10 December

Maison Alex/Harry

I greeted Jennifer at the door when she arrived. She wore the kind of outfit that made me think she must also own a beret. She complimented me on my earrings while taking off her coat and sing-songing a hello to Harry and Calum. I smiled my adult smile, which feels similar to my other smiles, but, when I see it in pictures, I remember I am 'adulting'. Based on its appearance, I'd call it a serene smile, though that seems so counterintuitive because 'adulting' is anything but serene.

When Calum echoed Jennifer's hello, he mirrored her pitches. I liked Calum. He had a lightness about him rare among Alex's friends and he played the piano on various kitchen surfaces. He and Alex chopped vegetables together while Eve and I set the table and looked busy. Harry and John were chatting in the corner of the room.

The evening's set-up was perfect. Each guest had brought with them a question. The first was served with Ottolenghi-inspired roasted cauliflower and green tahini.

Calum: Does anyone know a famous quote they think should be changed?

I wondered how, or whether, Dinner Party Conversation differed from University Conversation.

Jennifer: There's the W. H. Auden quote: 'If equal affection cannot be, let the more loving one be me.' Surely no one actually wants to be the 'more loving one'?

We cheersed.

> **Eve:** Didn't Eleanor Roosevelt say, 'No one can make
> you feel inferior without your consent'? I fucking feel
> sorry for her children

We cheersed again.

> **John:** I think the chronology of 'bittersweet' should be
> reversed, like the Greeks did it. Things are sweet and
> then they are bitter. Sweetbitter

The table applauded. John bowed his head earnestly. Eve
put her hand in his. Alex winked at me, mouthing, 'They're
great!' I'd been worried my housemates might not fit in. I
beamed with pride.

Moist falafel burgers, home-made lemony hummus.
Harry's question followed.

> **Harry:** Okay, I've got one: the type of people I struggle to
> work with are ...
> **Me:** That's easy – micro-managers
> **Calum:** Probably unreliable people
> **Eve:** People who are too diplomatic – waste of time
> **Jennifer:** Dictatorial chauvinists

No one could top 'dictatorial chauvinists'. I was up next: how
would you change the institution of marriage? I winked at
Alex, who rolled her eyes.

Calum: I mean, marriage has already evolved
   seismically – it's not defined by gender, it's not really a
   lifelong commitment, sexual fidelity is starting to feel
   old-fashioned …
Harry: Is it?

Calum tried to kiss Harry, who pushed him off, faux-appalled.

Me: So how would you evolve it further?
Jennifer: Okay, what if the state recognised the union
   of those promising to look after one another, but left
   romance and religion for each couple to sort out?
Calum: So less about sex and romance, more about care?
John: But then you could marry your friend or your
   sister! Marriage wouldn't be related to love!
Harry: Well, that would be the point! Love isn't the
   state's business
Jennifer: What if a framework existed in which each
   person nominated a special 'someone' who would
   care for them in sickness, assume their debts, even
   help raise children?
Me: Interesting
Eve: What if there were no financial or legal
   benefits at all?
John: But surely there has to be some sort of legal and
   financial system?
Eve: Expand your mind, Johnny
Alex: What if marriage contracts were renewable? With
   formalised points of reassessment

Harry: Oh, Alex

Tiramisu.

> **Eve:** Complete the sentence: if I were more secure in my
>   parents' love, I would be a . . .
> **Calum:** Pianist
> **Harry:** Philosopher
> **Alex:** I have no idea
> **Jennifer:** Academic
> **John:** Sommelier
> **Me:** Is it bad that I *am* pretty secure in my parents' love?

I was booed by the group. Laughter. It was a wonderful evening. Until–

> **Jennifer:** But you're not a musician, you're a consultant

25

WHAT HAPPENS WHEN YOU ZONE OUT?

We decided to plan a weekend away, visiting Sydney Cali in Oslo, where she was studying. Alex disappeared in Duty Free and I gravitated towards her perfume – Chanel Chance. I sprayed my palms then my neck. *Smell me by your scent and I'll smell you by mine.* I sprayed the little strip of paper and put it in the little leather case I used to keep my passport safe.

———

Me: I'm going to tell you about Cali
Her: Is it important to you that I like her?
Me: I don't know. I'm not sure she's very likeable
Her: Am I?
Me: More so
Her: Tell me about Cali
Me: Cali is very short – in height and manner. When we were younger, she wanted to be an artist, but I guess

now she prefers writing about art to painting. Since
we finished school, she's spent the years alternating
between travelling and studying. I think she's a
qualified scuba instructor these days

Her: Tell me about you and Cali

Me: I left her school, a Jewish school, when I was
eight and we stayed friends. We stopped talking
when we were about 17. It was really very silly. She
basically realised she was making all the effort in
our friendship and, instead of talking to me about
it, she quietly timed how long it would take me to
message her

Her: How long did it take you?

Me: A few months

Her: Ouch! That doesn't sound like you

Me: I'm glad you know present-day me

Her: Is that to say you don't identify with past you?

Me: I'm not falling for that. I'm the same kayak

Her: I think I don't want to know too much more. I'd
rather meet present-day Cali for myself

Me: Excellent idea

We hadn't heard the gate-change announcement, so we had
to run for the plane. We passed a pack of drunk men drinking. One was wearing a mask with a huge, erect penis for a
nose. It was really alarming. It looked like a *commedia dell'arte*
mask gone horribly, horribly wrong. I laughed because it was
the first penis I'd seen in a long time. I wondered whether
Alex was thinking the same. As we were running, I heard her

call, 'Do they smell like the boys you made out with in high school?' I called back, 'They look like them, too!'

Our plane neighbour taught us to say a few important words in Norwegian.

- Hello: *Hallo*
- Thank you: *Takk*
- Goodbye: *Ha det*

I gazed out the window into whiteness. It looked make-believe.

Her: Do you know why we have to keep our phones off on planes?
Me: I assumed it was something to do with signal clashes?
Her: Yes, exactly, I looked it up once because I don't like to follow rules I can't explain
Me: You're ridiculous

She turned to face me.

Her: I was just a cooler teenager than you
Me: Clearly. Do you know why they make us keep the window blinds up for take-off and landing?
Her: Actually, no ...
Me: Me neither. I used to think there was some sick rationale that, should the plane crash, someone wanted us to watch ourselves plummet to our deaths

Her: Somehow I don't think that's it

———

Her: Hang on, are you wearing my perfume?

———

When we arrived in Norway, I messaged Cali.

Amalia:
We're in Norway! X

Cali:
OMG me too

Cali met us at the station dressed in more layers than I'd ever seen her wear. Her hair was as dark as I remembered, tied in an angry bun. She had the same huge blue eyes and a new nose piercing. She smelled of boys' deodorant. We boarded the pristine train to her university accommodation. Cali started laughing. She told us she couldn't wait for us to hear the train announcement. We waited. Finally, a smooth, somewhat seductive electronic woman's voice told us to *dørene lukkes*. The doors closed quickly and we were off.

    Cali: Isn't her voice so ridiculously sensual? I can't
       handle it! I want to meet her!

Alex laughed her real laugh and I realised this was going to be a brilliant weekend. I tried to imagine what the woman with the smooth, seductive, electronic voice looked like, but I couldn't add any dimensions to the sound. I asked Cali how she imagined the lady behind the voice.

Cali: She's definitely blonde and tall. And she only wears black and red

Alex laughed again. I tried to live the rest of the journey in Cali's imagination. The tall, blonde lady wearing black and red leaned over, sighed, and announced our stop in honeyed tones: *Kringsjå*.

The university accommodation was in the middle of a forest. When we arrived, Cali made us pasta and asked us about the kind of porn we watched. Neither of us answered, so Cali told us about the kind of porn she watched. She said porn helped the loneliness in Oslo. She used her toaster to light a cigarette and stood by the window while she told us about loneliness and the kind of feminism that deems porn okay.

Cali: Before I left Sydney, my therapist gave me anti-depressants 'just in case'. She told me to prepare myself for *the quiet*

Me: That sounds ominous. Have you taken any? How have you been?

Cali: I'm still not used to *the quiet*, but I haven't taken any pills. Actually, I've used the gym and masturbation instead

Her: Do you prefer the gym or masturbation?

Cali: They're the same really. You trade manual labour
   for endorphins

Alex snorted.

Me: Are you seeing anyone?
Cali: I'm in love with a guy called Bobby, who is gay
Her: That sounds futile and frustrating
Cali: I'm not in love with him in a sexual way; I just
   haven't found anyone I click with like he and I click
Her: What does it mean to be in love with someone not
   in a sexual way?
Cali: Well, you can really want to fuck someone and not
   want to date them, so why can't you really want to
   date someone and not want to fuck them?

I thought back to my piano chords.

Her: I'm sure there's a way to rebut that logic
Me: Didn't the guy from Queen write a love song about a
   woman despite being gay?

Love of my life, don't leave me . . .

Cali: Yeah, Freddie Mercury and Mary Austin! I think he
   left his mansion to her and not to the guy who was by
   his bed when he died
Me: So does Bobby feel the same about you?
Cali: For sure. We've discussed it and everything. I was

sleeping with a girl for a while, but she insisted on
keeping her clothes on during sex and refused to let
me touch her

Her: Jesus

Cali: I'm glad we did it, but I'm equally glad it's over.
Also, her name is Amanda, which is my mum's name

Cali dropped the cigarette from her balcony into the night.
We ate our pasta and spoke about national stereotypes. Cali
thought Norwegians 'behaved awkwardly'. Alex thought
national stereotyping was 'stupid and harmful'. Cali com-
mented on my changed accent: 'I've wanted to tell you this for
a while.' I thought of Zadie's essay 'Speaking in Tongues', of
the new voice she added to her old voice before the old voice
was usurped. *Same kayak, different accent?*

Cali had arranged a single mattress for Alex and me to
sleep on next to her bed. She had laid out a single sleeping
bag, which we unwrapped to make a blanket. When we
finally went to bed, Alex and I got The Giggles for no reason,
which happened sometimes. Occasionally, Alex would say
that our sleepovers felt like teenage slumber parties–

Friendly love

–and I would slowly kiss her hands, neck, jaw to remind her
of the difference.

Sexual love

Cali amped up her Aussie accent and warned, 'Just because you guys are cute, doesn't mean I won't chloroform the shit out of you if you don't let me sleep,' which obviously made us laugh more. I heard her laugh along.

The room was cold when Alex and I woke. We lay curled together on the single mattress, holding each other for heat. Alex had buried her head in my neck and decided that kissing me quietly, while my childhood friend slept deeply mere feet from us, would be fun. It was. The room seemed warmer. Alex stood quietly, pulling me with her towards the bathroom.

———

We spent the morning walking around a nearby lake. It was too cold to hold hands, so Alex put her hand in my pocket and massaged my palm while we walked.

   Her: You know we haven't spoken for a few minutes and
      you seem to be surviving the silence?
   Me: Oh, my God
   Her: Norway's changing you
   Me: I know! I just zoned out

Another moment of silence.

Her: What happens when you zone out?

Me: Actually, I've never thought about that before.
Excellent question

Her: You sound surprised

Me: Well, just now I was trying to imagine what Cali's
Bobby looks like – I've imagined him quite fat with
thick, floppy hair and small blue eyes. Sometimes I
imagine conversations that I'd like to have, like I'll
rehearse an anecdote. Actually, often I imagine awful
things happening – like us walking down this path
and a tree falling over and crushing us and no one
discovering our bodies for days

Her: I think that's called catastrophic thinking

Me: Alright, doctor

Her: Is it ever just still?

Me: Um, no. I don't think so. Unless I've got a song
in my head

Her: You ever try meditating?

Me: Actually, no. You?

Her: I actually just downloaded a meditation app. I'll let
you know if it's any good!

Me: Where do you go when you zone out?

Her: I think I'm a lot less imaginative than you. Like,
my brain heads straight to the practical. I make to-
do lists or I remember I need to message someone
or I think about an article I've read. Actually, I read
about zoning out once! Something about other
areas of the brain decreasing in activity when
we zone out – so it could become harder to move

or speak and your emotions might numb. Isn't
that weird?

Me: Yeah, that is weird

Her: When you imagine us being crushed, do you
feel anything?

Me: Of course – I feel fear. Wouldn't you?

Her: Maybe not immediately

We met Cali in a park populated with violent, kinetic statues.

Cali: I heard you guys have serious fun in the bathroom
together this morning. Good for you! I'm jealous

The sculptures were mostly of naked human figures, contorted into graphic images of humanity, both base and abstract: screaming toddler; dancing woman; man attacking babies (or babies attacking man?); an assortment of couples engaging in aggressive yoga-esque poses ...

The centrepiece of the park, *The Monolith*, was sculpted from a single, enormous piece of granite – hundreds of human figures climbing on and around one another, like plants competing for sunlight.

Alex disappeared to sketch a statue, giving Cali and I space to catch up.

Cali: So that's what love looks like

Me: You think?

Cali: I've never seen people interact the way you two do

Me: That's just blatantly untrue

Cali: That's what we all want

Me: Cal, how are you really?

Cali, sighing: I've had lots of time to think

Me: Terrifying

Cali: I'm not sure why I do these things

Me: Like spend six months studying in Norway?

Cali: Like spend six months here and six months there and three months there. It's like I'm scared of commitment or intimacy or something. I build these surface-type connections with people and we'll say, 'I love you' and 'I miss you.' Then we say goodbye and we never see each other again

Me: Do you love them?

Cali: Of course not. But, at the time, I always think I do

Me: Are you happy?

Cali: Hmm. I don't know. Are you?

Me: . . . I think so

Cali: Why the hesitation?

Me: She's going to break my heart

Cali: Or you'll break hers. Or you'll stay happy together. That's what loving someone means. It makes you vulnerable

Me: I can't do vulnerable

Cali: Me neither. Try country-hopping?

Me, nudging her with my elbow: Great idea!
    Hook me up?

———

We met Bobby, Cali's gay crush, at a Norwegian pub with roast reindeer on the menu. Unlike my imagined Bobby, the real Bobby was tall and spaghetti-like. His keychain read: 'I heart your mum.' He had one of those voices that sounded like something was lodged in his throat, sort of scratchy but not abrasive. Cali and Bobby were odd to watch together. He was slow and goofy and a bit twee and she was quick and severe and alert.

Her: So how'd you two meet?
Bobby: At the gym, actually
Cali: Bobby sweats more than I've ever seen
    anyone sweat
Bobby: Cali doesn't sweat at all. It's yin–yang
Me: Then what happened?
Bobby: Then she asked for my number!
Me: Forward, Cali!
Cali: He was so obviously gay
Her: Obviously how?
Bobby: Yeah, obviously how?
Cali: For starters, you were checking out every guy that
    walked past you

Cali demonstrated. Standing up, she ran her fingers through her hair, puffed her chest, jutted her chin forward, and alarmed a passerby with a suggestive eyebrow bounce.

Eventually, the conversation fractured and Cali and Bobby talked without us.

Me: I once met a man whose broken heart cost him his
    singing career

Her: He gave up?

Me: He was so heartbroken, his voice just ... died

Her: What would happen if your heart was broken?

Me: I wouldn't lose my voice, I don't think

Her: No, you wouldn't

Me: What about you?

Her: I don't know what I'd lose – my mind?

Me: You wouldn't lose your mind

Her: No, I wouldn't

Cali and Bobby had stopped talking. They watched us in fascinated silence.

———

We met up again the following morning to take the train to Bergen. On the train, I noticed Cali rummaging through her backpack and asked if she needed something. She handed me a boiled egg wrapped in cling film and continued to rummage.

Cali: I'm looking for snus

Me: What's snus?

Bobby: Oh, my God, how have you not heard of snus?

Cali: Snus stops people topping themselves in
this weather

Her: Is it like tobacco?

Bobby: It's more popular than smoking in Norway!

Cali: Do you want to try it?

Me: No

Her: Yes!

The train from Oslo to Bergen is meant to be the most beautiful train ride in all of Europe. We made sandwiches for the journey and brought along a pack of cards. Cali made a habit of sneaking off into first class and returning with coffee and tea.

Stop 1: we babbled excitedly about the snow.

Stop 2: we gazed out the window, enthralled by sunlit, sparkling snow.

Stop 3: we jumped off the train and covered ourselves and each other with snow.

———

Fløyen is a 'city mountain' in Bergen, famous for its funicular railway, the only railway of its kind in Scandinavia. It was night when we rode to the top. Bergen seemed covered in colourful fairy lights, like a snow-speckled university dorm. At the top of the mountain, the icy air scratched. From so high up, the lights below merged to form a river of glowing lava snaking through the city.

———

Bergen Airport has a huge sign outside that reads: 'Bergen?' The question mark made us chuckle. *You tell us, Norway, is it?*

26

Do you find giving up easy?

Amalia:
I did it.
I booked a singing lesson at the Royal Academy of Music!!

Alex:
You're going to rock it!!

———

I felt deep, visceral envy, walking the halls of the Royal Academy. Music. Everywhere. On the walls, carved into the railings, in the air. *So this is what life could have looked like.*

The teacher was sitting at the piano when I arrived. Thick glasses, thin hair, warm smile. He began by asking me to describe my singing experience. I told him that I'd been singing classically since my early teens and that I'd studied music at university, but had since taken a job in the city to–

New singing teacher: Kill time?

What an awful thought.

Me: Save some money, learn some skills

The answer came automatically. He seemed sceptical, which alarmed me. We began with scales. He played my starting note. Suddenly, my vocal cords felt dusty. I cleared my throat. He waited. I breathed in to sing, but my diaphragm didn't expand in the way that I was used to. Fine. Still, we climbed the piano, semitone by semitone.

There was a horrible airiness to my sound that I didn't recognise. I ran out of breath before the phrase ended. I felt weak. Gently, he asked me to repeat the scale. I cleared my throat. Again, I breathed deeply, but didn't feel the familiar expansion. My vibrato was wobbly, almost weary of me.

New singing teacher: When did you say was the last
     time you practised?
Me: About six months ago, if I'm honest

We went 'back to basics'. He patiently explained to me how a singer 'should breathe'. *I know this, of course I know this, why isn't my body listening to me?* I began to panic, which made my voice feel constricted. I felt my shoulders tense, then my jaw. He dragged out the scales as long as he could before suggesting we try an aria. I decided to sing a slow, exquisite aria by Ambroise Thomas, 'Connais-tu le pays?' – an aria about missing and longing. The piano introduction left me glassy-eyed.

Connais-tu le pays où fleurit l'oranger?
Le pays des fruits d'or et des roses vermeilles,
Où la brise est plus douce et l'oiseau plus léger,
Où dans toute saison butinent les abeilles,
Où rayonne et sourit, comme un bienfait de Dieu,
Un éternel printemps sous un ciel toujours bleu!

(Do you know the country where the orange
     flowers bloom?
The land of golden fruit and crimson roses,
Where the breeze is sweeter and the birds
     fly lighter,
Where bees forage in every season,
Where shines and smiles, like a blessing from God,
An eternal spring under a forever-blue sky!)

The teacher raised his head. I noticed it, too – a hint of the warmth I recognised as my voice, rich, crimson. I clung to it.

Hélas! Que ne puis-je te suivre
Vers ce rivage heureux d'où le sort m'exila!
C'est là! C'est là que je voudrais vivre,
Aimer, aimer et mourir!

(Alas! That I can't follow you
Towards that happy shore, from which Fate exiled me!
It's there! It's there that I want to live,
Love, love and die!)

At the end of the lesson, he wished me luck with my consultancy job and told me to message if I'd like to organise
another lesson. I paid him the £80 and left. Of course, no one
on the Tube asked whether I was okay while I sobbed. God,
I missed home and I missed this part of me that was home. I
nearly called Alex, but we'd been doing so well that I couldn't
risk being needy.

———

Me: I can't sing any more
Eve: Don't be stupid, you're just rusty
Me: What if it doesn't come back?
Eve: Amalia, you need to chill out

I was yelling at her. I didn't want to yell, but the pain in my
throat almost felt good, like I was punishing my voice for its
betrayal. I tried to soften my tone.

Me: What if I've fucked up my entire life?
Eve: You have not fucked up your entire life
Me: I can't breathe
Eve: I think you should sit down, mate

———

I was struggling to sleep, so I downloaded the meditation app Alex had mentioned. I 'enabled notifications', which came in the form of quasi-motivational but slightly patronising messages: *Could thinking a problem is a problem be the only problem? Now is a good time to meditate. Now is good, too. How about now?*

——

My shoes were biting into my heels while my project manager lectured me. He had one of those high, whiny voices that scratched at my sensitive hearing. His hair was greasy. His skin was slimy and I just wanted to scream. I kept silent. After the lecture, he asked me a few questions about a spreadsheet I'd been working on.

Later, he called me back into his office.

Project manager, whining: Amalia, I wanted to speak
   to you about your ... general manner. I'd like you to
   please count to three before you answer my questions
Me: I'm sorry?
Project manager: I feel that you answer my questions too
   quickly and therefore haven't thought them through
   well enough
Me: When I answer your questions, does my answer
   imply I haven't heard you properly or thought
   through what you've said?
Project manager: No, I suppose not. But, still, it is
   important that I feel heard
Me: Right
Project manager: The same goes for our clients

I left without saying anything more. I lingered outside the office for a while, feeding the anxiety, stoking the rage. Again, I didn't message Alex.

———

Alex and I were meant to meet for dinner, but I bailed last minute. I wasn't in the right mindframe for us.

———

I felt myself slipping, but I didn't want to let on. We messaged less – a sad symmetry with her university withdrawal. I began to resent her for not being there, despite not explicitly asking for help.

———

It was 9 a.m. and the meditation app asked me: *What is something you have appreciated about today?*

———

Finally, we had dinner together at her house. Guilty for my absence, I wanted to buy her flowers. The only ones they were selling by my work were so very ugly – a leathery texture, an off-pink colour, and the smell of faux-floral detergent. Plastic-wrapped. I bought them anyway. I could tell immediately she didn't like them.

She didn't mention my withdrawal or seem fazed by our muted messaging. I felt unnoticed. She pulled me into her bedroom and left the lights on. She took things slow. There was no moaning or sighing from either of us. Instead, a soundtrack of breathing and sucking. I couldn't get into it. I pulled back and asked if she wanted this – sex, me – and she looked puzzled. This confused me, too. She teased that she was easing into it and said we could speed things up if I wanted to. I said I didn't mind.

Naked, finally, the heat she radiated marginally melted my anger; I only realised I was angry when I felt it melting. I didn't know why I was angry. She made me cum, but I didn't want to. I didn't know why I didn't want to. She whispered 'fuck' after she came, which was good. I was relieved she'd enjoyed it. Could she tell I wasn't into it? We were both less wet than usual and, when she asked if I wanted to 'keep going', I knew it was because she knew I didn't. She'd never asked before. I wanted to leave. To run. But, as soon as we stopped and she rolled over, all I wanted was to be enveloped by her. *What's wrong with me?*

The next morning, we had coffee and talked about the news as she read from the *Guardian* app on her phone. The world was fucked. US gun laws are fucked. When Harry came into the kitchen, he was manic. Investment banking is fucked. He slammed a cupboard closed and it made me jump. When she kissed me goodbye, I felt proud that I didn't have the urge to dissolve into her warm lips.

—

John: Are you doing okay, Amalia?
Me: I'm fine, I'm just ... things aren't great with
    Alex again

That wasn't it, but I'd found a perfect means of displacing my career stress.

Eve: What's going on?

Me: She's just . . . not really there for me

John: What makes you say that?

Me: It's just a feeling. I don't know how to describe it.
    I'm struggling at the moment and it's like she hasn't
    noticed or, if she has, she doesn't care

Eve: I'm sure she cares

Me: What if she's not actually in love with me?

Eve: What would make you say that?

Me: I can't think about this right now

John: Amalia, it's normal not to get through your 20s
    in one piece

Me: I feel shapeless

They exchanged a worried look as I left the kitchen.

———

Scribble.

> *I'm thinking it doesn't make sense*
> *That I'm speaking of love in past tense*
> *And so I try to write in rhyme*
> *But, by the time I think I might,*
> *It's nonsense.*
> *It's night and I'm dreaming of incense,*
> *Of your perfume in my bedroom*
> *While the ugly flowers I bought you bloom*
> *In your living room.*
> *It's bright.*

Oh, it's day, so I stay.
By the way, do you know?
Does it show there's no melody left in me?
And I weep for the rest of me,
For the empty space where the music used to be,
So I sleep to stop the tears.

———

So I tested her the childish way that Cali tested me while we were at school. *I'm not going to message. I am going to see how long it takes until she messages me.*

Two fucking days.

Alex:
Mali, come over for dinner tonight? I'll cook for us?

———

I asked to sleep on the couch. I wanted to hurt her. She looked hurt. I didn't like hurting her. I set up on the couch. I realised I didn't want to sleep on the couch. I went to her bed. I lay beside her. We didn't touch. We didn't say anything for half an hour. But I can't do silence, as you know.

Me: I don't think you're in love with me
Her: I think you're having a bad night and we should
talk in the morning

Why won't you tell me you're in love with me?

Me: I feel like I'm going to throw up

She touched my hands lovingly and I felt insane, like I was losing my mind.

You said you loved me or were you just being kind? Or am I losing my mind?

Me: I don't want to break you into loving me
Her: Please, Mali, let's sleep

She put her hand on my chest to calm me.

Me: I don't trust you. I don't trust us
Her: Please, Mals

She reached over and touched my hand. She gently played with my fingers and turned over my thumb so that my little thumb freckle was just next to her finger. She stared at it and I saw her eyes turn liquid, her cheeks flush, and her beautiful face light with a definite sensual hunger. I knew then that she owned this freckle, that every time I looked at my freckle I would see liquid eyes and sensual desire.

Sexual love

While she slept, I wished with everything left in me that I could see in the dark. That was the last time I would see her in bed. I only got her silhouette.

———

The night we actually broke up, I tried to steal her helmet. I'd spent the day in front of a single spreadsheet. It was a dull, nothing day. The meditation app asked me: *When did you last take a deep breath today?* The man sitting next to me on the Tube was wearing a pair of those fluorescent orange workwear trousers. He had the name GINA tattooed in block capitals on his left forearm, a clown smoking a cigar on his right. When a pregnant woman entered our carriage, he jumped up as though his seat had grown teeth and attacked him. Strange thought.

We'd arranged to meet in an East London bar where we could draw naked people. She was late to meet me, so I ordered a can of some craft beer. I read the back of the can: *I am a fruity, funky IPA. I go well with deep conversation and rimmed hats. Drink me and talk to someone.* There were two men next to me in matching suits and coral scarves who asked me who I was waiting for.

Coral scarf 1: You look like you're waiting for
someone special
Coral scarf 2: Hot date?
Me, smiling: Something like that
Coral scarf 1: Give *them* our best

I thought to plug into Spotify, but I'd been struggling with music since the singing lesson at the Royal Academy. When Alex arrived, the coral scarves smiled at one another. I don't think she noticed. I felt the nervous adrenaline ripple through me again. I told her I wasn't much in the mood to draw and she suggested we go get dinner. We walked down to Spitalfields Market, chatting casually about this and that for however long.

Sitting at the market, we drank too much wine. Suddenly, words spilled out of me, spreading and infecting the air between us. I told her that I felt too insecure, too unsafe in our relationship. I just kept speaking, spewing out words and words. So many words.

Me: I'm completely falling apart and you're so
   fucking far away!
Her: I was trying to give you space!
Me: I don't want space! I want you!
Her: Well, I'm not a mind reader, Amalia
Me: This isn't working

She paused. She appeared unsteady, breakable, and she asked me if I was seriously considering us exiting each other's lives. She really used the word 'exiting', like we were leaving a highway or trapped inside a building. I said yes, but without rational thought that 'yes' had implication and consequence. My voice was a different colour – a paler, colder colour – and it sliced sharply through the air.

Her: I think you're having a rough time at the moment
    and I don't know how to help you
Me: I need you to be there for me, that's all
Her: You can't rely on me for everything, Mals! I'm also
    struggling! I feel like I've completely lost my bearings
    in London. I don't know how to prioritise you and my
    work. But you! You're so sure about us and I envy you
    that surety!
Me: What makes you think I'm so sure?

Silence. I wanted to escape into the wine. To immerse myself
in it. To disappear. I imagined our language dying the
way languages sometimes die and my jaw felt too heavy
for my face.

*Zadie Smith pleasure icy poles. Birthday resolutions. Band-aid
goodbyes. 'Rainbow lorikeet' perfect. The same kayak …*

I couldn't look at her, so I looked at the couple behind her.
They were sitting opposite each other and held hands across
the table. But they also held their respective phones to their
respective ears as they talked enthusiastically to other people.
What do you think – dysfunctional or loving?

I forced myself to look at her.

Reader, I couldn't tell you what happened after I met Liam
on the Tube, just like I couldn't tell Alex or Eve or anyone. But
I'm telling you now, like I told Alex then.

Me: I fucked someone else when we first
    moved to London
Her: What?

> **Me:** After we'd had that fight. My Tube broke down and
> it was just me and this American guy in the carriage
> and I went home with him

Then she flicked a switch. I watched the sun leave the sky eyes. The light faded and everything went dark. She left money on the table and walked out.

I felt like I was falling, gravity's ruthless fingers tearing at me, pulling me down. But the falling feeling kind of brought me pleasure. How high I must have been soaring to be falling for so, so long. I never thought myself capable of reaching those heights.

Fuck.

I followed her.

Outside, I tried to say something mature like, 'I guess this is it then.' But could only think: *I want my mum.* And my heart cried. We'd made it to the corner of the street before I crumbled and sobbed without tears. I fought to control the tearless heaving. I tried again – 'I guess this is it then' – and this time I managed the words, though they sounded strangled. She nodded slowly.

> **Her:** I'm not upset you fucked that guy, we'd basically
> broken up then anyway

Who are you reassuring?

> **Her:** But we can't keep hurting each other like this
> **Me:** Do you find giving up easy?

Her: I think we need to let go of something that
    obviously isn't working

I had never seen her face so empty of light. I couldn't think
of anything more to say. All my thoughts imploded into pure
energy and I started to shake. Every part of me vibrated at
this distorted frequency. She unlocked her bike. I panicked
and grabbed her helmet so she couldn't leave me. She didn't
smile or laugh or flinch. She didn't react at all, she just waited
for me to give it back. I didn't. Then she simply mounted her
bike, intent on cycling without her helmet, so I gave it back.
She wasn't looking at me or looking at anything because her
eyes were hollow. *Come back to me, Alex. Please don't leave me.*

Me: No, no, no, no, you know you don't want to do this

She put her helmet on.

Me: No, no, no, no, just stop, what are you doing? You
    know we can't do this again

She got on her bike.

Me: You wouldn't seriously cycle away from us like this

She cycled away from us like that. The streetlights created
some artificial, anaemic moonlight that made me crave
home and hate England. I was worried that, if I started
crying real, wet, salty tears, I'd cry for the rest of time. I

walked past a shop window and stood next to it wondering whether or not to punch straight through it. I was so alone. I wanted to see the shards of glass protruding from my fingers. I wanted to feel warm, red blood dripping down my palm. I decided not to punch the glass.

The graffiti by the station read:

Oh, God, make small
The old star-eaten blanket of the sky,
That I may fold it around me and in comfort lie

Fuck you, too.

On the Tube platform, someone I didn't know accidently touched my back and I momentarily believed he had tried to push me. I had no phone signal on the Tube and no urge to do anything except stare out the window into the nothing, hoping to feel nothing. Everything felt unnatural. A mechanical woman's voice: 'There are beggars and buskers on this train. Please do not encourage their presence by supporting them.'

I cried tears. I sobbed. Eventually, I stopped. The half-poems returned.

She cycled away
You need to let her go
Stop asking if I'm okay
I don't fucking know

Impossibly, my room was the way I'd left it that morning – the pile of books in place of a bookshelf, the dishevelled-but-made bed and its grey–white blanket, a well-watered Sainsbury's pot plant, a series of mismatched paintings, our drawings of the naked man.

I can't think it's over.
I can't think.
It's over.

Once when I was a child at school, my science teacher put too much sodium into a beaker of water. It fizzled and then, with a hiss, the glass exploded, shattered into a million pieces and spat glass in a million different directions. A shard of glass pierced the ear of a boy in my class. The teacher fainted. He was fired. When I woke, I felt that explosion inside me. Then I turned to ash.

Her fingers were matches
They lit my skin on fire
I'm broken and burnt
I don't want to rhyme

The morning after, I accidentally cut my hand on that sharp bit that locks the door. *I hurt myself trying to lock you out, Alex.* I stood there, hypnotised by this bright blood already starting to clot. I couldn't feel it hurt.

Me: *Where do you go when you zone out?*
Her: *My brain heads straight to the practical. Actually, I*
  read about zoning out once! Something about other areas

*of the brain decreasing in activity when we zone out. Your
emotions might numb. Isn't that weird?*

*This cut will scar and the next time you look at my hands you won't
recognise them, just like I don't recognise them and you won't know
me, just like I don't know me.*

I avoided Eve and John in the kitchen. Then I went to work.

27

DO YOU STILL IDENTIFY WITH
YOUR UNIVERSITY SELF?

A week had passed since I'd nearly stolen her helmet.
Each day was just a slight, irrelevant variation on the one
before. Each day came with a fantasised parallel version
of itself – a version where we didn't break up. It helped
balance the despair.

The third date on the slips of paper Alex had gifted to me
was approaching.

Alex:
Hey, the last graduation gift I bought you was tickets to
an opera at the Barbican – Dead Man Walking

Do you want to go with me? Or are you telling me so that I go with
someone else? I didn't know how to reply. And I was terrified
to see an opera, given my crumbling voice.

Eve had gone back to Essex to visit her parents. John

was alone in the kitchen cleaning a cafetière. He didn't
notice me enter.

Me: I think I'm going to meet Alex on Friday night to
    see an opera
John: Why are you telling me this?
Me: I don't know
John: I do – you want me to tell you not to go
Me: Do you think I should go?
John: No, I don't. And neither would Eve
Me: But I want to
John: I know you want to, but someone has got to break
    this cycle
Me: It's a really good opera and I'm sure they're
    great tickets!
John: Who bought the tickets?
Me: They were a gift to me
John: I'll go with you
Me: You hate opera
John: I've decided I'd like to give it another go

———

Amalia:
Al, we probably shouldn't see this opera together

Alex:
I agree

I couldn't help myself.

Amalia:

I miss you

I watched her type, then delete whatever she'd written. Then she typed again.

Alex:

I miss you too

How did we get here?

———

I couldn't help but love the opera. The principal singer's voice was hot honey and my throat warmed and tingled with her vibrato. The familiarity of it made my stomach flip. It was almost sexual. John slouched beside me. For just a moment, during a particularly nectary note, I let myself imagine he was her. I'd want to take her hand and place it on my throat. I'd ask her if she could feel the tingling. I'd whisper so she would move closer to me and then I'd kiss the shallow dent below her throat. I'd watch her head arch in exquisite pleasure and I'd catch it in both my hands and kiss her soft lips so tenderly that she'd moan with the music's swells.

I forced myself to return to reality.

John looked handsome in his crisp, navy button-up shirt. I noticed one girl smile at him as we walked out of the theatre together. She looked at me awkwardly when we made eye contact. It was strange to suddenly look like a heterosexual couple, living heterosexual lives, going on a heterosexual date. Older heterosexual couples walked past us, smiling sweetly.

I was pleased when John suggested we grab a drink to dissect the opera. We found an empty bar nearby. The dark-haired, dark-eyed bartender asked if we were together and both of us chortled. We replied that we were 'sitting together'. John told me that he thought the story was a lot more gripping than he'd expected an opera story to be. I was pleased. He asked what Alex and I would have spoken about, had she been here instead.

Me: We'd probably debate whether the rapist really felt remorse and whether the nun was right in what she had said to the families of the victims

John: And?

Me: And we'd agree on most things because we agree on most things

John: Neither of you endorse the death penalty?

Me: No, do you?

John: Probably not for most crimes, but I think someone like Hitler deserves to die

I flinched, but I don't think he noticed.

John: Don't you think?

Me: How do you decide when a crime is bad enough that it deserves the death penalty?–

Her: *What is the right amount of violence when responding to violence?*

Me: *If you respond to violence with violence, it never ends*

Me: –I just kind of see the death penalty as
    formalised vengeance

John: Well, Nietzsche thinks that this idea of 'debt',
    in how we conceptualise punishment, is a way
    of understanding how 'bad consciences' came
    into the world

Me: Right. But I don't think prison should be about
    punishment. I think it's important to remove threats
    from society, sure, but to punish them feels wrong
    and hypocritical

John: But what about deterrence? Like, if there isn't a real
    punishment for inhuman acts, surely people would be
    more likely to commit them?

Me: Are there lower murder rates in countries that
    impose the death penalty?

I didn't let him answer.

Me: Or, even better, would you kill someone if you knew
    you wouldn't be punished?

John: Have you read Nietzche's *Human, All Too Human*?

Me: What do you think, John?

John: It's just that you kind of agree with him. We
    rationalise cruelty as moral duty

In bed that night . . .

Alex:

So how was the opera?

Amalia:

It was very good actually, how are you doing?

Alex:

Tell me about the music

Amalia:

I LOVED the nun's kinda childish musical theme – its innocence so perfectly complemented a story about guilt

Alex:

Send me a link to the music?

I sent her a link to the music.

Amalia:

I don't know what to do about us

Alex:

Me neither, Mals
Part of me thinks we should stop speaking, at least for a while

Amalia:

Stop all contact?

Alex:

Yes, for a while

Amalia:

Is that what you want?

Alex:

I think so

Amalia:

Okay, then let's stop speaking

Alex:

Please take care of yourself

Amalia:

And you

———

I got out of bed and put on a coat. I walked the streets feeling ugly and wild and confused and empty and hollow and barren and lost and lonely.

———

Alex. Just writing her name. Fuck. *It's like I'm losing my mind . . .*
  What fractures when we're together? Is it just bad timing? Have we ruined us? How could you even imagine that we should stop speaking?
  I couldn't think of anything else to write, another crumpled

bit of paper in the pile of unfinished, unsent letters. Then I couldn't write. I'd lost my words.

Amalia:
Cali, hey
Alex and I broke up
I don't know what to do

Cali:
Fuck Mals that's shit, I'm really sorry, are you okay?

I couldn't think straight and I couldn't stop thinking. It's impossible to think without words. Isn't it? Is thinking the opposite of emotion? Nothing made sense. 'With the torment of his own mind unleashed upon him.' *Please don't leave me with my thoughts.* I relied on songs to understand instead.

'Before and After You' – Jason Robert Brown, 2014
My after-her was filled with her even though she wasn't there. I heard her voice narrating my day-to-day. I knew exactly where she'd be almost every hour. There was something almost masochistic about knowing. Every morning, I stared stupidly at her stops on the Tube map, eyes flicking between where she worked and where she slept.

———

One morning, I dressed in silence. The underwear was already halfway up my legs before I realised it was hers.

I had the urge to take it off and bring it to my mouth. I wanted to taste it or wrap it around my neck or rip it into pieces. I carried on dressing. Over the course of the day, I'd move around in my seat just to feel it there, pressing into me.

'New York' – St Vincent, 2017

I wondered whether social media giants knew we'd broken up based on the sudden end to our messaging. They'd also probably know I was still in love with her by the way I stalked her empty Instagram. At least they couldn't see me panic when I saw she was online. Maybe they could.

'SOS' – ABBA, 1975

Often, when I opened my phone's Facebook app and saw she was online, I had this urge to sort of stroke the side of my phone. A desperate act of misplaced affection. So I stroked my phone. Really affectionately. I think it was the idea of the two of us being connected in some sort of way, even if that was both of us having the same app open. It did, it made me feel connected to her. And then there was the added thrill of wondering whether she had noticed that I was also online.

———

Dear Amalia,

It feels funny posting you a letter rather than leaving it in your college mailbox. We're growing up, aren't we? Do you still identify with your university self? I suppose university wasn't so long ago, though everything feels so different here in London.

I miss you and I love you – it's important you know that. So much of me wants to come see you, but I know that, if I do, we'll fall back into each other and carry on repeating this cycle. And you know as well as I do that it hasn't worked between us. We keep hurting one another and we need to break the pattern.

I think you were right – I am more distant with you now than when we were friends. I think part of me felt so much pressure to make this work, so that I wouldn't lose my 'person', that I couldn't properly be 'present' with you the way we were in your first two years of university. Gosh, that feels like a long time ago.

I feel like we have grown up around each other. So much of you is part of me. Sometimes it feels wonderful, sometimes suffocating. As clichéd as it sounds, I think we need to grow apart and become whole again. On which note, I need to tell you something. I've put myself forward for a two-year placement in Paris. In theory, I'd leave next month.

I hope you take care of yourself and that you have people to take care of you. I hope that you finish your time in management consulting and then get onto a stage as quickly as possible.

I hope to be there, cheering you on, when that day comes.

But, for me to be there and really be there, we need time apart.

I love you. I always will.

Your Alex

I wondered what she wanted me to feel reading her letter. How could she be so calm, so sure it was best for us to do life without each other? Again, I felt abandoned. I sat down, neck curled, head in hands. Then I felt anger. Deep, intense, violent, brutal, fierce, powerful anger. This thunderous, feverous rage excited me. It. Felt. So. Fucking. Good.

Fuck past versions of me – I wanted to be a new kayak. Fuck feeling abandoned and pathetic. Fuck you, Alex.

Amalia:
Liam, hey, hope you've been well.
How would you feel if I visited you in Warsaw this weekend ... ?

Liam:
Amalia, hey!
That'd be awesome!
I'll cancel all my plans (I don't have many plans dw ;))

I paid extra for a window seat so I could watch London grow small and irrelevant.

Amalia:

Sorry for not replying Cal, I'm fine – or I will be fine.
I've just booked a ticket to Warsaw this weekend to fuck
a guy I met on the Tube

Cali:

Mals, I love you ya know and I'm all for wild and reck-
less, but that doesn't sound healthy, mate

———

Eve and John were stuffing red peppers with a fluffy mixture
of feta, egg, and black pepper when I told them.

> **Eve:** I remember when you fucked that keyboard player
> after you and Cate broke up, but this is different,
> Mali – creepy Tube guy? He could be a fucking
> serial killer!
> **John:** Warsaw is an awfully long way for a booty call
> **Eve:** You're an adult, it's up to you – but, if you come back
> with all your limbs and organs, I'll be impressed

28

TELL ME, IS LOVE IN MY HEART?

The night before I left for Warsaw, I tried to meditate. The app told me to listen for the noises that surrounded me. I was meant to be 'present in the sounds'. I listened. There were no sounds.

'Need You Now' – Lady A, 2010
I hadn't taken my passport out of its case since our trip to Oslo. I opened the case to check my passport was there. The smell of her enveloped me. I could almost taste her. Chanel Chance. I breathed in deeply. The little slip of paper with her perfume had bled and stained my passport. I felt euphoric. But guilt made me pause. I inhaled again, deeper. Longing. I flicked through the passport to find my face. Instead, a young girl looked back at me. Her eyes were so big. She was so young and so far away. Maybe I didn't identify with her after all.

On the Tube to work, I noticed the woman opposite me was

wearing a T-shirt that said '1800-don't-call-him'. We made eye contact and I smiled and gestured to my own shirt so that she'd know I was smiling at hers. Then I realised that it probably just looked like I had smiled at this woman and then stroked my breasts. Excellent. I was comforted by the fact that, given the T-shirt slogan, she was probably too straight to think I was hitting on her. *Do completely heterosexual people ever second-guess a smile from another person of the same gender?* I supposed it depended on how 'gay' you presented and, by this point, I'd given up on the androgynous dressing. The woman was eating raisins, which made me think of failure. It's a strange sentiment to associate with raisins, but I can't help but think that grapes end up either as wine or as raisins, which means that raisins are the failures. When I worry about wrong decisions, I think of raisins and wine.

'Addio, del passato' – La Traviata, 1853

———

I took a new route from the station to the office, passing a second-hand store. In the window, among an eclectic array of mismatched glasses, vases, teacups and saucers, was a gas mask. Gaunt face. Hollow eyes. I froze. I was back in the gas chamber from my childhood visit to Auschwitz. I could see the scratch marks on the walls. Then–

Dizzy. I felt like I was spinning, spiralling. No, I didn't feel. I was outside my body watching myself spiral like some bored, mildly concerned voyeur.

Then I heard my heart beat erratically – acute disso-
nance – and I believed I was going to die. The panic felt like
something I was choking from, that I'd swallowed from the
air around me. Black and silver spots distorted my vision.
I couldn't find the oxygen in the air. I stood there, choking,
alone, until a stranger asked me if I was okay.

————

Project manager, whining: Don't type too hard, Amalia,
  you might break a nail!

He smirked at his own pathetic joke while leaning uninvited
over my laptop, hands on hips, stale breath polluting my air.

Project manager: Amalia, I'm here because your
  spreadsheet is completely impossible to understand.
  It's a pretty bloody simple job I've given you, even for

a music graduate. You'll need to start from scratch. It's going to be a late night for you, I'm afraid

My voice was dusty from the hours of silence. I felt slightly unhinged.

> **Me:** I think it's pretty easy to understand and so does the other associate who's using it for data extraction
> **Project manager:** Well, I'm your boss and I say it's rubbish, so fix it

Silence.

> **Project manager:** Did you hear me?
> **Me:** Sorry, I was just counting to three so as not to damage your ego
> **Project manager:** I beg your pardon?
> **Me:** I was counting in my head so you felt heard, and so your ego wasn't bruised by a quick-thinking music graduate
> **Project manager, shouting, spitting, raging:** I don't know who you think you are, but girls like you do not talk to their managers like that. Now finish that spreadsheet and send it to me tonight and, if it's good, maybe I won't have you fired

I did not finish the spreadsheet before I left the office for the airport. I left my work pass on my desk along with my work laptop and the work iPhone they'd given me. I was in the elevator when my phone buzzed.

Eve:

Mali, there's someone at our house with a suitcase who claims she's your best friend??? (I'm insulted)

Me:

What?

Eve:

Cali? (Her accent is much stronger than yours)

I have quit my job. I am on my way to the airport. I am not coping. I need to escape.

Me:

Eve, I'm on my way to the airport

Eve:

Cali says 'don't you dare'

And I agree. Just come home

I don't know what to do.

Eve:

Please, Mali!

———

Cali: Fuck, no, was I going to let you go to Warsaw, your mum would have killed me

Eve: I like her

Me: Yeah, you guys will get on

Cali: What was your plan exactly? Fuck random man you met once on a Tube, then come home feeling rejuvenated?

Me: I should text him and tell him I didn't get on the flight

Eve: Your priorities need work, Mali

Me: Also, I think I quit my job today

Eve: To be honest, maybe that's a good thing – your job sounded horrible

Cali: What are you going to do for money?

Me: Since when do you ask responsible questions?

Cali: Since you're being completely irresponsible! Speaking of money, you're paying for my flight over here, right?

Me: That's fair, I guess

Eve's eyes widened.

Eve: Did you fly here all the way from Australia?

Cali: No, no, I've been studying in Oslo

Cali insisted that, since it was her first time in London, we do something 'fun and kind of touristy'.

———

Amalia:
Liam, I'm really sorry but something came up at work and I can't come to Warsaw this weekend

Liam:

No way! I was so excited!

No sweat – hope it's all okay!

Rain check?

Pretty sure we'd have a great time ;)

———

'You Must Love Me' – Evita, 1978

———

Cali and I were the last to be admitted Upstairs @ Ronnie's.
She was shivering with her whole body and insisted she keep
her coat on. It was black and far too big and it consumed her
slight frame.

> **Cali:** I know, I know, I'm drowning in this coat. It's my
> mum's. I wasn't going to buy a brand-new winter coat
> for six months in Oslo

I agreed.

> *Her: Why do we say 'drowning' when clothes are too big?*
> *Me: I don't know*
> *Her: Maybe it's because you look as though you're a tiny*
>   *person in a huge sea*
> *Me: Maybe*
> *Her: Are you drowning, my sweet love?*

Cali smiled because she couldn't read my thoughts. I smiled back because she couldn't read my thoughts.

> **Me:** I'm sorry, it doesn't normally snow in
>   England in March!
> **Cali:** Well, I *am* only here for the good weather – what
>   a let-down. Okay, let's drink, I'm buying. What
>   do you want?
> **Me:** Red wine, please
> **Cali:** House okay?
> **Me:** Perfect

It's my favourite flavour.

The man who led the band moved as though his saxophone were an extension of his dick. Ludicrous to watch, but, if you closed your eyes, he was brilliant. I tried to let the music revitalise me, like a defibrillator. She arrived back with two full glasses of house red. We drank quickly.

> **Cali:** Do you want to tell me what happened with Alex?
> **Me:** Honestly, I wouldn't even know what to say
> **Cali:** Maybe you need a prompt

She gestured to our paper coasters, each marked with a quote. Hers said: *What does your soul look like?*

> **Cali:** Far out, London's very intense, isn't it?
> **Me:** I'm sure it's a lyric or something. Jazz is very intense

It was a terrifying idea, what my soul looked like. I told Cali that it probably looked like someone had taken a bite out of it. She rolled her eyes, which was the desired effect. I don't remember what she said next because I was imagining my soul as a glittering black lake. I imagined a whirlpool starting in the centre of the black lake. And growing. I'm sure I shuddered.

> **Cali:** Look, I'm not much into selfies, but I want to tell
> your mum you're not fucking some guy in eastern
> Europe and I'm sure she'd enjoy a picture of us
> together, so smile

On her phone screen, I noticed my lips had cracked from the cold. The cracks were filled with red wine residue. They looked raw and bloody and angry. Though the rest of me looked very calm. It's alarming when your outsides don't match your insides. Why wasn't I screaming? I should have been screaming. Screaming felt like the right thing to be doing.

> *Me: Alex, why do we scream?*
> *Her: Do you want the boring, Paleolithic-based answer or a*
> *more interesting, less true musing?*
> *Me: The latter, please*
> *Her: I think we scream for the same reason we swear.*
> *Sometimes words don't cut it*
> *Me: Where are you? What are you doing right this minute?*
> *Are you thinking about me?*

Cali: So what's happening with your singing?

Me: I went for a lesson at the Royal Academy of Music

Cali: I'm sure that's impressive, but I've never heard of it

Me: It was awful, I was shit

Cali: You were probably out of practice. When's your
next lesson?

Me: I never booked one

Cali: Oh, so you want to keep being shit?

Cali disappeared again to the bar and I closed my eyes so I could enjoy the music without the saxophone-as-dick visual. She returned with two shots and some paper between her teeth. She'd tucked a pen behind her ear. The shots were an off-pink colour – the kind you dress your bridesmaids in if you're an insecure bride. Cali put both of the shots in front of me. I obliged without question or protest. They were smoother and more tasteless than I'd expected, like the liquid rolled over my tongue without engaging any taste buds.

Cali: Okay, once those have kicked in, you get seven
minutes to write something. Anything

Me: Why?

Cali: Because Bobby made me do this when I was
struggling in Oslo and it really helped me

Me: I'm sorry, I haven't even asked how you're
finding Oslo

Cali: Tonight can be about you, as long as
tomorrow's about me

Me: Deal

She slid the shot glasses away and replaced them with the receipt, blank side up, and pen.

Me: Did he see this in a film?

She ignored me and set a timer on her phone. I didn't write for the first minute, but then I felt a little too dramatic or ridiculous – or both – so I wrote for the remaining six. My writing was very small.

> I know you say it's over, but every night we fuck while I sleep.
> When you stuck your fingers inside me on the last night we
> fucked in real time, you created a hole. You clawed up my cunt to my
> heart and you ripped it out while I came so I wouldn't notice. Sly.
> You keep my heart on your bedside table where a clock should be.
> Good morning, my darling. I hope you slept well.

I gave Cali the receipt when the timer told me to. She folded it without reading it and gave it back to me. I'm still not really sure of the point of the exercise, but I think I felt something splinter.

I wanted time to stop. Brian Thill taught me that waste = object + time. Time ruins things.

Heartbreak = love + time.

Death = life + time.

But will healing = heartbreak + time? How does denial fuck with that equation? *Alex, I want time to stop so we can heal separately and not miss a moment of each other's lives.*

———

Outside, the moon reminded me of me because it was just a pale sliver of itself. My eyes filled with tears, but I didn't feel like I needed to cry.

———

'Erbarme dich' – Bach, 1727

Schaue hier herz und augen weint vor dir bitterlich

(Look here, heart and eyes weep bitterly for you)

———

Amalia:
Hi, thank you for my consultation lesson at the Royal Academy.
I'm sorry it's taken so long for me to write again.
Would it be possible to arrange another?
Best,
Amalia

———

After my vulgar receipt poem, the words came home. They arrived all at once, filling me. I can't say why. I don't know why.

Wordlessness + time = . . .

My self-destructive mission had failed. Or rather, it had been thwarted by Cali. And my words came home.

I arrived in Stratford, grabbed my notebook and wrote in a fantastic frenzy that reminded me of the way we sometimes used to kiss. It reminded me of the way she licked her ice cream in the wind the night she tried to memorise the moment when the wind was in my eyes and the lights were in my hair.

Dear Alex,

    Once we saw a play where our favourite character asked the less cool character, 'Who would you look for in heaven?' They both agreed that they wouldn't look for anyone they actually knew. Alex, would you still look for me in heaven? As your lover? As your friend?

    Bon voyage. I hope Paris is Rainbow Lorikeet perfect. I hope you find your Zadie Smith icy poles soon enough and, perhaps selfishly, I hope you don't become a completely new Kayak.

    I love you, too.

    Your Mali

_____

So, reader, is it possible to enjoy a love story when you know it will end in the kind of heartache that slices time?

_____

AFTER HER

I wondered whether anyone had ever sat on the vibrant red chaise longue in the corner of our dressing room. It had too much of a personality to be sat on. The swirling armrests reminded me of Hokusai's *Great Wave* and I smiled my adult smile, remembering Cate's tattoo. *Sweet nostalgia for past lovers? At 26? Surely not.* The armrest swirls were not dissimilar from the blonde ringlets the soprano next to me was shaping. The Countess. Her red lipstick matched the velvet.

I hummed softly, checking my voice hadn't run away from me. No, it was still there. Warm. Nerves tickled my chest, but I didn't mind them. They were more excited than dreadful. I adjusted my wig in the mirror, straightened my tie. It had been strange, watching them transform me into a man, but here I was: short, slick hair, sharpened jawline, darkened brows. Music from the stage trickled into our dressing room through tinny speakers and I closed my eyes to listen.

Cherubino to the stage, Cherubino to the stage.

The Countess: *Toi toi toi*

——

Backstage was bustling, I was surprised that people were making so much noise so close to the action. I rolled my shoulders and stretched my neck. Tobias, the head of props, handed me the rose I would carry onto the stage. He patted my back paternally. The nerves were fiercer now, less a tickle than a squeeze. I raised my eyebrows at him and he whispered, 'All you can do is concentrate on your very first line and trust that the rest will follow.' I nodded. We both turned to watch the action on stage before he gave my back a gentle nudge. Lights. Every part of me caught fire.

> *Non so piú cosa son, cosa faccio.*
> *Ogni donna mi fa palpitar.*

> (I don't know what I am or what I'm doing.
> Every woman makes my heart beat faster.)

The Count appeared and I dashed away to hide behind a chair. From my new vantage point, I dared to let my eyes wander away from the action, away from the conductor, into the audience. The first few rows were silhouettes, the rest a dark smudge broken only by vivid, white lights. *My cue to exit.* I left the stage. The nerves had disappeared. Already, I was itching to get back. I greeted Figaro, who would drag me into the next scene. He was covered in sweat.

Voi che sapete che cosa e amor,
Donnè, vedete s'io l'ho nel cor.

(You who know what love is,
Tell me, is love in my heart?)

How is it already the finale? The stage was packed with bodies. A glorious moment of silence. Then, the most simple and beautiful melody. Shivers overwhelmed me.

'*Contessa, perdono*' ('Countess, forgive me'). Another stretched moment before the Countess forgave him. Soon, I joined the chorus and together we crept into this intimate musical moment. My eyes were glassy.

My body shook with our final note. I froze and steadied my gaze. I fell out of character as the audience applauded. I prayed that they couldn't see how much I was sweating. The Countess looked at me out of the corner of her eye. She winked. I smiled just as the curtain was closing, then nearly collapsed right there on the stage. But I couldn't collapse because the curtain was rising again as the rest of the cast reassembled to take their bows. We stood in a line at the front of the stage. I looked up, into the lights, closed my eyes, and bowed. Then I looked into the crowd and smiled at the single woman standing in the third row. I wondered whether she knew she was the only person standing. *Are you standing for me?* She waved. I fought the lights for a better view. Then I felt birds in my stomach, much fiercer than butterflies. I was pulled backwards by the other soloists as the curtain lowered.

ACKNOWLEDGEMENTS

Thank you to my agent Judith Murray, who not only completely changed my life, but is, objectively, The Best.

Thank you to Chris White, a patient genius, editorial wizard, and all-round wonderful person. Thank you to everyone else at Scribner and Simon & Schuster, especially Kaiya Shang, Becky McCarthy, Amy Fulwood, and Sian Wilson in the UK and Anna O'Grady, Racheal Versace, and Caitlin Withey down under.

To Juno Roche for your expertise and patience, and to Madeleine Ellis-Petersen and All About Trans for putting us in contact.

To my writing club, Ellie Shearer and Jenn Schaffer-Goddard, for your giant brains and hearts. I am so thankful for my fortnightly shower in your brilliance and support.

To early readers for your feedback, love, and encouragement: Naomi Morris Omori, Kathy Peacock, Livvy Bowen, Alicja Ciesielczuk, and Lisa Solomon.

To Jose Miguel Romero, for your sultry Spanish poetry and salsa inspo.

To Chloé de Canson, for lending me your astounding brain. *Our pink flower*

To Lell, for your Yoda wisdom.

To Leo Munby, for your generous musical genius. *Elevator ding*

To Naomi Morris Omori, for your initial (completely unfounded) support and excitement, and then for your continued (more founded) support and excitement. I wouldn't have written this book without you.

To Kathy Peacock, for reading at least 6 drafts of this story (and then some), for your unending support, regular updates, and tough love. You're a genuine, positive, totally marvellous, perfectly wonderful star.

To Soph, for blurring pleasure and joy in my every day. For your deep, beautiful, chocolate-filled love, dances in the kitchen, and sailboats.

To my pals who have had nothing to do with this book – any excuse to say I love you.

To my family in Australia, South Africa, and Canada who mean everything. I love and miss you every day.

To my mom and dad, Gabbi and Greg, for everything.